Independently
and very,

Millionaire Bachelors

But what these glamorous,
die-hard loners don't know is
that they're each about to
meet their match…and these
women deserve moonlight and
roses and promises of forever!

Dear Reader,

Welcome to Desire.

We start this month of fabulous Desire stories, with the final books in the ROYALLY WED series featuring the Stanford dynasty. **To Wed a Royal** has stories from reader favourites Valerie Parv – *Code Name: Prince* – and Carla Cassidy – *An Officer and a Princess*. Look out for more royal stories later in the year…

Another dose of opulent settings and sexy, wealthy men comes in the form of **Millionaire Bachelors**, which finishes THE MILLIONAIRE'S CLUB series with Sheri WhiteFeather's *Tycoon Warrior* and continues the Leanne Banks trilogy MILLION DOLLAR MEN with *Millionaire Husband*. (The final story in Leanne's MILLION DOLLAR MEN is in next month's **Millionaire Marriages**.)

Finally, **Made For Love** is wild and tempestuous reading; it pairs *Cowboy Fantasy* by the always marvellous Ann Major with Dixie Browning's moving *More to Love*—two more popular writers would be hard to find!

Enjoy!

The Editors

Millionaire Bachelors

SHERI WHITEFEATHER
LEANNE BANKS

SILHOUETTE®
DESIRE™

First published in Great Britain 2002
Silhouette Books, Eton House, 18-24 Paradise Road,
Richmond, Surrey TW9 1SR

MILLIONAIRE BACHELORS © Harlequin Books S.A. 2002

The publisher acknowledges the copyright holders of the
individual works as follows:

Tycoon Warrior © Harlequin Books S.A. 2001
Millionaire Husband © Leanne Banks 2001

Special thanks and acknowledgement are given to Sheri WhiteFeather
for her contribution to The Millionaire's Club series

ISBN 0 373 04743 6

51-0302

Printed and bound in Spain
by Litografía Rosés S.A., Barcelona

SILHOUETTE®
DESIRE™

is proud to present

Millionaires Galore!

Rich, renowned, ruthless and sexy as sin

Millionaire's Club - January

MILLIONAIRE MD *by Jennifer Greene*
WORLD'S MOST ELIGIBLE TEXAN *by Sara Orwig*

Millionaire Men - February

LONE STAR KNIGHT *by Cindy Gerard*
HER ARDENT SHEIKH *by Kristi Gold*

Millionaire Bachelors - March

TYCOON WARRIOR *by Sheri WhiteFeather*
MILLIONAIRE HUSBAND *by Leanne Banks*

Millionaire Marriages - April

MILLIONAIRE BOSS *by Peggy Moreland*
THE MILLIONAIRE'S SECRET WISH
by Leanne Banks

1201/SH/LC26

TYCOON WARRIOR

by
Sheri WhiteFeather

SHERI WHITEFEATHER

lives in Southern California and enjoys ethnic dining, summer pow-wows and visiting art galleries and vintage clothing shops near the beach. Since her one true passion is writing, she is thrilled to be a part of the Silhouette Desire line. When she isn't writing, she often reads until the small hours of the morning.

Sheri also works as a leather artisan with her Native American husband. They have one son and a menagerie of pets, including a pampered English bulldog and four equally spoiled Bengal cats. She would love to hear from her readers. You may write to her at: PO Box 5130, Orange, California 92863-5130, USA.

This book is dedicated to my Millionaire's Club sisters, Jennifer Greene, Sara Orwig, Cindy Gerard and Kristi Gold. I hope we can do it again sometime.

Special thanks to Lee Bundy for being my mom and my personal assistant, Joan Marlow Golan and Karen Kosztolnyik for inviting me to do this series, TSgt. Gerard Howard for answering questions about the United States Air Force, and Harold (Little Bull) Hull, Jr. for putting me in touch with a former Navy SEAL. Here's to secret Apaches and telephone conversations that never existed.

One

Retired air force lieutenant Dakota Lewis sat upright in a leather recliner, studying his home. Would the ranch look the same to Kathy?

Of course it would, he told himself a second later. He hadn't changed a thing. Not one cowboy novelty, not one Indian artifact. She would recognize every cow skull, every antler, every ceremonial pipe.

An ensemble of cedar, pine and mahogany made up Dakota's living room. He hadn't chosen pieces that belonged in sets. He preferred eclectic furnishings—hacienda-style trunks, tables topped with clay-colored tiles, mirrors framed in tooled leather.

He turned his attention back to his guests. They weren't discussing the mission at this point. Someone had made a reference to his wife. Was it Aaron Black? Sheikh Ben Rassad? Dr. Justin Webb? It wasn't Matthew Walker because Matt wasn't married.

No, but he was engaged. Happily engaged.

Hell, Dakota thought. What was wrong with him? The other men in the room were his friends, his peers. He had no right to envy them. They were all members of the Texas Cattleman's Club, the most exclusive gentlemen's club in the state. They were all wealthy—filthy rich, some might say. And they were all either happily married or happily engaged.

All except himself.

Dakota's estranged wife was due to arrive at his ranch any minute. Kathy had left three years before, a choice she hadn't even bothered to explain. Dakota had come home from an assignment to find her gone—her side of the closet empty, the scented lotions she favored no longer lined up on the bathroom counter. Two years of marriage shot to hell, and Dakota didn't know why. He had loved his wife, was certain she had loved him, too. Yet she'd walked out on him, saddling him with an emotional wound festering deep in his gut.

A wound that had become exceptionally active today. The top-secret mission the Cattleman's Club's members had come to discuss involved Kathy. She was the Foreign Service consular being teamed with Dakota. Together they would fly to Asterland, a small European country on the brink of a revolution.

The doorbell rang. Dakota excused himself from the other men and strode toward the entryway. Checking his watch, he tightened his jaw. Thirteen hundred hours. She was right on time.

Kathy stood on the other side of the door, slim and elegant, her thick, hard-to-hold hair coiled in a neat chignon. She wore a beige pantsuit and an emerald blouse that intensified the color of her eyes. Cat's eyes, he'd always called them. Exotic eyes and fire-tinted hair, features that belied Kathy's proper nature.

Neither spoke. Instead their gazes locked, and they stared at each other for what seemed like the longest moment of Dakota's life.

"It's good to see you," she said finally, extending her hand.

Polite pleasantries, he thought. What else could he do? This was business, and Dakota viewed his work as the number-one priority in his life. He wouldn't let anything stand in the way of an assignment, not even the pain shooting from his gut to his heart.

"It's good to see you, too," he responded, clasping her hand as though her touch wouldn't affect him. It did, of course. Her hand felt small and feminine, her skin soft and warm against his own.

He invited her in, cursing the memories threatening to surface. Her fragrance drifted to his nostrils like fresh strawberries smothered in cream. Kathy preferred scented lotions to heavy perfumes, aromas that never failed to make Dakota hungry.

Suddenly he fought the temptation to uncoil her hair, let it fall across her shoulders. He hadn't forgotten the woman he loved, hadn't forgotten how she looked soaking in the tub, her fiery tendrils slipping free from the pins that secured them, her long, sleek body creamy and smooth.

How many times had he watched her slide a washcloth down her arms and over her breasts? And how many times had he carried her, soaking wet, to their bed?

"Dakota? Are the others here?"

Kathy's question jarred him back to reality. Damn it. He stood in the tiled entryway, his hormones battling for control. How in the hell had he let that happen?

"Yes, they're here." He escorted his estranged wife to the living room, hating himself for the moment of weakness.

Like the Texas gentlemen they were, the other men rose as Kathy entered the room. Aaron Black came forward to hug her. How easily Kathy embraced Aaron, Dakota thought, wondering why a fist of rivalry gripped him hard and quick. Not only was Aaron blissfully married with a baby on the way, he was also a good friend, the American diplomat who had introduced Dakota to Kathy nearly six years before.

Kathy shook hands with the others, and soon they settled into their seats.

As Kathy crossed her legs, Dakota poured her a ginger ale from the wet bar. He didn't stop to ask her preference. He knew what Kathy's favorite soft drink was, and he still stocked the bar with it.

She thanked him quietly, the ice in her glass crackling. He poured himself a cola, opting to keep his hands busy. The urge to loosen her hair had returned.

How different they were, he thought, how opposite. Kathy was renowned for her grace and diplomacy, whereas Dakota was as rough-hewn as his taste in furniture, often solving matters with force.

Lifting his cola from the bar, Dakota took a swig, wondering if he should have spiked it with rum—something, anything to take the edge off. How could a woman skilled in conversation walk out on her husband without the slightest explanation? How could she ignore what they had meant to each other? The love? The passion?

Dakota didn't need to ask Kathy where she had been for the past three years. He already knew. She had gone to Washington, D.C., to serve in the Bureau of Consular Affairs, leasing a spacious apartment in an exclusive suburb and furnishing it with antiques. Prior to that, she had been on an extended leave of absence, debating whether to end her career. For Kathy, living abroad in the Foreign Service had become stressful. She wanted to remain in Texas. Or so she'd said.

Regardless, locating her in Washington had been easy. Keeping his distance had been the tough part. But Dakota figured Kathy didn't want to be confronted, didn't want him standing on her doorstep, demanding to know why she had left. So consequently, Dakota's pride—his hard-baked masculine ego—had managed to keep him at bay.

Sheikh Rassad drew Kathy into the meeting, pulling Dakota in as well.

"Are you familiar with the events leading up to this mission?" Ben asked her. "Are there any details that are not clear?"

"Aaron briefed me," she responded. "I know the Lone Star jewels were stolen. And I'm also aware that they've been recovered." She sat with her usual graceful posture, giving the sheikh her undivided attention. "Albert Payune, the Grand

Minister of Asterland, masterminded the robbery, intending to use the jewels to fund a revolution. Which is where Dakota and I come in. It's our job to make sure that revolution doesn't happen."

The sheikh leaned forward. "Aaron informed us that you are well acquainted with the king and queen."

"That's true. I'm very fond of the royal family, and I don't intend to see them lose their country." She placed her glass on a coaster, sending the sheikh a reassuring smile. "I've already made arrangements for Dakota to accompany me to Asterland for the queen's birthday ball. And since he will be visiting as my guest, his presence won't arouse suspicion."

Dakota listened, although he had already been briefed by Aaron. The plan had been carefully orchestrated. Dakota's initial arrival in Asterland must appear to be of a personal nature. And what could be more personal than traveling with his wife? They wouldn't need to fake their cover, at least not on paper. They would be playing themselves.

Almost.

They would have to pretend to be in the midst of a reconciliation, a couple mending their marriage.

Dakota glanced at Kathy, and she barely returned his gaze. She appeared poised and professional, but he could sense her uneasiness. The same uneasiness that swept through him.

How were they going to pull this off if they couldn't look at each other? Couldn't relax in each other's presence? Dakota glanced at Kathy again, his chest constricting with a familiar ache. Somehow, someway, they would have to. The future of a country was at stake. And this mission was far too risky for mistakes.

Kathy exhaled a quiet breath. When Aaron asked Dakota a question, he shifted his attention, giving her the opportunity to study him.

The years had been good to Dakota Lewis, aging him in a way that made him even more handsome, more rugged. He was half Comanche and half Texan—a tall, solid man with eyes that changed from brown to black, depending on his mood. His profile presented a determined jaw and high, slanted cheekbones. Everything about him boasted masculinity. His midnight hair, although short by most standards, was slightly longer than the military style he had worn while on active duty.

Active duty? Aside from allowing his hair to grow, retirement hadn't changed Dakota Lewis. He'd gone from Special Forces assignments to privately funded missions without a hitch in his long, powerful stride. Danger flowed through his veins like liquid; it was his life force, his blood. Kathy considered men like Dakota adrenaline junkies—men who would never give up the fight, the need to save the world.

Of course, adrenaline junkies didn't settle down with their wives. Instead they left them behind, left them alone to wait and wonder, praying frantically for their husbands' safe return.

How many assignments had he been on since she'd left? Did he miss her the way she had missed him? Or had his work filled the void? Dakota had loved her—that much she knew. Only he hadn't loved her the way she'd needed. Dakota's work had always come first. Kathy couldn't bear being second-best in her husband's heart.

And then when she'd lost the baby—

Her breath hitched. Oh, God. Don't think about the baby. Not here, not now. She placed a hand over her stomach. When would the pain go away, the ache of losing Dakota's child? How many years would have to pass? How many years before she stopped wishing every dark-haired toddler she saw was hers?

Dakota turned toward her, and she removed her hand from her stomach. Kathy had learned long ago how to keep her emotions in check, and she wouldn't give herself away now. Dakota didn't know about the baby. He had been in the Middle East tracking gunrunners when she'd miscarried—alone and afraid, missing her husband and crying for the baby they would never hold. A child she had wanted desperately.

"How well do you know Albert Payune?" Sheikh Rassad asked, catching Kathy off guard.

She lifted her chin and concentrated on the mission, the reason she had agreed to fly to Asterland with Dakota.

"I know Payune well enough to form an opinion of him," she responded. The sheikh's interest in Payune didn't surprise her, nor did his active participation in this meeting. She knew the sheikh's new bride had been formerly promised to Albert Payune in an arranged marriage. "Payune is a clever man, but he's arrogant, too. Much too vain to be considered charming. He isn't likable, but he knows how to command attention. He prides himself on power. Craves it, one could say."

"The perfect profile of a revolutionist," Aaron added. "It's quite possible Payune's sanity borders on his desire to succeed."

Matthew Walker joined in the conversation, mentioning his fiancée—Lady Helena of Asterland, a cousin to the royal family—a lady who shared Kathy's opinion of Payune.

Only Dakota and Dr. Webb remained silent. The doctor sat patiently, but Dakota rose from his chair and crossed the room, heading toward the cowhide-covered bar.

Kathy watched him. He moved like a long, fluid animal stalking his prey. It was the Comanche in him, she thought. The warrior preparing to count coup, his mental focus merging with his physical being. She recognized the look, the walk, the adrenaline charge that took him into the next battle, the next mission. This would be the man going after Albert Payune.

Had Dakota acquired another scar since she'd seen him last? Another mark of valor?

Kathy knew every inch of his body, every taut muscle, every hard ridge and flat plane. She also knew his hands were mildly callused, capable of inflicting pain or pleasure, depending on his objective. She had always been on the receiving end of pleasure, those large callused hands surprisingly gentle against her flesh. Dakota Lewis was as skilled a lover as he was a warrior.

Don't think about that now, she told herself. Focus on the mission. The reason she had agreed to help the Cattleman's Club.

When the meeting ended, the other men departed, leaving Dakota and Kathy alone. She clutched her handbag and stood. Suddenly the smell of wood and leather made her homesick. The ranch looked the same, the living room cluttered with rustic charm. Pillows, lamps, paintings, bronze statues—every piece told a Western story.

Was the bedroom the same? Had he kept the items she had chosen? The canopy bed, the hand-painted dresser, the horse weather vane sitting atop a Chippendale desk? The ranch belonged to Dakota, a custom-built home he had helped design ten years before. But when Kathy had married him, he'd asked her to redecorate the bedroom—fill it with her flair, her flavor. So she had combined formal antiques with Western relics, candles with cowboy boots, Waterford crystal with carved wood. The end result had pleased Dakota, especially the massive bed.

A bed Kathy had no right to remember. She didn't belong in this house. Loving Dakota didn't mean she could live with him, wait months on end for him to return from the missions that consumed him.

How ironic that they would come together for an assignment, for one of the secret operations engineered by the Texas Cattleman's Club. The members of that prestigious club weren't just established businessmen. They were Lone Star warriors, men who vowed to serve and protect.

Only Dakota hadn't protected her. He hadn't been there when she'd lost the baby.

"I think we should have dinner together tomorrow night."

Kathy blinked, then glanced up. How long had she been standing in the middle of Dakota's living room? And how long had he been watching her? "To synchronize our plan?"

"To get used to each other." He placed several empty glasses on top of the bar. "We can't go to Asterland like this. Acting like strangers. No one will buy our cover."

She let out an anxious breath. Right. The reconciled couple. The Foreign Service consular and her husband. "We still have some details to work out about the mission."

"We can do that over dinner. Which means avoiding a

restaurant. There are too many ears out there. I don't want to take the chance of being overheard.''

And she didn't want to have dinner with him at the ranch. She couldn't bear the familiarity. "How about my hotel suite? We can order in."

"That's fine."

He walked her to the door, and as she turned to say goodbye, their eyes met.

Yes, she thought, struggling to hold his gaze, they needed to get used to each other. Three years, too many missions and a secret miscarriage had created a lot of distance between them. Pretending to be a reconciled couple wasn't going to be easy.

The following evening Kathy stood before a full-length mirror in her hotel room. She wore a white suit, gold jewelry and low heels. Reaching into her blouse, she lifted a long chain. Her wedding ring glittered on the end of it, a brilliant-cut diamond surrounded by emeralds. It was foolish, she knew, to wear it in such a manner, but she didn't have the strength to part with it completely.

It reminded her of wishes and dreams, a house full of children and growing old with the man she loved—a life where terrorists and gunrunners didn't take her husband away from home. As she slipped the chain inside her blouse, the ring thumped against her heart, out of sight but not out of mind.

Kathy tilted her head. Her hair was loose about her shoulders, the way Dakota liked it best. Quickly she twisted it into a neat chignon, her fingers working the heavy strands with deft precision. This wasn't about what Dakota liked. This was a business meeting, a professional dinner engagement.

When the room-service waiter delivered the meal, Kathy stood nearby, watching him set the table. Dakota would be arriving at any moment. She signed the bill and forced a smile, telling herself to relax. She had been in the company of dignitaries and heads of state. One tall, ex-military man, a dark-eyed Comanche, had no right to twist her stomach into a pretzel.

Five minutes after the waiter departed, a knock sounded at the door. She answered it, keeping her head high and her posture straight but not stiff. "Hello, Dakota."

"Hi." He smiled, a brief affection that gentled his raw-boned features.

She used to kiss the scar on his chin, she thought. And the one on his belly, too.

Kathy took a step back. What a thing to invade her mind—that masculine stomach, rippling with hard-earned muscle.

"Come in. I took the liberty of ordering our meal ahead of time."

"Great." He walked into the suite, his voice more casual than she had expected. But when he made a beeline for the phone and began dismantling it, she realized his tone was for show.

He talked about insignificant things as he swept the set of rooms for bugs, electronic devices that might have been planted by someone posing as part of the hotel staff. Kathy had already done a search, but she appreciated Dakota's professionalism. With her anxious behavior, she could have missed something. She wasn't accustomed to providing her own security.

"What are we having?" he asked, indicating his search had turned up clean.

"Prime rib," she responded, wishing she could relax the way a proper hostess should.

Tonight Dakota looked a little dangerous—black trousers, a black jacket and eyes as dark as his clothes. He used to complain that he didn't blend in well, that men in his field shouldn't stand out in a crowd. Of course, men in his field were masters of disguise, and he played the game to perfection. Kathy knew he had altered his appearance many times, his height the only feature he couldn't change.

"It smells good," he said.

"Yes, it does."

He scooted back her chair, and she took her seat, thinking they weren't off to a very good start. There was no level of comfort between them. None whatsoever.

She poured the wine, her hand steadier than her heart. He sat across from her, watching every move she made, his gaze filled with questions. Clearly he wanted to know why she had left.

Kathy wasn't ready to talk about personal matters, wasn't sure if it would even matter. Retired or not, Lieutenant Dakota Lewis was, and always would be, the ultimate soldier—a man drawn to the heat of battle. A wife longing for babies and domestic bliss had no place in his life.

Dakota reached for his wine, and Kathy toyed with her salad. But before the silence threatened to swallow them, he spoke. "Tell me about your relationship with the royal family."

"I consider Queen Nicole a friend," she answered, relaxing a little. "She is part American and enjoys having another American woman to talk to. Although she was born in Asterland, she was educated in the States and has a fondness for our culture."

"When were you assigned to the consulate in Asterland? You've been in Washington for the last three years."

So he knew where she had been. Well, of course he did. She couldn't very well hide from a man like Dakota, nor had she intended to. She had wanted him to come to her, wanted him to profess that she was more important than his work, that he would retire for good.

"I wasn't assigned to Asterland. I was brought in to handle a situation that involved Prince Eric." Queen Nicole's young son, a dark-haired little boy who had stolen Kathy's heart. "Prince Eric had gotten into trouble at a prestigious New England boarding school. He was on the verge of being suspended because his classroom behavior was too disruptive. And since the school officials weren't being particularly cooperative, Queen Nicole requested that an American consular assess the situation and report to her."

Dakota cut into his meat. "Your report must have impressed the queen."

"Prince Eric turned out to be a delightful child, which led me to believe his classroom behavior needed further investigation." Kathy adjusted the linen napkin on her lap. "With the queen's approval, I brought in an educational psychologist. And the psychologist diagnosed Prince Eric with attention deficit disorder. Personally, I feel the boy had been treated unfairly. A learning disability isn't something that warrants a suspension."

Dakota smiled. "You've always been tuned in to kids. You could have been a teacher."

Or a mother, she thought, swallowing the lump in her throat. Prince Eric had come into her life soon after the miscarriage, and bonding with the young boy had helped ease the pain of losing her own child. "The queen transferred him to a boarding school that specializes in learning disabilities. He's doing well now. A determined fifth-grader."

"It's hard to believe Prince Ivan came from the same family."

"I know." Kathy pictured Prince Ivan. He was Eric's older brother, a grown man who abused his power and shamed his family. He had also been a menace to the town of Royal, a threat to the Cattleman's Club. But in the end, a cowardly act had consumed him. Rather than return to Asterland to face his family, the prince had committed suicide. "Ivan is dead now."

Dakota placed his fork on the table. "But he's still creating trouble. Or his past deeds are. He's the one who convinced the king to appoint Payune to the position of Grand Minister. Payune and Ivan were thick as thieves."

And at one time, the king, clearly blinded by parental love, had intended to abdicate the throne to Ivan. "Prince Eric is nothing like his brother. He will make a fine king someday."

"That's good to know. But if we don't stop Payune, young Eric will never get that chance." Dakota trapped her gaze, his dark eyes riveting. "I hope to God Payune buys my cover. And yours, too. I'm going to have to convince him that you're a double agent."

Kathy tried to look away, but couldn't. Dakota held her there, caught in his magnetic gaze. She wasn't able to respond; her mouth had gone dry. She reached for her wine, took a small sip.

His husky voice sounded gentle, low. "I'm sorry, sweetheart. I hate doing this to you, but I don't know how else to reach Payune."

Sweetheart. Kathy felt a pool of warmth settle deep in her belly. Dakota had used that endearment the first time they'd made love.

Show me what you like, sweetheart. Put my hands—

Oh yes, those hands. Those strong, callused hands—fingertips stroking her breasts, sliding lower, slipping between her thighs. He used to watch her climax, smile and watch, masculine pleasure alight in his dark eyes. Afterward they would kiss, and he would enter her, push himself deep inside, make it happen all over again. Every explosive, glorious sensation.

"Kathy?"

She started. "Yes?"

"Are you all right? Did that upset you?"

Yes, she wanted to say. It unnerves me that I can't stop thinking about us. That I can recall your touch, your smile, the feel of your mouth covering mine, the weight of your body, the rock of your hips. "No. I came into this mission knowing we would have to fool Payune. I'm prepared to play my part."

"You're absolutely sure? You don't have any second thoughts?"

"I'm ready for this assignment," she said, struggling to maintain her composure. "Aaron briefed me on all of the details." Dakota would present himself as a Texas billionaire willing to fund Payune's revolution for personal gain. And she would be painted as Dakota's shrewd wife—a woman who used a government job to her best advantage.

"Don't worry about me," she added. She wouldn't allow her thoughts to stray, wouldn't allow those disturbing images to cloud her mind. Because recalling Dakota's touch was possibly more dangerous than the mission.

Two

Kathy wore her hair up again, Dakota noticed, but the dry Texas wind had disturbed it, loosening several long, bright strands. She wore casual clothes—jeans and a short-sleeved cotton blouse, her shoulder nearly brushing his.

A bronze statue of Tex Langley, the founder of the Texas Cattleman's Club, stood like a monument behind them.

They sat on a park bench, but they weren't lounging on a leisure day. This was business, another meeting place where they wouldn't be overheard.

Sheikh Ben Rassad and his wife, Jamie, sat on the other side of the bench, a newly married couple looking far too much in love. Dakota resisted the urge to move closer to Kathy, to allow their bodies to touch. Although last night's dinner hadn't been a failure, it wasn't a complete success, either. They weren't exactly used to each other yet.

Dakota dug a booted heel into the grass. Maybe he should just kiss her and get it over with. Pull her onto his lap. Tug her hair loose. Slam his tongue into her mouth and devour the woman he had married.

After all, she was still technically his wife.

He glanced up at Ben Rassad. Yeah, right. Kiss Kathy now, here at the park, in front of his happily married friend. What the hell was he trying to prove? That he was an egotistical, envious idiot?

Dakota lifted a bottle of water and brought it to his lips, wetting his mouth and cooling his thoughts. Strange how things had worked out for Ben. The sheikh had been assigned to watch over Jamie when she needed protection, then ended up falling for her in the process. The feisty young woman had originally been a mail-order bride for Albert Payune, a union arranged by Jamie's father and Payune himself.

Luckily, Payune had backed out of the deal and never pursued Jamie any further. Which, in turn, had prompted this meeting—second-guessing Payune's actions—the man Dakota intended to take down.

"So, do either one of you have any idea why Payune had advertised for an American wife?" he asked, dividing his gaze between the other couple.

Jamie shook her head. "No, but we've talked about it. Tossed ideas back and forth."

"Like what, for instance?"

"Vanity, perhaps," Ben said. "Payune may have desired a young wife to boost his ego. Texas women are renowned for their beauty." He reached for Jamie's hand and held it lightly. "But there is also the possibility of revenge. Payune might blame the town of Royal for Ivan's suicide, and he planned to take one of our women as payment."

Dakota mulled over Ben's words, deciding anything was possible where Payune was concerned.

"I tend to think Sheikh Rassad was right the first time," Kathy said. "That Payune's ego was involved."

"Really?" When Dakota turned toward her, his hand brushed hers—an accidental touch that sent an electrical charge straight to his heart. He forced himself to concentrate on the discussion, but failed miserably. He noticed Kathy's hand was bare. She wore no rings. The wedding band he'd placed on her finger was gone.

Dakota looked over at Ben and Jamie. Both sat patiently as though waiting for Kathy to expound on her theory. Apparently he was the only one losing his train of thought. Damn it. He knew better than to allow his heart to get tangled up in this mission. Kathy had left him, and that was that.

Tightening his jaw, he turned toward her again. "So you think Payune wanted an American wife to make himself look good?"

She nodded. "It would enhance his public image in Asterland. Queen Nicole is well received in her country. And since she is part American, Payune may have been trying to find a wife he considered comparable to her." She shifted her gaze to Ben. "A beautiful Texan, just as Sheikh Rassad pointed out."

Dakota frowned. "If that's the case, then why did Payune let Jamie go? My contact in Asterland says he's no longer pursuing a wife, American or otherwise."

Kathy smoothed the wind-blown strands of her hair. "I don't know. But I've always had the feeling that Payune is enamored of Queen Nicole. Of course she's madly in love with her husband. She isn't the kind of woman to have an affair, and I'm sure Payune knows that."

"But he wants her." And in Dakota's opinion that made Albert Payune even more dangerous. Could there be an assassination plot brewing? If the king were killed during the revolution, Queen Nicole would be left a widow, free to accept Payune's affection. And if Payune controlled the queen and Prince Eric, then, in a sense, he would control Asterland, too.

Dakota figured Payune had three options: overthrow the Asterland government through a revolution, dispose of the entire royal family or kill the king and marry Queen Nicole.

But how could Payune possibly think the queen would turn to him? If she loved her husband, she wouldn't embrace the man who had assassinated him.

Or would she? Was Kathy wrong about Queen Nicole? Maybe the queen wasn't as madly in love as she claimed to be.

Wives, it seemed, changed their minds about such matters. Dakota knew firsthand that love wasn't all it was cracked up to be.

They were both experienced flyers—more than experienced. Kathy had lived abroad most of her life, and Dakota was a pilot, a man who belonged to the sky. But not today. Although they rode on a private, luxurious jet owned by a prominent member of the Cattleman's Club, they were anything but relaxed.

The pilot, thank God, was another retired air force officer, someone Dakota trusted implicitly. Flying to Asterland with Kathy was difficult enough, and the last thing Dakota needed to concern himself with was the competency of their pilot.

Kathy sat across from him in a cushioned chair. The jet offered an upscale, home-like setting, a penthouse apartment in the sky. Kathy fit right in. Dakota supposed he did, too— on the outside at least. He'd been born into money, even if he was the bastard son of a hard-nosed land baron, a man who'd left him a sizable inheritance. Dakota didn't fashion himself after his father, but he'd done his damnedest to earn the older man's respect.

Kathy paged through a magazine. It wasn't difficult to assess that she wasn't absorbed in its contents. Her mind was elsewhere. And rightly so, Dakota supposed. This mission had sucked both of them in, drawing them into an imminent vacuum.

Placing the magazine on a table, she looked up and asked, "Are you sure we're doing the right thing?"

Good God. She had second thoughts? Now? They were halfway to Asterland. "What do you mean?"

"Not involving the king and queen. I don't like deceiving them."

"We're not deceiving them. We're keeping this mission under wraps to protect them. The less people involved, the safer we'll all be."

Kathy frowned. "But it's their country."

And she was thinking with her heart instead of her head,

Dakota thought. Her friendship with the queen was blinding her judgment. "Kathy, we don't know how many cabinet members are actually part of the revolution plot. If the king or queen put their trust in the wrong person, it would blow our operation sky-high. We can't take that chance."

And Dakota had some concerns about Queen Nicole and Albert Payune. "Besides, how well do you really know the queen? She could have stumbled into an affair with Payune. That might be the reason he quit looking for a wife."

Kathy narrowed her eyes. "Queen Nicole hasn't *stumbled* into affair, Dakota. I already told you she wouldn't do something like that. She loves her husband."

And I thought you loved me, he wanted to say. "So women don't cheat on their husbands? They don't get themselves tangled up with other men?"

"Some do, I suppose. But not most. That's a man's game."

She picked up the magazine again, and Dakota kicked his legs out in front of him. A man's game. Right. He hadn't even looked at another women since she'd been gone. He studied Kathy's professional attire, her slim, fashionable figure. When she flipped a page, he caught sight of a gold band glinting on her finger. She wore her wedding ring, the diamond and emerald design he'd had custom made for her.

Don't take that as encouragement, he told himself. She'd put it back on for show, for the sake of their cover. "So have you been with anyone?" he asked, his voice gruff. "Did you leave me so you could sleep with another man?"

Kathy's complexion paled. "I can't believe you're asking me something like that."

He felt his muscles tense. Technically, they were still married. Neither had filed for a legal separation, much less a divorce. He had a right to know. "Well?"

"Of course not." She lifted her chin and met his gaze, her eyes locking onto his. "What about you? Have you been with someone?"

"No." He shook his head and made light of his loneliness, the years he'd waited for her to return. "The way I figure it, we've still got that piece of paper between us." As well as the vows they had taken.

For better or worse. Until death do us part. He had meant every word.

She let out an audible breath, her eloquent vocal skills suddenly failing her. "I suppose it was best that we…discussed this issue. I…we…don't need any personal distractions on this mission."

Yeah, and wondering if your spouse had a new lover would certainly fall under the category of a personal distraction. "I agree. Now that it's out in the open, I won't mention it again."

"Good."

Her smile was tight, but the fear in her eyes had faded. Fear that he had been with another woman. The thought made him a little smug, as well as confused. If things like that still mattered, why hadn't she come home before now?

Dakota dragged a hand through his hair. She isn't home, Lieutenant Lewis. This is an assignment, a fake reconciliation. Get your facts straight.

They remained silent for the next twenty minutes, she, occupying herself with another magazine, he, staring out the window at the night sky. He would have rather been piloting the plane than sitting idle, thinking about how much he missed a closeness with his wife. Sure, they had spent some time away from each other, but due to the nature of his work, those separations couldn't be helped. And their reunions used to be nice. Damn nice. Nothing like this one.

"Dakota?"

He turned away from the window. "Yes?"

"Why didn't you ever tell me the Lone Star jewels really existed?"

While he'd been thinking about her, she'd been thinking about the recovered jewels. Well, at least one of them had her mind on the mission. "Only those associated with the Texas Cattleman's Club were supposed to know they existed."

"Because of the legend?"

"Yes."

"So the story about that soldier is true?"

Dakota nodded. A Texas soldier had found the jewels during the War with Mexico and had brought them to Royal after the war, intending to sell them and make his fortune.

"When he came home, oil was found on his land. So he believed just owning the stones was lucky, and that they should remain in Royal."

"And now the Cattleman's Club protects them, and everyone else thinks their existence is just a legend. A story passed down from generation to generation."

"Yes, but Payune came across the truth somehow."

Kathy leaned forward, clearly engrossed in their conversation. But then she loved jewels, and the Lone Star gems were a rare, stunning collection. Too bad she would never see them, he thought. He would enjoy watching her eyes glow—those gorgeous green eyes.

"Any idea how Payune found out about them?" she asked.

"It's possible Prince Ivan had something to do with it. When he was in Royal, he asked a lot of questions. It would stand to reason that he heard about the legend. He probably told Payune about it."

"And Payune discovered the legend was true, from his comrade, Robert Klimt—the man who had stolen the jewels." Kathy reclined in her chair. "I'm so glad they were recovered. They haven't been safeguarded all these years to end up in the wrong hands."

"Funding a revolution no less." Dakota rose and headed toward a small wet bar. "Do you want a cold drink?" he asked.

She shook her head.

"Then how about a cup of hot tea?" He knew she added one teaspoon of sugar and a splash of cream to her tea. He wondered if she remembered little details about him or if she had chosen to forget. It wouldn't be hard to recall that he drank his coffee black or that he considered hot sauce a breakfast staple.

"No, thank you. I'm fine."

He poured himself a tall glass of soda water and returned to his seat.

Kathy placed the magazine on her lap. "Are you concerned about the queen's ball? I know how much you dislike social functions."

Dakota cocked an eyebrow at her. He didn't dislike all social functions, just the ones that required a tuxedo and served champagne instead of beer.

"No, I'm not concerned about it. I've been to plenty of fancy affairs." And they made him uncomfortable as hell, even the familiar Texas Cattleman's Club events. Dakota had spent more years in war paint and combat gear than he had in uniform. This ball, he figured, would be the worst part of the mission. Next to Kathy, he would probably look like a big, snorting Brahma. James Bond he wasn't. Not all undercover agents were that damned debonair.

"So you don't want me to brief you on royal protocol?" she asked.

Dakota scowled. "No, Miss friend-of-the-queen, I don't. I know how to behave around royalty. As you might recall, I spent twenty years of my life serving in the United States Air Force. I've picked up a few manners along the way."

She nibbled her bottom lip, then broke into an amused smile. "Miss friend-of-the-queen?"

He couldn't help but return her smile. Kathy knew him better than anyone. She knew darn well how he felt about attending the queen's birthday ball. "If the glass slipper fits, Lady Katherine."

She tossed her magazine at him. He ducked and shot her a playful grin, recalling how many times he used to tickle her on the living-room floor.

Dakota picked up the magazine, his grin fading. Somehow those tickling sessions would inevitably turn into foreplay. Hot, sexy kisses. Rubbing against each other through their clothes.

He looked over at Kathy and noticed her smile had disappeared, too. Just as well, he thought. The less tender memories they made, the better. Because when this assignment ended, they wouldn't be going home together.

The cottage the queen provided sat on a grassy cliff, the ocean below crashing upon a private stretch of beach. A cool, yet comfortable, sea breeze misted the May air, and clouds drifted lazily across an azure sky.

Kathy had stayed in the isolated cottage on several other occasions, and she adored the quaint, European charm. Window boxes displayed an arrangement of colorful flowers, and leafy vines clung to a white trellis. A scattered-stone walkway led to the front door. Inside was a collection of art and antiques, a cozy living area, two bedrooms, a fully stocked kitchen and two bathrooms decorated with hand-painted fixtures. French doors in each bedroom opened onto a lush, well-tended garden. A wrought-iron table sat amid perennial blooms in what Kathy considered an outdoor breakfast nook—a place to sip coffee and breathe the sea air.

The first thing Dakota did was search the cottage for concealed microphones, but Kathy expected as much. A frown furrowed his brow, she noticed. Was he preoccupied with the mission, or had he noticed the romantic ambiance—the vases of long-stemmed roses, the extravagant chocolates placed upon the master-bedroom bed? The big, quilted bed the queen's servants must have assumed Kathy and Dakota would be sharing?

He completed the search, and she stood beside their luggage. "We won't have daily maid service," she said. "There's a little bungalow behind the garden that was built as servant's quarters, but it's vacant. We've been provided with enough food, towels and linens to last through the week."

"Good. The less people around the better." He turned to look at her. "How did you manage that, anyway?"

"I informed the queen we wanted to be alone. She's fanatical about seeing to her guests' personal needs."

He frowned again. "Of course, our cover. Sorry, it was a stupid question."

With an answer that made them both wary, she realized. A married couple requesting privacy meant long, sensual baths, sipping wine by candlelight, feeding each other aphrodisiacs.

"I'll take the smaller bedroom," he said.

Kathy didn't respond, instead she followed him as he lifted her luggage and carried it to the master bedroom.

He placed her suitcase and garment bag on the bed, then turned toward the French doors and gazed out. "It's pretty here."

She moved to stand beside him. "There's a fountain in the center of the garden." And she thought of it as her own private wishing well, even if her wishes had yet to come true. "This cottage is in a world of its own."

"But it's not our world." With rigid shoulders, he turned away from the view, his mood switching from light to dark in one abrupt motion. "I have to meet with my contact soon. We can't get caught up in flowers and fountains. We're not on a holiday."

"I'm well aware of why we're here." Angry now, she continued to study the foliage. She wouldn't allow him to spoil the allure of her garden, a place where mystical creatures made magic. She wanted to believe that fairies fluttered around the flowers, and mermaids splashed in the ocean below.

"Kathy?"

She turned toward him with a hard stare. "What?"

He handed her one of the chocolates from the bed, an apology in his voice. "Truffles. They're your favorite."

She bit into the candy and savored the richness, the gentleness in his tone. "Is that why you offered me this room?" A silk-draped room with all the elements Kathy adored— scented candles, fresh-cut flowers, lace-trimmed sheers.

He smiled, but it fell short of reaching his eyes. He was worried, she realized. Worried about the mission, worried about being in an isolated cottage with his estranged wife. There was still so much distance between them, so much unnamed hurt. But how could she tell him that he hadn't loved her enough? That she needed more?

"You should unpack and get settled in," he said.

"I will." She searched his gaze. "Who is your contact, Dakota? Have I met him before?"

He shook his head. "No, but he's someone I've known a long time. A former intelligence officer, another skin."

Kathy knew that meant Dakota's contact was Native American. "Comanche?" she asked.

"Apache. Goes by the name Thunder. If something goes wrong on this assignment, he'll get in touch with you, Kathy. He vowed to look after you."

She didn't want to think about something going wrong, but she couldn't pretend the danger wasn't real. A man in Royal had been murdered by one of Payune's anarchists, and now they were on Payune's soil.

"Is Thunder a mercenary?" She knew Dakota didn't consider himself a mercenary because serving merely for pay wasn't his objective.

Dakota nodded. "Yes, but that doesn't make him someone you can't trust. He took a bullet for me. I owe him my life. We even look similar, like brothers."

Feeling an emotional chill, she crossed her arms. How many bullets had Dakota dodged? How many times had his life been spared? "Do you want me to unpack for you?" she asked, hoping he would understand why she had offered. She needed to place his clothes in the closet, his shaving gear in the bathroom. She used to unpack for him whenever he came home from an assignment. To her it meant he would be staying, at least for a while.

He didn't answer. Instead he remained motionless, staring at her. Her husband stood so close, she could see every eyelash, every pore in his sun-baked skin. And now she remembered how it felt to stroke his face. That intense face—smooth in some areas, rough in others.

Kathy moistened her lips. She wanted to grip his shoulders, lean into him and press her body against all that male hardness, feel her bones dissolve while his tongue stroked hers.

"You better go," she heard herself say.

She had no right to want him, not now, not after all the

tears she had cried, the baby she had lost. Dakota would forever be walking away. There would always be another assignment, another mission—something more important than
his marriage.

He left the cottage, and she decided not to unpack for him.
Touching his clothes would only make her ache.

Hours later Dakota returned from his meeting to find Kathy
in the garden. Rather than disturb the moment, he watched
her. She stood beside the fountain, wearing a pale cotton dress
that billowed softly in the breeze. Her hair fell loose from its
confinement, long silky strands framing her profile. She belonged in the setting, he thought. The foliage reached out to
her, colorful blooms and lush greenery graced by her presence.

He felt like an intruder. But he had some news, and it
couldn't wait. Bad news, it seemed, never could.

"Kathy?" he said softly.

She turned. "Oh, hi. I didn't know you were back."

"I haven't been here long." He hated to spoil the serenity,
the beauty of what he had come to think of as her garden.
Her enchanted garden. He had no right to be there. Dakota
wasn't a dreamer. To him life consisted of reality—hard,
strong doses of it.

"Any new information?" she asked.

He nodded. "A valuable necklace was stolen last night,
and Thunder is convinced Payune is responsible." Dakota
shifted his stance. "It belonged to the Duchess of Olin. A
rare ruby heirloom that will command a substantial price on
the black market."

"Now Payune has another means to fund his revolution."

"That's right. He couldn't get his hands on the Lone Star
jewels, so he went after the next best thing."

Kathy frowned. "How are we going to get around this?
You can't very well infiltrate Payune's operation if he doesn't
need the money you intend to offer."

"True. But Payune is still powerless until he fences the
necklace." Dakota felt a surge of adrenaline rush through his

veins, nervous energy he couldn't shake. This mission had become even riskier, and his wife was his partner. That thought didn't sit well. "I have to retrieve the necklace. Steal it back, so to speak."

Kathy's face paled. "How's that going to work? Payune will become suspicious of everyone who comes into contact with him. If the necklace is taken from him, he'll know that someone is trying to stop him from funding the revolution. And it won't take him long to look in your direction, not once you approach him with your cover."

"This won't affect my cover." Dakota resisted the urge to pace, to stalk the garden path. "The Duchess has a paste copy of the necklace. It's the one she wears in public, and it's extremely high quality—identical to the original. So all I have to do is switch them. Payune will never know he was robbed."

"Not until he tries to fence it and discovers it's fake."

"True, but that's the beauty of this plan." Because Kathy was still frowning, Dakota sent her a roguish grin. "Payune will think he nabbed the wrong necklace to begin with, rather than suspect foul play."

She chewed her bottom lip. "It could work."

"It has to. We don't have much time. Thunder thinks the necklace will be fenced right after the ball. Late that night. He has a pretty good handle on who's backing the sale."

"The ball is three days from now."

"Which is why I've secured a meeting with Payune tomorrow. I need to establish my cover before he tries to sell the necklace. If I wait to approach him, he just might put two and two together."

A light breeze blew the loose stands of Kathy's hair. "When are you going to switch the necklaces? You have to do it before the ball."

"Don't worry about it, sweetheart. I'll let you know when I've got the details worked out." Dakota was going to need her help. And Thunder's, too. It would take the three of them to pull this off.

He motioned toward the stone path leading back to the

cottage. "Why don't we go inside? I could use a cup of coffee." He had more news. Something that would take an emotional toll on Kathy, something he hated to tell her.

While Kathy brewed a pot of coffee, a wave of homesickness washed over Dakota. Not for Texas, but for her. He missed having her nearby, watching her do simple tasks. Her feet were bare, and more of her hair had come loose. He could almost imagine them snuggling in front of the TV, eating popcorn the way they used to.

Life had never been particularly simple for Dakota, but being married to Kathy made the world a better place. She brought out the good in him. Or at least he'd thought so. Kathy must have felt differently. A woman didn't leave a good man.

She handed him a cup of the dark brew. He carried it into the living room while she doctored hers with sugar and cream.

He lowered himself onto the sofa, and she entered the room and sat across from him in an overstuffed chair.

"I can tell there's something else going on," she said. "What is it?"

"You won't like it."

"Dakota. Quit stalling. That isn't like you."

"You're right." He wondered why he was trying to protect her from someone else's life. "There are rumors circulating about the king and queen."

She placed her coffee on a nearby table. "What kind of rumors?"

"That their marriage is in trouble."

She pushed a stray lock of hair away from her face, her posture suddenly tense. "I don't believe it. People like to make things up. Create scandals. That happens to every royal family."

"Don't hide your head in the sand, Kathy. Plenty of couples have problems. And royalty are like everyone else in that regard." Our marriage failed, he wanted to say. And we were supposed to be happy. Why not a king and queen?

She thrust her chin in a stubborn gesture. "This does not mean Queen Nicole is having an affair with Payune."

"I didn't say it did."

"But that's what you're thinking."

"No, it's not." He was thinking about his own life, about why Kathy had walked out on him. He wished to hell he knew what he had done wrong. But now wasn't the time to ask. Dakota had to concentrate on retrieving the stolen necklace, on trapping the revolutionists and sending them to jail.

This mission wasn't about the hole in his heart. It wasn't about the woman seated across from him, messy locks spilling out of her proper hairdo, her long slim body draped in a summer cotton dress. This romantic little cottage wasn't home, and he would do well to remind himself of that. Every chance he got.

Three

Kathy couldn't sleep. Tired of tossing and turning, she slipped out of bed, then stood before the French doors. She knew her garden was out there, and beyond it a grassy terrain dotted with wildflowers. Below the hills, a midnight ocean crashed upon the shore. She gazed out, but it was too dark to see anything but an eerie reflection of herself.

A woman in white silk, her hair a long, tousled curtain. She looked like a mysterious shadow. A faded image. The silhouette of a lady longing for her lover.

Suddenly she could see this woman, this shadow of herself, roaming the hills, the wind whipping through the night, a sheer nightgown clinging to her skin. She was naked beneath the gown, waiting for her lover to come to her. He was forbidden, she knew. But she wanted him. Wanted to tumble to the ground with him, tear at his clothes and feel his mouth ravage hers.

What am I doing?

Shaking off a sexual chill, Kathy reached for her robe. A thirty-two-year-old woman should know better.

What she needed was food. A sandwich might be a poor substitute for a good night's rest, but it would keep her mind off foolish fantasies.

Belting her robe, she made her way to the kitchen. She flipped on the light. The room was spotless. The appliances were white, the wallpaper a tiny floral pattern. The appeal was homey, but kitchens usually were.

Kathy opened the refrigerator and removed a package of ham. After spreading a small amount of mayonnaise on two slices of bread, she reached for the mustard. It was her favorite—a spicy French condiment. In her haste to combine the two flavors, she ended up with a glob on her finger. Lifting it to her mouth, she froze. The chill returned. This time it slid down her spine like a masculine hand brushing her skin.

She was being watched. She could feel his eyes on her. She hadn't heard him come into the room, but she felt him there.

Watching every move she made.

She squared her shoulders and turned. He stood in the open doorway, tall and silent, his stare dark and intense. He wore a pair of drawstring sweat pants, riding low enough to expose his navel. He looked big and powerful, almost frightening. His eyes were so black, his pupils no longer existed. He had spiked his hair with restless hands, the glossy strands a startling shade of midnight blue. A trick from the light, but it startled her just the same.

The muscles along his stomach rippled with each breath he took. Hard, barely controlled breaths.

He was angry. Or aroused. Neither thought gave her much comfort.

She wanted to leave the kitchen, retreat to the safety of her room. But she couldn't. Her sandwich was half made, and Dakota blocked the doorway. She had no choice but to continue her task, to convince herself his presence hadn't unnerved her.

"I can't sleep," he said.

Turning back to her sandwich, she barely glanced up.

"Neither can I. But then we both drank coffee later than we should have.''

Although she avoided his gaze, she knew it remained fixed on her. He couldn't know about her fantasy, about what her imagination had conjured, yet she sensed he did. In her mind, she had been waiting for her lover. Her forbidden lover. And now he was here—the man she wasn't supposed to want.

The coffee hadn't kept him awake, Dakota thought. She had.

It had been three years. Three years since he'd made love, since he'd felt her warm, willing heat. And she stood in the kitchen wearing a silky robe, her hair spilling gloriously over her shoulders—that fire-tinted hair he ached to grasp, lift to his face.

She didn't look his way. Instead she continued to make her sandwich. No, he couldn't sleep. Because he had tossed and turned, remembering every kiss, every tantalizing taste. He had even considered going outside, walking the cliffs as if he would find her there. As if she would be waiting.

"Maybe I should eat, too," he said. He wasn't hungry, but he couldn't think of another excuse to get close to her, to stand beside her and torture the hell out of himself.

"Oh, okay." She moved to allow him room at the butcher-block isle.

He came forward, grazing her shoulder as he reached for the bread. She slipped by him to rinse a tomato. And when she turned back, her robe fell open.

He wasn't a painter, a man who made images come to life, but at this moment, this incredible, breathtaking moment, he sought to immortalize her. Kathy's nightgown was as filmy as a lace curtain, as sheer as a summer rain. Her nipples brushed the surface, and he imagined the fabric cool and sleek against her skin.

He lifted his head, and their gazes collided. The tomato fell from her hand and rolled onto the butcher block. And then nothing moved. Nothing made a sound.

"What's happening?" she whispered, her voice barely audible.

He heard her, yet he didn't. Her robe was still open, and heat rose between their bodies like steam. He knew they fought to breathe the same air.

Outside the wind grew angry with lust, forcing its way through the trees. He could hear it rattling the windows.

He fought the urge to push her to the floor, tumble and roll, tear at the wisp of silk and lace she wore. Wild, forbidden lovemaking. The wind was challenging him to take her. His loins hardened, his pulse quickened, his mouth went dry. He moistened his lips and imagined tasting hers.

What's happening?

The wind howled again, and Dakota gripped the counter. Damn the wind. Damn the ache in his groin. He stared at Kathy; she stared back at him. Her eyes shone like emeralds. Sensual. Catlike.

Damn her.

Damn them both.

"Nothing's happening," he said, masking the arousal in his voice, the huskiness that nearly made him hoarse. "Your robe came undone, and…"

She moved like lightning, a blur before his eyes. When he focused again, her robe was belted, snug and secure. She picked up the tomato as though trying to backtrack, make that other moment disappear.

She glanced at him quickly, then looked away. She couldn't meet his gaze, yet only moments ago those green eyes bore brazenly into his.

This was so damn awkward, he thought. It shouldn't be, but it was. He had seen every inch of her, caressed her most intimate places. They had showered together, licked beads of water off each other's skin. They weren't sexual strangers. Yet they were. Three years spanned between them—an eternity.

"Maybe we should talk about it."

"There's nothing to talk about." She studied the tomato she had cut into even little slices. "We're making sandwiches."

"I'm not hungry. I only said I wanted a sandwich so I

could get close to you. But I'm okay now. I got through it, and so did you." He tossed his bread in the trash. "This is only our first night. We'll feel better in the morning. Normal." The wind would calm and the sexual pull would pass. Daylight would make everything all right.

She glanced up. "Do you think so?"

He could hope. "Sure. We just have to get used to each other."

Much to his relief, Kathy smiled—a small, delicate tilt of her lips. "Maybe I'll pass on the sandwich, too," she said. "It's been a long day, and I could use some sleep."

Dakota finally slept, not a deep, soundless sleep, but enough to help him function the following morning. He knew he would find Kathy in the kitchen. He could smell breakfast, the homey aroma of bacon sizzling and eggs frying.

He stood at the bathroom sink and splashed water on his face. A shower could wait. He couldn't recall the last time Kathy had cooked for him. It was a good sign, he thought. Apparently she had decided to put what had happened behind them.

As casually as possible, he entered the kitchen. "Good morning. Is there anything I can do to help?"

She turned away from the stove, and for a moment, a suspended moment in time, their eyes met. And held.

He stood, riveted to the floor, the tiles cool against his feet. Don't let it happen again. Not now. Not today.

She blinked, and the air in his lungs whooshed out.

"You can set the table."

"Sure. Okay." He opened the appropriate cabinet and removed the dishes. "The bacon smells good. A great aroma to wake up to."

"I figured we could both use a hearty breakfast." She motioned to the coffee pot. "It's strong and dark, just the way you like it."

"Thanks." Sidetracked now, he left the table half set. Pouring himself a mug of freshly perked coffee, he leaned against the counter and sipped. Was Kathy worried about his meeting with Payune? Was that the reason for this special treatment? Or was she trying to prove how normal staying in the same house could be?

Her hair was coiffed to perfection, he noticed, the fiery tresses twisted neatly, two pearl combs making an elegant statement. Her skin glowed flawlessly, her makeup applied with skill. She wasn't dressed to go out, but he sensed she would be before long.

Realizing breakfast was ready and he'd neglected his domestic duty, he gathered some silverware and napkins. The kitchen table matched the butcher-block isle, and a bay window presented a spectacular view.

She filled their plates and took a chair. He sat across from her and smiled. She had placed his favorite hot sauce on the table. Apparently she had supplied the queen's servants with a list of foods to provide, right down to brand name selections—items imported from a variety of continents.

He lifted the bottle, then poured the spicy sauce over his eggs. "You remembered."

"Of course," she responded in an easy voice. "How could I forget? You practically refuse to eat breakfast without it."

Was she as relaxed as she seemed? Or was she drawing from her social skills to fool him? Dakota thought Kathy would make a hell of a poker player. She could bluff with the best of them. He had no idea what was actually going on in her mind.

His one-track mind, on the other hand, had taken a dangerous turn. He imagined destroying her proper hairdo, bathing her lips with strawberry preserve, then licking it off with slow, erotic strokes. Apparently his social skills, as well as his table manners, weren't enviable qualities. It didn't take much to fuel his sexual appetite—a sunny kitchen and a tasty breakfast did him just fine. Now last night's haunting didn't seem quite so odd. The woman had been wearing see-through silk.

"Do you have an appointment later?" he asked.

"Tea with the queen. The palace is sending a car for me this afternoon."

A long, black limo, no doubt. He cocked his head. "That sounds downright snooty. Why didn't you tell me before now?"

She buttered her toast. "I always have tea with the queen when I'm invited to Asterland. This is nothing out of the ordinary. It won't arouse suspicion."

He shoveled a forkful of eggs into his mouth and swallowed, enjoying the trappings of a home-cooked meal. "Routine or not, you still have to keep me informed about everywhere you go, everything you do. Don't take anything for granted while we're here. Okay?"

She nodded solemnly. "Okay."

Dakota savored a slice of bacon, and Kathy added cream to her coffee, a drink he assumed she had diluted with extra water. He knew she preferred a milder brew.

She studied her cup, and he assumed her mind was on her audience with the queen.

Today they would both slip into their respective roles.

Hours later Dakota arrived at Albert Payune's home. A crenellated gateway, reminiscent of a medieval structure, led to the entrance of the Grand Minister's estate. The house itself wasn't quite so foreboding, but it reflected European craftsmanship with its stone-by-stone construction.

A butler escorted Dakota to a dimly lit office furnished with a large mahogany desk and leather wing-back chairs. But what caught Dakota's eye was an impressive collection of swords. Displayed on the paneled walls, they wielded military power, something Payune obviously admired.

"The Grand Minister will be with you shortly," the butler said, his English heavily accented.

"Thank you," Dakota responded, exaggerating his drawl. Today he was a big, tall, rich Texan—a businessman eager to make an unethical deal.

He didn't scan his surroundings for a safe. He knew Payune wouldn't keep the stolen necklace in his office. He would probably secure the heirloom jewels in his private quarters— the master suite where he slept. Thunder was working on a diagram of the estate, so it wouldn't be long before Dakota would have a floor plan to back up his instincts.

Minutes later Payune entered the room. A man in his early fifties, he stood with his shoulders squared and his head held high. He was neither tall nor broad. He was of medium height with a medium build, his physique toned and trim. He wore a dark suit with a silk ascot tie. And although his hair was thinning, he wasn't foolish enough to style it in one of those ridiculous comb-overs. Albert Payune carried his vanity with pride. He had an impeccable quality about him, but power-hungry rulers often did.

Payune extended his hand, and they exchanged a proper greeting.

Dakota had dressed carefully for the occasion. He couldn't present himself as a showy, loud-mouthed American, because that would belie his military background. But he still wanted to be easily identified with Payune's image of Texas, so he had worn a pair of custom-made cowboy boots and a 5X Royal Stetson he'd removed upon entering the house.

"Please, have a seat, Lieutenant Lewis."

"Thank you." Dakota settled into one of the wing-back chairs while Payune walked around to the desk. Referring to a retired officer by his rank was accepted as proper protocol, and a man in Payune's position would naturally adhere to decorum.

The butler appeared with a silver tray, offering both men snifters of brandy. When the servant departed, Payune lifted his eyes to Dakota.

"So you have come to discuss a business venture?"

"Yes, sir, I have." Dakota met the other man's detached gaze. "My partners and I intend to open a resort in Asterland with the biggest, grandest casino imaginable. But our only stumbling block is King Bertram." And for the sake of this mission, a proposal for the resort had been presented to the Cabinet under the guise of a Texas corporation. A proposal Dakota knew the king would not approve.

"I see." Payune swirled his brandy. "Am I to understand

that you want me to influence King Bertram to reconsider his stand on this matter?''

''In a manner of speaking.''

''You realize the king believes our country could not successfully support a venture such as yours. Our neighbors in Obersbourg have converted a portion of their palace into an exclusive gaming casino. How many resorts are tourists willing to visit? Asterland is still quite obscure.''

''So was Obersbourg before they opened their casino.'' And Dakota knew damn well Payune didn't intend to rule an obscure little country. He wanted to put himself and Asterland on the map. ''I'm talking about a full-scale resort—a five-star hotel, a spa, a country club and a PGA quality golf course. I have some of the wealthiest men in Texas in on this deal. And we don't intend to take no for an answer.''

Payune's demeanor was no longer detached. ''I've seen your proposal. And I must admit, it was quite impressive.''

''And so is the fact that you're going to govern Asterland someday.''

''You're mistaken. Prince Eric is heir to the throne.''

Dakota chose not to comment further. The Grand Minister was playing the loyal Cabinet member, feigning disinterest in the crown.

Payune placed his hands on the desk, then linked them together. ''As I said, the proposal for your resort was impressive, but I am puzzled by one thing.''

Dakota sipped his drink even though he had never acquired a taste for brandy. ''And what would that be?''

''Why, your wife, of course. Is she aware of your venture?''

Dakota's heart took a quick, forward leap. ''She's not only aware of it, she supports it without reserve.''

''But she is also a high-ranking Foreign Affairs consular.''

Dakota kept his gaze focused on his opponent. ''That's right, she is,'' he said, his tone implying Kathy used a government job to her best advantage. If Payune assumed Kathy's friendship with the royal family had been manipulated to influence the king to approve the resort, then all the better. But before the other man concentrated too deeply on Kathy, Dakota continued, "I was hoping, sir, that you would help me get this project off the ground. If anyone can make this happen, you can."

Payune sat with his head tilted at a regal angle. "I appreciate your confidence, but I do not see how I can."

"Maybe you could take some time to think it over." Dakota paused a beat, then leaned forward and dropped a hint about the impending revolution, making damn sure the other man wouldn't forget this meeting. "My partners and I are willing to make it worth your while." A cash settlement he hoped Payune would be in dire need of within a matter of days. "And with your involvement, I'm sure King Bertram would no longer stand in our way."

Kathy walked with Queen Nicole along a stone path. Both women adored flowers, and strolling the castle gardens after a tea had become one of their favorite moments to share. Azaleas, poppies, tulips, irises—Kathy couldn't begin to name them all. There were also bridges to cross, statues to admire, bodies of water rippling with sunlight.

"This is like stepping into a painting," Kathy said.

The queen smiled as they passed a lily pond, then stopped to breathe the country air. "And today we are in a Monet."

Kathy turned to look at her friend. She thought Queen Nicole was one of the most beautiful women she had ever seen. With jet black hair and violet-blue eyes, she could have been a model. Even at fifty-three, she had a face and figure cameras loved. But for Kathy there was no envy, only admiration.

"You have been quiet on this visit," the queen said. "Are you not well?"

"I'm fine. It's just been so long since I've shared a home with my husband." At least, she thought, that was a portion of the truth. She couldn't lead the queen to believe that her personal life was in perfect order, that her supposed reconciliation with Dakota had no flaws. The queen had come to know her too well for such a charade.

"You have not told him yet, have you?"

"About the miscarriage? No. And I'm not sure I can."

The other woman guided her toward a bench overlooking a sweep of irises. "If you want to have a life with him again, then you must."

But I'm only pretending I want a life with him, Kathy thought. So what good would it do to tell him about the baby? They couldn't alter the past. Dakota hadn't been there when she'd needed him. There was nothing either one of them could do that would change that.

"You could forgive him," the queen said as though reading her mind. "There is healing in forgiveness."

Kathy watched a butterfly light upon a flower. "I know." But how could she forgive him when she knew his work would always be more important than their marriage? "We're still attracted to each other." A dangerous attraction, she thought. "I can't think clearly when I'm around him."

No, she couldn't think, but she could feel. And fantasize.

She could still see herself waiting for him on the cliffs. Waiting for him to pull her to the ground, tear her nightgown and cover her body with his. And for one haunting moment last night, she knew he had wanted the same thing—desperate, forbidden lovemaking—a union they would have regretted later.

Queen Nicole sighed. "I have no right to give advice."

Jarred from her wayward thoughts, Kathy turned, then studied her friend's sad expression. "Forgive me for asking, but are the rumors true? Is your marriage troubled?"

"Yes, very troubled. Losing Ivan has put a strain on our relationship. The king refuses to mourn his son. He cannot cope with what Ivan did."

Kathy hadn't been prepared to discuss Prince Ivan, but she could see that the other woman needed to confide in some-one—someone she trusted. "Most men don't grieve the way women do. They tend to keep their feelings inside."

Queen Nicole's voice quavered. "But the king is still too hurt and too angry to grieve. And until he forgives Ivan, our lives will never be the same." She lifted her face to the sun as though the warmth would help. "I, too, was destroyed by what Ivan had done. But he left us a note. He begged for our forgiveness.''

Kathy knew Prince Ivan had arranged a car accident that had taken the lives of a neighboring princess and her lover. Plus he'd tried to force the princess's sister, Anna, to marry him and merge their countries. So in remorse and shame, the Asterland prince had committed suicide rather than face his family. "I'm sorry. I wish there was something I could say."

"I grieved for my son when I buried him, and I found it in my heart to forgive him. I ask nothing more of the king."

"I understand."

Together they rose from the bench and walked side by side in companionable silence, the garden offering solace. Kathy had never doubted the queen's love for the king, nor had she suspected her of having an affair with Payune. And now Dakota could put aside his suspicion. What troubled the royal marriage was not another man.

Footsteps sounded on the walk, and a child with a radiant smile appeared. Ten-year-old Prince Eric had slipped through a path of trees, his fretful, red-faced nanny on his heels.

The queen laughed. "He is so full of energy."

And so beautiful, Kathy thought. The young prince had inherited his mother's jet-black hair and easy manner. His skin was tanned from the outdoor activities he enjoyed at his American boarding school, and his eyes were dark like the king's.

Like Dakota's.

Kathy realized Prince Eric looked the way she imagined a child of hers and Dakota's would look. Immediately she thought about the baby she had lost—the little boy or girl who should be toddling beside her.

"Mother, you told me I could visit with Kathy," the boy said.

"Yes, but I did not say you could give Nanny a wild goose chase." The queen cupped her son's cheeks, then whispered. "Nanny is not so young anymore. You must show her the courtesy befitting her age."

"Yes, ma'am," he responded.

Kathy knew the boy wanted to fidget. She couldn't help but smile. Prince Eric glanced over at her with a gleam in his dark eyes. When his mother released him, he came toward her with a proper greeting, and she responded in kind.

The hug that followed made her a little misty-eyed. "I've missed you, young sir."

"And I, you." He stood gazing up at her. "Mother says I may go to the ball. At least for a little while."

"I'm glad. I'll be there, too."

"Is your husband going to escort you?"

Kathy resisted the urge to skim his bangs from his eyes. "Yes, he is."

"So I will meet him?"

She thought of her lost child again. Dakota's child. "Yes," she said softly. "I would like very much for the two of you to meet."

Kathy sat beside Dakota in their rental vehicle, heading down a winding country road toward the beach. They had dressed for a casual outing, but Kathy assumed Dakota had business on his mind. They had a lot to discuss. The queen's birthday ball was tomorrow evening, and the necklace switch still hadn't been made.

Dakota parked the utility vehicle, and they remained silent for a moment. The private beach presented a narrow stretch of sand and a clear blue ocean bathing a scatter of large, jagged rocks.

Kathy smiled to herself. Mermaids lounged on the rocks when no one could see them, she thought—their long, luxurious hair blowing in the breeze, their iridescent tails swaying to the rhythm of the sea. Were there mermen? Or did the mermaids sing their siren's song for human males—men who didn't believe in fairy tales.

Men like Dakota.

"Let's go," he said.

He carried a blanket and a backpack, and she trudged beside him in a pair of lace-up boots. It wasn't a swimsuit day. The wind blew with a brisk chill, and the ocean roared with

foaming waves. Both she and Dakota wore sweatshirts and
jeans.

He picked a spot away from the tide and secured the blanket the best he could. They sat beside each other, and Kathy
waited for him to speak. She could have kept silent for hours
just watching the sea, imagining schools of glittery fish and
sunken treasures sparkling with gold.

"Have you ever been through the maze at the palace?" he
asked.

Kathy turned. "Just once. Prince Eric wanted me to play
hide-and-seek with him, but I ended up getting lost. He had
to rescue me, even though he was the one hiding. I felt a little
foolish." And somewhat frightened. The garden maze was a
labyrinth of tall, dark-green shrubs, a puzzle that had made
her feel like Alice in Nightmareland.

"Did you ever make it to the center?"

She nodded. "Prince Eric guided me there." And she recalled a white gazebo, a porch-type swing and a lovely arrangement of seasonal blooms. "It was pretty, but not quite
worth the trouble."

He frowned. "So you wouldn't remember how to get to
the gazebo on your own?"

Kathy pushed a strand of hair away from her face. She had
worn her hard-to-hold hair in a practical ponytail, but already
wispy tendrils were coming loose. "Heavens, no." She studied the crease between his eyebrows. "Why? What's going
on?"

"I'm going to switch the necklaces during the ball."

She had no idea what that had to do with the garden maze,
but, regardless, his plan made no sense. "You can't. You're
a guest at the ball. Nobody can be two places at once."

"It's the only time I can make the switch, the only time I
can be absolutely certain of Payune's whereabouts." He sent
her a wicked grin, his teeth gleaming. "And you're wrong, I
can be in two places at once."

That slash of white in an otherwise dark face made him
look like a rogue. She had to tell her girlish heart to behave.
"I hope you're going to explain."

He moved closer. "Of course, I am. This plan involves you."

And that nightmarish maze, she thought with sudden doom. "Go ahead."

"Okay. We'll attend the ball—drink, dance and make our presence known to Payune. Then at 2030, we'll take a walk—stroll through the maze and neck a little on our way to the gazebo."

Her heart bumped. "Neck?"

The roguish grin returned. "Kiss, nibble, paw each other like lusty teenagers."

She couldn't catch her breath, so she forced herself to gulp the sea air. She didn't want to kiss him. Well, maybe she did. But because she did, she knew she shouldn't. "That's hardly proper behavior at a royal ball."

He raised an eyebrow at her. "Don't get your sequins in a snit, Kathy. This is part of the mission. Payune might be watching us. He may even decide to follow. But if he sees us wrapped in each other's arms, he'll figure we're just out on a romantic, moonlit stroll."

How did Dakota know her dress had sequins on it? she wondered testily, wishing she had brought an alternative ball gown. "Payune is going to be that suspicious of us? Enough to follow us outside?"

"Hell, yes. He's not a stupid man. He understood the direction I was taking yesterday. I'm a former air force officer from Royal, Texas, with a Foreign Service consular for a wife. And to top it off, we're asking to be part of his revolution." Dakota blew a windy breath. "I'd say that makes us the most interesting couple at the ball."

He was right, of course. But necking for the sake of the mission irked her. Everything Dakota did was for some top-secret assignment, and now that included kissing her. "So what happens next?"

"We go to the gazebo, retreat to a dark corner, and I slip away. From there I break into Payune's estate, switch the necklaces and return before anyone knows I'm gone."

Panic rose in her throat as the sound of the ocean crashed in her ears. "You're going to leave me in the maze? Alone?"

His voice gentled. "No, sweetheart. Thunder will take my place. In the dark, we're virtually twins. Same height, same body structure."

Wonderful. She would be trapped in the maze with a stranger while Dakota took all the risks. "Why can't Thunder switch the necklaces?"

"Because breaking and entering are my areas of expertise, not his."

Kathy got a mental picture of a cat burglar—a tall, shadowy figure dressed in black. Dakota would do his part, and she would have to do hers. "It's a good plan," she said, reminding herself the future of a country was at stake.

"Thanks." He removed a sheet of paper from his backpack, and it snapped in the wind. "Now all we have to do is memorize the key to the maze."

"Is that a diagram of it?" she asked, leaning toward the paper.

He nodded. "Looks like one of those magazine puzzles, doesn't it?"

"Yes, it does." The pattern of the hedges had been outlined, along with a red line marking a zigzag path to the gazebo. She assumed the resourceful mercenary named Thunder had provided it.

"Come sit here so we can study it together."

Here, Kathy realized, undoubtedly meant between those long, denim-clad legs and against that big, broad chest. She frowned at the map. Didn't he have another copy? "Why do we have to share?"

"So we can snuggle. Payune won't buy our cover if we flinch every time we touch." He adjusted his position to make room for her. "Since we have to get physical at the ball, we may as well get used to the idea now."

Sure. Right. For the sake of the mission, she thought, hiding her frown. Settling herself between his legs, she leaned back, then held her breath. In spite of the chill, a sudden, unwelcome heat blazed through her body.

"Relax," he whispered, slipping his arms around her waist.

She let out the breath she was holding and tried to focus on the sway of the ocean, the color of the sand, the sprinkle of broken sea shells surrounding their blanket. But her concentration wavered. All she could think about was the pressure of her bottom nestled between his thighs.

He moved closer and nuzzled her neck. He smelled like a familiar brand of aftershave, the one he had always worn. She swallowed and searched for a place to rest her hands.

"You still feel stiff," he said.

Well, so did he, she thought, lowering her hands to her own lap. But then his stiffness was beneath his zipper, and that probably didn't count.

"I'm fine," she responded. But when he tugged at her earlobe with his teeth, she wasn't fine. She wanted to turn her head and capture his mouth, remember the first time they had kissed. The last time. Every time in between.

He held the maze key out in front of her. The paper rippled in the wind. "Don't let it blow it away," he told her.

She grabbed it and held on for dear life. She felt him removing the decorative band from her hair, dislodging her ponytail. She knew he liked her hair loose, liked to run his hands through it, liked to mar her proper image.

"Do you still think about me, Kathy?"

In bed. He wanted to know if she climbed under the covers at night and thought about him, imagined the stroke of his tongue, the rock of his hips. That hard, powerful body thrusting into hers. "Yes."

He placed his hand over hers, then began tracing the pattern of the map. When his jaw brushed the side of her cheek, his beard stubble grazed her skin. "I think about you, too. About all the things I used to do to you." His voice turned low—hushed and aroused. "The naughty things you used to do to me."

Kathy moistened her lips.

The naughty things you used to do to me.

Suddenly the secluded beach called out to her—the allure of the wind, the scent of the sea, the passion of the sky. Now she remembered the last time they had made love. The way they had rolled over the bed, tugging at each other's clothes. His labored breathing, her hand closing over his arousal. The forceful kisses, the soft moans, the silky sensations. She had lowered her head to taste him, take him into her mouth while he'd fisted her unbound hair and raised his hips, his gaze following every urgent stroke.

"You used to watch," Kathy heard herself say. You watched that night, she thought, that wild, bittersweet night.

"And you used to make me crazy," he responded, scraping his jaw against her cheek once again. "So good. So crazy."

Her heartbeat thudded in time with his, but she knew he wouldn't kiss her, wouldn't ease the forbidden hunger flowing through their veins. Instead he would make them both wait until tomorrow night. The mission, Kathy thought. As much as they lusted after each other, they still needed an excuse— even for a kiss.

Four

Dakota walked down the hall, then stopped when he saw Kathy through her open doorway. She stood in front of a full-length mirror, checking her appearance. When she smoothed her dress, he allowed himself a long, languorous look.

The emerald-colored gown clung to her curves in a lithe, elegant shimmer. The fabric, a watery satin, caught the light each time she moved. The neckline, decorated with a row of sequins, revealed a hint of cleavage. Her skin looked warm and smooth next to all that icy green.

Her hair, he decided, had been styled with him in mind. It fell loose about her shoulders in thick, scarlet waves, both sides adorned with a diamond-and-emerald-studded comb. It appeared deliberately messy, yet fashionable. He could touch it, twine it around his fingers, lift it to his face, and no one would know. It was, Dakota thought with a smile, a hairstyle created for lovers.

When she turned his way, her hand flew to her heart. "Oh my God! You scared the daylights out of me. How long have you been standing there?"

Long enough to get turned on, he almost said, his smile tilting a little crookedly. "Just a few minutes."

Her eyes, he noticed, had been enhanced with a smoky liner. The dark, sultry illusion made them appear even more catlike. "You look incredible, Kathy."

She tilted her head, and diamonds winked at her ears. "Thank you."

She slipped into satin pumps, and he wondered what she had going on under her dress. A corset-type bra? Silk panties? A garter belt and thigh-high hose? He moved into the room so he could enjoy her mouthwatering scent. He knew she had layered her favorite body products: powder, lotion, a strawberry mist. She smelled good enough to eat, so he imagined lathering her with whipped cream—a taste from her nipples—a line down her belly—a sweet, sexy flavor between those long, gorgeous legs.

She would purr, he decided. Press herself against his mouth and make throaty little sounds.

When she glanced up, he shoved his hands in his pockets and feigned a casual air. He wasn't behaving like an officer or a gentleman. But damn it, he wanted her. Wanted to bathe her with the afterglow of a warm, wet orgasm.

"You look handsome, Dakota."

He blinked, his blood still pumping lust through his veins. Struggling to focus, he glanced at his starched white shirt. He wore a traditional black tux with a pair of onyx cufflinks. Kathy had always liked the way he looked in formal attire. "Oh, yes. Thanks."

She opened a sequin evening bag and placed a lace handkerchief, a gold compact and a tube of lipstick inside. Then reaching into the closet, she removed a shimmering green jacket that matched her sleeveless dress. "I'm ready."

They walked toward the front door, then he turned and headed into the kitchen. "I forgot something." Opening the fridge, he removed a windowed box. "It's a wrist corsage." A delicate floral design he couldn't resist—a white orchid with gold ribbon and a spray of baby's breath shimmering with emerald glitter.

"How did you know?" she asked, reaching for the flower, her voice soft with feminine wonder.

"That it would match your gown?" he watched her slip the corsage around her wrist. "I didn't. I ordered it because it reminded me of you." And because he knew it would complement the diamonds and emeralds sparkling on her finger— the engagement ring and wedding band he had given her.

An hour later they arrived at the palace, then stood with the other guests in a receiving line, waiting to pay their respects to the royal family. The king stood tall in a uniform that displayed his commander-in-chief status. Dakota assumed Payune drooled inwardly over that uniform, since the impressive armed forces rank came with the crown.

The queen glittered in a diamond tiara and a sparkling gown, and young Prince Eric wore a serious expression, even though boyish excitement brightened his dark eyes.

The ballroom dominated nearly an entire floor. Crystal chandeliers glimmered from the ceiling and leaded-glass doors led to the gardens. Tables in the dining area were set with candles, polished silver and fine linens. A velvet curtain with gold tie-backs signaled the entrance to the dance hall.

Dakota wasn't the least bit nervous, but he was no longer out of his element. Tonight's agenda put him in control. The ball was now a crucial part of the mission.

As the festivities got underway, Kathy spoke to a great number of people—most of them as noble as their prestigious European titles. Dakota kept one eye trained on Albert Payune and noticed the Grand Minister kept an equally close eye on him.

Kathy excused herself from an elderly duke, and Dakota escorted her to the expansive buffet. It was, he thought, the most impressive spread he had ever seen. Each delicacy was a work of art, but Kathy had told him that renowned chefs from around the world had been flown in to prepare the menu. Serving platters brimmed with deviled quail eggs, gingered capon, crab soufflé, tender meats, fresh vegetables and exotic fruits. The dessert tables displayed decadent cakes, parfaits, tortes, tarts and meringues.

They filled their plates and sat beside each other in their designated seats. Kathy sampled a lobster crepe, then looked up and smiled. Their gazes locked in an intense stare, and Dakota knew their minds had connected. Yesterday's erotic admission billowed between them like a warm, sensual cloud. Both still fantasized about being in each other's arms—aroused and naked.

Her tongue darted out to taste the crepe, and he nearly groaned. He wanted to kiss her. Here. Right now. In front of the king and all of his fancily attired court.

But as other guests occupied their table, Dakota reined in his hormones. And while they ate their meal, they engaged in varied conversations.

On occasion Dakota glanced at Payune from across the room and noticed Payune kept stealing glances at the queen.

After dessert and coffee, the king and queen danced the first waltz. Dakota and Kathy stood with other guests, watching the royal couple glide across the floor.

"They look so right together," Kathy said, her voice tinged with sadness.

Dakota frowned. His wife was still upset by the queen's troubled marriage. Or was it the reminder of their own broken vows that she thought of tonight? He sensed this was not the moment to ask her to dance. Instead he suggested they explore the alcoves in the ballroom, and she readily agreed.

The first windowed section held a pair of seventeenth-century Venetian chairs, and the second displayed borders of rose-covered silk and a marble table.

Kathy examined a gilded vase on the table, and Dakota moved closer. "Did you wear your hair like that for me?" he asked, studying the tumbling red tresses she normally struggled to contain. He would not allow her sadness to linger. Not tonight.

She hesitated, then met his gaze, her eyes as illuminating as her gown. "Yes," she said softly.

"Because you knew I would want to run my hands through it?"

"Yes," she whispered again.

He skimmed her cheek. She hadn't reapplied her lipstick. Her lips were moist and slightly parted, just waiting for his. Dare he kiss her now? Inside the palace?

He dropped his hand. He couldn't. There were too many guests milling about, too many foreign dignitaries, dukes and counts, lords and ladies.

"Excuse me. Ma'am? Sir?" a voice said.

Dakota cursed his lack of focus. Someone had managed to approach without his knowledge. And at the very moment he had been debating a kiss, no less. He raised an eyebrow at Kathy. She, too, seemed surprised. Unsure of what to expect, they turned simultaneously.

Prince Eric stood before them. In spite of his regal posture and proper tuxedo, the boy's appearance made Dakota smile. The child's thick black hair rebelled from a slick side part, a cowlick fighting desperately for control. Apparently the young prince had hair as hard to tame as Kathy's.

They responded to the boy as protocol dictated, and Dakota decided Prince Eric owned not an ounce of pretension. He was being groomed to rule an old-world country, but his manner put both Dakota and Kathy at ease.

"Are you a United States Air Force lieutenant?" the boy asked Dakota, clearly wondering why he wasn't in uniform.

"I retired from duty four years ago," Dakota told him.

"Are you a pilot?"

"Yes. Do planes interest you?"

"Yes, and cowboys, too," came the youthful response. "I attend a boarding school in America."

Dakota resisted the urge to slip Kathy a sideways glance. He supposed he looked like a forty-one-year-old cowboy with his rugged skin and hard-earned crow's-feet. His Texas drawl certainly fit the cowboy mold. Dakota didn't have a lot of experience with children, so the last thing he had expected was admiration from an adolescent prince. It boosted his pride with a masculine sort of awe.

"So you like horses, then?"

Prince Eric nodded, his voice a little quieter. "But I prefer a Western saddle to the hunt seat," he said as if the admission might earn him a European scolding. A security officer in the royal service stood a non-intrusive distance away, keeping a careful eye on the boy.

Dakota smiled. He doubted the stoic-faced guard had heard, and even if he had, who would tattle on a future king?

For a moment Dakota thought to invite the child to his ranch. He could teach the young prince about Comanche horsemanship. In Dakota's culture, a boy didn't merely learn to ride. He had to be a trick rider, practice picking up objects while his mount traveled at full speed. And the ten-year-old prince, with his rebellious hair and dark, curious eyes, would make a quick study. European royalty, he thought, with a Comanche soul.

Dakota shook off the notion, realizing he had allowed an unexpected paternal urge to get the best of him. He couldn't extend an invitation to Price Eric, he thought, a twinge of regret constricting his chest. Who would explain his true marital status? Who would tell the child that Kathy no longer lived at the ranch? It was bad enough the young Prince would be burdened by his parents' personal problems. He didn't need to be dragged into Dakota's as well.

After Prince Eric departed, Dakota and Kathy returned to the main ballroom. As they left the charming alcove, Kathy's heartbeat quickened. Heading toward them was Albert Payune, his steely blue eyes focused directly on her.

There was no way to avoid him. Soon they would come face-to-face with the man who had been watching them for most of the night. Did Payune know that Prince Eric had looked upon Dakota with youthful admiration? Or that Dakota had smiled affectionately at the child? The rightful heir to the Asterland throne?

Payune shifted his gaze to Dakota. "Lieutenant Lewis," he said in a formal greeting. "Are you enjoying the ball?"

"Yes, thank you. And you, sir?"

Such stifled pleasantries, Kathy thought, her pulse refusing to relax. How could Dakota stand there looking so calm?

Because it was his job, she reminded herself. Her husband thrived on danger.

"It is a lovely affair," Payune responded in an unemotional tone. He turned to Kathy, trapping her with a cool smile. "Mrs. Lewis, you look simply stunning."

She forced herself to meet those frosty blue eyes. "Thank you."

He held her gaze, and she knew he was testing her, waiting to see if she squirmed. She lifted her chin a notch, even though she feared the pounding of her heart would give her panic away.

"Your husband came to see me the other day," Payune said. "We had quite an interesting chat."

She glanced briefly at Dakota. He didn't come closer, didn't coax or comfort her in any way. But the Grand Minister studied them with keen interest. Assessing their body language, she assumed.

"Yes, he told me," she said. "And I do hope you will consider his offer."

"We shall see. For now, it is much too grand a night to concern ourselves with business." He reached for her hand and brushed his mouth over her knuckles in the same manner he had brushed off her statement. "But I would be honored, Mrs. Lewis, if you would save me a dance."

"Of course." She wanted to snag her hand back and wipe it on her dress. Even his lips were cold.

Dakota moved in with a smile, touching her with sudden familiarity. She did her best not to collapse in his arms.

"My lovely wife promised me a tour of the gardens. Didn't you, darling?"

"Yes, I did. The grounds are breathtaking."

"Do not detain her for too long, Lieutenant." Payune split his cool gaze between them. "I am looking forward to that dance."

The instant Kathy and Dakota stepped outside, she allowed herself a nervous shiver.

"Are you cold?" he asked. "Do you need your jacket?"

"No, I'm fine. The air feels good." She took a deep,

cleansing breath. Already she could smell sweet, earthy scents rising from the flowers. She would draw from their beauty, she thought. Their magic. Surely the palace gardens had resident fairies, little winged creatures who would keep them safe.

They walked arm in arm for a short while, taking the stone path that would eventually lead to the maze. As they came upon the queen's traditional rose garden, he spoke in a hushed tone. Other guests explored the grounds, their voices a distant buzz.

"You did fine, sweetheart."

"He's suspicious of us."

"Of course, he is. I expected as much. He isn't the sort of man who puts his trust in others. Not even those he considers allies."

And that worried her. Payune might accept Dakota's offer, might bring him into the revolution, but her husband would be watched. Maybe too closely.

Before she could ask if he thought they were being followed, Dakota stopped to draw her into his arms. Needing him, she came willingly. He dipped his head and his breath fluttered across her cheek, then brushed her lips.

The kiss was tender and protective, and she welcomed it from deep within her soul. Roses flourished all around them— a gathering of soft, velvety petals—long, sturdy stems and prickly thorns. Beauty and danger, her mind warned.

This man.

This moment.

Their tongues touched lightly, ever so lightly. It was a tease, an awakening. He tasted of Russian vodka. Just a little, she realized, just enough to induce a slow, warm intoxication.

She let the sensation steep her, heat and melt and pull her into a dreamy state. He licked her bare shoulder, grazed it with his teeth. She clung to him, felt a shift in his stance. She inhaled his cologne, wanting to breathe him into her lungs, into her body.

He nuzzled her neck, then lifted his head and brought his face next to hers. "We have to go. We can't stay here."

"I know." Somewhere in the back of her foggy mind, she heard voices. Someone was speaking French. A language as fluid as their kiss.

Although flood lights lit the gardens, shadows danced across their path—dark, leafy shapes—tall, billowy figures. Their feet scraped the stone walk, scattering pebbles. The natural perfume from the roses had disappeared. Beyond them lay an endless carpet of grass, and in the distance a dark, ominous structure.

The maze stood like an ancient castle, ghostly and foreboding. The music from the palace seemed ghostly, too—a lonely waltz drifting into the shadows.

"It looks haunted," Kathy said. And if someone followed, they couldn't be sure. Payune could have sent a tail—a dark figure who blended into the night. There were too many shrubs, too many trees in which to take cover.

They cut across the grass; it was damp and freshly mowed. She felt her shoes sink into the moisture.

The opening of the maze beckoned, and she feared that first step. It would swallow them, and then Dakota would disappear.

They followed the path they had memorized. It went on forever, twists and turns, fake passageways, clever openings. There was enough light to keep from stumbling, but not enough to make her feel safe.

The gazebo surfaced like a mirage, but it, too, seemed haunted. The swing rocked on its own, just a little, just enough to frighten her. A spray of flowers grew from the soil—blooms too unusual and too exotic to name. Nothing felt familiar. Nothing felt right.

The night had eyes, she thought.

Dakota took her hand and guided her into a corner—a tall, rectangular shape that led to another geometric cove.

And then his mouth came down on hers.

Hard.

So hard she locked her knees to keep herself from falling. There was no time to think, no time to dwell on ghosts and swings and heady-scented flowers. His hands, those big, powerful hands circled her waist and pulled her flush against him.

This was no phantom lover, no figment of her imagination. He was real, solid, built of bronzed flesh and unyielding bones. She explored the breadth of his shoulders, the tapering of his waist, the muscles that jumped in his stomach.

And while arousal flooded her system, he played with the zipper on her dress, sliding it down, then back up again—cupping her bottom, pressing heat against heat.

She heard sounds. Her sigh. His low growl. The slice of her zipper.

He delved into her hair, and she felt it fall into his hands, tumble over his wrists and down his arms.

He kissed her, over and over, sipping and tasting. Her nipples tingled against the silk of her bra, the satin of her dress.

They made love through their clothes, she thought. There was no other way to describe the sleek, sliding motion. The pressure building upon need. The hot, fumbling strokes.

But they didn't have long. It would end too soon—this glorious, wicked sensation. And it wasn't enough, not nearly enough.

He gentled the kiss, then drew back to look at her, his breathing a series of husky pants. Moonlight slashed across his face—the razor edge of his cheekbones, the sensual shape of his lips, the hard, smooth line of his jaw.

"I wish I could take you. Here. Right now."

She understood, and the thought made her dizzy. He wanted to lift her dress, remove her panties, untuck his shirt, open his trousers.

Suddenly she didn't care if the night had eyes. She could almost feel him moving deep inside her, each powerful thrust urging them to completion. "Then stay with me," she whispered.

He rubbed his forehead across hers, his voice quiet—broken words only they could hear. "I can't. You know I can't."

Yes, she knew. But the fear had returned, and she didn't want to lose him. It was always the same fear, the one that had surfaced soon after she'd married him. He would go away and never come back.

Don't do this to me, she wanted to say. Don't make me remember why I can't be your wife. Not now. Not while I'm here in your arms.

"Close your eyes," he told her.

She did as he asked, and he carried her to the connecting cove. As her feet touched the ground, he kissed her. A touch that fluttered across her lips like the elusive wings of a butterfly.

She could still smell the woodsy scent of his cologne, but when she opened her eyes, she looked into the shadowy face of a stranger. Dakota was gone, and in his place stood the man called Thunder.

Payune's estate wasn't far from the palace, and Thunder had left everything Dakota needed, including a vehicle that took him to a grassy field laden with foliage. Dakota parked between two gnarled old trees, then brought the night optics to his eyes. He could see the stone wall that surrounded the Grand Minister's estate. He had studied the floor plan of the sprawling estate, and he knew the home contained three safes. The necklace could be in any one of them, but he was banking on the one located in the master suite.

Dakota adjusted his gloves. He had already slipped on a pair of dark coveralls and changed his shoes. There was nothing left to do but switch the necklaces and return to Kathy's waiting arms.

What would happen to Kathy if he foiled this mission? Dakota started across the field, his mind suddenly troubled. Thunder would take care of her. The other man had given his word.

A burst of masculine rivalry surged through his veins like a charge of angry adrenaline. Yeah, that was all he needed. A guy who looked like himself taking care of his wife.

His face shielded by a ski mask, Dakota scaled the wall, grateful Payune wasn't a fan of guard dogs. Or dogs in general. All Dakota had to think about was the household staff,

and a skeletal crew at that. Apparently Payune didn't trust
employees of the royal service any more than he trusted a
Doberman or a rottweiler not to turn on him. But then Payune
was a man who had plenty to hide, and people as well as
dogs could usually smell a rat. Especially if they lived under
the same roof with one.

Taking to the shadows, Dakota disengaged the alarm, a
tedious task of stripping and rearranging wires. He did the
same with the phone lines, knowing he would have to reverse
the process after he switched the necklaces.

Dodging flood lights and a security camera, he ascended
the terrace like a mountain climber claiming Mount Everest,
then stood beside the door that led to the master suite, his
back to a stone wall.

Get in and get out, he told himself. Kathy was waiting.

Frowning, he picked the lock. That's right. Kathy waited
in the maze, in a dark, cozy corner with Thunder—an Apache
with the heart of a rogue and a smile to match. Women loved
the hell out of that guy. And Dakota trusted him. Until now.

Payune's private suite came into view, but Dakota didn't
waste time assessing the man's ostentatious taste in art and
antiques. There were three sets of connecting rooms. He
turned to the wall that contained the built-in safe and grinned.
This was too easy—a scene from an outdated television show.
An aristocratic portrait with a stolen necklace behind it.

He went to work on the safe and what he didn't find had
him cursing under his breath. That out-dated television script
had just thrown him a Hollywood curve ball. There wasn't a
ruby in sight.

The library or the office? he asked himself. Which safe was
it in? He checked his watch and thought about Kathy. With
Thunder.

He slipped out of Payune's suite and took up residence in
an unlit corner of the hallway. The servants' quarters were in
the back of the house, and he could only hope the household
staff had tucked themselves in for the night. And if not, he
had already mapped out every escape route imaginable.

The stairs descended in a circular motion, a slick polished

banister guiding the way. He took each step soundlessly. But as he made his way toward the library, he spotted a flood of light streaking beneath the kitchen door. Not a security light like some of the others burning throughout the estate. This bright flash said that someone was working in there.

His senses went into full alert. Freshly baked bread. A pot of simmering soup. The contented hum of a plump, elderly cook.

Footsteps sounded. Foreign voices spoke. Maids, two of them. He stood like a masked statue, his body molded to the side of an antique hutch taller and wider than himself. The women entered the kitchen, and he heard feminine chatter and bowls clanking. Apparently the cook had prepared a late-night meal.

When the rat is away, Dakota thought, his mouth splitting into a grin—the household staff will gossip and play.

A push of pure adrenaline led him into the library. He went right to his mark, pulled out the false front on a bookshelf and uncovered the safe.

The rubies glittered like blood, and a surge of excitement shot straight to his groin. With his mind on his wife, he slipped the necklace into a pouch, leaving the fake for Payune.

Years of experience kept Dakota on track, even though Kathy occupied his thoughts. He completed the job and returned to the palace grounds. With a pounding heart, he followed the twists and turns in the maze, then stopped when he saw them.

Kathy and Thunder.

They stood near the gazebo, leaning toward each other, their shadowed faces much too close. Thunder could have been him, Dakota thought. No one would suspect that the man gazing into Kathy's eyes was an imposter. He looked like her husband.

Her lover.

A knot of jealousy twisted Dakota's gut. He mimicked the caw of a raven, signaling his return—a call Thunder would recognize.

The other man leaned a little closer to Kathy, then took her hand and guided her toward the section of the maze where Dakota waited. Kathy didn't seem aware of what was happening, but Dakota knew she couldn't see him, not when a tall, dark shrub stood between them.

"I'll be right back," Thunder whispered as he moved away from her.

Like hell you will, Dakota thought, even though he knew Thunder didn't intend to keep his word.

A moment later, the two men came face-to-face, but neither dared speak. Dakota handed over the pouch containing the necklace, and Thunder grinned before he stole into the night, letting Dakota know he had enjoyed every minute of his assignment.

Wonderful. His wife and the guy who had taken a bullet for him. How was that for an equation?

Dakota slipped around the hedge and, in spite of the darkness, Kathy recognized him instantly. She threw her arms around his neck and practically melted in his arms.

He stroked her hair and smiled. Apparently he had been missed.

Their mouths came together then, more in relief than passion, but an overwhelming pleasure squeezed his heart. At that mind-spinning moment, he felt loved.

Beautifully, thoroughly loved. An illusion, maybe. But a damn good one.

"We can't stay," he whispered as they came up for air. "We have to go back." The job had taken longer than he'd expected, and they couldn't afford to arouse Payune's suspicion anymore than they already had.

"I know," she responded, stroking his face as though his features might disappear if she didn't touch him.

They walked back to the palace, but before they re-entered the ballroom, Kathy stopped and let out a breath. "Do I look a mess?"

He smiled. Her hair fell about her shoulders in gorgeous disarray and her cheeks as well as her lips were flushed. "You look thoroughly kissed, sweetheart."

She didn't return his smile. "I have to freshen up before anyone sees me." She glanced down at her shoes. "Oh, goodness. They have grass stains."

He suppressed an amused grin. Her shoes were green to begin with, an emerald satin that matched her dress. "I don't think anyone will notice. But I'll escort you to the nearest powder room, so you can get yourself together. Okay?"

"Thank you."

"Kathy?" He took her hand. "Afterward, will you dance with me?"

She went stiff, her hand suddenly cold. "I promised *him* a dance."

And Payune would be waiting, Dakota thought. "Don't worry, you'll get through it. And if he tries to monopolize your time, I'll cut in." Dakota wanted to hold her, just once more. In spite of the sexy things they had said to each other earlier, he knew they wouldn't be sharing the same bed tonight. Stars still lit up the sky and flowers still scented the air, but the moment had passed.

"What am I supposed to say if he asks where we've been? We've been gone a long time, Dakota."

He guided her to the door. "Just tell him we got lost in the maze." It was, he thought, as close to the truth as they could admit. Even to themselves.

Five

Two days after the ball, Dakota entered Albert Payune's home, an invitation extended by a phone call early that morning. The butler escorted him to the parlor, and Payune told the servant not to disturb him. Besides Payune, there were three other men already in the room. Dakota recognized all of them. Two were low-level Asterland cabinet members—willing participants in the impending revolution, he assumed.

And the third?

Dakota locked gazes with the average-looking man. He could have been anyone's neighbor, European or American. With his wavy brown hair and relaxed stance, he didn't appear to have a sinister bone in his body. Dakota knew otherwise. Mark Delray, as he had just been formally introduced, was a hired assassin. They had never met before, but Dakota had seen Mark's photograph in a top-secret military file. Different name, but that average, nice-guy face was one he wasn't likely to forget.

Someone was going to be murdered. Today, tomorrow or

possibly the day after. Soon, he thought, the assassin would strike soon. Dakota glanced around the room and hoped to hell he wasn't the intended recipient of Mark Delray's hit.

Kathy had practically worn a hole in the carpet. What was taking so long? Where was Dakota? She peered out the window. Dusk had begun to settle in the sky. A bright orange sun was setting, a silvery moon hiding somewhere, waiting to take its place.

Feeling claustrophobic, she headed out the front door and down the scattered-stone walkway until she reached the grassy cliffs. She needed to breathe, needed to feel the wind on her face.

There was no one to call, no one to spill her worries to. How long could a meeting with Payune take? Dakota had left six hours ago.

Six hours. Six days. At the moment she couldn't distinguish the difference. All she knew was that he hadn't returned, and she feared for his safety.

Thunder would contact her if there was trouble. She tugged on an errant strand of hair as it fell free from its pinned coiffure. What if Thunder didn't know Dakota was in trouble. What then?

She stared out at the hilly terrain. The beauty mocked her mood. The sky was ablaze with a fiery glow and wildflowers dotted the hills with a lavender hue.

She spotted a familiar SUV in the distance, a white Mercedes ML moving up the winding road. "Thank you, God," she whispered.

Dakota parked the vehicle, and she stood watching him, the wind playing havoc with her hair. She couldn't run to him, no matter how much she wanted to. If she took that first step, she would probably burst into tears and cry in his arms, shake uncontrollably and kiss him senseless.

So she waited instead, her feet bare, the hem of a pale blue dress billowing in the breeze, her heart as fiery as the setting sun. Suddenly she wanted to kiss him, taste and tug and pull him to the ground. She wanted to feel those muscles bunch beneath her hands, hold him and never let go. He was safe. He was safe.

He exited the car, then caught sight of her. For a moment he stood motionless, watching the way she watched him. And then he smiled, a flash of white in that dark handsome face.

He came toward her, then stopped just shy of touching. "It's over," he said. "Or it will be in the morning."

"Over?"

"Payune and the others will be arrested tomorrow. I found what I needed to know and passed the information to Thunder."

"And Thunder contacted the Royal Police?"

Dakota nodded. "Payune is expecting the money tomorrow, but that's not what he's going to get."

Kathy released a sigh of relief. If her feet weren't planted so firmly in the grass, she might have lost her footing and toppled over. "You did it."

"We did it," he corrected gently. "I couldn't have pulled this off without you."

She blinked back a collection of tears. The sun had disappeared, but the sky was still a haven of color. Magenta streaks blazed through slashes of orange and beams of midnight blue. It was beautiful, and so was he—this tall, powerful man.

"Kathy?"

"Hmmm?"

"They were going to kill the king."

Her heart went still, much too still. But rather than respond in a frightened voice, she waited for Dakota to continue. "It wasn't Payune's original plan. But when he heard that the royal marriage was in trouble, he got this insane brainstorm."

Dakota pulled a hand through his hair, spiking the thick, ebony strands. "Payune tried to convince me that the king was emotionally disturbed, just like Prince Ivan."

Kathy's heart was no longer still, it pounded with a hard thump. "They were going to murder King Bertram and make it look like a suicide."

"That's right. And in Payune's warped mind, Queen Nicole would have eventually turned to him for solace. Of course Payune didn't admit to any of this outright, but one of the other cabinet members got my attention on the sly."

"How?" she asked, picturing Dakota in that risky situation.

"He was pouring drinks for everyone. And when he handed mine over, he whispered, 'follow me.' I knew he meant after the meeting. At first I was concerned that I was being set up for a hit. But then, something—instinct, I guess—told me he was going to make some sort of confession." Kathy fought a shiver, and Dakota continued. "So after the meeting I followed him to a deserted road."

"And he told you about Payune's plan?"

"Yes, he did. And he's willing to cooperate with the Royal Police. He never expected this to come down to murder, but he didn't know how to approach the police without arousing Payune's suspicion."

Kathy battled another chill, realizing how often Dakota had been exposed to dangerous situations. "How did this cabinet member know you were out to get Payune?"

"He didn't. He just figured an American businessman wouldn't want to be implicated in the assassination of a king."

She tipped her head and looked up at the sky, then back at Dakota. "I'm so glad it's over."

"Me, too."

They stood staring at each other, and she nearly lost her breath. "I'm going to miss this cottage." And she would miss him—those piercing black eyes and that Comanche smile.

"It is kind of magical." He moved closer, brushing his body against hers, his lips just a heartbeat away.

A pounding, drumming heartbeat.

He lowered his head, and she closed her eyes. There was no time to think, to rationalize. There was only Dakota's mouth covering hers.

He tasted as clean as the elements, as spicy as the scent of his cologne. She stood on her toes and clung to him. Heat burned throughout her body, making her breath catch in her throat. She arched to feel as much of him as she could, but it wasn't enough.

While he kissed her, she tugged his shirt from his trousers, then unbuttoned it, searching for muscle and male flesh. The wind snapped the tails of the fabric, pulling it away from his chest. She grazed him with her nails, and he shifted his hips and deepened the kiss.

His hands were suddenly everywhere, all over her, sliding and roaming. He went after the front of her dress, popping buttons as he did. Dragging his lips down the column of her neck, he unhooked her bra. Kathy moaned and bit his shoulder. Dakota tongued her nipple.

She held him against her breast and watched him suckle. A blade of moonlight glinted off his hair, and she realized dusk had slipped into darkness. Her bra remained slack, falling against her body.

No, there was no time to think. No time to care about anything but how he made her feel. She had become part of this enchanted world—the cliffs and the trees and the ocean crashing below. She pictured the waves rising and swelling, bathing the rocks in crystalline sheets. Just as Dakota bathed her—with his mouth, his tongue.

She buried her hands in his hair while he licked, then pulled on those short spiky strands as he closed his teeth around her. It was gentle. It was rough. An ache that brought both pleasure and pain.

When he stepped back to look at her, a light breeze blew across her nipples, chilling them.

"Tell me you want more," he said.

Her breath rushed out of her lungs. "I do." She wanted everything. Every touch, every kiss, every slick, hot sensation he could give her. "I want more."

As he pushed her dress from her shoulders, Kathy felt it pool at her feet in a flutter of pale-blue lace.

Their gazes locked in a magnetic pull. His eyes were black against the night, dark and compelling. And his face, so close to hers, was hard and smooth and mildly abrasive. She stroked his skin, memorizing him beneath the stars.

He didn't remove her panties. Instead he skimmed her

tummy, then slid his hand under the elastic. She rocked against his hand, and he stroked—a gentle, rhythmic pressure.

He pushed a finger deep inside, and she gasped. More. Yes, she wanted more. He kissed her, took her mouth while he made her unbearably wet.

She tasted desire in his kiss, felt it blaze like a neon moon. She gripped his shoulders and lost herself in his touch—his hand moving between her thighs, those long, callused fingers teasing and arousing.

Deeper.

Wetter.

"Let it happen," he whispered.

She had no choice. The wind rushed through her hair, spilling pieces over her shoulders and down her arms. One strand adhered itself to her nipple, to the moisture he had made. His fingers surged into her with exquisite force. Desperate, she kissed him so hard, they both gasped for air.

Need clawed like talons, and she rubbed against his hand—against the pressure, the friction, the fire she couldn't control.

And then suddenly the world stilled, and there was nothing but the sound of her release. She heard it rip from her throat and echo into the night before she closed her eyes and let herself tumble.

Kathy collapsed in his arms, so Dakota held her in a soft, quiet moment. The moon sent fiery streaks through her hair, and her skin glowed with a passionate sheen. She was beautiful. So beautiful. Bathed in the afterglow of the climax he had given her.

He brushed her cheek, and she made a kittenish sound. She was still dazed, still caught between silk and sensation. He ran his hands down the sides of her body, down the long, lithe curves. Her tummy was flat, her hips lean yet womanly, her breasts full, nipples taut and aroused.

He was aroused, too. So damn aroused.

His shirt flapped in the wind, and he wondered if she was cold. She wore nothing but a pair of lace panties. Blue lace and smooth, creamy skin.

"I'm taking you inside." He swept her into his arms, and she clung to him, her hair falling free from its confinement. It spilled over her shoulders like a scarlet ribbon, reminding him of Christmas and birthdays and all the holidays he had missed holding her.

Tonight they would make up for lost time. Tonight, he thought, carrying her to the master bedroom, they would make love.

He placed her on the bed and turned on a lamp. An amber bulb lit the room, illuminating with a soft glow. There were fresh flowers on the nightstand, and he knew she had picked them. They were wild, the same lavender blooms that dotted the cliffs. Everything in the room was decidedly feminine— pillows the color of champagne, window sheers trimmed in lace, a quilt as silky as her skin.

It made him feel erotic, a little forbidden—a man stealing into a lady's chamber at night.

Oh, yes, he thought, as he unbuckled his belt, this cottage was haunted. A sexual haunting he had no will to stop.

"Let me touch you," she said.

"Go ahead," he challenged, his shirt gone, belt undone, trousers unzipped. "Touch as much as you want. Wherever you want."

Painfully aroused, he stood before her while she sat on the edge of the bed and looked up at him. She skimmed his belly, gently abrading him with her nails. And then she leaned forward and pressed her mouth to the scar just below his navel.

His stomach was corrugated with muscles, and each and every one of them jumped, sending a cool, clean shiver straight to his groin.

Damn it. He closed his eyes, then opened them, realizing they had forgotten something. One simple, important little thing.

"I didn't bring any protection." Three years of celibacy had left him without a reason to think about it. Until now. "Tell me we can risk it." They had taken risks before. But Kathy knew her own body, knew when it was safe.

"I..." Something flashed in her eyes. Pain? Sadness? He couldn't be sure, wasn't certain if he wanted to know. Suddenly their emotions were too close to the edge. They were half naked, looking into each other's eyes, stripping each other's souls.

He skimmed her cheek. "Kathy?"

Her breath hitched. "I want you to love me."

"Then I will."

He discarded his boots and shed his belt, then lowered himself to the bed. She reached for his trousers, and together they battled to remove them.

Soon his pants landed at the foot of the bed along with his briefs. She still wore those pale blue panties, so he slipped them off, tugging the lace from her hips.

The sheets smelled sweet, like Kathy, like fresh-picked berries on a summer morning. He imagined living there, in this bed, with her by his side.

They could feed on each other, sustain themselves with sex. Luscious, wild strawberry-scented sex. It was an insane notion, but it made him smile.

And then she reached between their bodies, and every coherent thought slipped from his mind. He surged hot and greedy into her palm, and she closed her fingers around him.

His pulse pounded. He wanted to slam into her, take her as hard and fast as he could. Yet he wanted to savor and touch and kiss and make the urgency last.

Pinning her to the bed, he cuffed her wrists with his hands. Her hair was everywhere, a mass of scarlet ribbon tangling over her shoulders, down her arms, across the pillow. One silky wave curled around one taut, rosy nipple. She was his fantasy. She had always been his ideal, and he had wanted her from the first moment he had seen her.

She looked up at him, seducing him with those exotic green eyes. She must have been a cat in another life, he thought. A lean, leggy creature with claws.

She struggled against his restraint, rising to nuzzle his chest, purring like the feline he imagined her to be.

He smiled and held her down again. Hot and restless, she moved beneath him, challenging him to take her, to make her wet and slick and quivering with lust.

Dakota nearly lost his mind. Releasing her wrists, he slid down her body, over those smooth, feline curves. Placing his mouth against her, he kissed between her thighs. Kissed and licked while she bucked and made throaty little sounds.

He could hear the wind outside, knew it had picked up speed. The same speed as the rhythm of his heart. The beating, the pounding, the rush of excitement.

He tasted her release, felt her orgasm rise and swell, but it still wasn't enough. Not nearly enough.

He needed more. So much more.

Dakota rose above her, then entered her with a deep, sensual stroke. She raised her hips, and together they moved in unison—lovers who relished the pleasure, the warmth, the familiarity of each other.

They couldn't stop kissing, touching, feeling—giving sensation, taking it back.

They rolled over the bed until she straddled him, rode him while he watched. Her hair fell forward, a portion of it still pinned, the rest tangling over her body like fiery vines. She was a goddess, he thought, an enchantress, a mermaid from the sea, a siren from the sky. She was everything he had ever wanted in a lover.

He couldn't think about missing her because she was here, riding him, milking his body with hers. Heat shot through his belly and blazed through his loins, begging for a release. Begging for the strength to hold on. Just one more minute, one more warm, wet spiraling second.

She grasped his hands, locked on and held. He watched her, his vision blurred, his need edgy. And when that last second spun out of control, he threw back his head and let himself fall.

Hours later Dakota opened his eyes, trapped between waking and sleeping. The room was dark, not pitch black, but still too dark to focus. Someone touched him. A hand in his hair, fingertips skimming his shoulder.

He didn't stir. Instead he wondered if he dreamed, if he wasn't awake at all. He slept alone each night, yet there was a woman beside him. The lotion scent of her skin drifted to his nostrils, melding with the lusty lingering of sex.

Kathy. His mind came awake, and his body responded. He grew hard and achy between his thighs—the kind of pressure a woman could relieve. But not just any woman. He wanted his wife.

He turned, shifting in her direction, and her breath caught. He could see her shadow—the outline of a heavenly body with tumbling hair.

"I thought you were asleep," she said.

"I was." He squinted to bring her into focus, but she was still ghostlike. It was the cottage, he thought. The haunting. "You don't have to stop touching me."

"I stayed awake because I wanted you again." She slid down beside him, her leg brushing his. "Before morning."

He struggled to make sense of her words. If she wanted him she could have him now and in the daylight. "We won't turn into pumpkins. Or whatever happens in fairy tales."

"Maybe we will." She ran her hands down the front of his body, over the planes and ridges, muscles that formed his stomach. "Maybe tonight is just a fairy tale."

A tightness, a pain constricted his heart. He understood why she had remained awake. Tomorrow their loving would end. She wasn't offering to come back to him, to become a part of his life again.

What they had was now. His haunting. The darkness that shielded their past and kept them from a future.

He should have turned away, but he couldn't. If this moment was all they had, then he'd take it.

He reached for her, and she moved into his arms. They kissed and then caressed, their hands slipping into a languid rhythm. It was like dancing on a wave, floating on the edge of a dream. Yes, he thought. She was a mermaid, a goddess of the sea. And he couldn't keep her. Nor would he try.

After tonight, he would let her go.

"Kathy," he whispered her name, and she lifted her hips to accept his penetration. His deep, warm strokes.

There were no urgent thrusts. No groping or fumbling. No torn clothes or breathy pants. This was quiet, gentle loving— a joining that came from the heart.

And one Dakota would never forget.

Two days later Kathy held a gold vase, a gift from Queen Nicole and King Bertram. It was truly over. Albert Payune, the other revolutionists and the hired assassin were in jail. The cabinet member who had cooperated with the police would receive a lesser sentence for exposing the murder plot.

She studied the sparkling sapphire imbedded in the vase. King Bertram was a gracious man. Both he and the queen had thanked Dakota and Kathy personally, offering a valuable gift in honor and gratitude. The Asterland government had also promised that Payune would not be able to spread the word that the Lone Star jewels actually existed. The legend would be protected.

"Kathy?"

She turned to the sound of Dakota's voice. He hadn't stepped foot in the master bedroom since the night they'd made love. She had awakened that morning to find him gone. Later she'd discovered he'd left the cottage to roam the hills, then tie up the loose ends of their mission.

"Have you finished packing?" he asked.

"No, but I'm nearly done." She tried to avoid his gaze, but couldn't quite manage. Those Comanche eyes held her captive, trapping her in deep, dark emotion.

"It's beautiful, isn't it?" He motioned to the vase. "Kind of an unusual shape, though."

Should she tell him? Kathy wondered. Tell him why her vase had a curved indentation and his rounded on one side? Apparently he hadn't examined them closely enough to make the connection. "They're a set."

He blinked. "What?"

"The vases."

He reached for the jeweled object, a small frown creasing his brow. She watched as he ran his hand over the gold, following the shape. "It means something, doesn't it? Something significant?"

Kathy released a quiet breath. "They represent love. They're very old and valuable. There aren't that many in existence, and in Asterland when they're given as a gift, they're always given to a couple, sometimes on their wedding day."

Kathy glanced down at her hand and realized she still wore her wedding ring, the diamonds and emeralds Dakota had given her. She noticed Dakota still wore his, too. But he had chosen white gold and onyx. A design that didn't resemble a wedding band—a ring that rarely interfered with his undercover work. It was a piece of jewelry that looked natural on an Indian man, whether he wore it on his left hand or switched it to his right.

"Love." Dakota cleared his throat as if to clear away a sudden huskiness. The discomfort in his eyes wasn't hard to miss. "You didn't tell the queen about our cover, did you? She thinks we've reconciled. That we're making a fresh start in our marriage."

"I didn't have the opportunity to tell her." Kathy folded a blouse and placed it in her suitcase, giving herself something to do. "And after she and the king gave us the vases, it seemed too late. The gesture had already been made."

Shifting the object in question, Dakota's frown deepened. "Mine fits against yours." He lifted his gaze. "Like our bodies."

"I think that's the idea." She knew her voice sounded rigid, but she couldn't relax her throat. He had practically abandoned her after they'd made love. But then what had she expected? For him to say that he would retire for good? That their marriage was more important than the next mission? Sex wouldn't change that, no matter how incredible it had been.

To ease some of the tension building in the room, she took the vase and placed it on the bed. "I don't think the symbolism was meant just for us. I think the gift was also the queen's way of saying that she and the king are trying to work through their differences.'' And for that, Kathy was deeply relieved. Not only did the monarchs truly love each other, they had a child to consider—a ten-year-old boy.

''That's good.'' Dakota stood with impeccable posture, a military stance that fit his tall, broad stature. ''They're a nice family,'' he said, revealing an affection for Prince Eric that mirrored her own.

''Yes, they are.''

Telling herself not to dwell on dark-eyed children, she glanced at the wilting wildflowers on the nightstand and realized the extent of her loneliness. She hadn't been in the mood to walk the cliffs, enjoy the scent of the ocean or pick lavender flowers. All of those pleasures reminded her too much of Dakota. Even the garden was a sad reminder. Making wishes and imagining fairies seemed foolish now.

''Are you going back to D.C.?''

She looked up. ''No, I'm not. I'm leaving the Bureau.''

''For good?''

''Yes. I gave my notice before we came here.'' A decision that had been a long time coming.

Dakota hooked his thumbs in his jeans, suddenly looking more like a cowboy than a retired air force officer. Why hadn't she noticed his Wranglers and embroidered Western shirt before? His lizard-skin boots and tooled leather belt? He had well-dressed Texan written all over him.

Kathy closed her suitcase. Maybe she hadn't wanted to notice. Maybe she found the image just a bit too sexy.

''So what are you going to do?'' he asked.

''Head up a satellite office for my parents' business.'' Her grandfather had founded a successful import/export company. Kathy's family had been living abroad for as long as she could remember. So joining the Foreign Service had seemed like a natural step. But now she wanted to live in the States, someplace other than the Capitol.

''So where are you going to set up shop, so to speak?''

She lifted her chin. ''In Royal.''

His jaw nearly dropped. "You mean Texas? Where I live?"

She narrowed her eyes. "As you may recall, I lived there once, too." After Dakota had retired from the air force, Kathy had taken an extended leave of absence from the Foreign Service, hoping for a quiet, domestic life at the ranch, one Dakota had never given her. In spite of his retirement, the dangerous missions continued. "I like Royal. I have friends there."

"Of course you do." He softened his voice. "So you've rented an apartment already?"

"No, but I intend to. I've already arranged for a moving company to ship my belongings to Royal."

"Oh."

They stood in awkward silence after that, Dakota staring at his boots and Kathy reorganizing cosmetics in her makeup bag, hoping to look busy enough for him to just leave her be.

Finally he lifted his gaze and broke through the quiet. "You're welcome to stay with me. You know, just until you find a place."

Her heart leaped forward with a hard thump. "Do you think that's wise?"

"Why wouldn't it be?" he responded a bit too easily. "Since we've already gotten each other out of our systems, it just might be possible for us to be friends. There's certainly no harm in trying."

Gotten each other out of our systems. Maybe Dakota was right. Maybe it was time to accept him as a friend. She had lived in limbo long enough. And so had he. They both needed to come to terms with their broken marriage and move on with their lives.

"Thank you." She forced a casual smile. "I promise I won't wear out my welcome."

"Don't worry about it." He returned her smile, then offered to carry her suitcase out to the car. This tall, gorgeous man who still made her heart beat much too fast.

Six

Dakota was back in Texas and wondering if he'd gone crazy. He'd left Asterland behind, but he'd brought Kathy with him—to the ranch, the house they'd once shared. She was in the guest room he'd offered, and she'd been holed up in there all day.

He squared his shoulders and headed in the direction of her room. They couldn't hide from each other. Both had agreed to embrace friendship.

He knocked, then stepped back a little. Embracing friendship wasn't the same as embracing each other.

She opened the door, and he cursed a sudden, unwelcome jolt of lust. Her hair, damp from a late-day shower, fell loose about her shoulders. And she wasn't wearing a bra. He could see the faint outline of her breasts through a printed cotton dress.

"Hi," she said.

"Hi." Dumbstruck, he couldn't think of another thing to say. Why had he gone to her room? What had he hoped to accomplish?

"Are you settled in all right?"

"Yes. Thank you."

So polite, he thought, so proper. Even with damp hair and no bra. "Are you hungry? It's lunchtime," he added hastily. Her nipples were erect, poking against the flowers on her dress.

She tucked a lock of wet hair behind her ear. He could smell her shampoo. "Are you fixing lunch? Or are you going out?" she asked.

"I thought I'd fix something here. Mrs. Miller did some shopping for me this morning." And he didn't have the slightest idea what to make. Lunch had been an afterthought, just something to talk about.

Kathy let the door fall open. Behind her Dakota could see the unmade bed. The sheets probably smelled like strawberries by now, like her hair and her skin.

"So Mrs. Miller still works for you?"

He pulled his eyes away from the bed. "Yes, and she hasn't changed a bit."

Kathy smiled. "Same starched gray hair, same white uniform, same squeaky white shoes?"

"That's her." And the housekeeper's non-meddling, get-the-job done personality suited him just fine.

"Can you give me a few minutes before lunch? I still have to dry my hair."

"Sure. No problem."

He made his way to the kitchen, opened the refrigerator and rummaged through the groceries. What in the hell had possessed him to invite Kathy to stay with him? Self torture? He hadn't gotten her out of his system. Not by a long shot.

Forcing himself to concentrate on food, Dakota decided on grilled cheese sandwiches and a black bean salad. The salad took a lot of dicing and slicing, but it contained some of his favorite ingredients: bell and jalapeño peppers, onions, cilantro, parsley and Roma tomatoes.

Kathy entered the kitchen just as he poured the Southwestern mixture over a bed of lettuce and garnished it with lime wedges.

"I should have known you would make something spicy."

He glanced up to acknowledge her, and when she turned toward the dining room, he noticed her dress was one of those great little backless numbers. Talk about spicy. "You know me. A creature of habit." Hot food and sleek redheads. His tastes would never change.

While she took it upon herself to set the table, he grilled the sandwiches. Maybe spending time together at the cottage had made things easier on them. They fell into a domestic pattern as if it were routine. But then, it used to be. They had always shared kitchen duties.

They sat across from each other at an early Texas table scarred with over a century of wear. It suited Dakota's lifestyle as well as the rugged surroundings. His home wasn't a showcase for wealthy living, nor was it actually a working ranch. He owned horses because they gave him pleasure and steers because he enjoyed hosting an occasional Friday-night jackpot for amateur cowboys. And since his ranch hands tended to the animals as nonintrusively as Mrs. Miller tended to the house, he was able to protect his personal life. No one gossiped about Dakota Lewis. Not anymore. He had worked damn hard to be regarded as something other than a billionaire's half-breed, bastard son. High society, he knew, wasn't always kind.

He looked across the table at Kathy. She ate the food he'd prepared, even scooped a diced jalepeño into her mouth. In spite of the disciplined, air force officer image he'd carved out for himself, she used to tell him that he liked everything hot and fast, that he lived on pure heat and adrenaline.

Dakota watched her sip a frothy glass of milk. As if Miss proper-and-pretty had room to talk. The woman was downright wicked in bed, and the stuffy society types she'd dated before him hadn't satisfied her need for hot, fast sex.

"When is Mrs. Miller coming back?" Kathy asked.

Dakota blinked. Answering a question about his no-nonsense housekeeper while he had been thinking about hot-and-fast sex with his gorgeous wife wasn't an easy transition for his male brain to make.

"Wednesday afternoon." He reached for his coffee, hoping the caffeine would snap his senses back in order. "Her schedule hasn't changed." The older lady didn't live at the ranch. Instead she worked four days a week, whether Dakota was home or away on an assignment.

Kathy lifted her napkin. "Does she know I'm here?"

"Yes, I told her."

"So she understands it's just a temporary stay?"

He tried not to frown. "Yes." It hadn't been easy telling the housekeeper that his wife was sleeping in one of the guest rooms. His pride, he supposed, along with his heart, had taken a bruising just saying the words out loud. "There won't be any misunderstandings." Nor would he pressure Kathy about why she had left in the first place. Eventually he would ask, but for now he would do his best to concentrate on friendship.

Dakota tilted his head, pushing the brim of his Stetson back a notch. West Texas was a sight to behold, even before the break of dawn. The moon peeked through a menagerie of clouds as they moved across a vast, deep-blue sky.

Dakota turned toward Ben Rassad. "Do you paint?" he asked, wondering how someone would go about capturing a crescent moon or a shifting cloud.

"No," the sheikh answered. "But I appreciate those who do."

Ben, too, seemed mesmerized by the sky. But Dakota supposed once a man lived in Texas, there was no turning back. The Lone Star state flowed through his veins, whether he was an Amythrarian sheikh or a Comanche pilot.

"The others should be here soon," Dakota said, focusing on their purpose. The Texas Cattleman's Club didn't normally hold pre-dawn meetings in the middle of a park, but this meeting was probably the most significant gathering this group would ever have. The recovered Lone Star jewels would be hidden on this brisk May morning. The private park, which housed the Cattleman's Club and an old adobe mission, also offered acres of greenery. Neither the exclusive gentlemen's club nor the historic mission was visible from the spot they had chosen, but the park, with its tree-lined paths and seasonal blooms, was as familiar to Dakota as his own home.

"Tex is waiting," Ben noted.

Dakota smiled. In 1901, Tex Langley had founded the Texas Cattleman's Club, and these days the rugged oil baron stood in the form of a prestigious bronze statue erected just a few feet away.

Dr. Justin Webb and Matt Walker arrived together. And like Dakota, both the surgeon and the horse breeder sported Western hats and boots. Minutes later diplomat Aaron Black joined the group, and the men greeted each other quietly.

Other than nesting birds and curious squirrels, there wasn't a sign of life seen or heard within miles. The gated park was deserted, and the road that led to it as dark as the night sky.

"So this is it," Matt said, studying the designated location.

Dakota nodded. A small reflecting pool was under construction. The forms had already been set and the rebar was in place, leaving rows of soil between round metal rods. All they had to do was bury the tiny, sealed case containing the priceless gems and wait for the unsuspecting contractors to arrive to pour the concrete.

While the other men stood in the shadows, Dakota dug a deep, narrow hole with a small camper shovel, and Matt placed the airtight case inside. Their only light was a solitary beam from a flashlight. Even the moon respected their silent task, its crescent shape slipping behind a cluster of trees.

The jewels had been originally hidden in a secret passageway in the old mission, and securing them this time seemed simple by comparison. But Dakota knew what each man had risked in an effort to recover the gems. Their lives, as well as those of the women they loved, had been laden with danger. The triumphant moment belonged to all of them.

Dakota stepped away from the burial site. The moon had resurfaced, bathing the ground with a soft silver glow. It seemed fitting somehow—ceremonial to a Comanche who believed Mother Earth provided all things sacred.

Leadership. Justice. Peace. Those three words shone in the eyes of every man present. The Lone Star jewels. A red diamond, a black opal and a two-carat emerald, represented an unspoken mantra—lifelong values they vowed to uphold.

With satisfied nods, Ben, Matt and Justin departed. They had agreed beforehand that Aaron and Dakota would wait for the construction crew.

The diplomat headed out to his truck and returned with a thermos and two plastic cups. He placed them on a nearby bench. ''Shall we?''

''Sure,'' Dakota answered. ''And I'm glad it was you and not Justin who supplied the coffee.''

Aaron poured the steaming brew, and they grinned at each other in the dark. It was a running joke that the doctor had acquired a taste for week-old sludge that accumulated in the bottom of a pot.

''So how does it feel to be back on American soil?'' Aaron asked.

''Good. It's where I belong, I suppose.'' Even if an edge of restlessness had begun to set in. For Dakota the end of an assignment often left him anxious.

The other man lifted his coffee. ''If you get hungry, my wife sent along some pastries. They're in the truck.''

''Thanks. Maybe later.'' Although Dakota considered Aaron a close friend, they went on to discuss insignificant things. Aaron wasn't one to pry, and Dakota wasn't one to offer details about his personal life. Aaron already knew that Kathy had left the Foreign Service and was staying with Dakota until she found a suitable place of her own. What else could be said of his broken marriage? Dakota had offered Kathy a guest room at the ranch so they could pursue friendship. He wasn't supposed to want her so badly, wasn't supposed to hurt every time he thought about the past. Admitting how he felt would solve nothing.

An hour after the sun came up, Aaron opened the gate for the construction crew, a trio of men who routinely repaired the hardscape at the park.

Dakota leaned against a tree as they poured the concrete. After the barricades were placed, he and Aaron would discuss another construction matter with the crew, but only for the

sake of their cover. The American diplomat and the retired
air force lieutenant would remain at the scene to protect the
Lone Star jewels one last time.

A small breeze billowed Dakota's jacket. Within days the
pool would be filled, and only those who had made a vow to
the Texas Cattleman's Club would know that three priceless
gems lay beneath the reflection of Tex Langley's statue.

Kathy knew she was alone. Dakota had left the ranch in
the wee hours of the morning. The master bedroom was next
to hers, and she'd heard his shower running at an ungodly
hour.

Squinting at the sunlight streaming through the windows,
she slipped on her robe, then stepped into the hall. Glancing
over her shoulder, she noticed Dakota's door was slightly
ajar.

She had no right to enter the master bedroom, but she
couldn't seem to stop herself. Immediately the bed drew her
toward it. She ran her hand along the wood and imagined
Dakota sleeping there, his long muscular body tangled in the
sheets. He was a light sleeper, a man who always seemed to
have something on his mind.

The room looked the same. He'd kept it just the way she
had decorated it. The horse weather vane still stood atop a
Chippendale desk, the window valances still matched the fabric on the canopy bed and a hand-painted dresser displayed a
collection of Indian baskets and crystal candelabras.

Kathy released a shaky breath. Still scanning the dresser,
she noticed a familiar item was missing. A framed photograph. A picture of herself and Dakota on their wedding day.
She moved closer and reached for the top drawer. Had he
buried it beneath his clothes? Or had he destroyed it?

"What are you looking for?"

Caught in the act, Kathy froze, her fingers wrapped around
the brass handle. "I apologize," she said as she turned toward
him. "I shouldn't have come in here."

He stood, tall and rigid in black jeans, leather boots and a lightweight jacket. The brim of a cowboy hat shielded his eyes, but she knew they were fixed on her.

"I asked what you were looking for."

He made her feel like a criminal, the woman who had once shared this room with him, slept in the canopy bed, kept her undergarments folded in the drawer she had been opening. "I wondered where our picture was," she answered honestly.

He jutted his chin toward the dresser. "It's in there. I couldn't look at it. Not every day."

"I'm sorry," Kathy whispered, not knowing what else to say. His tone was guarded, but pain edged his words. She knew she owed him an explanation, yet she didn't know where to begin.

Neither spoke after that, and Kathy felt the room closing in. She glanced back at the dresser and imagined their picture hidden beneath his clothes. It made her sad and guilty. He deserved better than a woman who had just walked away, a woman who couldn't bring herself to admit why she had left. But the loss of their child and the loneliness she had suffered wasn't something she could put into words. It wasn't fair, but it made her realize that she and Dakota had never really been friends. Their courtship had been a whirlwind romance based on passion, not communication. And their marriage had been much the same.

Dakota followed her gaze to the dresser. "I don't burn candles anymore. I don't know why I still keep them around."

She understood his meaning. Their wedding picture used to sit between the crystal candelabras, and they used to make love by candlelight, touch and kiss while blue and gold flames sent shadows flickering across their skin.

"I'm sorry," she said again. Sorry that she had hurt him. Sorry they hadn't been able to share more than just their bodies. But she knew he hid his deepest emotions. She had seen him laugh, but she had never seen him cry. Not even at his father's funeral.

He tossed his hat onto the bed. "I'm sorry, too. I didn't

mean to sound so harsh earlier. I just didn't expect to come home and find you in my room.''

She wasn't sure whether to leave him alone or stay and talk. He still seemed guarded, yet his tone had softened, his apology sincere. ''You left while it was still dark.''

''Texas Cattleman's Club meeting.'' He unzipped his jacket, then dragged a hand through his hair. ''We secured the jewels.''

And he seemed unsettled, she thought, a little edgy. But hiding the jewels meant the mission was truly over and he had become an out-of-work soldier again, a man without a purpose. Staying home never suited Dakota, and that was one of the reasons Kathy had left. She had wanted some normalcy in their marriage, but he had been satisfied with their whirlwind relationship, with stealing moments between his never-ending missions.

''Are you sure it's okay for me to stay here?'' she asked, wondering if it had been a mistake.

''Of course, it's okay.''

He came toward her, so close she could smell the wind on his clothes, the fading scent of his aftershave. She lifted her face to his and wondered if he was going to kiss her. If he did, she would kiss him back. She could feel the sexual magnet, the energy that drew them together. They couldn't talk, but they could touch. Yearn for each other.

He toyed with the collar of her chenille robe. ''What happened to the silky one?''

''I didn't think I should wear it around you.''

He moistened his lips. ''Afraid I wouldn't be able to control myself?''

She swallowed. ''It's been known to happen.'' He was too tall, too dark, too dangerously handsome. His mouth was inches from hers, his breath warm. He would taste like the elements, she decided, like a warrior who belonged to the night.

He skimmed her cheek with his, then stepped back and grinned. ''So you decided to wear this grandma getup instead?''

For a moment Kathy only stared. He'd gone from brooding to sexy to silly within the blink of an eye. And she remained in a daze, waiting for him to kiss her. She lifted her hand to her face, to the spot he'd just touched. "Grandma getup?"

"Yep. You look cute, though. Kinda sweet and fuzzy."

She couldn't find it within herself to return his smile. He teased her, but the humor hadn't quite reached his eyes. They were black, with a sort of feverish glow. He was aroused and pretending he wasn't. If she bumped against his fly, she'd feel the evidence of his desire. This was her punishment for invading his room, she thought. She should have stayed away.

He stepped back even farther. "Kathy?"

"Yes?"

"I danced with other women at the Texas Cattleman's Club ball. It was months ago, but I just thought I should mention it. You know I'm not one for fancy social events, but I felt more or less obligated to be there."

"And you felt obligated to dance." She tried to keep her voice steady. She had no right to be jealous. She had, after all, walked out on him. "It doesn't matter, Dakota. You didn't do anything wrong."

"Have you danced with other men?"

She sent him a twisted smile. "I danced with Payune. Remember?"

He didn't seem amused. "That's not what I mean."

"There were political functions in Washington. I suppose I danced a few times." But she couldn't remember who her partners were. "I don't understand why you brought this up."

"Because you've lived alone for three years. And I keep thinking that there must have been men interested in you. Someone must have asked you on a date."

The look in his eyes startled her. The macho, possessive glare. She had already told him that she hadn't slept with anyone, but apparently he couldn't stand the image of her even having dinner with another man. "I didn't go on any dates."

His gaze softened. "So what did you do?"

"Worked." Came home to an empty apartment and

thought about her husband, wondered what he was doing, wondered if his next assignment would be a greater risk than the last, if he would be captured or killed. "I adopted a dog."

"Really? That's great."

"I'm glad you think so because I'm picking Sugar up at the airport tomorrow. A friend from Washington is putting her on a plane for me."

"Sugar? That's your dog's name?"

Kathy nodded. "She belonged to an elderly lady who lived in my building. And when Mrs. Leone died, I just sort of inherited her dog. But Sugar is a little angel. I adore her." The Maltese had gotten her through some sad and lonely times, making her separation from Dakota bearable. "She loves everyone. And she's quiet. You won't even know she's around."

"Your dog is welcome here, Kathy. You have to stop acting like you're putting me out. I invited you, remember? We agreed to be friends."

"Yes, friends," she said, wondering if that was truly possible.

The following day Kathy returned from the airport with the Maltese in tow. She walked into the living room, and Dakota looked up from his newspaper and smiled.

The dog was pretty much what he had expected. Little old ladies had lapdogs that wore bows on top of their heads, and Kathy had inherited Sugar from a little old lady. He had to admit the pooch was cute—silky white fur and a face with round eyes and a delicate muzzle. He figured the Maltese didn't weigh any more than four or five pounds.

Placing the paper on the coffee table, he came to his feet. "So this is Sugar?" He reached out to pet the dog and received a high-pitched doggie yip in return.

Kathy's head whipped up. "What happened?"

"I don't know." Dakota nearly stammered. "I guess she's scared or something."

"But she likes people." Kathy adjusted Sugar in her arms. "She never acts that way."

"She just got off a plane, and this is a new environment. Hell, she's bound to be nervous."

"I suppose you're right." Kathy stroked the dog's head. "Maybe I should put her down and let her get used to the place."

Sugar decided she liked the couch. She curled up on a cowhide pillow, and Dakota thought she looked like a toy— a little, white fluffball on his rugged sofa. Yep, she was cute, even if he thought hair bows on canines were kind of sissy. But this one was a female, so he supposed that was okay.

He inched closer, then knelt to let the dog sniff his hand.

Sugar bared her teeth and snarled.

Caught completely off guard, Dakota jerked back, lost his balance and landed flat on his startled butt.

Behind him, Kathy gasped. "Oh, my God! Are you all right?"

"Of course, I am."

"Did she bite you?"

"No." With as much masculine pride as he could muster, he stood and squared his shoulders. He outweighed Sugar by a good hundred and eighty pounds. And he was an ex-military man trained in survival tactics. A former para rescuer who flew planes into enemy territory, rescued hostages, defused mines, tracked gunrunners across the desert. He had done it all, in and out of the service.

"I wasn't expecting her to snarl at me," he said, explaining away the humiliation.

"I'm so sorry. She's never done that to anyone before." Kathy reprimanded Sugar, and the dog dropped her ears and whined, making Dakota feel like a heel.

"I'm sure it won't happen again," she told him.

"Don't worry about it." He met Kathy's gaze, and she caught her bottom lip between her teeth. "Don't you dare laugh," he warned.

"Why would I?" she asked, a bit too innocently.

"Oh, I don't know. Maybe because your little dog knocked me on my ass."

"You should have seen yourself, Dakota."

Her lip quivered, and they both burst into laughter. But when footsteps sounded in the entryway, Kathy sobered immediately.

"That must be Mrs. Miller," she said.

Dakota nodded. He knew Kathy and the housekeeper hadn't seen each other yet, but he figured they were about to. Mrs. Miller would say a predictable yet impersonal hello before she began her chores.

Dakota studied his wife. As though suddenly conscious of her appearance, she fussed with the loose strands of her hair—that luscious, heavy hair she had twisted into its usual chignon. This afternoon she sported tan trousers and a lemon-colored blouse. Yellow suited her. Even the sunny robe she'd worn yesterday had turned him on. She'd looked as frothy as the meringue on top of a pie.

Mrs. Miller entered the room like a broom-wielding militant, shoulders back, head held high, short gray hair resembling a helmet. She could have been a nurse with her crisp white uniform and thick-soled shoes. It amazed Dakota that even after a thorough housecleaning, she departed as starched and white as she had arrived.

"Good afternoon, Lieutenant," she said, greeting him as she had for the past ten years.

"Good afternoon," he responded as the older lady turned toward Kathy.

He watched as they acknowledged each other. Kathy stepped forward and smiled. "It's nice to see you again."

"Thank you. It's a pleasure to see you as well."

The conversation was neither strained nor friendly. Dakota had no idea if Mrs. Miller liked Kathy, but he wasn't sure if the older woman liked him, either. The housekeeper rarely smiled, even during the holidays when she filled the cookie jar with red-nosed reindeers and jolly Santas.

Mrs. Miller smoothed her immaculate dress, then turned and spotted the dog curled up on the couch. "Oh, my."

"That's Sugar," Kathy said. "But she's a little nervous today."

As the older lady headed toward the sofa, Dakota searched

for a more appropriate warning. Be careful. Watch yourself. That adorable little fluffball is actually a junkyard Doberman in disguise. But before he could utter a single word, Sugar wiggled her behind and gazed up at Mrs. Miller with adoring eyes.

"Aren't you precious?" the housekeeper crooned in a sing-song voice Dakota had never heard the no-nonsense woman use before.

Kathy beamed like a moon in June, and within minutes she and Mrs. Miller were discussing Sugar's upkeep and habits. The dog ate a select brand of canned food, played indoor fetch games, required periodic trips to a groomer and enjoyed being walked on a silver leash that matched her glittery collar.

Dakota had never felt so left out, so big and undeniably male. And then it hit him. *Male.* That was it. Sugar probably didn't know what to make of him. She wasn't used to men. The Maltese had been coddled and protected by women.

He watched the pooch leap into Kathy's arms, watched as Kathy's expression turned soft and gentle.

Dakota swallowed around a lump in his throat. Somehow he was going to have to earn that little dog's trust. At the moment Sugar seemed to hold the key to Kathy's heart—a heart he longed to feel beating in time with his own. Because in spite of all of his friendship talk, Dakota couldn't deny the truth.

He was still in love with his wife.

Seven

L ater that afternoon Dakota offered to accompany Kathy on her home search. Royal had plenty of upscale apartment buildings since it was a bustling, exclusively rich town surrounded by oil fields and sprawling ranches.

The temperature rose to ninety degrees, but the West Texas wind blew, making the heat bearable. Kathy still wore the lemon-colored blouse, and her hair still rebelled from the pins struggling to secure it. Wispy tendrils fluttered around her face, reflecting sunlight like sparks of fire.

They took the stairs and followed the apartment manager to 6B, then waited while the woman unlocked the door. Kathy had specific tastes, but she hadn't been nearly as selective as Dakota. He had found fault with the previous apartments they'd looked at, but he had good reason. Plain and simple— he didn't want his wife leaving the ranch. He liked having her around. He wanted to keep her.

He loved her.

"This is nice," Kathy said as they entered.

Dakota frowned. "It's all right."

A gas fireplace dominated the living room and two large windows offered a spectacular view of Royal. The appliances in the spacious kitchen were new, and the dining area boasted a brass chandelier.

"That won't look right with your furniture," Dakota said. "It's too modern for antiques."

"It's fine," Kathy responded and moved on to explore the bedrooms.

The master suite presented another view, this one from a rather large balcony. Dakota couldn't find much fault, but he was damned determined to try. "I'll bet lugging groceries up and down stairs is a nuisance. And then of course there's that balcony."

Kathy stepped onto the feature in question. "What's wrong with it?"

He moved to stand next to her, out of earshot from the building manager. "Could be dangerous."

She sent him a strange look. "It seems sturdy enough to me."

"Of course, it's sturdy. I was referring to the rail. Sugar might be able to fit through the bars." He approached the rail, playing out his drama. "It's a long way down, sweetheart. And there's nothing to pad the fall. I don't think you should risk it."

Kathy studied the opening between the bars with a critical eye. "Sugar's body is bigger than that. She couldn't fit through there."

Dakota scraped a booted foot on the cement. He was certain Kathy would have given that scenario more thought. "Maybe you're right. But she could get her head stuck. Animals do that sort of thing all the time."

That appeared to do the trick. Kathy frowned and stepped closer to the rail. "You know, that's actually possible."

"Of course it is." He resisted the urge to flash an overly smug, overly macho smile. "Did you think I was making these things up? I've been trained to spot potential hazards.

And this apartment isn't right for you. I sensed it the moment we walked in.''

She gave him another one of those strange looks, and he lost the urge to grin, his machismo not quite so smug. Had he really said something that ridiculous, laid it on that thick? Trained to spot potential hazards? In an upscale Royal apartment?

"How about some lunch?" he suggested, hoping to distract her. Did he really want her to know that he was deliberately thwarting her effort to find a suitable place to live?

Kathy accepted his invitation, so Dakota decided on the Royal Diner, a typical greasy-spoon-type place that served typical greasy-spoon-type food. He had a hankering for casual atmosphere and a messy hamburger. He'd been to enough fancy balls and eaten enough deviled quail eggs to last a lifetime.

They scooted into a vinyl booth and grinned at each other like kids sharing a private joke. The paper placemat the waitress slapped in front of them boasted, The Royal Diner—Food Fit for a King! Yet King Bertram stopping in for a bowl of chili and finding it to his liking presented a ludicrous image.

Dakota ordered a bacon cheeseburger, and Kathy chose a club sandwich. He drank coffee while she sipped iced tea.

"I really thought I would find an apartment today," she said.

"You know what the problem is?" he asked without giving her a chance to answer. "You should be living in a house and not an apartment. Someplace with a yard for Sugar and privacy for yourself." Someplace like the ranch, he thought. He had a fenced yard the pooch could play in and a big canopy bed just waiting for Kathy.

"You know, I think you're right," she responded, her eyes sparkling with sudden enthusiasm. "I should start looking at rental houses instead."

Dakota wondered if he was an idiot. Here he was hoping to keep her, yet he hadn't asked why she'd left in the first place. Lifting his coffee to hide a frown, he took a sip. And why hadn't he asked?

Because deep down he feared the answer. Kathy might have left for a very simple, very devastating reason. She might have fallen out of love with him. And if that was the case, there wasn't much he could do about it.

Or was there? If she had loved him once, couldn't she love him again? If they spent enough time together, would those feelings come back?

The waitress delivered their lunch, and as they sampled their food, the jukebox played a country ballad. The sound of silverware clanking and voices chattering could be heard above the music, but the song managed to soothe Dakota's soul just the same. Kathy had chosen to live in Royal. That in itself seemed like a good sign.

He searched her gaze. "Do you ever think about the first time we met?"

A small smile touched her lips. "Charity dinner at the Texas Cattleman's Club. You were in uniform."

"And you were in white silk." A dress as cool and sleek as the woman wearing it. He'd taken one long, luxurious look and decided he'd wanted her. As to how he intended to win her over, he hadn't been sure. "I didn't think you would be interested. You were so refined, so elegant. Your type rarely gave me the time of day."

"My type?"

"You know what I mean." He took another bite of his burger and swallowed. "Do you think it was fate, us meeting like we did?" He had been stationed at Aviano Air Base in northeastern Italy at the time, but was home on leave. And she had come to Royal to visit Aaron before she left for Italy to replace a consular who had taken ill.

"That we met in Royal, but both ended up at the same Italian village?" She glanced down at her sandwich, then back up. "The Italy part might have been fate, but Aaron suspected I wanted to meet you. I think that's why he invited me to the charity dinner."

Stunned, Dakota leaned against the table. "I don't understand. Did Aaron mention me? Tell you I was a decent guy or something?"

Kathy stirred her tea a little nervously. "Yes, but I saw your picture first. Aaron had some photographs from a friend's wedding, and you were the best man. So when I came across your picture, I think I said something like 'Wow. He's gorgeous. Who is he?'" She clanked her spoon against the glass. "Pretty shallow, I guess."

Shallow? It was the best damn thing he'd heard in years. "Why didn't you ever tell me this before?"

"In the beginning it would have been too embarrassing. And later on, it didn't seem important. We never talked about how we had met."

Something in her voice bothered him. Something that said they weren't as close as he liked to remember. Dakota reached for his coffee, pushing his worry aside. Why dwell on the past? Instead he would do his best to focus on the future.

The following afternoon Kathy paced her bedroom, wondering what to do with herself. She couldn't seem to concentrate on anything other than overwhelming guilt. She could barely face herself in the mirror, let alone face Dakota every day.

Was he waiting for her to approach him? Waiting to hear why she had walked away from their marriage? A week had passed since they'd returned from Asterland, but she had yet to say a word.

It wasn't fair. He had a right to know. The baby had belonged to him, too.

Kathy slipped on a denim blouse, then zipped her jeans. She knew Dakota was at the barn, spending some time with the horses.

Exiting the house through the back door, she ventured into the Texas air. She could have taken one of Dakota's trucks, but decided the walk would do her good. Once inside the courtyard, she stopped to take comfort in her surroundings. Greenery had a way of soothing her, and the yard was lush with potted blooms. Beyond the Spanish tiles and rustic patio furniture lay a thick carpet of grass. This was her favorite spot at the ranch, a place to sip coffee in the morning and watch the stars light up the sky at night.

She opened the gate leading to the rest of the property. The land was flat, wide open and picturesque in a vast, Texas kind of way. As she walked, her boots kicked up dust. The soil wasn't fertile, but it reflected the sun in warm, golden shades.

The breezeway barn stood strong and solid, a building alive with the scents and sounds of the horses Dakota loved. He had an incredible facility, designed with the recreational cowboy in mind—an indoor and outdoor arena, fenced pastures, wash racks, a hot walker, an enormous tack room, hay storage and RV buildings. He didn't want for anything, she thought, except maybe the truth from his wife.

Kathy didn't need to enter the barn. Dakota stood beside a hitching post, saddling a big, black gelding. She couldn't help but admire her husband, the breadth of his shoulders, taper of his waist, those long legs covered in time-worn denim. And his rear, she thought, that taut masculine rear.

She walked toward him, and he turned and smiled, making her guilty heart flutter. He still affected her, still had a way of making her limbs watery and her breath catch.

"Hi," she said. "Are you going for a ride?" It was a dumb question with an obvious answer, but she couldn't think of anything else to say.

"Sure am. Do you want to join me? It's a great day to hit the trail. Not nearly as hot as yesterday."

Kathy brushed a stray hair from her eye. He sounded so relaxed, so friendly. And she was a nervous wreck, at least on the inside. Maybe on the outside, too. She couldn't seem to keep her hands still. She batted away another hair, a useless effort in the wind.

"Okay," she answered, thinking she would probably return to the ranch wobbly-legged and sore. "But I haven't been on a horse in a while. I'm a little out of practice." And anxiety-ridden. Could she really talk about the miscarriage today? Talk about their lost baby on this warm, breezy Texas day?

"Then you should ride Serenity," he said, suggesting Kathy's favorite mount. "She'll be good to you."

Serenity had been named well. The mare, a leopard Appaloosa, nuzzled Kathy in a gentle welcome. "She hasn't forgotten me."

Dakota placed Kathy's saddle on a nearby stand. "You're
not easy to forget, sweetheart."

And neither was he, she thought, sending him a shaky
smile. Not a day had passed without him entering her mind.

They mounted their horses in silence. The main trail led to
a dozen smaller paths, the next as boundless as the last. The
vegetation was sparse and the ground level for as far as the
eye could see, but the land was rich with history. Wars, cattle
drives, the building of railroads, the discovery of oil. Every
rock, every cactus, every speck of dirt told a story.

They rode for nearly two hours, with Kathy taking in familiar sights, scenery she enjoyed. In the distance, windmills
turned, pumping water from the earth.

"Do you want to stop?" Dakota asked as they came upon
one of the few shade trees on the trail.

Kathy nodded, anxiety setting in once again. If she intended to tell him, then it should be now, while they were
away from the ranch—away from the memories that lingered
in the halls of the house they once shared.

She slid from her saddle, and Dakota took Serenity's reins.
He hobbled the horses, returning with a blanket under his arm.
Dakota never traveled on horseback without a blanket. It was,
Kathy decided, the Indian in him, the nomad running through
his veins. The Comanche were a wandering tribe, a people
who had once roamed West Texas, then later fought to keep
the Lone Star plains as their home. Another piece of history,
she thought, another lost battle.

They sat beneath the oak and sipped bottled water.

"I'm going out of town tonight," he said.

Kathy's heart made a fast, nervous leap. "Another assignment already?"

He shook his head. "No. Business in Lubbock."

"Oh." She released an audible breath. Business in Lubbock meant the shopping centers Dakota owned. Commercial

property was the major source of his income. The Texas Cattleman's Club missions had nothing to do with money. "How long will you be gone?"

"A few days."

Apparently that was all the information he intended to share. But Kathy knew Dakota didn't enjoy the corporate world. It wasn't dangerous enough, she supposed.

He removed his Stetson and handed it to her. "You'd better wear my hat on the way back or you'll end up with a sunburn."

"Thanks." Kathy placed the hat beside her. She had the fair, sensitive skin common to most natural redheads, even though she lacked the freckles and fiery temper often associated with scarlet hair. But Dakota used to say that her passion was red, that her appetite in bed was the color of fire.

She felt her cheeks warm. "I'm probably pink already."

"A little." He tapped her nose in an affectionate gesture, and her nipples pebbled.

"This is nice," he said.

She blinked. "Nice?"

"The weather. The horses. You and me. It reminds me of our days in Italy."

It had been wondrous—falling in love with a pilot, holding his hand and stealing kisses in tiny cafés. Aviano Air Base was thirty minutes from the beach and thirty minutes from the mountains. A more romantic location didn't exist.

He reclined on the blanket. "Lie down with me."

Kathy caught her breath. She couldn't resist—not his crooked smile, his Texas drawl, the long fluid line of his body.

She lowered herself to the blanket. Being next to him was more than nice.

"I think we're turning out to be pretty good friends," he said. "Don't you?"

She nodded, knowing she couldn't bear to spoil this moment, this warm, tender feeling. She couldn't tell him why she had left. At least not today.

* * *

Kathy answered the phone at 10:00 p.m., surprised by the masculine voice on the other end of the line. Dakota rarely called when he was away on business.

"What are you doing?" he asked.

"Nothing, really." She glanced at her bed. Sugar was curled up on a pillow. "I was thinking I might make some hot chocolate. Maybe read for a while."

"Are you in the kitchen?"

"No. My room."

"And you're alone?"

Kathy gripped the phone. "Sugar's here."

Dakota sounded strange, not quite himself. She looked around nervously. Was he worried the house was bugged? He could be involved in another mission, something he hadn't told her about. Or someone from his past might have surfaced. Dakota had probably made plenty of enemies over the years.

"Are you on the cordless phone?" he asked.

Was he really in Lubbock? "Yes."

"Good. I want you to go to my room."

"Okay." Heart pounding, she walked down the hall, then entered the master bedroom. He hadn't made the bed before he'd left, but other than that, the room was tidy. Nothing looked disturbed, nothing out of place. "I'm here."

Dakota's voice softened. "Go to the closet and pick out one of my shirts."

Kathy frowned. His instructions were getting stranger by the minute, but he appeared to have a distinct purpose in mind, something he needed her to do. Meet him somewhere? Bring him a shirt? It made no sense.

She stepped into the walk-in closet. Neat, organized, very Dakota. Casual wear at one end, dress clothes at the other. She tried to ignore the empty rack that used to be hers. He hadn't filled the space. It remained vacant.

"What kind of shirt?" she asked.

"It doesn't matter. You choose."

She reached for denim, soft and well-worn—a long-sleeved

shirt with pearl-front snaps. She liked how he looked in blue, it made his eyes appear darker, his skin more golden.

"Do you have one?"

"Yes."

"Put it on the bed."

If they were being bugged, she thought, someone was listening to an odd conversation. But maybe that was the idea. She removed the shirt from the hanger and did as he asked. "Done."

"Good girl. Now tell me what you're wearing."

Kathy froze. She looked around, caught sight of the canopy bed—the tousled covers, his denim shirt. There were no electronic bugs, no old enemies lurking. She wasn't in any danger. And there was only one reason why she couldn't hang up on him.

His voice. The husky, sensual sound of his voice.

She adjusted the phone. "I can't believe you're doing this to me."

"I'm lonely, Kathy. I miss you."

She closed her eyes. She missed him, too.

"Are you wearing a dress?" he asked.

She shook her head, then realized he couldn't see her. "No." He wanted to see her, she thought. He wanted to picture her in his mind. She opened her eyes. "A blouse and a skirt."

"Nylons?"

"No. My legs are bare."

She heard him swallow. "Take your blouse off."

Kathy sat on the edge of the bed. Could she do this? Could she play this forbidden game? She touched his shirt. Dakota's scent lingered in the room, the woodsy note of his cologne drifting through the air.

"Kathy?"

"I'm taking it off," she said, reaching for the top button on her blouse.

"Is it green? Emerald, like your eyes?"

"Yes." But even if it wasn't, she would have told him what he wanted to hear. She wanted to fuel his imagination,

make him warm and aroused. She glanced at her hand and
realized she still wore her wedding ring. "Where are you,
Dakota?"

"In a hotel room."

She pictured him lying on a bed, his chest bare, his back
braced against a wooden headboard. His room-service dinner
would be untouched, except for a bottle of imported beer. She
could almost taste the alcohol on his lips, taste the intoxicating flavor.

"Are you wearing jeans?"

"Yes."

She let the blouse fall from her shoulders. "Are they unzipped?"

His voice turned rough. "As far down as they'll go."

Suddenly the image in her mind intensified. The contrast
of his skin against crisp, white sheets. The broad expanse of
his chest, the narrow line of his hips. His sex, full and erect,
pressing against his jeans.

Kathy couldn't stop the heat between her legs, the silky
moisture. "I'm in my bra and panties." She had dropped her
skirt to the floor, where it pooled at her feet.

Dakota groaned, and she knew he had lifted his hips. "Tell
me what you look like," he said. "Every detail."

She walked to the mirror, the phone cradled against her
ear. She looked aroused, her cheeks flushed, her lips slightly
parted. "My hair is pinned up, but it's starting to fall." Just
the way he liked it, she thought, tangled and messy. And the
color of her bra, she told him, was called autumn gold. She
had ordered it from a catalog, along with matching panties.
The bra was seamless and sheer, the panties decorated with
a hint of lace.

"I can hear the wind," she said, turning toward the window. She could almost feel it blowing through her hair, cooling her face. With her head tipped back and her eyes closed,
she unhooked her bra, then slipped off her panties.

"Are you naked?" he asked, his voice a husky whisper
above the wind.

"Yes." For him, she thought. Naked for him.

"Put my shirt on, Kathy. Put it on and climb under the covers. I want you in my bed."

The shirt could have been his hands. It caressed her, brushed her nipples, slid between her thighs—rough yet gentle.

And the bed. She pressed her face to the pillow and imagined him there. His scent. The weight of his erection. His mouth covering hers.

Kathy brought the phone to her lips and smiled. Tonight they would make love in their minds. Warm, wet, languorous love. A beautiful, erotic fantasy.

Kathy answered the door, and found herself face-to-face with Violet Tenewa, Dakota's Comanche mother.

"Kathy!" the other woman exclaimed. "Honey, I had no idea you were back."

"I'm not. I mean, I am, but…" How could she explain her presence at the ranch to her mother-in-law? "I'm just a temporary houseguest. Dakota invited me to stay until I find another place to live."

Violet's smile fell. "Oh."

Kathy stepped away from the door, praying this wasn't going to be an awkward reunion. She adored Dakota's mother. Violet was a striking, independent woman. Even at sixty-two, she looked as exotic as her name. Her silver-streaked hair fell in a straight, black curtain, complementing a golden complexion and deep-set eyes.

"Would you like to come in?" Kathy asked. "Dakota isn't here, but I'd love to visit with you."

"Thank you. I'd love to visit with you, too."

Kathy made a pot of coffee and warmed the pastries she had baked the day before. Coffee in hand, they sat in the living room, the aroma of cinnamon wafting between them.

"Where is Dakota?" Violet asked.

"He had some business in Lubbock. He's been gone a few days."

Violet reached for a cinnamon roll. "Have you heard from him?"

"Yes, he called." And seduced me over the phone, she thought, her skin suddenly warm. "He should be home later this afternoon."

Neither spoke after that. Small talk didn't seem appropriate. Kathy had walked out on Violet's son—a subject that certainly outweighed the weather.

"I'm sorry," Kathy said finally, struggling to find a simple way to explain the burden in her heart. "I never meant to hurt Dakota. When I left, I kept hoping that he would come to me. That he—" She paused, her eyes beginning to mist. "That he would tell me that I was more important than his work." She swallowed past the emotion and met the other woman's gaze. "I suppose that sounds foolish, especially to someone as independent as you. Your life with Jack was so unconventional."

"Oh, honey. It doesn't sound foolish at all."

Kathy scooted to the edge of the sofa. "Then you understand why I left?"

Violet pursed her lips. "I suppose I do. Except it's a little difficult for me to accept because he's my son. I want to believe that Dakota was a perfect husband, even if he wasn't."

Kathy's eyes turned misty again. "I never stopped loving him."

Violet squeezed her hand. "Now that part I truly understand. I know it's possible to love a man who always has other priorities. Who makes you feel like you're second-best in his heart."

Unable to conceal her curiosity, Kathy blinked away her tears. "Dakota's father?"

Violet nodded. "If Jack Lewis wasn't caught up in an important business deal, then he was attending a social function with his wife." She released a heavy sigh and went on, "I realize that I shouldn't have been involved with a married man, but I honestly believed he was going to divorce his wife and marry me. Jack and Sharon had one of those society marriages. There wasn't any real love between them."

"We've never talked about this before." Kathy knew Violet had been Jack's mistress, but she had no idea Dakota's mother had wanted something more. "I assumed you were comfortable with the arrangement."

"No, I never was."

"But you were with him all those years."

"Yes, all those years, and he was still married to Sharon. They even died together."

A boating accident, Kathy recalled. "I'm sorry. I had no idea." Which seemed disrespectful to Dakota's mother. Most women would prefer to be a wife than a mistress.

"I was nineteen when I met Jack. Nineteen and naive. I left him once, though. I was devastated that I was about to give birth, and my baby's father still hadn't made arrangements to marry me. So I went to South Dakota to stay with a friend." She sent Kathy a woman-to-woman smile. "Two months later I came back to Texas."

Kathy returned Violet's smile. "And presented Jack with a son."

"An illegitimate son. Something Dakota never let himself forget."

Both of their smiles faded. "But he hasn't made an issue of it, at least not to me. I was under the impression it didn't matter to him all that much."

"It mattered." Violet reached for her coffee, then took a sip. "Being the illegitimate son of a prominent man wasn't easy, even if Jack treated him well. Dakota tried very hard to legitimize himself, to be accepted by his father's peers. And I suppose serving his country was a way of proving his worth. Dakota enlisted at seventeen, a boy on the verge of manhood."

And now Kathy understood why her husband didn't enjoy high-society events. They reminded him of a time when he wasn't welcome. "It must have made things easier on Dakota that Jack and Sharon didn't have any children. At least he was Jack's only son."

"That's true, but his father being intimate with two women

was still a problem. I don't think Dakota understands the true concept of marriage—how much work is involved or how much a couple has to give of themselves. In that respect, Jack was a poor role model.''

Kathy nodded. It made sense. All of it. Unlike his father, Dakota had remained faithful to his vows, but he still didn't consider marriage the number-one priority in his life. His career had always come first.

''Dakota still doesn't know why I left. I can't seem to bring myself to say the words out loud. At least not to him.'' And that sounded like an excuse, Kathy thought. Feeble and unfair. But there was the baby she had wanted so badly—the part of her heart she had lost.

Violet frowned. ''Has he asked? Has he questioned you about it at all?''

''No.''

''Then maybe he isn't ready to face the past. Maybe he needs a little more time to sort out his feelings.''

Kathy cocked her head, considering the possibility. ''I hadn't thought of that.'' She hadn't thought of anything but her guilt, her secret, her own loss. But what Violet suggested provided a small measure of relief. Kathy wasn't ready to talk about the past, and Dakota wasn't ready to hear about it. ''After I left, did he confide in you? Did he say anything?''

''Not a word,'' the other woman responded in a soft, almost sad voice. ''At first he closed himself off completely, and later he threw himself into his work, doing all of those dangerous things that he does.''

Kathy lifted her coffee. Dangerous things. She understood that phrase well. ''So he—'' As a pair of boots sounded on the Spanish tile, she nearly spilled the hot drink.

Dakota.

''He's home.'' She looked up at Violet, and they both waited for him to enter the room.

Eight

While Kathy battled a bout of nervousness, Violet stood and approached her son. Had he overheard their conversation? Kathy wondered.

She stole a quick glance and decided he hadn't. It wasn't in Dakota's nature to eavesdrop.

"Mom." He hugged her, then stepped back. "It's good to see you."

"Kathy said you were in Lubbock."

He nodded. "I had some business to take care of with Dad's properties."

Kathy shifted on the couch. Strange, she thought, how Dakota still hadn't taken mental possession of the shopping centers Jack had left him. He still referred to them as his father's—a man who had influenced him more than she had realized.

Violet resumed her seat, and Dakota turned toward Kathy. "Hi."

"Hi." She met his gaze, her heart leaping into its teeter-totter mode. Why couldn't she look at him without experiencing a physical reaction? "I wasn't expecting you back so soon."

"I had a meeting this morning, but it ended early."

He held her gaze, and her heart continued to flutter. He wore a tan T-shirt, faded blue jeans and distressed leather boots—clothes too casual for a business meeting. Apparently he had changed before coming home.

Kathy chewed her lip. Were those the Wranglers he had worn during their telephone conversation? Unable to help herself, she glanced at his fly, then back up to his face. He flashed a bedroom smile and made her hot all over.

Are you wearing jeans?

Yes.

Are they unzipped?

As far down as they'll go.

Violet cleared her throat, and Kathy felt like a teenager who'd been caught lusting after an older boy. Her nipples tingled against her bra, not a good thing to happen when the older boy's observant mother occupied the same room.

Dakota looked away and pulled a hand through his hair. "So, Mom, what's going on? What made you stop by?"

"Do I need a special reason to come to your house?"

"No, of course not."

Violet's eyes, Kathy noticed, sparkled with amusement. But her big, strong, Comanche son revealed something rare—an embarrassed flush coloring his bronzed cheeks. Of course, he had been caught behaving like a teenager, too—sending Kathy a provocative, I'm-thinking-about-sex smile.

Dakota moved toward a leather recliner and sat. Careful, it seemed, not to cast his gaze in Kathy's direction. He focused on his mother instead.

Unwelcome silence ensued, and Kathy wished her heart would quit bumping against her breast. Violet couldn't possibly know that she had climbed into Dakota's bed while he was gone, or that his shirt had brushed decadently between her naked thighs.

Two or three minutes passed, but still no one spoke. They

just sat there, Kathy and Dakota avoiding eye contact, and Violet splitting her amused gaze between them.

"Actually I did stop by for a reason," she admitted finally.

Grateful for the reprieve, Kathy's breath rushed out of her lungs. Dakota, too, seemed grateful his mother had decided to let them off the hook. He leaned forward in his chair.

"As you know," Violet said, "I'm on the board of directors at the West Texas Indian Center, and we need some volunteers to help out with an event next Saturday."

"What kind of an event?" Dakota asked.

"A carnival to raise money for the Foster Care Mentor Program."

Apparently more relaxed, Dakota strode to the bar and poured himself a soda water. "Oh, yeah. You mentioned that program before."

Violet explained to Kathy. "Since we're not able to place all of the children in Indian homes, we're trying to secure weekend foster parents. It's actually called respite care, but we prefer to think of it as our Mentor Program."

"That sounds wonderful," Kathy responded. "Role models are important." Especially to kids from troubled homes, she thought sadly.

"So you'll help out at the carnival?" the other woman asked.

"I'd love to."

Violet looked at Dakota, and he placed his drink on the bar. "Sure, Mom. Me, too."

"Good." She smiled at both of them. "I should get going. I still have more volunteers to recruit." She hugged Kathy, then took her son's arm as he walked her to the door.

Kathy busied herself carrying coffee cups and the leftover pastries into the kitchen. A minute later, Dakota came in and grabbed one of the sweets.

"I enjoyed visiting with your mom," she said before the lone moment trapped them into another awkward spell.

"I imagine she was surprised to see you. I should have called her and told her you were staying here."

"That's okay." Kathy didn't want to think about telephone

conversations, not when she couldn't get the other night out
of her mind.

She rinsed the cups and placed them in the dishwasher,
then turned to see Dakota licking icing from a cinnamon roll.

He smiled that sexy smile, and she swallowed.

"Do you want a bite?" he asked.

She wanted to bite him. Kiss and nibble. Taste that warm,
dark, tantalizing skin.

Struggling to respond in a dignified voice, she cleared her
throat and then remembered why Dakota's mother had done
that earlier. "No, thank you," she managed.

Sugar trotted into the kitchen and saved Kathy's sanity. The
dog made a wide circle around Dakota to get to her.

"She still doesn't like me," he said.

Kathy opened a can of dog food, glad the Maltese had
given her another busy task. "I know, I'm sorry. I just don't
understand it."

"I do." He leaned against the counter, his shoulder nearly
brushing hers. "Sugar isn't used to men."

And he was definitely a man, she thought, cursing her qua-
vering heart. Dakota Lewis was as rugged as his gender came.

She filled the dog's bowl, hardly blaming Sugar for being
nervous around him. "Then I suppose it will take time."

Time she wouldn't allow herself to have. Soon she would
have to find another place to live.

Dakota knew he didn't have much time. Several days had
passed since he'd returned from Lubbock, and he'd barely
seen Kathy. She spent every free moment looking at rentals.
How was he supposed to win his wife back once she moved
out?

Call her? Make love on the phone?

The idea had merit, but it wasn't the same as a flesh-to-
flesh encounter. He missed holding her, missed being her husband.

And his progress with Sugar was slow, too. He opened the
box of dog treats he kept in his room and stuffed a few in
his pocket. He bribed the Maltese whenever Kathy wasn't

around, although it didn't appear to do him much good. The dog still wouldn't get close enough to take the treat from his hand. He would set it on the floor, and she would wait until he backed away before nabbing it.

He strode down the hall, then entered the kitchen where he found Sugar with Mrs. Miller. The dog danced happily around the older woman's feet as she cleaned.

He assessed the situation. Little white dog. Big, dark Comanche man. Unless he got some outside help, his chances were slim to none with that pooch.

"Good morning, Mrs. Miller."

She looked up from her sponge. "Hello, Lieutenant."

He stood at attention, but why, he couldn't be sure. Mrs. Miller was hardly his superior. "I need a favor from you."

She took a break from her chore. "Yes, sir. What is it?"

"I want you to help me make friends with the dog." He eyed Sugar and noticed her ears had perked. "I'm not having much luck on my own."

Mrs. Miller cocked her head, giving him the same curious look as the dog. "What seems to be the trouble, Lieutenant?"

Dakota didn't ease his stance. At the moment he felt far from casual. What he felt, he realized, was tense. Out of his element. "Sugar doesn't appear to like men."

"Oh, my. That could present a problem."

She glanced at the dog, then back at Dakota, her bottom lip quivering. Was she suppressing a smile? he wondered. No-nonsense, never-cracks-a smile Miller?

"I don't suppose we can put you in a dress," she said, her lip quivering just a bit more.

Dakota raised an eyebrow at her. He supposed the image was funny, but he hadn't pegged the housekeeper as the smart-aleck type. Deciding he liked this side of her, he grinned. "Why not? I've got great legs."

She finally smiled. And when she did, her entire face came alive. "I hope it won't come to that." She reached down and scooped up the dog. "Say hello to her. How you talk to an animal is important."

Okay, now he felt stupid. Sugar, her gold hair bow angled

like a crown, looked like the queen bee in Mrs. Miller's arms, just waiting for him to make an ass out of himself.

"Hi, Sugar," he said.

The dog turned her white fluffy head away, and Mrs. Miller snorted. "Your voice is too deep."

Dakota frowned, wondering what in the hell he had gotten himself into. "It's called testosterone. I can't help it." Hadn't they already discussed the fact that he was a man?

"Of course you can help it," she scolded. "Haven't you ever talked to a baby?"

A baby? "Actually, no." His lifestyle didn't lend itself to pink and blue bundles. Dakota didn't know diddly about kids, especially the diaper-clad variety.

Mrs. Miller tsked, and he wondered if she had given up on him. She placed the Maltese on the floor, then asked, "So what have you been doing to get Sugar's attention?"

He reached into his pocket and produced the doggie treats. The older woman made another disapproving noise. "I think we can do better than that."

"Better than that" turned out to be pan-fried bits of filet mignon. "Grandma's making you something special," Mrs. Miller told Sugar, who sat sniffing the air.

Grandma? Dakota shook his head. He sure as hell hoped that didn't make him the dog's—

"Daddy's going to help," the gray-haired lady added, shooting him a you-better-get-involved glance. "Aren't you, Lieutenant?"

Daddy seasoned the steak, thinking he'd just lost his mind. All this fuss for a five-pound mutt.

They waited for the meat to cool. Sugar let out a few anxious yips, wiggling impatiently on the floor. Dakota didn't make a move without Mrs. Miller's instruction. The housekeeper had taken charge, giving orders the way his mother sometimes did, outranking him with feminine skill.

"Now you can feed her," she told him. "One piece at a time."

He knelt and offered the treat. As badly as Sugar wanted

the steak, she didn't forget herself. She looked up at Mrs. Miller and whined, clearly pleading for help.

"Go on," the older lady urged. "He won't hurt you."

The dog inched closer and took the meat. Dakota grinned, feeling like he'd just scaled a mountain. He continued hand feeding Sugar, and by the time she'd devoured the last piece, the pooch was sitting on his lap.

Mrs. Miller smiled. "You realize we've just spoiled her for life?"

"It's for an important cause."

"I know," the woman said gently. "It would be nice if Kathy and Sugar moved in permanently. I like your wife, Lieutenant. You're good for each other."

"Thank you." His heart went soft. "I think so, too."

On Saturday morning, Kathy woke with the sun. It was too early to get ready for the carnival, so she brushed her teeth and slipped on her chenille robe, preparing to start a pot of coffee.

Sugar roused from her spot on the bed and followed Kathy into the hall. But as they passed Dakota's room, the dog nudged open the crack in the door.

"Sugar, no!" Kathy's warning came too late. The Maltese had already darted inside.

Without a second thought, Kathy went after her, then stopped when she neared the bed. Dakota was still asleep, the sheets tangled around his waist, the quilt kicked away from him. His face, she noticed, was dark and angular, the tiny lines around his eyes prominent in the morning light. Black hair spiked against his pillow, and beard stubble shadowed his jaw.

He looked warm and touchable, she thought. Like the man she had married, yet slightly changed. She wanted to tame his hair, skim his cheek. But she knew better. He wasn't hers anymore. Too much time had passed, too much heartache. And he was still a soldier. Soon there would be another mission. Dakota wouldn't remain idle for long.

So why was she here, standing in his room, longing for

what could never be? What had possessed her to get this close to him?

Good grief. Sugar. One long, stolen glance at Dakota and she had forgotten about the dog.

"Sugar," she whispered, looking around the room. "Come on, sweetie, we have to go."

A movement from the bed caught her eye, and a familiar being emerged from beneath the rumpled quilt—two black eyes, a mass of silky white fur and a half-cocked metallic bow.

Kathy sent the dog a scolding glance, keeping her voice hushed. "What are you doing in his bed? You don't even like him."

As if determined to defy Kathy's words, Sugar picked her way around the tangled sheets and settled herself right next to Dakota, snug against his bare chest.

Kathy had to smile. The big man and the little dog were an odd, but tender sight. Sugar's white paw rested on Dakota's arm, and he nuzzled closer, stirring in his sleep.

She turned to leave them alone, but only got as far as the door.

"Kathy?"

She turned back to see Dakota squinting at her. She should have known he would awaken. Dakota was a light sleeper. She assumed it came from his military background, night after night of sleepless combat. "I'm sorry I disturbed you. I was looking for Sugar."

"She's right here. Did I oversleep?"

"No. It's still early."

He sent her a boyish smile. "Wanna join us?"

She did. God help her, she did. "No. I'm already up. I think I'll just go start a pot of coffee. Maybe fix an omelet."

He glanced down at the dog, then straightened her bow in what seemed like a paternal gesture. Kathy steadied herself. The image in her head made her knees weak—Dakota with the child they should have had—a dark-eyed, dark-haired little girl dressed in ruffles and ribbons.

"Sweetheart?"

"Yes?" She responded to the endearment, hating that it made her weaker, more vulnerable, achy inside.

"If you give me a few minutes, I'll help you with breakfast."

"Just meet me in the kitchen when you're ready." She forced her legs to carry her down the hall, wondering how she was going to survive the carnival—an event overflowing with dark-eyed, dark-haired children.

Kathy started the coffee and by the time the hash browns were cooking, Dakota arrived with Sugar in tow. He had showered, shaved and zipped himself into a pair of jeans.

He made his way around her, the Maltese at his heels. Kathy couldn't help but wonder what had turned Sugar around. Had the dog looked at him this morning and decided he was just too gorgeous to ignore?

They fixed breakfast and sat across from each other at the dining-room table, their plates filled with potatoes and eggs.

"So, have you found a house yet?" he asked.

Kathy shook her head. "No." None of the rentals seemed quite right. They were all too big for one person, too spacious and lonely. She wanted charming and cozy, like the cottage in Asterland. Or a place that would make her feel warm and woodsy, like Dakota's ranch. She needed the perfect, permanent home, something her living-abroad parents had never provided.

"What about office space?" he asked, pursuing their conversation.

"I haven't looked." She had been too busy scouting Royal for a house that probably didn't exist. "But I guess I'd better start. My parents are anxious for me to get this location up and running."

He lifted his coffee. "Do they know you're staying with me?"

"Yes." And they approved. They didn't understand why Kathy had left Dakota in the first place. One lost baby, her mother had told her, didn't mean that she couldn't have another. And Dakota had been a soldier when she'd married him, so walking out on him two years later made no sense.

Kathy's pragmatic parents didn't understand the dreamer in her, the old-fashioned girl who wanted an enchanted garden, a house full of children and a husband who cared more about saving his marriage than saving the world.

Hiding a frown, she sipped her juice. Her mother had been the first to suggest Royal as a satellite location. That didn't mean her parents were playing matchmaker, did it? Her proper, professional, business-minded parents? No. That couldn't be.

A small, whining noise jarred Kathy from her thoughts. "Is that Sugar?" She looked around to see the dog sitting at Dakota's feet. "Is she begging?"

"No," he answered hastily. "She's just watching me eat."

Watching him eat? "You've been feeding her table scraps, haven't you?" No wonder Sugar followed him around like a lovesick fool. It was food she was after, not masculine attention.

Dakota winced. "Maybe I've given her a few bites here and there. But it wasn't my idea. Mrs. Miller put me up to it."

His boyish excuse sounded impossibly endearing. "And why would your housekeeper do that?"

"Because I asked her to help me make friends with your dog."

A burst of moisture rushed behind Kathy's eyes. She blinked, refusing to cry over breakfast. It had to be, she thought, the sweetest, silliest thing he had ever done. She smiled and reached across the table for his hand. "Sometimes you surprise me."

His fingers curled around hers. "You surprise me, too."

Sugar leapt onto Dakota's lap, and Kathy laughed. Suddenly she was looking forward to spending the day with her husband, even in the company of dark-eyed, dark-haired children.

Beneath the Texas sun, a small park in Midland had been transformed into a carnival, its grassy spaces filled with merriment. It wasn't a large affair, not the kind with those whiplash-type rides, but it was entertaining nonetheless. It reminded Dakota of being a kid himself, of the Halloween festival his elementary school used to host every October. His mother had been involved in that, too. Dakota figured being on the board of directors at the Indian Center was a lot like being a PTA mom for Violet Tenewa. Only these days, she had more than one child to look after. She had taken on a caseload of foster kids.

Dakota sniffed the air, the aroma of hot dogs and buttered popcorn teasing his senses. Kathy had been placed in one of the concession stands, and he could see her from his post at the shooting gallery. She wore slim-fitting jeans and a buckskin-colored T-shirt, a thick ponytail bouncing high on her head. She seemed right at home, filling cartons of popcorn and handing out candy apples.

Looking up from a customer, she noticed him watching her, then graced him with a quick, ladylike smile.

He returned the smile, feeling like a tall, love-struck adolescent, a Comanche youth just coming into his own.

They lost eye contact over the crowd, and Dakota glanced back at the prizes lined on the shelves—the stuffed animals and plastic toys. Suddenly he wished Kathy had been a part of his early years. Maybe if they had been childhood sweethearts, their lives would have been too connected for her to sever the tie as she had.

A middle-aged man placed a stack of tickets on the counter. "For the boys," he said, a friendly smile working its way across his face.

Dakota took the tickets and scanned "the boys." Three of them, each a different shade of brown. Foster kids, he thought, and a fair-skinned foster dad who believed in rainbows. It made him like the man, respect him for doing something Dakota would have never considered. Kids, no matter what their shape or hue, were foreign to Dakota.

"You're Violet's son, right?" the foster dad asked, as each boy claimed a rifle and studied the ducks moving across the target.

Nodding, he extended his hand. "Dakota Lewis."

The other man gave a hearty shake. "Bob Calhoun." He motioned to the child at the end of the row, his voice suddenly quiet. "That one's Jake. He's Comanche. Violet said I ought to mention that. You know, since Jake's in the program."

In other words, Dakota thought, Jake was in need of an Indian mentor. A Comanche, he supposed, wondering if his mom was lurking somewhere, watching his befuddled expression.

What did he know about being a mentor? Jake appeared to be about five, with thick brown hair and skin about the same color as Dakota's. A mixed-blood, he surmised, like himself.

The boy wiggled as he fired at the ducks, even though his tongue darted out in a gesture defining serious concentration. Dakota figured all kids that age were squirmy and active. No, he wouldn't know what to say or do with someone that small.

The tallest of Bob's boys earned himself a prize. Dakota let him pick through the toys, his foster brothers crowding him in excitement as he chose a plastic snake. He looked up at Dakota with a ready smile. "I'm Scott. Me and him are Cherokee," he said, nudging the boy on his left. "Just like Bob's stepdad."

So Bob had been raised in an Indian home. Somehow that made sense. The rainbow was a part of his upbringing. Dakota assumed Bob's stepfather was a mentor to the two Cherokee boys.

"Nice to meet you guys, I'm Dakota. I'm from the Comanche Nation."

"Cool." Scott put his arm around the third child. "So is Jake."

At the mention of his name, Jake flashed a gap-filled grin. He was the littlest of the bunch and the most wiggly. Dakota resisted the urge to smooth his hair. For an instant, Jake reminded him of Prince Eric.

The kids went back to their rifles, and Dakota returned to Bob.

"You know, Jake has a twin sister," Bob said. "Pretty girl named Jenny. She lives with us, too." He motioned toward another booth and chuckled. "She's with my wife. Those two are determined to bring home a goldfish."

Twins. He could only assume Jake and Jenny were a package deal. A boy and a girl who needed a Comanche mentor, someone who could help them stay connected to their roots. It made him wonder how they had ended up in foster care in the first place. Were they orphaned? Abused? Neglected?

When their tickets ran out, Bob and his lively brood said goodbye and headed in the direction of the goldfish toss, Dakota staring after them.

Fifteen minutes later, Violet arrived with Dakota's replacement. Rather than accuse his mother of setting him up, he strolled the carnival grounds with her, waiting for Kathy's shift to end.

"Tell me about them, Mom."

"Jake and Jenny?" She took his arm as they passed a vendor selling Texas trinkets. "Their father is Comanche, but he's been out of the picture for quite a while. And their mother is in rehab for drug abuse." When Dakota frowned, Violet squeezed his arm. "She's not a bad person, she just got caught up in something bad. She loves her kids, and she's working hard to stay clean."

"That's good."

"Jake and Jenny are perfect for the mentor program. They're doing well at Bob's, but he isn't familiar with Comanche practices." She stopped to gaze up at him. "They're sweet kids, and they're mixed-bloods, Dakota. Like you."

He let out a breath, confused by his emotions. "You don't have to push so hard. I've already decided to come into the center and find out more about the program. But, Mom—"

"Yes?"

"I can't make any promises."

She kept her eyes on his. "It's enough that you're thinking about it."

Was it? he wondered. Thinking and doing weren't the same thing. He didn't know if he had what it took to make a dif-

ference in Jake and Jenny's lives. What if they sensed his
uneasiness? His inexperience with kids? And how many Sat-
urdays would he be free to mentor? Thunder had already contacted him about the possibility of another assignment.

Nine

At dusk Kathy and Dakota sat on the lawn, the carnival twinkling around them. Enjoying each other's company, they sipped ice-cold lemonade and ate a variety of junk food.

Kathy savored the sweet, sugary taste of cotton candy melting on her tongue. Her fingers were sticky, but she didn't care. It made her feel young and free, a girl without a care in the world. She hadn't felt that way in a long time. Life had a way of crushing those moments.

Dakota munched on chili dogs dripping with melted cheese. He spilled a glob on his jeans, wiped it with a napkin and grinned.

"Do you ever wish we had known each other when we were kids?" he asked.

Kathy reached for her drink, the question surprising her. Dakota wasn't a dreamer. He didn't try to turn people or places into something they weren't. They had grown up worlds apart, and she assumed he accepted their differences. "I've thought about it." But the fantasy never played out quite right. "Since you're nine years my senior, I don't think we would have been friends."

"I forgot about our age difference." He chuckled. "And here I was picturing myself as your first lover. Sixteen-year-olds parked in an empty field, kissing and groping."

She laughed, too. "When you were sixteen I was seven. And when I was sixteen, you were twenty-five."

After polishing off two chili cheese dogs, he attacked a carton of fries. "So much for that romantic illusion."

Kathy leaned back, wondering what had made him imagine such a thing in the first place. Was it the carnival? The teenagers holding hands and stealing kisses? When dusk arrived, so had the Texas youth—long, lanky boys in cowboy hats and girls with fresh, pretty faces.

"I didn't know kissing and groping in the back of a pickup was romantic," she said, angling her head to study him. He had been long and lean as a youth, too. Or so he appeared in the photographs his mother kept in leather-bound albums. And his first vehicle had been a shiny red Ford, much like the truck he drove today.

"It is to sixteen-year-old boys." Lifting a fry, he dunked it into a plastic cup brimming with ketchup. "And I did my fair share."

"Should I be jealous?" Once the words were out, she could have kicked herself. They might be legally married, but they were no longer a couple. Jealousy didn't fit into the equation.

He didn't appear to notice her blunder. Either that or he was having too much fun reminiscing to care. "You know who drove the boys in Royal wild?" he said wistfully. "Lori Lynn Thorton and her thirty-six-double-Ds."

Kathy found herself amused. He sounded ridiculously male. "Was she your first?"

"In my dreams, maybe." He shoved a fry into his mouth. "Lori's older brother was a body builder. Mr. Universe or something. I swear, the ground rumbled when he walked." Dakota went after another fry. "Hell, Lori's probably still a virgin."

"Yes," Kathy quipped, nudging his foot with her own. "Poor Lori Lynn and her double-Ds. She probably joined a convent. Took a vow of chastity."

He pushed back, his boot against hers. "Yeah, and Mr. Universe probably has love handles and a beer belly by now."

They looked at each other and laughed, their feet still touching. It felt strangely intimate, she thought. Casual and loving.

When their laughter faded, Kathy let the wind caress her face. The air was light and stirring, the noise from the carnival almost dreamy and far away. And the sky, she noticed, was painted with streaks of lavender and soft shades of blue.

She finished her drink and thought about what Dakota had called his romantic illusion. No, he hadn't been her first lover, not in the literal sense, but he had been the first man to awaken her desires. To bring her to a mind-spinning climax, to melt her bones and heat her skin, to leave her dizzy and trembling.

He knew, of course. During a fainthearted moment in Italy, she had told him. And he had reacted with sheer masculine pleasure, pushing his tongue into her mouth and carrying her swiftly to his bed.

She remembered how incredible that moment had been, how smooth and seductive, the mountain air blowing in through an open window, billowing the curtains.

Wondrous love. Deep, possessive strokes. She could still feel him moving between her legs, promising a lifetime of forever. He had asked her to marry him that night, his eyes dark and intense, waiting for an answer.

"Kathy?"

She placed her cup against her forehead, realizing how warm she had become. How suddenly warm. "Yes?"

"Are you okay?"

She blinked and lowered the cup. "What?"

"You seem a little out of it."

"I'm thirsty," she said, as if that should account for her dazed behavior. "My drink is gone."

He handed her his, and she placed her mouth on the straw,

thinking she could taste him there. It was, of course, her imagination, her weakness. The part of her that still fantasized about him, that let herself remember the past.

"I was just thinking about Asterland," he said.

She allowed the lemonade to cool her, then took another slow, steady sip for safe measure. They had made love in Asterland, and that was something she hoped he didn't want to discuss. Not now, not while her body was already wandering in that direction. She couldn't pour the drink over her skin, even if it craved something cold and wet.

"You were?"

He nodded. "I was wondering what you thought of Thunder."

Relief flooded her system. Thunder she could deal with. "I liked him. He was nice."

"Nice?" Dakota made a disbelieving face. "Women don't refer to him as *nice*."

Her senses, thank goodness, were returning. And to prove it to herself, she handed Dakota the lemonade. "Then how do they refer to him?"

"Oh, I don't know. A hunk. A flirt. A womanizer. Something along those lines."

"Well, I thought he was nice. The perfect gentleman."

The look he gave her could have split hairs. "Now I know you're lying."

And now she knew her conversation with Thunder hadn't reached Dakota's ears.

Dakota misses you, Kathy.

He told you that?

No, but I recognize the signs.

"Did you know Thunder was married?" she asked.

Dakota's jaw nearly dropped. "Well if that's the case then he's been cheating big-time. Boy, did he play a number on you. Pretending to be blissfully wed."

She shook her head. Trust a man to jump to that conclusion, especially a man whose father had kept a wife and a mistress. "He's not married now. It was a long time ago."

"So he's divorced?" Dakota asked, his tone quieter.

She nodded. "He didn't say why. Just that things didn't work out." And it was Thunder's wife who had filed the papers, that much Kathy sensed.

Dakota drew his knees up. "I guess I shouldn't have said what I did. But he's never mentioned an ex-wife to me. Then again, we rarely talk about our personal lives."

No, she thought, but they go on missions together, dodging bullets and trying to save the world. How ironic that neither one of them could save something as sacred as a marriage. They were more like brothers than they knew.

"I just spoke to Thunder a few days ago." Dakota collected their empty food containers and shoved them in a bag. "He might need my help."

Kathy's heart slammed against her chest. "With what?" she asked, although she knew. An assignment. An undercover mission. More bullets. More danger.

"Thunder has been tracking the leader of a prominent terrorist band for years. And just recently, he got another lead. Whether or not it will pan out remains to be seen."

She forced out a breath. "So if it pans out, he'll need you."

"Yes, but it will probably be a while. Thunder could be tagging this lead for months. He won't bring me into it until he's certain that he's on the right track."

How could Dakota sound so casual, so relaxed? Didn't he know what news like that did to her?

Of course, he didn't. And he never would. Because even if she told him, it wouldn't matter. She was back in Royal, and Dakota was caught up in another mission.

A knot formed in Kathy's stomach. Soon she would have to contact an attorney about filing for divorce. What other choice did she have?

Dakota Lewis was a soldier, not a husband. Nothing would stop him from pursuing his life's work. Ending their marriage was the only answer. Even is she still loved him.

The weekend wasn't over. The sun rose on Sunday, even if Kathy's heart refused to shine. The decision she had made yesterday left her cold and shaken.

Divorce. The word sounded so final, so permanent—a legality she had been avoiding for three long, hopeful years. Three years of waiting for Dakota to come to her, to choose their marriage over his work. But hiding her head in the sand wasn't going to change the facts. She was back in Royal, and Dakota hadn't thought twice about getting involved in another mission. When Thunder needed him, he would go. And she would be left alone.

Again.

Remembering where she was, Kathy took a deep breath and told herself to relax. The weather was perfect for a poolside barbecue, and Sheikh Rassad had gone to great lengths to entertain his guests. A buffet table displayed a variety of side dishes, many from Ben's homeland, including several large platters of *hummus* and baskets of pita bread. Of course, the thick prime cuts of beef being seasoned for the grill were pure Texas.

Kathy studied her host and decided he and his wife were an unusual, stunning pair. Ben stood tall and lean, a proper man with copper skin and exotic gray eyes. Jamie, on the other hand, was petite, blond and as spirited as her smile.

"They make an interesting couple, don't they?"

The comment came from Aaron's wife, Pamela. She sat next to Kathy, nibbling on a small variety of salads. Pamela had a quiet charm about her, a former elementary school teacher with twin dimples and a scatter of freckles.

Kathy smiled at the other woman, thinking her young students must have adored her. "Yes, they do."

Pamela reached for her drink. "The food is wonderful. I've never had some of these dishes before." She pointed to a bulgur wheat salad on her plate. "This is my favorite."

"It's called tabbouleh." Kathy was familiar with Middle Eastern food. One of the advantages, she supposed, of being a world traveler. "It's fairly simple to make. I'm sure Ben's housekeeper will give you the recipe."

"I'll have to ask her. I'm eating as healthily as I can."

Of course she was, Kathy thought, with a tug of admiration

and a twinge of envy. Pamela was five months' pregnant, her tummy a small mound beneath a light cotton blouse. Aaron would be a father in the fall.

Kathy resisted the urge to place her hand on Pamela's stomach, to feel the flutter of life. She remembered being pregnant all too well—the thrill, the maternal warmth. She knew the stages of prenatal development, the miracle growing and changing in Pamela's womb. The miracle that had once lived in her womb.

Refusing to dwell on her own loss, Kathy pictured Pamela's child instead. Tiny fingernails forming, a strong, steady heartbeat, an active little creature kicking its legs and sucking its thumb.

"Are you hoping for a boy or a girl?" she asked, knowing it must be the universal question posed to a mother-to-be.

"It doesn't matter. A boy who looks like Aaron would be wonderful. But having a daughter would be special, too. All those adorable, frilly little clothes." Pamela placed her hand on her tummy in a natural gesture. "If my doctor requests an ultrasound, we're going to ask the technician not to tell us what the baby is. We like the old-fashioned idea of being surprised."

Kathy nodded in agreement. Waiting and wondering had to be one of the pleasures of expectant parenthood—choosing two sets of names, decorating a nursery with either sex in mind.

Pamela kept her hand on her tummy, even when she turned to glance over her shoulder, drawing Kathy's attention to Aaron and Dakota.

The men stood Stetson to Stetson, each with a bottle of beer in hand. Kathy assumed the party was for the Texas Cattleman's Club members who had recovered the Lone Star jewels. It was a close-knit group, and Ben seemed happy to provide a casual, festive afternoon.

Kathy amended her thought as Matt Walker and his fiancée, Lady Helena, headed toward her and Pamela. The party was for the *couples* who had recovered the jewels, those who shared a common bond. She supposed in that sense, she and Dakota were a couple, too.

Matt placed Lady Helena's plate on the table and lingered for a moment, his hand on her shoulder. She looked back at him with quiet intimacy, and Kathy and Pamela exchanged a glance, their hearts tugging. Lady Helena was still recovering from substantial burns, making the use of her left hand nearly impossible. She also walked with a slight limp, but that didn't make her any less beautiful in Matt's eyes.

"Ladies." He stepped back and tipped his hat, brushing his fiancée's cheek before he detoured to the ice chest and joined Dakota and Aaron.

Lady Helena took her seat and followed his progress. "The women are sampling the buffet, and the men are drinking beer." She smiled and placed a napkin on her lap, her movements careful and slow. "I don't suppose they will be interested in food until those steaks are grilled."

"Deep down, they're just cowboys," Pamela said, indicating the masculine show of boots and trophy belts. "Even the sheikh."

Lady Helena nodded. "That may be true, but he is the only man keeping his wife exceptionally close by."

"I noticed that, too," Kathy added. But she also noticed the tender smiles passing between the newly married couple. The sheikh's young bride all but glowed.

She glanced at her plate, a lump forming in her throat. It made her long for the days when she and Dakota had first fallen in love. The romance and passion, the stolen glances and heartbeats of excitement.

Could she really divorce him? Take that final, devastating step?

Pamela rose. "I can't resist another helping. Just one more salad before the main course." She rubbed her protruding tummy. "And I do have the excuse that I'm eating for two."

As the pregnant woman flashed her dimples and headed for the buffet, Kathy and Lady Helena laughed. Aaron's wife was a true delight.

A quiet, reflective moment ensued, and Kathy gazed out at

the scene before her. A Texas-style terrace led to the pool, but an arrangement of pillars and statues resembled the ruins of a classic temple. The sheikh's ranch was a Royal oasis—a unique blend of culture and eclectic architecture. Beyond the pool, an array of colorful blooms charmed the Western landscape with tropical beauty.

"Kathy?"

She met Lady Helena's gaze and realized the other woman had been watching her. "Yes?"

"Thank you so much for what you did. I owe you and Dakota my deepest gratitude, but I don't know how to repay you."

Kathy's eyes misted. Lady Helena was the daughter of an Asterland count, and she had been waiting to return to her homeland to plan her wedding. But the threat of Payune's revolution had kept her from fulfilling that dream. And now that Payune was in jail and her country was safe, Lady Helena and Matt Walker would fly to Asterland to arrange a traditional European ceremony.

"We've already been rewarded by the king," Kathy responded. "And your happiness is gratitude enough. The way Matt feels about you makes it all worthwhile."

"Thank you." The blonde tilted her head. "He is such a wonderful man."

And they deserved a long and happy marriage, Kathy thought. Their union was just beginning—as hers and Dakota's was ending. But she had no right to envy Lady Helena, no right to fixate on the emptiness in her own soul. Today was a celebration, a party of goodwill and cheer.

Pamela returned to the table and the three chatted until a friendly commotion caught their attention. Kathy turned and found herself staring. The last of the guests had arrived. Dr. Justin Webb and his wife Winona apologized for being late, but no one minded their tardiness. Angel, their six-month-old daughter, had just awakened from an overdue nap.

The baby, graced with golden curls and bright blue eyes, clung to her mother with a chubby-cheeked smile. And at that tender moment, Kathy's arms began to ache. She wanted the chance to hold Angel, for as long as the child would allow.

Dakota was having a wonderful time. The steak was thick and juicy, the grilled corn dripping with butter, the beer cold and thirst-quenching. Ten adults gathered at one long table, eating great food and exchanging lively conversation.

He sat next to Kathy, thinking she'd never looked prettier. She wore a breezy spring dress and strappy beige sandals. Her hair fell loose about her shoulders in a shining burst of scarlet waves. He also noticed that she couldn't keep her eyes off the baby.

Little Angel was propped on Winona's lap, waving her hands and making kiddy sounds. And although she had already eaten her own mushy food, that didn't stop her from attacking the contents on her mother's plate.

How did parents do it? he wondered. How did they entertain someone so small? Did they baby-talk and make goofy faces from sunrise to sundown?

"Would you like me to hold her?" Kathy asked Winona. "I've finished my meal."

The other woman removed a squished strawberry from the little girl's hand. "Are you sure you don't mind?"

"No, not at all. I couldn't eat another bite. I've been to the buffet table twice, and you're just getting started."

"In that case, I accept." Winona sent Kathy a grateful smile and came around to their side of the table. Placing her daughter on Kathy's lap, she told the child to be good.

Dakota wondered if that was possible. In spite of Angel's ethereal name, a devilish glint shone in those big blue eyes. Then again, cherubs smiled the way she was smiling, their cheeks pink and chubby.

Her smile widened, and he grinned. She had one tooth, one tiny white chip poking out of her gums.

While Angel bounced on Kathy's lap and laughed, Dakota made one of those ridiculous faces just to amuse her. But when Kathy looked over to see the child's source of entertainment, he stopped acting like an idiot and picked up his corn. Making faces was one thing, getting caught quite another.

Angel laughed again, and he bit into his corn. The cherub seemed pleased that they'd fooled Kathy, even if he hadn't intended to make a game of it.

"What are you giggling about?" Kathy asked the baby.

Me, Dakota wanted to say. He had made Angel laugh. And it felt good, he realized. Babies had never paid much attention to him in the past, but he supposed that was partly his own fault. He wasn't overly animated nor did he have a smooth, soothing voice. He was big and broad and uncertain of how to connect with a being so much smaller than himself.

But he had done all right today. Angel seemed to like him.

Kathy fussed adoringly with the little girl, brushing a curl from her eye, fixing her T-shirt when it rolled up her belly. Angel sported a casual yet lacy outfit, complete with matching socks and a ruffled collar. Sugar and spice, Dakota thought. The description fit the child and his wife. They made a beautiful, feminine picture.

From across the table, Winona and Justin watched, pride glittering in their eyes. Angel was their miracle, a baby who had literally been left on Winona's door step. Dakota couldn't help but wonder how it would feel to save something as precious and tender as a child. At the moment, it seemed far more important than anything he had ever done.

A jolt of unexpected longing constricted his chest. Would a child have made a difference in his marriage?

He glanced at Kathy, and Angel laughed again, catching him off guard. He grinned back at her, but this time his wife turned and trapped his gaze.

"So you're the reason she's been giggling all this time?"

He shrugged, his grin still in place. "I guess she thinks I'm funny looking."

The smile that spread across Kathy's face was as sappy as his, and he thought this had to be the strangest, most heartwarming moment they had ever shared. He felt warm and wooly and kind of stupid inside, but he liked the feeling so he kept smiling, even if a flutter of self-consciousness had crept in.

There probably wasn't a person at the barbecue who hadn't noticed his uncharacteristic behavior.

Angel leaned forward and held out her arms, and Kathy's expression softened. "She wants you to hold her."

His pulse jumped, and something akin to panic shot through his veins. Hold her? Him? The big, brutal soldier? What if he dropped her? Damaged the little imp for life? Or what if she decided he wasn't so entertaining up close? What if she squirmed and cried?

Angel made a loud, impatient noise and waved her dimpled arms, demanding the attention he was afraid to give.

"Okay, now. Don't fuss." He placed his hands around the child's waist, handling her as carefully as a ticking bomb. A feminine temper tantrum would only make matters worse.

Angel came to him readily, no tears, no tiny-female fits. Instead she hugged his neck and snuggled against his shoulder. He looked across the table at Justin, who studied him from beneath a straw Stetson, a father watching his baby girl cuddle in another man's arms.

"She smells good," Dakota said, nuzzling the child.

Justin cocked an eyebrow, a slight quirk to his lips. "Did you think my daughter would smell bad?"

Dakota flashed a chagrinned grin. "No." But he hadn't expected to feel like the sun had chosen to shine exclusively on him. Angel's body was soft and warm, her skin a blend of sweet, comforting scents—powder and lotion and flowers blooming along heaven's pearly gates. He stroked her back, then patted her bottom, the rustle of diaper a curious sound.

Angel wasn't exactly still, but she wasn't a concealed bundle of explosives, either. She toyed with his shirt and moved her head back and forth, her hair tickling his chin.

I want one, he thought, turning to meet Kathy's gaze. A shimmering, misty gaze, he noticed. A woman thinking she wanted one, too.

Was it possible that their sudden fantasy could already be taking shape in Kathy's womb? They had made love in Asterland without protection, and mistakes often produced miracles.

Before Dakota could monopolize Angel's time, the baby decided she wanted to try her luck with Ben. She latched onto the sheikh, and the transfer was made. Ben got a syrupy look on his face, and Dakota laughed. One bright-eyed little girl was turning the Texas Cattleman's Club macho militia to mush.

Within twenty minutes Angel had charmed her way around the table, until Justin claimed her for good. Once she was in her daddy's arms, no other man stood a chance.

After the dishes were cleared, the sheikh's loyal housekeeper appeared with a frothy cake, pastel icing dotted with sugared roses.

Ben nodded to the elderly woman and guided his wife to the head of the table. "We would like to thank all of you for coming to our home," he said. "This is a special time for Jamie and me, and we are proud to announce that—"

"I'm pregnant!" his spontaneous young bride blurted, raising the hem of a pale blue blouse just enough to expose a glimpse of her navel.

The customarily proper Ben laughed and kissed her smartly on the lips, and a blast of excitement followed. The women rushed Jamie with exuberant hugs, and the men clapped Ben on the back and pumped his hand. Even Angel squealed in baby wonder.

Dakota congratulated the beaming couple, then stepped back to absorb the joy, the sheer enchantment of life.

God permitting, he and Kathy would be next.

Ten

Kathy exhaled a ragged breath, her emotions a mass of conflicting energy. Being happy for your friends and sad for yourself presented an uneasy combination. She craved a cup of herbal tea, her Irish grandmother's remedy for relaxation.

"Can I get you anything? Tea? Coffee?" she asked Dakota, slipping off her sandals. Bare feet helped, too. And curling up in an oversize chair.

"No, thanks. I had coffee at Ben's." He removed his hat and hung it on a nearby rack.

She nodded and headed into the kitchen. Searching through the tea bags, she chose a lemon flavor promising to lift her spirits. Tea from the microwave wasn't as soothing as tea from the stove, so she set the water to boil and waited.

She could hear Dakota playing with Sugar, tossing the dog's favorite ball so the Maltese could romp down the hall. The chipper little bark should have snapped her out of this confusing depression, but somehow it only managed to intensify her loss.

Kathy carried the steaming brew into the living room, then frowned when Dakota and Sugar followed. She wasn't up for company or conversation, but she couldn't explain why she needed a few quiet moments of solitude. It would mean alerting Dakota to her mood, something she preferred not to do.

Dakota settled onto the sofa, and Sugar leaped up beside him, a striped ball in her mouth. She dropped it and nudged him, pursuing lapdog attention. He obliged with several gentle strokes. Satisfied, Sugar closed her eyes, one paw guarding the ball.

They made a touching pair, a domestic sight that hurt Kathy's grieving heart. She sipped the lemon tea, praying for the promised lift. Wallowing in self-pity at the expense of someone else's good fortune placed her in a selfish, unhealthy light, even in her own bleak eyes.

She knew better. God help her, she did.

Tucking her feet beneath her, she studied the fireplace. Although the weather wasn't permitting, she imagined burning logs just to calm herself. Winter was her favorite season— mistletoe, evergreens and the woodsy scent of a crackling fire.

"I had a great time. Didn't you?" Dakota asked.

"Yes." But it had been too much for one day. Too many happy couples, too many pregnant women. One moment at the barbecue she had been fine, the next floating through the reverie and wishing Angel was the baby she had lost.

"Are you tired, sweetheart?"

She glanced up from her drink. "Do I look tired?"

"A little. But you look pretty, too."

She wanted to squeeze her eyes shut and make the world go away. How could she look appealing, the woman who wanted to cry because her friends were either getting married or having babies? She didn't deserve pretty.

The tea wasn't working. Kathy's emotions were fighting a losing battle. And contemplating divorce while others found happiness was the self-inflicted culprit. She had spent the past three years pretending divorce wasn't a viable option. At least not to her. If Dakota had made the choice, then she would have told herself that he'd never really loved her, that it had all been a mistake. But that hadn't happened. No papers were served, no irreconcilable differences charted. Instead they stayed in limbo, legally married with no future to speak of.

And wasn't that worse? she asked herself. Worse than no decision at all?

"You seem happy," she told Dakota. Which, of course, made her even more sad. There would be someone else in his life someday. Someone who understood the soldier in him, who supported his causes. He was too magnetic, too easy to fall in love with, too attractive to ignore.

"I do feel good," he announced. "But I enjoy casual get-togethers."

Kathy tilted her head. Maybe he would choose a string of lovers instead of just one. Sex without serious commitment worked for plenty of men. And wasn't that the lifestyle he had leaned toward before their relationship developed? People did that after divorce, didn't they? Reverted back to their old ways?

Not everyone, she thought. She couldn't see herself dating at all, let alone the type who had come before Dakota—Ivy League heirs who appreciated proper, mundane dinners and suggested she cut her unruly hair into a more suitable style.

She would rather remain alone and remember the tall, dark-eyed man waiting for her on the cliffs. Her forbidden lover. The husband she couldn't keep.

She released a weary sigh. How typical. And tragic. Casting herself as the heroine in an ill-fated legend—a woman wandering through life like an aimless shadow, her heart longing for what could never be.

As Dakota removed his boots and placed them under the coffee table, Sugar stirred, then settled beside him again. "Angel sure is a cute little girl." He shook his head in amazement. "Imagine discovering a baby on your doorstep. Thinking you hear an abandoned kitten, but going outside and finding a child instead."

Because Kathy couldn't bring herself to picture such a confusing yet magical scenario, she responded simply. "Winona and Justin are wonderful parents."

He sought her gaze. "Yes, they are. In that regard, it was the right doorstep."

And ours was the wrong one, she thought, wishing those dark eyes weren't exploring hers. Why was he watching her so closely? Did he sense her uneasiness?

She set her tea on a nearby table and tried to relax. She didn't want to be found out. Not now, not with the dark cloud of divorce weighing on her mind, with images of Dakota finding other lovers.

"Kathy," he said, still studying her.

It was too late, she realized. He was going to ask why a festive barbecue had made her so sad. She held her breath and waited, wondering what she would say, how she would convince him that she was fine.

"Is there a chance you might be pregnant?"

Oh, God. She gripped the cushioned chair, her heart tackling too many beats. "Why would you—?"

"We didn't use protection in Asterland."

"I'm not." She let out the breath she had been holding, forcing her voice to remain steady. Every cell in her body ached, right along with her pounding heart. "You don't need to worry."

"I wasn't worried. I was actually hoping." He paused to shift his posture, move closer to the edge of the sofa. "I've never really thought about having kids. At least not consciously. And then today it hit me."

Dizziness swept through Kathy, making her legs weak. She untucked them, then placed both feet on the floor, searching for solid ground, for stability she couldn't quite find.

"I'm not pregnant." And his wish, his hope had come much too late. Their baby was gone.

"Are you sure? Did you take one of those drugstore tests?"

"There was no need." She felt as though she were floating outside herself, pushing away pain from the past. Pushing as it drifted toward her, waiting to connect. "I didn't miss my period."

"Oh." He dropped his gaze, then lifted it a second later. "We should have had kids when we had the chance, when

things were right between us.'' Reaching for Sugar, he
stroked the dog's sleeping form. ''I can't help but think it
would have made a difference in our marriage.'' His smile
was a little sad, a little wistful. ''You would have made a
terrific mother. And I could have learned to be a dad.''

Kathy didn't burst into tears. Instead they trailed slowly
down her cheeks, one right after the other, burning as they
went.

When Dakota leaned forward, she held up her hand to ward
him off, to keep him from coming closer. It was time to tell
him about the baby, but she couldn't if he touched her.

''Don't,'' she whispered. ''Just give me a minute.'' A minute for three years of loneliness. It sounded absurd.

Wiping her eyes, she stared at her husband, the man who
waited with a concerned expression. The man who suddenly
wanted to be a father.

Dakota knew he had said something hurtful. Somehow he
had hurt Kathy without meaning to. ''Tell me, sweetheart.
What's wrong?''

She continued to stare, more through him than at him, her
red-rimmed eyes vacant, the sound of her voice distant.
''There was a baby. But I miscarried. Three years ago.''

''I don't understand.'' He blinked, struggling to grasp her
words. It wasn't something he expected to hear, to comprehend. ''Why didn't you tell me when you found out you were
pregnant? When…?'' He let his next question drift, unable
to say it out loud.

''Because you weren't here. Not during any of it.'' Her
voice broke a little, and he knew she forced back another
flood of tears, another knot of emotion. ''I had no way to
reach you. You were on a mission. Gone for months.''

And she had lost their child. The baby he had thought about
today. The baby they should have had. He tried not to picture
her, but his mind's eye refused to listen. He saw her in his
head—her tummy swollen, the life inside her flourishing one
week, its tiny heartbeat gone the next.

''Did you tell anyone?''

''I was waiting for you.'' She brushed at her dress, her

fingers curling until they clutched the fabric. "I didn't suspect I was pregnant until weeks after you'd gone. So I waited, hoping you would come home soon."

"But I didn't." And to him, one day of the mission had seemed like the next. It had been a long, grueling ordeal—a dangerous operation that kept him from contacting his wife. "I thought about you, always." But that hardly mattered, he realized. His thoughts hadn't protected Kathy or their child.

She glanced away. "I thought about you, too. Wondered exactly what you were doing, who you were with, if you were safe. I was happy about the baby and worried about you at the same time."

He didn't know how to respond, not through the overwhelming pain and guilt. Was it stress that had caused her to lose their child? "How far along were you?"

"When I miscarried?" Avoiding eye contact, she released an erratic breath. "Almost three months. Eleven weeks. I was just getting over the morning sickness."

Suddenly her answer made it all too real. Too vivid in his mind. He should have returned from his mission to find a healthy, happy, pregnant wife. He should have kissed her tummy, brought her breakfast in bed, shopped for teddy bears, chosen a color for the nursery.

"It happened at home," Kathy said. "In this house. I suppose I should hate staying here, but for some reason I don't. Maybe because I was happy here once."

Dakota prayed she could be happy there again, that they could get through this. He didn't want to lose his wife. Not a second time.

"Were you alone?" he asked.

"Yes. I came home from the market and while I was putting away the groceries, I got this terrible cramp." She clutched her stomach as though still feeling it. Feeling the loss of their child. "I called the doctor right away, but I knew it was too late." Rocking a little, she stared into space, into the memories filling her head. "I didn't buy much at the store. I had this craving for a peanut butter and banana sandwich."

Someone should have been there with her, he thought.

No, not just someone. He should have been there. Her husband.

She kept her hands wrapped around her middle. "I don't even like peanut butter. Not really."

Dakota wished she would look at him, scream and yell, tell him that she hated him. It would be easier to bear than watching her droop like a wilting flower, delicate petals ragged and torn.

"I'm sorry," he whispered. "So sorry."

Finally she turned, "I left this house two weeks later. I couldn't stay here. I couldn't wait for you anymore. I didn't just lose our baby. I lost us."

"I know." He remembered coming home to find her gone, to find himself living with emptiness. "Let me help you get ready for bed. You're exhausted. You should lie down." Dakota rose to his feet. He needed to hold her, and she needed warmth and comfort. Her eyes were still edged with tears. She wasn't through crying. Tonight they would spill from her heart.

She didn't take the hand he offered, so he stepped back, a lump forming in his throat.

"I don't need your help," she said, her voice quiet. "I fell apart a long time ago. I'm not falling apart now."

But she was, he thought. She was barely holding on. She had waited so long to tell him about the baby. Much too long.

She stood and faced him. "We can't change what happened. It's over. It's done. And I don't want to talk about it anymore."

Dakota nodded and let her pass, not knowing what else to do. On silent feet, she walked down the hall toward her room. The day had shifted into night, early evening with an early moon shining through the living-room windows.

After closing the blinds, he left the sleeping dog on the sofa and carried Kathy's cup into the kitchen. Leaning against the sink, he pictured her there, three years before, pregnant with his child.

His child.

Today he had held a baby for the first time—a tiny girl

who smelled sweet and powdery, a girl with fair hair and bright blue eyes.

Pouring the leftover tea down the drain, Dakota watched it disappear. Like Angel, their baby would have been beautiful. It would have inherited his Comanche skin and Kathy's Irish smile—a child whose dark hair would have shimmered in the sun with streaks of auburn.

Dakota sank to the floor, mourning the life he had never got to know—a son or daughter who should have grown into a wondrous little being.

Two hours passed before he glanced up at the clock. While he'd sat on the floor, trapped in emotion, what had Kathy been doing? Battling exhaustion? Hugging her knees to her chest?

Rising, he pulled a hand through his hair. He couldn't leave her alone. Not tonight. They both needed comfort, whether they lay awake or succumbed to sleep.

A pale glow spilled from beneath her bedroom door. He stood, gazing down at the light. It wasn't her bedroom, he corrected, a frown taking root in his brow. It was the room they had decorated for guests. Kathy didn't belong there. She belonged with him.

He didn't think to knock. Opening the door, he slipped inside.

She was awake, wearing the same sleeveless dress, her hair a golden shade of red—a fiery halo enhanced by the illumination of a single amber bulb. Fragility sprinkled over her like a spring rain, each teardrop as delicate as spun glass. Some clung to her lashes, others slid down her cheeks.

How could she look so lost, yet so beautiful?

Their eyes met, but neither spoke. She held a pillow against her stomach while another supported her back, cushioning the headboard. The quilt was rumpled, the sheets only mildly disturbed.

He wanted to carry her to his room, to the bed they once shared, but he doubted she would welcome such a powerful intrusion. If he touched her, it would be with her permission.

He stopped in the center of the room, praying she wouldn't

turn him away. He should have knocked, respected her privacy.

"Can I stay?" he asked. "Can I sit with you?"

She nodded, and he came toward the bed.

"You should try to sleep." He reached for a tissue on the night stand, then settled beside her. Tilting her chin, he dried her tears.

She leaned into him, her head on his shoulder, the scarlet halo vivid against the white background of his shirt. He intended to get her a nightgown, to dress her for bed, but he didn't want to lose the connection. So he held her instead.

Even in the amber light, he saw shadows beneath her eyes, pale lavender circles, swollen from tears. She felt as fragile as she looked, her slim, elegant body draped in a wrinkled dress.

"I should have told you sooner," she said. "I meant to."

"It's okay. None of this is your fault." He lifted the sheet and tucked it around her. Pressing a kiss to her forehead, he felt her breath stir against his neck just as her eyes drifted closed.

And while she slept, he thought about how much he loved her.

Kathy awakened at daybreak and found herself next to Dakota, a printed sheet balled at their feet. They were both dressed in the clothes they had worn yesterday, but his shirt fell open and the top button of his jeans lay undone. His belt was gone, she noticed. Sometime in the middle of the night he had removed it.

He looked rumpled and gorgeous, his jaw shadowed with just a hint of beard stubble. And his hair, as black and coarse as a winter night, spiked against a pillow. The bedding suited him, the wash of Sante Fe colors complementing Indian skin.

Allowing her gaze to roam, she locked onto his hips, onto those unfastened jeans. The waistband of white briefs were barely visible, and a stomach rippling with muscle moved with the inhale and exhale of sleeping breaths.

She glanced away deliberately, but came back a moment

later. Was he aroused? Drifting in and out of naughty dreams? His fly bulged, a masculine rise beneath deep-blue denim.

Palms itchy to touch, she lifted her gaze, and it collided with his.

Blushing wasn't welcome, but her cheeks heated just the same. She had been caught studying his hips, his navel, his sex.

They stared at each other, neither sure what to do or say. She hadn't expected to feel this way, not on the morning after an emotional cry. But last night's tears had vanished with the dark, and now Kathy couldn't think beyond the awkwardness of lust.

He arched a long, sturdy body, stretching a mass of muscle and sinew, and she swallowed, her throat dry as dust.

"Morning," he said, his voice still rough from sleep.

"Hi." Her nipples pebbled against her bra, chafing uncomfortably. "We slept in our clothes." Obvious as her statement was, it was the only coherent sentence that came to mind. Her bra was, after all, part of her clothing.

He grabbed hold of his shirt tail. "Yeah, we did."

Kathy nearly smiled through her nervousness. Apparently he lacked vocal skills on this odd morning, too.

A second later, a heavy breath expanded his impressive chest. She chewed her bottom lip and decided he didn't need to say anything brilliant or compelling.

Even as she told herself having him would be wrong, her rational side refused to obey. She struggled for control and lost.

She needed him. One last time.

"I don't want to talk," she said. Not about important things. That would spoil the moment. The slow, shy heat slipping between them.

"Then we won't. Not now." He moved closer, just enough to send a silk-wrapped shiver down her spine.

"Touch me," she whispered, inviting his caress.

He unbuttoned the front of her dress with infinite care, and the gentleness made her dizzy. The simple white bra and cotton panties weren't designed for seduction, but she saw pleasure shining in his eyes as he discovered them.

Their mouths came together, and they sipped from each other, sunlight spilling like wine. She removed his shirt, then brought her hands to his chest and smoothed her palms over warm, solid flesh. He had the body of a warrior, strong and toned, with a line of dark, silky hair that grew from his navel to his sex.

Kathy reached for his fly, lowered the zipper and smiled when his stomach flexed with a taut quiver.

He kissed her again, this time hard and deep, tongue to luscious tongue. She swayed with sensuality. Dakota was half-naked and fully aroused. As he unhooked her bra, a groan rose from his throat.

"Tell me what you want," he said, trailing a finger down her belly.

Her bra went slack, her breasts aching. "You. I want you."

"Where?"

Battling her next breath, she pressed her thighs together. Suddenly she wanted him there, his mouth and his tongue, but she couldn't bring herself to voice the words.

He nipped her ear. "You said it on the phone that night. I asked what makes you crazy, and you told me."

But he had been miles away in a hotel room, not poised above her, waiting for an answer. "Then you already know."

Removing her bra, he lowered his head and nuzzled her nipples. She slid her hands into his hair and struggled to hold onto the short, spiky strands. He was teasing her, moving slowly down her body, turning heat to hunger, satin to sensation.

"Is this what you want?" He lifted her hips and brushed his mouth over her panties, over the swatch of virginal cotton.

"Yes," she whispered. "Please. Yes."

He complied, pulling her panties down and discarding them. She clutched the sheet and let the fever take control. The blinding heat and cool shivers. The moisture. The edgy need of knowing what came next.

"You taste sweet," he said, opening her fully, licking and sucking, pressing her erotically against his mouth.

Kathy clung to the fever, holding fast and tight, until the stab of his tongue, the deep, wet strokes drove her to a quick and ruthless climax.

In the next spiraling moment, he was naked, nuzzling tenderly. "Do you want me to use protection?"

Barely recovered, she nodded, and he reached for his wallet on the night stand.

"I kept hoping this would happen between us, but I didn't know where or when, so..." His words drifted as he fingered the foil packet. "Are you sure we should use it?"

Her answer came out shaky. "Yes."

"Okay." He lowered his mouth to hers, stealing her breath and the sudden sadness with it.

Now, they both knew, was not the time to talk about babies.

Sheathed in a condom, he entered her, sliding hard and heavy between her legs. She touched his cheek and arched to accept him, thinking how much she loved him. How much she would miss him.

Their eyes met, and they slipped into a smooth, sleek rhythm, watching each other with longing and intensity.

She wrapped her legs around him, and he made a primal sound. She welcomed every sensation, every shiver, every ragged pulse. He kissed the side of her neck, breathed in the fragrance of her hair. She could feel his heart beating against hers, pounding as he withdrew and entered her again, heightening the magic. The pleasure of making love.

Desire swam in her head, like the flow of a long, luxurious current, the water warm and inviting. Touching him, she lingered over the play of muscles, over powerful arms and a stomach tightening with each sexual thrust.

Pressure battered upon need, and the water rose like a tide. Desperate, she took his mouth, kissed him until greed devoured. Him. Her. Both of them together.

They shuddered and strained, arched and bucked, then fell in each other's arms, lovers forbidden once again.

Eleven

Kathy slipped on her robe. She wanted to stay in bed with Dakota all day, but she knew that would only prolong the inevitable. "I have to leave soon."

He wore his briefs and nothing else—nothing but skin as smooth and solid as a bronze statue. "Why? Where are you going?"

"To look at a house."

Dakota frowned and reached for his jeans. "Why can't you stay here with me? This is your home. This is where you belong."

She sat on the edge of the bed while he stood and zipped his Wranglers. Watching him, she tightened the belt on her robe. "No, it isn't. Nothing has changed. You know about the baby, and we made love again. That doesn't solve the turmoil in our lives."

"So we'll make things right." He skimmed her cheek with callused fingers. "We just need some time, that's all."

She blinked, willing herself not to cry. He made it sound

so simple. "I didn't leave because I lost the baby, Dakota. I left because you weren't there when I needed you."

"I know." His voice turned rough with tenderness. "But I'm here now, and we can start over. We can have other children. I love you, Kathy. So damn much."

An arrow lanced her heart, magnifying the ache already there. His claim wasn't enough. The dreamer in her wanted to believe that love healed all wounds, but deep down, she knew better. "You're going on another mission with Thunder."

He sat beside her. "But that could be months from now. Or it might not happen at all."

"What if we decided to stay together and I was pregnant months from now?" Couldn't Dakota see that the cycle would repeat itself?

"Then I wouldn't take the mission. Thunder could get someone else to help him. It doesn't have to be me."

Such easy words to say, she thought. But they wouldn't be easy for him to fulfill. She studied him, this dark-eyed, dark-haired man she had married. He looked every bit the warrior, his face leaner, bones more pronounced. His work suited him, the missions that kept him focused. It was all he had ever known. An honor-roll student at seventeen, he'd graduated from high school early, gone to his parents and told them that he wanted to join the air force. And, recognizing his determination, they'd granted their consent.

Kathy couldn't compete with that, and she would be foolish to try. She had learned her lesson well. "You would go crazy staying home," she told him. "I've seen how restless you get."

"But we're not talking about for the rest of my life—" He paused, then held her gaze, his eyes as dark and cloudy as a foggy night. "Are we?"

She took a breath, let it out slowly. Dakota's panic had already set in. It surfaced in his expression, the muscle working in his jaw, the lines beginning to crease an otherwise smooth forehead.

If only dreams could take the form of reality. She wanted

to keep him forever, live in the fantasy of her choosing. But Dakota was what he was—a soldier who could never be a conventional husband.

"Kathy?" he persisted.

"I can't expect you to change, and it wouldn't be right to ask you to try." She lifted her chin and tried to keep her thoughts calm and logical, her hands folded quietly on her lap. She had fallen apart last night and couldn't bear to let it happen again. "We don't want the same things. We're too different from each other."

He stood, his shoulders broad, his chest bare. He looked big, powerful and combating a myriad of emotion. "Opposites attract. It's what brought us together."

"And what pulled us apart." Her hands fumbled now, looking for something to do. "You wouldn't be content to stay home. You agreed to help Thunder with his mission because that's who you are. A soldier out to save the world."

He rolled his shoulders, the muscles bunching. The movement reminded her of a caged animal fighting its confinement. The battlefield was Dakota's wilderness, she thought, his natural element. And civilization, no matter how much he conformed to it, would always be his cage.

"I was a soldier when you married me."

"I know, but you only had a year left of active duty." She smoothed her tangled hair, hating that she couldn't keep her hands still. "I was eager for you retire. Eager for us to settle down."

"You never told me that. You never said a word."

"I didn't think I had to. I assumed that's what retirement meant to you, too."

He sat beside her again, the bed shifting from his weight. "It scared me a little. Being retired, I mean. I was thirty-seven years old and idle for the first time in my life. I couldn't imagine lounging around in my socks. Or fishing half the day away. Reeling in some poor unsuspecting trout when I could be making a difference somewhere." He turned to look at her. "But I liked the idea of you being home, safe and secure, waiting for me. That part felt right."

And it was the part she couldn't handle. Kathy wanted to pretend this wasn't happening, that their marriage wasn't ending. Yet she wanted to lure him back to bed, back into her arms, into that current of sleek, silky possession. "Sex is the only thing we have in common. It's the only form of communication that works for us."

He glanced at the tumbled sheets. "Is that why you slept with me?"

"No." She brushed his hand, then drew back, the contact too familiar. "I needed to hold you again. To make love with you just one more time."

Breathing shouldn't hurt, but as Dakota inhaled the strawberry-scented air, an overwhelming pain rose in his chest. The room smelled like her, like lotion and shampoo. Why hadn't he noticed that before? He loved her fragrance, her sweet, feminine aroma.

He pulled a hand through his hair. The room smelled a little like sex, too. A hint of the lovemaking they had just shared.

Just one more time.

It couldn't mean anything else. Kathy was leaving him. And this time it would be for good, the final act he had feared all along.

"You're divorcing me, aren't you?"

She clutched the front of her robe, her hand as shaky as her voice. "It's the only thing left to do. The only thing that makes sense. We'll never be able to get on with our lives if we don't end it."

He laughed, a bitter, humorless sound. "And here I thought if we spent enough time together, you would fall in love with me again." His eyes burned, but he knew he wouldn't cry, at least not outwardly. Tears would only humiliate him, and he already felt a sense of emasculation.

"Spending time together makes me hurt," she said. "And I don't need to fall in love with you again because I never stopped loving you."

Her admission should have pleased him, given him a measure of satisfaction, a glimmer of hope, but he couldn't see beyond the despair of divorce. "That makes a hell of a lot of sense."

"Have you ever looked up *love* in the dictionary? Read its various meanings?" Still clutching the robe, she tilted her head. "I have. I know them by heart."

Dakota wasn't in the mood for a collegiate rendition of love. "You know almost every word by heart. In a variety of languages. Why would this one be any different?"

"Because I used to think there were some definitions missing." Kathy steadied her gaze to his. "It doesn't say that love heals. And it doesn't say anything about happily-ever-after, either. But now I understand why those things aren't mentioned."

Because love hadn't healed her broken heart, he realized. And because she had lost faith in happily-ever-after.

Studying her, he frowned. What had happened to his wife? To the woman who relished fairy tales, who dreamed of knights in shining armor and ladies in long, flowing dresses?

I happened to her, he thought. The man who spoiled her fairy tale, who left her alone when she needed him most.

"I still believe in love. Or I want to." He reached for her hand, held it lightly in his. "Can't we start over? Give it one more try? If you don't want me to go on any more missions, I won't. I'll stay here with you instead."

"That won't work." She curled her fingers, her nails grazing his palm. "Eventually you would resent me for clipping your wings. For holding you down when you're desperate to fly."

"You're wrong. I could never resent you." True, he had no idea what staying home would be like. He had never been completely comfortable in a quiet, domestic setting. Making a difference in the world was the only thing he knew, the only true calling he'd ever had. And he used to think that Kathy understood that, loved him for it. But she was right. They didn't communicate well.

Dakota glanced at his rumpled shirt. He had to admit that the idea of giving up his work made him nervous. What would he do with himself? How would he fill his time? And would he lose a part of himself? The man who needed to make a difference?

The questions, the insecurities were boundless. This wasn't something he could have predicted, and it made him disoriented. But if Kathy asked him to stay home, he would. At the moment that didn't appear to be an option. She seemed convinced it was too late.

He linked his fingers through hers, but she tugged her hand away. Not in anger, he thought, but in pain. She was wounded, as fragile as a fledgling with a damaged wing.

She stared straight ahead, her voice quiet. "After I left, I prayed for you to come to me."

And say the words he was saying now, the words that were suddenly too late. How could he blame her for being wary? For not believing in him?

She rose from the bed and headed toward the dresser. "I should get ready to go." She fumbled through the top drawer, gathering fresh undergarments.

She still looked fragile. But the unexpected shyness struck him most of all. They had made love less than an hour before and now she balled a pair of lace panties in her fist as if it embarrassed her to let him see them.

It made him feel like a stranger, a lonely soul aching for familiarity. If she divorced him, this is how it would end. They wouldn't remain friends. There would be nothing left but faded memories.

And then she would meet someone else.

Dakota tensed against the pain, the fear he couldn't dismiss—Kathy finding solace in the arms of another man.

Who would be her next lover? A handsome young politician searching for the perfect partner? Or maybe a widower who already had children, someone who understood her need for family?

She motioned to the connecting bathroom. "I'm going to take a shower now. I don't want to be late for my appointment."

He nodded. Her appointment to look at a rental house. God. How could he lose her? How could he let this happen?

Dakota watched her disappear into the other room, wishing he knew how to save his marriage.

Two days later, Kathy stepped into the kitchen, following the aroma of Colombian coffee.

Mrs. Miller stood at the counter rinsing dishes. She turned and smiled, and Kathy greeted her, surprised by the house-keeper's chipper expression. She could only assume that the older lady's newfound friendship with Dakota was the cause.

Kathy poured herself a cup of coffee and diluted it with hot water, noting the strength had been brewed for Dakota.

"Can I fix you some breakfast?" Mrs. Miller asked.

She added sugar and cream to her cup. "No, thank you. This will do."

"Lieutenant Lewis is in the backyard. He wants to talk to you when you have some time."

"Oh." She looked up, a twinge of nervousness setting in. "All right."

Crossing to the back door, Kathy walked through the court-yard, then stopped when she saw Dakota. He stood, leaning against a shovel, staring at a section of freshly tilled ground. Long and lean in a pair of threadbare jeans and a simple T-shirt, he was a striking sight to behold.

Sugar sniffed around his feet, pawing the earth, her white muzzle dusty with compost.

Kathy moved froward, telling herself to relax. It wasn't easy being around Dakota. Divorce still hovered over them like a murky cloud. "I think my dog is going to need a bath," she said, conjuring an airy voice and a manufactured smile.

He adjusted the shovel. "True, but she's been having a blast out here."

"So I see." Sugar dropped a stone into a hole she had dug and proceeded to bury it. She reminded Kathy of a mischie-vous little girl playing in her Sunday best. A fancy gold bow and a heap of rich soil presented an amusing combination.

They didn't speak for a few minutes. Instead they watched

the dog, the sun shining brighter than usual. It was, Kathy thought, a beautiful day to be outdoors. It almost chased that cloud away, making her forget the turmoil in her life.

"When did you take up gardening?" she asked, breaking the silence.

He grinned a bit boyishly, a white flash against tanned skin. "This morning."

As her heart forgot its natural beat, she glanced away from that devastating smile and studied the trays of potted herbs. Gardens were her weakness, even though she had never attempted to start one herself.

"I've always been fascinated by herbs," he said. "Their healing and cooking properties. But I never asked my gardeners to plant them because it's something I wanted to do myself."

She didn't need to ask why he had chosen to pursue this task. He was home and feeling idle, needing to fill his time, the restlessness that normally left him eager for another mission.

Maybe he had the right idea. Kathy itched to dig in the dirt, to lose herself in manual labor, as well. Dakota wasn't the only restless soul. "Mrs. Miller said you wanted to talk to me."

He nodded. "Thunder called earlier."

"He did?" She looked up at the sky, focused on the vast, dream-like serenity before allowing the harshness of reality to overwhelm her. "About the mission?"

"Yes. He still doesn't know if it's going to happen or not, but he should have more information in a few weeks." Dakota implored her to meet his gaze. Beneath the brim of a tan cowboy hat, his eyes sought hers. "I told him I wasn't sure if I was available. That he may want to consider contacting someone else."

Her mouth suddenly dry, Kathy swallowed. "Do you want to be available?"

"Not if you would prefer I stay here."

"This should be about what you want, Dakota. The decision has to be yours." Reaching up, she secured a bobby pin.

Her topknot was loosening, spilling errant strands of hair. It made her feel messy and disorganized, not in control.

"I'm confused," he admitted. "I love you desperately, and I want to stay married and raise a family. But I'm having trouble making a conscious choice to give up my work. If you ask me to, I will. Right now, that's the best I can do."

"I appreciate your honesty. But I don't want to be responsible for forcing you to stay home." In time it would destroy him, and she couldn't live with the emotional destruction it would cause. Neither could she live with the nature of his work, no matter how desperately they loved each other. "It looks like we're at a crossroad."

"I suppose," he said, his expression grim. "How about if we take a couple weeks to think about it? Don't make any decisions until then. You won't move out or file any papers, and I'll take some time to deal with everything that's happened." He paused to study her. "You haven't found a house yet, have you?"

"No." And what he proposed seemed logical. A few weeks of reflection would give them the opportunity to prepare for what lay ahead. The calm, she thought, before the storm. "I did lease an office, though. Not far from the Royal Diner."

He managed a smile. "I guess you won't go hungry at lunchtime." The smile faded, and he adjusted his hat. "Will you give it a couple of weeks, Kathy?"

"Yes." She fixed her hair again, nearly jabbing a bobby pin into her scalp.

"Good." He leaned the shovel against a shiny red wheelbarrow, but it slid to the ground with a thump. Sugar barked at it, then went about scattering dirt.

The dog's busy paws were the only movement. Dakota and Kathy both stood silently, nearly frozen like statues. It reminded Kathy of the recess bell at one of the elementary schools she had attended. She couldn't recall which school exactly, but she remembered that her playmates used to freeze in silly positions when the bell rang. Kathy, of course, never acted foolishly. She always stood with impeccable posture, her hands at her sides.

"So you're ready to set up shop?"

She blinked, only hearing a portion of his question. "I'm sorry. What?"

"Your office. Are you anxious to get things going?"

She shook away the recess-bell memory, wondering if she had been a dull child, too mature for her own good. "Yes, I'm looking forward to it."

"So what is it you'll be doing? We haven't talked about it. Other than it will be a satellite office your folks asked you to head up."

"I'll be managing the export operations for domestic companies my parents are affiliated with. Besides hiring distributors and reps, I'll be in charge of advertising, marketing and promotions. There's plenty to do."

"Sounds like you'll need help."

She nodded. "As soon as I get the office set up, I'll be interviewing for a secretary and an assistant."

"Well, I'm glad you found a convenient location."

"Me, too."

A hush fell over them again, the kind of silence that had them staring at each other in discomfort. She fussed with her hair for something to do, and he dug his work boots into the soil.

How could she divorce him? she wondered. Sever their tie completely? Then how could she not? He was willing to give up his work for her, but it wasn't what he truly wanted to do. And she hadn't anticipated a complication like that. In her dreams, Dakota never regretted the decision. He was eager to leave the danger behind.

But those were glorified fantasies, she reminded herself. This was reality. Kathy looked away from Dakota. In two weeks they would discuss their decisions. *Two weeks.* What could possibly change in such a short amount of time, other than Thunder's details about Dakota's next mission?

"I guess I better get these planted," he said, indicating the trays of potted herbs.

Kathy should have nodded her head and used this moment to escape, but suddenly she didn't want to. She wanted to lift the plants to her nose and inhale each sweet, earthly fragrance.

"Do you need some help?" she heard herself ask.

"I—" He paused to look at her, move his gaze from the top of her head to the tips of her Italian shoes. "In those clothes?"

She lifted her chin under the tight scrutiny. "I'm wearing jeans." And a white cotton blouse with a lace collar. And butter-soft leather flats sporting a designer label. She should have said that she intended to change, but that seemed dull and proper, like a child who didn't have enough spunk to make the freeze bell enjoyable. "Yes, in these clothes. My blouse can be laundered." She slipped off her shoes and stood in her bare feet. "And I like the feel of dirt between my toes."

He arched a black brow. "More like mud since we're going to be watering these plants."

She shrugged. "That's okay."

"All right." He didn't smile, but he sounded amused. "Then let's get to it."

Sugar, her nose and paws still covered in compost, sent Kathy a doggie grin when Dakota turned his back to retrieve the plants. Surging with excitement, she patted the dusty Maltese. Her first gardening experience. She felt like an eager virgin.

Dakota set the trays near their work area. "I hope you know more about this than I do."

She placed her shoes out of the line of fire. "That depends on how much you know."

"Gee, I'm so glad you offered to help," he said, his voice tinged with pleasant sarcasm. "Now I know we're going to kill every last one of these. By tomorrow morning they'll be needing a decent burial."

"We'll do no such thing." She lifted a plant she thought was dill, then checked the label with a smug expression.

"They're going to be healthy and happy. We'll even talk to them if we have to."

Dakota shook his head. "If you say so."

"I do." She sniffed the dill. "This one makes a fabulous dip."

"It's good for an upset stomach, too," he added. "My mom used to make a tea out of it with white wine."

"See." Kathy smiled and placed the pot back on the tray. "We know more than we think we do."

"A barefoot woman, a dirty dog and three bags of compost." He handed her a pair of work gloves and grinned. "What more could a man want?"

"Nothing, Lieutenant Lewis." She grabbed the gloves and stole his hat, her heart tagging longingly after his. "At the moment you've got it all."

Twelve

$\mathbf{D}$akota was nervous. He hated to admit it, but it was true. Kathy had promised to be home by 1500 hours. And he sure as hell hoped she was on time. This afternoon, patience wasn't his strongest virtue.

Jake and Jenny were due to arrive at 1530. This would be their first unchaperoned visit with Dakota. Seven-year-old twins. What in God's name had he gotten himself into? What did he know about mentoring second graders?

He checked his watch and cursed. He couldn't do this without Kathy, at least not today.

Striding into the kitchen, he removed a half gallon of milk and considered taking a swig from the carton. It used to burn his mom when he did that during his teenage years. But what good would it do to defy her in his own house? She wasn't even there.

He retrieved a glass and shook his head. Great. Now he was punishing his mom for nudging him into the mentor program. He poured the milk and swallowed it in one long, thirsty gulp.

A feminine sound rapped his attention. He cocked his head. The sexy snap of high heels on the entryway. Dakota left his glass on the counter and followed the clicking noise.

Catching sight of Kathy, he stopped. A cream-colored jacket nipped her waist and a matching skirt exposed long, slender legs. Suddenly aroused, he glanced at her feet, not surprised that she made a pair of professional-looking pumps sound wicked.

He moistened his lips, and she adjusted the briefcase in her right hand. How many of these silent, hungry moments would he be forced to endure? Dakota couldn't think of a damn thing to say. In fact, he couldn't think at all, not beyond the visceral emotion of wanting her.

Almost a week had passed since their agreement, six days of torture. Neither seemed any closer to a solution. He wanted her to remain his wife; she wanted him to be content giving up his work.

"I did my best to get here on time," she said.

Dakota's mind stumbled for a moment, then kicked into gear. The kids. She had come home to help him mentor. "I appreciate it. How was your day?"

"Fine. I'm still interviewing." She placed her briefcase on a small antique table in the foyer. "How are you doing?"

"Okay."

"Are you sure? You seem tense."

He pulled a hand through his hair. "I'm a little nervous about this, I guess. You know, having the twins here." It was, he supposed, the center of his anxiety this afternoon. That and wanting his wife. Missing her. Praying she wouldn't divorce him.

She stepped closer. "You shouldn't be. You've already spent time with Jake and Jenny."

"At their house, with Bob, his wife and the social worker present. Somehow, this doesn't feel the same."

"But you've been approved for the Mentor Program. That has to mean something."

He wished his misgiving wasn't so obvious. It made him feel inadequate. But he supposed his limited experience with children spoke for itself. He couldn't pretend that being certified as a weekend foster parent made him an expert.

"I'm anxious to meet them," she said.

"I'm glad." He needed her today, more than ever. "They're twins, but they don't seem that much alike. But there is the boy-girl thing, I suppose." He led Kathy into the living room. "I'm worried that they're a little small for their age. When I first saw Jake I thought he was around five. But he and Jenny are seven."

"Children develop in stages." She gave him a reassuring smile. "I'm sure they'll catch up."

Dakota worried more for Jake then Jenny. He remembered some of the smaller boys in school being picked on. But that wasn't a cross he'd had to bear. The unkindness he'd endured had come in the form of whispers and unclean looks. Not so much from kids but from adults. His mom may have been an active PTA parent, but she had also been sleeping with a prominent member of the community—a married man.

Kathy glanced at her watch. "I should change."

Dakota nodded. "Slip on a pair of jeans and boots. The kids are interested in seeing the horses." Which he hoped would be his saving grace. At Bob's house there had been all sorts of toys to entertain the twins.

She moved past him, the picture of professional beauty, her wild hair coiled in a tidy topknot, her designer suit simple yet elegant.

Sugar roused from her favorite napping spot and followed Kathy. She stooped to greet the dog, and Dakota tilted his head. Too bad, he thought, that Kathy hadn't leaned forward. He would have enjoyed a little more leg, a glimpse of thigh. Cradling himself between those creamy thighs occupied a good portion of his thoughts these lonely, troublesome days.

The doorbell pealed. Dakota let out a breath and answered the summons.

"Hi." He invited Bob and the children into the house. Bob wore a mail carrier's uniform, signaling the end of a workday. The kids were dressed for the ranch. Jenny had a dark-haired doll with her, and Jake had his hands in his pockets. Both stared up at him with curious faces—wondering, he supposed, how much fun he was going to be.

Dakota smiled, wishing he were more like Bob. The other man had a relaxed, easy manner, an unmistakable dad-like quality.

They chatted in the entryway and, before Dakota knew it, Bob hugged the kids and said goodbye, leaving Dakota on his own.

He guided the twins into the kitchen and offered them a soda. He had asked Mrs. Miller to stock up on kid-type food, so now the cupboards were filled with crackers, chips and snack cakes oozing with gooey filling.

"My wife is getting her boots on," he said. "Soon as she's ready, we'll head out to the barn."

Jake wiggled and hummed while he drank an orange pop, and Dakota was glad the boy hadn't chosen one of the caffeine colas.

Jenny, her dark-brown hair fashioned in two long ponytails, placed her doll on the counter.

Dakota studied the toy. "Hey, she's wearing boots. And fringe, too." The doll appeared to be attired for a Texas hoedown. "What's her name?"

The girl gave him a look that said he had just asked the dumbest of dumb questions. "Barbie," she replied.

And everybody, including Dakota, knew who Barbie was.

Insecurity looming over him, Dakota wondered if he should ply the kids with snacks. Or would that spoil their dinner? Mrs. Miller had suggested hamburgers with a side of macaroni and cheese, then ice cream for dessert.

Kathy entered the kitchen and saved the moment. "Well, hello." She flashed a radiant smile. "I've heard a lot about the two of you."

Five minutes later they walked to the barn. And as Jake bubbled with excitement and Jenny reached for Kathy's hand, Dakota's heart gave a warm, yearning lurch. With a light breeze blowing and spring blooming, he felt a sudden, amazing sense of family.

* * *

Kathy held Jenny's hand, wondering how many times she had dreamed of moments like this. Herself and Dakota enjoying the ranch, dark-eyed, dark-haired children beside them.

Jake, who carried a bag of carrots for the horses, had a charming grin, just crooked enough to make him look mischievous. And Jenny, precocious, ladylike Jenny, was a child beyond her years. They were both delightful, enchanting in their own special way.

Upon entering the barn, Dakota directed them to the first occupied stall. "This is Kathy's mare," he said. "Her name is Serenity."

The horse came forward and poked her head out, pleased by the introduction.

"Can I give her a carrot now?" Jake asked, eager to make friends with Serenity.

Dakota smiled. "Sure. But let me get you something to stand on, then show you how to feed a horse correctly." He found two empty crates and placed them on the barn floor, helping each twin onto one. Next he cautioned both children to keep their hands flat and offer the carrot in their palms. "Otherwise the horse might nip your fingers."

Jake laughed as Serenity took the treat from him, and Jenny held perfectly still watching the animal with curious intensity. "She has spots like a leopard," the girl said.

Dakota glanced at Kathy, and she could see that Jenny's observation impressed him. "That's because Serenity is a leopard Appaloosa. All Appaloosas have spots, but the leopard appy is white with dark spots, kind of like the jungle cat."

Jenny turned toward the next stall. "What kind is this one? It doesn't have any spots."

"Nomad is a quarter horse. He's my personal favorite, the one I ride most of the time." The horse snorted and Dakota stroked its nose.

"Nomad wants a carrot, too," Jenny told Jake, moving her crate so the boy could accommodate the animal. She assumed the role of the older, wiser sibling, even though she had entered the world only minutes before her brother.

Taking a step back, she looked up at Dakota. "You called Serenity a mare. Does that mean she's a girl?"

"Sure does."

"What's a boy horse?"

"Nomad is a gelding."

"Oh." She stood quietly for a moment, pondering his answer. "Then what's a stallion?"

Dakota's head whipped up to catch Kathy's gaze. She smiled and shrugged, amused by his shocked expression. Apparently he had no idea how bright and curious a young child could be. He would have to handle this one on his own, she thought. Jenny and Jake were his charges.

He frowned, then let out a heavy breath. Jenny waited patiently for his response, her head cocked.

"A stallion is boy, too."

"So Nomad is a gelding and a stallion?" Jenny prodded, confused by his simple answer.

Dakota swallowed, and Kathy placed her hand on the girl's shoulder, wondering if she should come to Dakota's rescue. The big, tough soldier looked as though he had lost his voice.

"No," he said finally. "Nomad isn't a stallion. He's called a gelding because he—" Dakota paused, possibly rethinking his statement. "He won't ever be a father."

Jenny studied the horse with an expression bordering on pity. "So Serenity and Nomad can't have babies together?"

"That's right. But Serenity could have a foal with a stallion if she wanted to." He appeared to notice Jenny's sympathy for the quarter horse. "And most people ride geldings instead of stallions. So you don't have to feel bad for Nomad. He's not particularly interested in being a dad."

Her worried expression softened. "A foal is a baby horse?"

Dakota nodded, relief bringing a smile to his lips. "You don't miss anything, Jenny. Do you?"

"Neither do I," Jake interjected in typical kid fashion, making sure he didn't lose out on any attention. "Can I ride Nomad, Dakota?"

"Not today, sport. I'd have to give you some lessons, and

I can't do that without making sure it's okay with your social worker first.''

"You can ask our mom, too." Jake pushed his bangs out of his eyes. "Mrs. Newberry takes us to see her every other weekend. You can come with us.''

Kathy assumed Mrs. Newberry was the social worker. She glanced at Dakota and waited for him to answer.

"I'll talk to Mrs. Newberry," he said. "And we'll let her decide when I can meet your mom. All right?''

"Kathy, too," Jake added. "I want Kathy to meet our mom, too.''

Her heart tugged. Being included in something so important to Jake felt wonderful, but it tied her to Dakota in a way that made her sad. Next week they were supposed to discuss their marital status—the choices they needed to make. Choices Kathy was afraid to face. If she asked Dakota to give up his work, he would. But she couldn't see basing their reconciliation on a forced issue, on his desperation and guilt.

She met Dakota's gaze, and he smiled, making her heart hurt even more.

He hoisted Jake up, and the boy laughed. Kathy still had her hand on Jenny's shoulder, the connection easing her a bit. Today was for the children.

"In the old days, one of the first things a Comanche kid learned to do was ride," Dakota said. "Both girls and boys were taught to ride with and without a saddle. But the boys had to try harder because they were expected to do tricks.''

"How come?" Jake asked, interest alive in his dark eyes.

"Because it was part of their training to become warriors. When a boy was young he had to learn to pick up objects from the ground while his horse was running full speed. At first, these were small, light objects." Dakota placed Jake back on his feet and continued. "But as the boy grew older, heavier things were used. So by the time he became a man, he was able to rescue an injured warrior. Pick him up from the ground and swing him across his horse.''

"But that must have hurt the guy who was bleeding," Jake said, clearly searching for the logic in Dakota's story.

"Maybe, but it was better than leaving him there to be killed by the enemy. And usually two men performed this task together, both lifting the fallen warrior at the same time. There wasn't much else they could do. They didn't have ambulances in those days."

Jenny gazed up at Dakota. "Can you ride like a warrior?"

He smiled at the little girl, then knelt to bring himself to her level. "I've never rescued anyone on horseback, but I can do a few tricks."

Kathy struggled with her next breath. Maybe he had never lifted a fallen comrade onto his horse, but he had spent a good portion of his life flying into enemy territory and rescuing downed airmen who would have otherwise died. And hostages, Kathy thought. How many innocent civilians had he rescued? Dakota Lewis was more than a warrior. To those he had saved, he was a hero.

"Will you ride for us?" Jenny asked. "Show us some tricks."

"Sure."

He winked at the girl, then glanced at Kathy. She managed a shaky smile and told her lovelorn heart to be still. Now wasn't the time to miss him.

Jake and Jenny went home and evening brought moments of reflective silence. Although sadness had edged portions of the day, Kathy couldn't deny how much she had enjoyed watching Dakota with the children.

He would have made a loving, attentive father.

She excused the thought and concentrated on loading the dishwasher instead. She had no business drifting over that emotional line.

Dakota came up behind her. She heard his booted footsteps, smelled the faint note of his cologne blending with the earthy scents of hay and horses.

She turned to look at him, unable to control the attraction rising inside her. The excited flutter. The yearning. The need to hold and touch.

"Would you like to sit outside for a while?" he asked. "Maybe have a glass of wine?"

"That sounds nice." She dried her hands and released the top button on her blouse, certain fresh air would do her good.

He poured two glasses of zinfandel and offered her one. She accepted the drink, and he opened the backdoor. Wine in hand, she slipped past him, leading the way to the courtyard.

Just as she'd imagined, the air was cool and fresh. She took a seat at the wrought-iron table and tipped her head to the sky. "It's a beautiful night." A vast strip of velvet showcased a glitter of stars, and a three-quarter moon shone with a silvery haze.

Dakota settled across from her, angling his chair so he could stretch his legs. The heel of a boot scraped the courtyard's Spanish tile. "It was a beautiful day, too."

Kathy nodded and studied her husband. The illumination from the patio lamps highlighted his eyes and shadowed those arresting cheekbones. She thought his face resembled that of a nineteenth-century warrior, a man marked by a hardened lifestyle, the risks that had become part of his nature. When he lifted his wine, it struck her how delicate the glass seemed in his large, callused hand.

"Children are amazing, aren't they?" He smiled and rolled his shoulders. "Active, too."

She couldn't help but return his smile. Now he looked like a forty-one-year-old warrior uncovering one of the seven wonders of the world. "You were terrific. Jake and Jenny adore you."

"Thanks. I couldn't have made it through the day without you, though. I think I would have been overwhelmed."

"I'm glad I could help."

How polite they were, she thought. Two people on the verge of ending their marriage, of abandoning the love they still felt. It made no sense, yet it made perfect sense. They cared too much to destroy each other with anger. So they held on by their thumbnails, afraid to let go.

"This must be how parents feel," Dakota said. "You know, after their kids are in bed."

Because her thoughts had strayed in a different direction, it took Kathy a moment to comprehend his words. "You mean the quiet? The close of a busy day?"

"Yeah. I'm tired, but it's a good kind of tired. Rewarding."

In spite of the wine, she vowed to keep a clear head. His admission pleased her, but slipping into a fantasy would only end up shredding her emotions. Jake and Jenny were someone else's children.

They sat quietly after that, both lost in thought. She gazed into the backyard where their herb garden flourished, spilling sweet, harmonious scents into the air. Breathing in that air, she shook her head. The garden wasn't theirs, it was his, along with the rest of the ranch. She had only been borrowing his possessions, stealing into his life. The temporary wife, longing for more.

"Kathy?"

She placed her glass back on the table, wondering if he had read her mind. His tranquil expression had tightened. "Yes?"

"Do you remember me mentioning that Thunder called last week?"

She nodded. It wasn't something she was likely to forget, nor was the fact that Thunder would be calling again, expecting Dakota's final answer. "You discussed his latest mission."

"Among other things." He kept his legs stretched out before him, his boots dark against the clay-colored tile. "I asked Thunder about his marriage. It wasn't any of my business, I suppose, but I asked him anyway."

"And did he tell you?"

"Yes. His wife lost their baby, too."

Kathy couldn't breathe. For one lonely moment all the pain came rushing back. Forcing oxygen into her lungs, she willed herself to sit and listen, to keep her eyes dry and her hands steady.

"It wasn't like our situation, though," Dakota said. "They got married because she was pregnant, so when she miscarried, their relationship ended. He said there was no reason to stay together."

"And do you believe that was all there was to it?" she asked.

"No, but I didn't see the need the press Thunder about it. To me, it was obvious that he had loved her. I could hear it in his voice."

Kathy's hand wasn't as steady as she had hoped, so she avoided lifting her glass. "Did it help? Talking to someone else who has been through it?"

"In a way, yes. And now that I know about Thunder's child, I understand why this mission is so important to him. The terrorist he's been tracking is responsible for opening fire on a group of tourists. One woman was eight months pregnant. And although she pulled through, the baby didn't."

A lump formed in Kathy's throat, but she didn't respond. She dropped her hands to her lap and waited for Dakota to continue, knowing he had more to say.

"I want to be here for you, be the best husband possible." He glanced up at the sky as though drawing emotional strength from the elements. "Yet I want to help Thunder catch this guy. For the baby who didn't survive the shooting. For the baby Thunder's wife lost. And for our baby, the child we should have had."

She kept her hands on her lap, her fingers numb from gripping her jeans. "I'm confused. Are you asking for my permission to go? Or are you asking me to tell you to stay home?"

"Neither. You said the choice has to be mine, and you're right. But I do want you to understand why I'm considering this mission, and why the decision is weighing on me. It isn't giving up my work that scares me. It's giving up the good I can do."

"What about us?" she asked, blinking back tears. "What about our marriage?"

"That's the hardest part." He trapped her gaze, his voice breaking a little. "Because losing you scares me most of all."

Thirteen

———

Dakota walked into the backyard, then stopped when he saw Kathy. She knelt at their garden, mothering the plants. She didn't appear to be aware of his presence, so he remained silent, taking the opportunity to admire her.

Her hair, shimmering in the late-morning sun, cascaded over her shoulders. She sported a blue work shirt tied at her waist and a pair of faded jeans, cuffed at the ankles. Because her feet were bare, he smiled. She really did like the feel of dirt between her toes.

He moved closer, his smile fading as anxiety coiled in the pit of his stomach. His decision-making two weeks were up. And Thunder would be calling for an answer. Soon. Most likely today.

As he approached, his boots made slight indentations in the grass. The garden, small enough to look cozy yet large enough to require stepping stones, thrived just beyond the lawn.

Kathy turned, gazed up at him and shielded her eyes with

her left hand, where the wedding ring he'd given her still sparkled. She hadn't removed it since they'd returned from Asterland.

Why? he wondered. Was she hoping she wouldn't have to? Hoping he would live up to her fantasy and give up his work? The decision that scared him senseless.

"Hi," she said.

He knelt beside her. "How long have you been out here?"

"A while. It's so peaceful."

It was, he thought, as a warm breeze blew the loose strands of her hair. The Texas sun offered warmth and an illusion of safety, something he knew Kathy needed. But it wasn't her own safety she feared for, it was his.

He wanted to brush a strand of hair from her cheek, but he kept his hands still instead, not trusting himself to touch her. Even the lightest caress might lead to a kiss. And that was his illusion of safety. His need.

"Were you talking to our plants?" he asked, knowing she had already watered them hours before. The soil remained slightly damp, just enough to make the ground cool.

"Maybe a little," she admitted. "They looked sort of lonely."

He scanned the herbs. But to him, they didn't look lonesome at all. They grew in pretty clusters, keeping each other company with a variety of shapes and colors. It was Kathy who appeared lonely, she who seemed to long for companionship.

She fingered a sprig of parsley, then drew back. "They're not our plants, Dakota. They're yours."

He frowned, pressure creasing his brow. "That's not true. Everything here belongs to both of us."

She shrugged. "Legally, maybe."

He didn't like the direction their conversation was headed. It sounded like divorce talk, common-law jargon. Rather than continue on the same vein, he said what was in his heart. "I love you, Kathy."

She lifted her gaze to his, her eyes as green as their surroundings. "I love you, too."

Dakota took a deep breath. Such beautiful words. Shouldn't they be enough?

Maybe they were, he thought, at least for the moment. Suddenly the tension eased between them, making the sun feel warmer, the plants smell more fragrant. He picked a grouping of leaves and tucked them behind Kathy's ear, giving in to the need to touch her.

"Peppermint." Before the leaves could slip from her hair, she secured them, brushing Dakota's hand as she did. "It's my favorite."

"I know. Mine, too." The scent was cool yet comforting, as clean and refreshing as a playful kiss on a spring day. It was, he realized, the way being married to Kathy made him feel.

Enraptured. Being with her brought joy and contentment. And so did everything else he wanted to share with her—the ranch, the horses, the newly planted herbs. And the children. Jake and Jenny, who basked in the attention Kathy favored upon them.

"I made sun tea." She pointed to a jar sitting in the center of the yard.

Dakota smiled. It looked like an offering, a gift to the elements, to the beauty of the morning. Strange how something so simple could seem so important. So homey. "Do you think it's ready?"

She nodded. "Are you thirsty?"

For a kiss, he thought, telling her he would love a glass of tea.

"Just give me a few minutes. I'll add some ice and sugar."

"And mint." He plucked more leaves and handed them to her, thinking she looked like an island goddess, with her emerald-colored eyes and bare feet.

"And mint," she repeated.

He watched her walk across the grass and lift the jar. As she proceeded to the house, her hair blew around her like a vibrant curtain, each strand shining beneath the sun.

Dakota studied the garden. They were common herbs, but they fascinated him, made him feel connected to the earth

Maybe he would take another trip to the nursery and let the kids get involved. He remembered seeing a mint that smelled like chocolate. Jake and Jenny would probably get a kick out of planting that.

Glancing up, he noticed Kathy coming toward him, minus the iced tea he'd been expecting. "Isn't it strong enough?"

She stood for a second, her expression strange, her eyes cloudy. "You have a phone call."

"Oh." He came to his feet, then stopped, reality taking hold. He didn't need to ask who was on the other line. He already knew. It was Thunder, awaiting his answer. The decision Dakota had momentarily forgotten about.

Kathy walked beside Dakota. They entered the house together, neither speaking. She'd known this day would come, and she'd known how it would make her feel. Alone, sad, lost.

Dakota paused in the kitchen and stared at the telephone. "I'll take it in the study," he said. The study was the room Dakota used for personal business.

Kathy nodded, and he lifted his hand and grazed her cheek, his touch gentle. She wanted to lean into him, kiss him, hold him. But she didn't. The phone call wouldn't disappear, and she couldn't pretend it wasn't important, that it didn't symbolize the end of their relationship.

They stared at each other, both silent. Finally he turned away and exited the kitchen, leaving her alone.

Kathy studied the blinking telephone. She stood dead still until the light quit flashing, an indication that Dakota had picked up the line in the other room.

The jar of tea sat on the counter, the freshly picked mint beside it. Returning to her task, she filled a glass pitcher with ice and poured the tea into it. She had to keep herself busy, keep herself from tears.

Kathy added sugar to the drink, then watched it sink to the bottom of the container and crystallize.

How could two people in love be losing each other?

Her heart constricted. Deep down, she knew the answer.

And it shamed her. She hadn't given their marriage a chance, hadn't believed in the power of love.

It was her fault, all of it. She was the one who had left, who had walked out on her husband without an explanation. He had been a soldier when she'd married him, that fact remained. And she had loved him for being strong and caring, for trying to make the world a better place.

But she had left him for the same reason.

Because she had blamed him for the loss of their child. Blamed him for something that was out of his control.

As Kathy stirred the tea with a wooden spoon, ice cubes clinked against the pitcher. Dakota wanted to dedicate his next mission to the baby they had lost. And he wanted to make the world a safer place for future children.

Children he hoped to have with her.

How could she fault him for that? How could she divorce a man with that kind of honor and integrity?

She couldn't. God help her, she couldn't. Dakota's passion for justice was part of his spirit, part of the warrior she had fallen in love with. And she had no right to ask him to be less than what he was. If she had to share him with the world, then she would.

The tea forgotten, Kathy began to pace. How long would Dakota's phone call take? How long before she could look into his eyes and tell him that she wanted to remain his wife, no matter what the cost?

Thirty minutes passed, and Kathy's decisiveness turned to anxiety. What if Dakota no longer trusted her? What if she had ruined their chance at happiness? How could she convince him that she wouldn't run away again, that she would wait for him, mission after mission?

She wasn't sure what to say, what to do to prove herself.

"Kathy?"

She spun around at the sound of her name.

Her heart in her throat, she stared at Dakota. His T-shirt was untucked, his jeans soiled from the garden. He had raked his hands through his hair, leaving the short, ebony strands in disarray. But to her, a more handsome, more noble man didn't exist.

"Yes?" she asked.

"We need to talk."

Kathy came toward him, her limbs shaky. They headed for the living room where Sugar snuggled on a leather recliner. The dog's ears perked when she saw them. Kathy sat on the sofa, and Dakota stood in the center of the room as though gathering his thoughts.

"I told Thunder I'm not taking this mission," he said.

His admission startled her, causing a quick, unexpected gasp. "You can't do that. You can't give up something that's so important to you."

He sat beside her. "Other things are important, too." He turned to face her, his voice quiet. "And I don't want to lose you."

"But you can't do this just for me."

Dakota took her hand. "It isn't just for you. It's for me, too. Something happened over these past few weeks, Kathy. Moments of contentment I hadn't understood until now. I want to wake up everyday with you beside me. And I want to grow beautiful things together. Flowers, babies."

She wanted that, too. She longed to see her tummy swollen with his child, longed to feel the flutter of life. She slipped her fingers through his, grateful for the physical connection. "But what about the terrorist? What about your need to catch him?"

A frown creased his forehead. "It still exists. But saving my marriage is more important. Even Thunder understood."

"I shouldn't have asked you to make that choice." She looked into his eyes and prayed he would accept her words, believe the truth in them. "I want you to take that mission."

He shook his head. "But I can't leave you alone."

She lifted their joined hands. "Yes, you can. And I promise to wait for you. Forever if I have to."

"You're forcing me to go? I decided to stay home, and you're forcing me to go?" A smile tugged at the corner of his lips. "We're quite a confused pair."

Kathy felt like smiling, too. Crying, smiling, holding him inside her heart. "We're in love. I think it goes with the territory. And I'm not forcing you to do anything. But I think we both need closure, and this mission is it."

"Like starting over where we left off?"

She nodded.

"Does that mean we should renew our wedding vows?"

Her breath rushed out her lungs. He trusted her. She could see the depth, the beauty, the emotion in his eyes. "Do you want to?"

He took her in his arms. "What do you think?"

Before she had the chance the answer, he kissed her, his mouth, his tongue brushing hers. Kathy meant to deepen the kiss, but he drew back.

"If I take this mission," he said. "Then it's going to be my last one. Okay?"

He didn't honestly expect her to argue, did he? "If that's what you want."

"It is. There are other ways to make a difference. The world is full of orphaned and abandoned kids. Children who need parents." He gazed into Kathy's eyes. "I hope you're interested in a big family." A grin teased one corner of his lips. "I'm really into this dad thing."

She closed her eyes, then opened them, testing the dream, the perfection of the man she had married. Not only did he want to raise their own babies, he wanted to adopt. He wanted to give his home and his heart to those who needed him. He would still be saving a piece of the world, but this time with love. He couldn't have said anything that would have pleased her more. "A big family is all I've ever wanted."

"Then that's what we'll have."

She pictured the ranch, alive with tiny faces and happy voices. "I think Jake and Jenny will approve."

"I'm glad they've become a part of our lives. But it's even more important that they have a caring mother, someone who's trying hard to win them back."

"You're incredible, Lieutenant Lewis." She stood and held

out her hand, offering him the security of her touch. The warmth of her body. The start of their future.

Dakota accepted her hand, and she led him to her room. There she collected the gold vase the king and queen had given her. She handed it to Dakota, and they proceeded to the master bedroom. Sealing their emotional declaration, he placed her vase beside his, joining the two pieces as one. Next he removed their wedding photograph from his drawer and centered it between two candles.

Lighting the candles, he smiled, anxious to see the fiery glow dance over Kathy's skin. It was daytime and the sun streamed through the windows, but the candles added a touch of magic, an element of quiet romance.

They turned toward each other and began to undress. While he removed his own clothing, he watched her untie the blouse at her waist, slip the faded jeans from her hips. Her bra and panties fluttered to the floor in a wisp of yellow lace. And then she stood naked before him—a seductive angel, her hair falling in tantalizing waves.

They came together in a kiss, her aroused nipples brushing his chest, his hands sliding down her back, over lean, luscious curves. She smelled as fresh as the Texas breeze, like the mint leaves still tucked behind her ear.

"I love you," he said.

"I love you, too." Her voice was breathy, soft and alluring. "Always."

She nuzzled his neck, then slid her mouth down the center of his chest until she dropped to her knees and kissed his navel. His stomach muscles jumped as her hair tickled his skin. He knew what she intended to do, and he had no will to stop her.

She closed her fingers around him, setting the rhythm for her tongue, her mouth. Dakota lowered his head and watched, his blood running through his veins like a warm river. A current of pure need.

Candlelight shimmered in her hair, sending streaks of gold tumbling through the scarlet mass. He tugged a handful, reveled in the texture while she seduced him with slow, intoxicating strokes, her mouth gentle yet greedy.

She kissed her way back up his body, and they tumbled onto the bed, pulling at the covers as they did. He couldn't get enough of her. This woman who was his wife, his lover, the lady of his heart. She had given him the most important gift of all. She loved him for who he was, for the man life had made of him. He couldn't ask for anything more.

He licked the tips of her breasts, smiled when her eyes glittered like emeralds. Beautiful Kathy. She arched as she reached for him, playful as a kitten, erotic as a cat.

He settled between her thighs, took comfort in being there.

"No protection this time." She slid her hands through his hair. "I want you inside me, only you."

Dakota touched her cheek. Not using protection might make her pregnant. He understood her wish, her hope. She had found healing in their reunion, just as he had. The past was over, the hurt and the pain gone. Tonight was perfect for creating a new life.

He entered her, found her warm and willing, wet and inviting.

Together they moved, peppermint leaves and candles scenting the air. He was home, Dakota thought. Wrapped in the luxury of forever.

Epilogue

Dakota, attired in a buckskin shirt, led a pinto, an exceptional horse he had purchased for this occasion. Pinto horses had been prized by his Indian ancestors for their color and stamina.

Stopping at the fence that separated the courtyard from the path that led to the barn, he waited, the horse patient beside him.

A gathering of guests waited as well, quiet and respectful of the ceremony about to take place.

Kathy's father, Harold, opened the gate and escorted his daughter onto the dirt path. Stunning in a three-piece buckskin dress, she took Dakota's breath away. The beadwork was bright and intricate, the leather heavily fringed. Her hair fell loose about her shoulders, shimmering like fire beneath the Texas sun.

Dakota offered Harold the pinto, a ceremonial gift representing a bride price in the Comanche culture. As the older man guided the horse back to the corral, Kathy came forward and reached for Dakota's hand.

Their eyes met, and they smiled. This was the renewal of their wedding vows. No words were exchanged, but the message was clear. In a modern version of an ancient tradition, Kathy had just accepted Dakota as her husband. It was simple, yet beautiful—a moment neither would ever forget.

A whoop of appreciation sounded from their guests, and Dakota and Kathy turned to the festive commotion.

Dakota scanned the sea of faces and spotted his mom, Kathy's mother and Mrs. Miller, the three looking happy and proud. A beaming Jake and Jenny stood with their full-time foster family, and beside them were the men and women who had participated in the Lone Star jewel mission.

Sheikh Rassad, wearing a kaffiyeh with his traditional robes, held his wife's hand. Dr. Webb and Winona took turns entertaining baby Angel, and Aaron and Pamela caught Dakota's eye and smiled. But the couple who seemed to relish the ceremony most deeply were Matt Walker and Lady Helena. Soon they would be married, too.

Within a heartbeat, hugs and good wishes were granted, along with laughter and handshakes. Angel squealed and flashed Dakota a one-toothed grin. He nuzzled the little girl's cheek and winked at Kathy. Making babies was constantly on their minds.

Dakota escorted his bride to the courtyard where buffet tables of catered food and a tall, white cake awaited. A band had been hired to play soft country ballads—music to sway by.

As the guests filtered into the festively decorated area, Dakota kissed Kathy's hand. The Lone Star jewels mission was over, but he knew the hidden stones still sparkled.

Leadership. Justice. Peace. The secret mantra the Texas Cattleman's Club members had chosen to honor still guided their lives. But so did another word.

Love.

Each man, including Dakota Lewis, had found his one true

love. The woman who would share his home, his soul, his world. The woman who had become the shining gem of his heart.

*   *   *   *   *

Look out for more from
Sheri WhiteFeather later in the year.

MILLIONAIRE HUSBAND

by
Leanne Banks

LEANNE BANKS

is a national number-one best-selling author of romance. She lives in her native Virginia with her husband, son and daughter. Recognised for both her sensual and humorous writing with two Career Achievement Awards from *Romantic Times Magazine*, Leanne likes creating a story with a few grins, a generous kick of sensuality and characters who hang around after the book is finished. Leanne believes romance readers are the best readers in the world because they understand that love is the greatest miracle of all. You can write to her at PO Box 1442, Midlothian, VA 23113, USA. An SAE with return postage for a reply would be greatly appreciated.

This book is dedicated to the stock jock
with *cojones*, brains and heart.

Thank you for everything!

One

Another day, another hundred thousand dollars. With the exception of the nagging pain in his abdomen, Justin Langdon was feeling pretty pleased as he climbed the steps to Edward St. Albans Elementary school. The *St. Albans Chronicle* didn't call him their top stock jock for nothing. Popping two antacids, he thought the beautiful thing about the stock market was that a shrewd man could make money when it went up and when it went down. Justin believed in doing both.

After a childhood spent at the Granger Home for Boys, Justin had worked a day job and put every penny he had on making money in the stock market.

His tightwad days of eating beanee weenees had paid off, and he was now a multimillionaire. He was damn sure he wouldn't be eating cans of beans anymore. If his financial success occasionally rang hollow, he didn't dwell on it. Besides, two of his highly successful alumni buddies from the Granger Home for Boys had talked him into joining them in a secret, tax deductible, charitable foundation, the Millionaires' Club.

Justin still had moments of doubt over his commitment to the Millionaires' Club, but he would do his duty. He walked through the hallway of the aging elementary school toward the sounds of young children. Justin's charity assignment was to investigate the after-school program to determine whether the Millionaires' Club should donate and how much.

Absently rubbing his stomach, he rounded the hall corner and peered into the noisy classroom. A curvy woman with a mop of red curly hair and dressed as a *J* led the youngsters in a song of words starting with the letter *J*. Was this Amy Monroe, the director of the program? Her feminine curves and one hundred and fifty watt smile nearly distracted him from the fact that the red costume clashed with her hair. She gestured and danced for the children, encouraging them when their volume grew. He'd never seen so much enthusiasm inside one single person before.

"Jack, jam, Japan, jar!"

Justin's stomach clenched and he frowned. It must be the noise, he thought, but he couldn't deny Miss Monroe's effectiveness. He was almost tempted to join in the chorus too.

Amy spied him and waved at him. "Come in and join us," she called, then smiled at the children. "Join starts with—?"

"*J!*" they chorused.

Justin moved into the room and slid into a too-small chair. His stomach seemed to nag him more than usual, but he pushed the pain aside, telling himself it was the result of overexposure to so many noisy children at once.

Justin didn't hate kids. From his upbringing, however, he'd learned that a wife, ex-wife and children constituted the biggest sucking sound a man could possibly experience in his bank account. That lesson had been driven home to him month after month when his divorced mother received the child support payment from his dad and subsequently shopped till she dropped. She and Justin always ended up with more month than money left, eventually necessitating his move to the Granger Home for Boys. Justin had vowed never to put himself or anyone else he cared for in that position again in his life. That meant no marriage and no kids.

Amy Monroe's curves distracted him again. His no-marriage rule didn't mean no dating, he told himself, remembering his good friend Michael's advice for him to drag himself away from the computer and get out more.

"See you Thursday," she said, dismissing the class. "We're doing *K* then."

Justin stood as the kids stampeded past him. A hush immediately descended on the room, and he met Amy's gaze. "You're Amy Monroe, the pre-school special-program coordinator," he said.

She nodded. "And you're Justin Langdon. I received a message that you might be coming to observe, but no explanation." She gave him a curious glance. "Do you have a child you want to enter into the program?"

"Oh, no. I'm doing some research on your program. You looked like you were getting through to them," he said. "I'd like to hear more about it. Can I take you to dinner tonight?"

Amy Monroe felt a sliver of temptation and ignored it. She also ignored the fact that Justin Langdon's intelligent gaze perked her interest. She ignored his chiseled bone structure and the curve of his lips that hinted at sensuality. She told herself not to think about how his broad shoulders promised strength and protection. She ignored the hum of electric awareness shooting between them. She ignored all these things because she had to ignore them. Although Amy couldn't remember the last time she'd joined a handsome intelligent man for dinner, she knew she had no room in her life for dates. She shook her head. "I'm sorry. Tonight's bad."

He shrugged. "Tomorrow night then?"

"Tomorrow's bad, too. Actually every night for the next year is probably going to be bad."

He blinked. "Why?"

"Three reasons," she said and decided to kill all the interest at once. "Their ages are five, three and three. My kids," she said, because since her sister and brother-in-law had died eight weeks ago, Emily, Jeremy and Nick had become her kids.

Justin Langdon blinked again. If she didn't know better, she'd swear he even turned pale with disbelief. "You have three children," he said. "I didn't see a ring—"

"Oh, I'm not married. I've never been married."

"I can see why you'd be busy, then." Justin rubbed his stomach absently. "Is there a restroom?"

"Sure, right through that door," Amy said, pointing to the rear of the room. She grew concerned at the odd expression on his face. "Are you okay?"

He made a vague sound and headed for the restroom.

Amy frowned. She realized children frightened many men, but she hadn't expected his look of near-nausea. Shrugging, she quickly put the classroom in order so she could leave. Hearing a strangled cough, she felt a tinge of uneasiness. "Mr. Langdon," she called, knocking on the door. "Justin, are you all right?"

He coughed again.

Her uneasiness growing by the second, she knocked again. "Mr. Langdon, are you decent?"

"Yes, but—"

Amy pushed open the door and saw that the man's handsome face had turned ashen. He held a paper towel in his hand stained with bright red blood. "Nose bleed?"

He shook his head. "I coughed."

Alarm tightened her chest. She didn't know what the blood meant, but she knew it wasn't good. "You need to get to the hospital."

Justin protested the pushy woman for about forty-five seconds until he felt the urge to cough again. Then he focused his energy on not coughing and fighting the light-headed feeling that settled over him like a thick fog. In the occasional moments the fog lifted, Justin noticed Amy Monroe drove her Volkswagen Beetle like a bat out of hell and swore in a very un-teacher-like fashion at drivers who moved too slowly to suit her.

Pain burned through his gut, stealing his breath and sense of humor. He felt her quick glance of concern.

"Breathe," she told him.

"In a minute," he muttered, hating the combination of pain and fuzziness.

"No," she said. "Breathe. You're tensing up. That makes the pain worse. It's like childbirth. If you breathe, you can stay on top of it."

"You should know," Justin said and drew in a ragged breath. Lethargy dragged at him. He felt as if someone was pressing two hundred pound weights on his eyelids. If he could just rest for a few minutes...

"Mr. Langdon! Justin!"

Wincing at the pain, he didn't open his eyes. "What?"

"We're almost at the hospital."

He'd never felt so tired. It occurred to Justin that he should thank her for bringing him. He struggled to open his mouth, but couldn't. Frustration swirled inside him.

The car jerked to a stop and he felt a flurry of activity. He heard voices.

"—coughing up blood," Amy Monroe said. "I think his stomach is hurting."

"...ulcer. He may need surgery," a male voice said.

Justin tried to protest, but again he couldn't. He focused all his energy on opening his eyes and found himself staring into Amy Monroe's worried gaze. He opened his mouth. "Thank—"

She put her finger over his lips and shook her

head. "Save your strength. We were all put on this earth for a reason. You're one of my reasons today. Breathe," she said and brushed her soft mouth against his cheek.

Justin felt himself wheeled over the pavement through the doors. The pain mounting, he stopped fighting and allowed his eyes to close. The hospital faded away and his world turned dark.

"Emergency surgery," he heard a woman say, and then he heard no more.

A vision wafted through his mind. His good friends Michael and Dylan shook their heads. "So young," Michael said.

"What a waste," Dylan said. "All he did was work and worry about money."

Michael's wife Kate took his hand. "He never really got it," she said sadly. "I think he was right on the edge, but he never really got it."

Got what? Justin wondered.

"He fought it," Dylan said.

Fought what? Justin wanted to know.

Michael nodded. "I can't believe he didn't have a will. He would turn over if he knew how much the government was getting of his fortune."

Will! Panic sliced through him. He'd never made a will because he'd always assumed he had time. He broke into a cold sweat. Was he dead?

Kate wiped a tear from her eye. "I wish he could

have had more. It feels like such a waste. I can't imagine getting to the end of my life and knowing I could have made a difference, but didn't. I can't imagine never loving someone. It's such a waste,'' she said and Michael took her into his arms.

Justin wondered if he was dead. All the things he'd intended to do later raced through his head. Worst of all, however, was the incredibly empty feeling that engulfed him. His throat tightened with dread. Had his life really been all for naught? He'd been so busy trading and adding to his wealth, adding to his financial security that he couldn't even see anything, let alone anyone else.

What had he done to make the world a better place?

The regret felt like a tidal wave, drowning him with a thousand should-haves.

If you're out there, God, I'm sorry. I've screwed up big time. If you can give me a second chance...

Ridiculous notion, Justin thought. If Justin were God, why would he give Justin a second chance? What had Justin done to deserve another chance?

Well, hell, Justin thought. Maybe God wasn't a self-centered jerk like Justin was. Maybe God was smarter and better than he was. Maybe God was nicer. Maybe God believed in second chances.

If you can give me a second chance, I'll try to figure out the real reason you put me on this earth and get it done.

* * *

Justin wished whoever was putting fifty-pound bags of cement on his eyelids would stop. He frowned, concentrating with the effort to open his eyes.

"Looks like he's waking up," a familiar voice said. Through the fog of his mind, he tried to place the voice.

"Hey, Justin, welcome back to the land of the living," another familiar voice said.

Justin blinked and looked into the faces of his two friends, Michael Hawkins and Dylan Barrows.

"You gave everyone a scare," Michael said, his observant gaze crinkled with concern. It occurred to Justin that Michael seemed more human since he'd married and become a father.

"I know you've been dragging your feet on this after-school reading program donation," Dylan said, "but was surgery really preferable?"

Justin felt a grin grow inside him. He gave a rough chuckle. Pain sliced through his side. He swore under his breath. "Show some mercy, Dylan."

Dylan shook his head. "You look like a truck ran over you."

"Thank you," Justin said wryly.

"No, really," Dylan said, his face growing serious. He gave Justin's arm a quick squeeze. "You need to take better care of yourself. I don't want anything bad to happen to you. Even if you are a cheapskate, you're a good guy.''

A fleeting image of his Scrooge-like dream oozed through his mind and his humor faded. ''Maybe not good enough,'' he muttered to himself.

''I hate to run, but I booked this charter last week,'' Dylan said regretfully. ''I'll rest easy knowing you're okay.''

''Charter to Rio or Paris?'' Justin asked, mildly curious. Dylan was always running here or there. At times, it almost seemed as if Dylan was running from himself.

''Neither. The Caribbean. Weekend in Belize. Maybe you can go with me when you're feeling better.''

''Blonde or brunette?'' Justin asked.

Dylan cracked a grin that didn't extend to his eyes and waved his hand. ''Neither this time. I invited Alisa Jennings, but she turned me down flat. Third time this month.''

''For someone with a healthy ego, you seem to have none where she is concerned.''

''Glutton for punishment, I guess. I'll just do a little fishing and diving and a lot of thinking.'' He glanced at his gold watch, then back at Justin. ''Take care, bud. I'll see you when I get back. You too, Michael.''

As soon as Dylan left, Justin met Michael's gaze. ''Dylan? Thinking?''

"He's pretty hooked on Alisa."

"I'm surprised he didn't just go on to the next one. Dylan always seems like he's got a string of women waiting for him."

"I think he and Alisa were more involved than he admits."

"That's what I always thought," Justin said, fighting a sudden weariness.

"But enough about Dylan. You look like you're ready to drift off again, so I'll leave—"

"Just a minute," Justin said. "I, uh…I guess I could have croaked."

"Yeah," Michael said with a nod.

His chest tightened and he brushed the sensation aside. "I thought about everything I hadn't done."

"Like going to Belize?" Michael asked with a grin.

Justin shook his head. "No. Important stuff." Strange emotions tugged at him and he shrugged. "You seem like you're at peace. Why?"

"Oh, that's easy. Kate and the baby. When it's all said and done, everyone and everything else might leave, but I know I'll still have Kate." He paused. "And I like what I'm doing with you and Dylan. It's fun and more." He chuckled to himself. "Kate says the three of us suffer from a fraud complex about our wealth. I guess giving some of it away makes me feel less like a fraud." Michael studied him. "You need to rest," he said. "You'll be okay."

Distantly aware of Michael leaving his room, Justin struggled with the haze settling over him. He thought about what Michael had said and shook his head. He couldn't believe his purpose had anything to do with being a husband and father. Closing his eyes, Justin decided he would just have to keep looking.

Three weeks later, Justin still had a gnawing sensation inside him but, thank goodness, it had nothing to do with an ulcer. Needing to thank Amy Monroe for getting him to the hospital, he found her address and drove to her house after the stock market closed. He pulled into the driveway behind Amy's Volkswagen. He scanned the area and noted the large older two-story home in a neighborhood filled with oaks, weeping willow trees and kids, at least a dozen kids.

Snatching the bouquet of roses from the passenger seat and getting out of his car, he climbed the small, slightly tilted porch and rang the doorbell. A little girl with lopsided pigtails quickly appeared and stared him up and down. "A man is at the door," she yelled at the top of her lungs.

Just then, two toddler boys raced to the door and stared at him. One poked his thumb in his mouth.

Twins, Justin noted, thankful again that fatherhood was not part of his purpose.

Amy appeared, dressed in shorts that emphasized her long shapely legs. Affectionately ruffling the hair of one of the twins, she glanced at the flowers and Justin in surprise. Her gaze searched his and she smiled.

Justin's heart gave an odd, unexpected jump.

Amy opened the door. "Come in. I called the hospital a few times to make sure you survived my driving. How are you? Was it an ulcer?"

"I'm much better," he said and nodded. "Yes, it was an ulcer. After surgery, the treatment was antibiotics." He had felt sheepish when he'd learned his emergency could have been prevented with a simple prescription.

"Guys hate going to the doctor, don't they?" she mused.

"This one does," he said and extended the bouquet of roses. "These are for you. Thank you for saving my life." Flowers weren't nearly enough, but Justin wasn't stopping there. He had other plans for Amy and her after-school program.

"You're welcome," she said, taking the roses in her arms. The two tykes wrapped their arms around each of her legs.

Justin couldn't blame the little guys for wanting to be close to her. She radiated a combination of optimism, feminine strength and nurturing that would draw boys, both little and big, and she wore her undeniable sensuality like a spellbinding exotic perfume.

She glanced down at the boys. "Oops. I've forgotten my manners. Justin Langdon, allow me to introduce my kids, Jeremy, Nick and Emily. Smell the beautiful roses," she said dipping the bouquet to pint-size level, then she turned to Emily. "Would you mind getting me a vase with water, sweetheart? There's one under the sink. Dinner's almost ready, so everyone needs to wash up."

Faster than a speeding bullet, the twins detached themselves and tore out of the room.

"Me first!" Nick said.

"*Me* first!" Jeremy said.

"Chicken and dumplings is one of their favorite dinners," Amy explained. "Comfort food. We're very big on comfort food since my sister and her husband died."

Justin frowned. "Your sister died recently?"

Amy nodded, sadness muting the lively glint in her brown eyes. "And her husband. The children lost mom and dad in one day."

Justin digested the new information. "They're not your children?"

"They're mine now," she said firmly. "And they're staying with me regardless of what any social worker says about my age or anything else."

Justin got the uncomfortable impression that there was a story here, a story he'd just as soon not hear.

Emily reappeared and tugged on the hem of Amy's shirt. Amy bent down while the little girl whispered to her. Amy's smile emanated amusement and a hint of challenge. "Emily wants to know if you'd like to join us for dinner. The food should be safe, but our dinner table, uh, culture, may test your ulcer medication."

Justin glanced at two pairs of brown eyes and was surprised at his visceral response to both. Emily's gaze held a tinge of sadness that tugged at him. He couldn't help remembering long-buried feelings of abandonment from his own childhood, and the knowing provocative dare in Amy's eyes affected him in a wholly different way. He could learn about the after-school program, he told himself, justifying his immediate decision.

"I'd love to stay," he said, getting a sly sense of satisfaction from Amy's double take.

"You're sure?" she said, and he had the odd sense she was really saying *Are you man enough for this?*

Justin felt the click inside him. It was a quality he kept hidden from most people, a deadly serious determination to meet a goal, to prove himself. He'd experienced the sensation only a few times in his life and learned it was like flicking a lighter in a room filled with gasoline. It was what had won him

a scholarship to college and what had kept him going during his years of eating cans of beanee weenees before he'd made his first million.

Something about Amy Monroe brought the same
flame to life. She was a woman with sunshine in her
eyes, a body with dangerous curves and even more
dangerous dependents—children. He didn't know
why, but he had the inexplicable urge to show Amy
he was man enough for anything she might need.

Two

"**I**'d like to expand the program to at least five more elementary schools in this district," Amy said, responding to Justin's question about her after-school program at the same moment she saved Jeremy's cup from a spill. "I'd really like to make it county-wide, and if you want to know what I wish before I blow out the candles on my birthday cake, I'd love to see this spread all over the state, then the whole country." She paused, studying Justin's face. She knew some people felt overwhelmed by her dreams, but she sensed he understood at the same time he was amused.

"Amy, the Empress of Literacy," he said.

He made it sound more sexy than mocking, but perhaps that was just because *he* was sexy.

"I can't deny it," she said. "Two and a half hours per week could make a huge difference in the lives of the children who participate in the program."

"What do you need to make it happen? Money?"

"That would help," she said. "Teachers interested in helping with the program would find it more inviting to know their time and experience would be rewarded. The program also needs more exposure. It would be great if we became the darling of a women's organization, or a corporate sponsor decided to take us on, but since I became a mom," she said, smiling at Nick, Emily, and Jeremy, "I've had three of the best distractions in the world living with me." She noticed Nick squirming in his seat. "Bathroom?"

The little boy nodded. "I don't wanna miss dessert."

"Scoot. I promise to save some for you." After Nick left, she met Justin's inquiring gaze. "He waits a little too late sometimes," she explained. "Are you allowed to eat chocolate?"

His lips twitched, and his eyes flickered with a dangerous sensuality. "I'm allowed to eat anything I want," he said in a low voice that made her wonder what it would be like to be the subject of his undivided attention.

Distressed at her thoughts, Amy bit her lip and banished a wayward provocative image from her mind. If this was how she reacted to being dateless for six months, how would she act after a year? She cleared her throat and stood. "Good, then you can have a piece of the candy bar cake Emily and I made this afternoon."

Nick skidded into the room. "I'm back."

"Did you wash your hands?"

The little boy paused too long.

Amy chuckled and patted his head. "Finish the job and use soap."

"Are you a teacher like Aunt Amy?" Emily asked Justin.

As curious as her niece, Amy glanced over her shoulder to watch his response.

He shook his head. "I trade stocks."

"Which brokerage?" Amy asked.

He gave a casual shrug. "I trade online."

She gave him a second glance. He didn't look like a gambler. "What do you do when the market goes down?"

"When the market goes down, I short stocks."

Amy frowned as she placed a slice of cake on a plate. "Short?"

"I'm not gonna be short," Nick interrupted. "I'm gonna be tall."

Justin chuckled. "This doesn't have anything to do with height. Shorting a stock technically means you borrow the stock at one price hoping to replace it at a lower price. You place your order at a hopefully high price, then get out when it goes down. It's called shorting a stock.''

"I've never heard of it.''

"Only in America can you make or lose money on something you don't technically own. It's not for the faint of heart,'' Justin wryly said.

"Oh, makes for ulcers?'' she asked.

He paused. "Partly,'' he grudgingly admitted. "But not making money at all would make more ulcers.''

"What's an ulcer?'' Emily asked.

"It's something in your tummy that makes it hurt,'' Amy said.

"When my tummy hurts, I throw up,'' Jeremy said, then eyed the cake and quickly added, "but my tummy doesn't hurt now. My tummy is smiling because it's going to get cake.''

"My tummy is smiling bigger,'' Nick said.

"Is not,'' Jeremy said.

"Is too,'' Nick said.

"Is—''

"If your tummies don't shut up, you might not get cake,'' Emily pointed out.

Complete silence followed. For sixty seconds.

The doorbell rang.

"Is not,'' Jeremy whispered.

"I'll get it," Emily said, bounding from the kitchen.

Amy frowned as she set plates of cake in front of each twin. "Who could that—"

"It's Ms. Hatcher," Amy yelled from the foyer.

Amy's stomach sank.

She felt Justin's curious gaze on her. "Hatcher?"

"One of the social workers," she whispered. "I don't think she likes me."

He stood. "Why do you need a social worker? You're the closest living relative, aren't you?"

Amy nodded. "Yes, but my sister didn't have a will, so it's complicated." She glanced at the cake and winced. "She won't approve of the cake."

"Cake?" Justin echoed in disbelief. "What's wrong with cake?"

Amy shoved her hair from her face with the back of her arm. "She'll find something."

At the sound of heavy footsteps, Amy greeted the social worker with a bright smile. "Ms. Hatcher, what a surprise. We were just having dessert. Would you join us?"

The older woman gave a sharp glance to the boys and the messy chocolate cake. The boys' faces and hands were covered with chocolate. She sniffed in disapproval. "Sweets at this time of night will make it difficult for the children to sleep." She looked down her nose at Amy. "And it's unsafe for little Emily to answer the door. You should know better."

"I was cutting the—" Amy began and stopped. She didn't know why Ms. Hatcher so easily succeeded in making her feel inadequate. Amy had been trained to teach, and although she hadn't been trained to mother, she was determined to be the mother her niece and nephews desperately needed. "I'm sure you noticed that Emily may answer the door, but she doesn't open it unless she knows the visitor. Is there anything else I can help you with?"

"The health department will be making an inspection next week," Ms. Hatcher grudgingly reported.

Amy felt a trickle of relief. Progress, at last. "That's great news. That means we're one step closer."

"There are other steps in the process," Ms. Hatcher reminded her, glancing at Justin.

He extended his hand. "Justin Langdon. I met Amy through her after-school program. I'm sure you're familiar with the impressive results of her work."

Surprised at the alliance he offered, Amy met his green gaze and sent him a silent thank-you.

"I'm aware that Ms. Monroe has set a full plate for herself," Ms. Hatcher said. "You may see me to the door," she said to Amy.

Amy followed the woman to the foyer and endured Ms. Hatcher's lecture. After the social worker left, Amy leaned against the door. It was amazing how one person's presence could suck all the joy out of the air. Amy resented it. She didn't understand what Ms. Hatcher had against her. Although their first encounter hadn't been stellar, the woman couldn't seem to get past it. Amy knew the woman didn't approve of her. She disapproved of Amy's youth and the fact that she wasn't married. She seemed to disapprove of everything about Amy, yet the woman clearly didn't have valid grounds to prevent Amy from gaining custody of the children. The only thing Ms. Hatcher could do was make things difficult for Amy, and that was what the woman was doing.

Amy sighed and returned to the kitchen. The twins were licking their fingers and Emily had eaten the frosted perimeter and left the un-frosted center on her plate. All three faces were smudged with chocolate, all three content. Amy's heart twisted. Heaven help her, she loved these kids.

"We hated it," Justin said in a deadpan voice, lifting his empty plate and meeting Amy's gaze with a knowing look in his eyes. "You should have given us gruel instead."

"What's gruel?" Emily asked.

"Yucky, gross soup," Amy said, her lips twitching at Justin's joke. "Now you need to prove Ms. Hatcher wrong and get ready for bed."

All three groaned in unison.

"Why is that lady always so cranky?" asked Nick.

"She's mad at Aunt Amy because Aunt Amy slammed a baseball into her windshield and broke it," Emily said.

Amy felt Justin's intent gaze. Heat rose to her cheeks. "I apologized and paid for the repair," she felt compelled to say.

"She's still mad," Emily said, sadly shaking her pigtails.

"She needs to eat more cake," Jeremy suggested. "Can I have one more piece?"

"May I," Amy corrected. "And no, sweetie, you may not. First person ready for bed gets to pick the first bedtime story."

The three stampeded from the kitchen, leaving the room in abrupt silence.

Justin chuckled and shook his head. "You broke her windshield the first time you met her."

"It was an accident," she said, clearing the dishes from the table. "And it was technically before I met her." She shrugged. "How was I supposed to know she was going to pull into my driveway?"

"She reminds me of someone," Justin said.

"Named Atilla?" Amy asked, turning on the faucet to rinse the dishes.

"Close," he said. "I thought a house had already fallen on her."

Amy smiled at his reference to the witch in *The*

Wizard of Oz. "I'm sure that somewhere underneath her gruff exterior—"

"—lies a heart of stainless steel." His expression turned serious. "Can she prevent you from getting custody of the kids?"

Amy felt a ripple of unease. "I don't think so," she said. "She can just make things difficult. She doesn't approve of me."

"Any reason besides the baseball?"

"I'm too young, too employed, too single." Amy figured she would remain single for the rest of her life, and that was fine.

"And you smile too much," he said in that deadpan voice that made her smile at the same time her stomach danced. "You laugh too much. And her biggest objection is probably that you aren't ugly enough."

Not ugly enough. A forbidden pleasure rippled through her. "I'm not?"

He shook his head and stepped closer. "You need warts and an extra eye."

"You suppose she would like me then?"

"Maybe," he said. "You still might not be ugly enough even with warts and an extra eye."

She looked into his green eyes and wished she had a little more time and just a smidgeon more freedom. He was the most interesting man she'd met in a long time, and his mere presence in her house reminded her she was female. Amy heard Nick gargle. She had no time and no freedom, so she'd best just store up this moment for a rainy day.

"Thank you for coming tonight, Justin Langdon," she said and following a wayward impulse, she kissed him. Her mouth should have landed on his cheek. Instead, she pressed her lips against his surprised mouth. In two seconds, she caught a hint of his fire, his musky scent, and the taste of chocolate. The combination was seductive. She pulled back.

"Do you kiss every man whose life you save?" Justin asked.

Surprised at herself, Amy struggled for breath. "I don't save many lives. I used the Heimlich maneuver on a first grader when he tried to swallow an entire hot dog and he cried on me." She bit her lip. "Thank you for putting in a good word for me with Ms. Hatcher."

"Aunt Amy!" the twins chorused.

Regret and relief warred inside her. "I need to go. Can you let yourself out?"

He nodded, looking at her thoughtfully.

"G'night," she said. "And don't get your shorts in such a twist that you get another ulcer." She left him and the dishes, knowing the dishes would be there when she returned, but he would not.

Three stories, five songs, and lots of hugs later, Amy tucked first the boys, then Emily into bed, and softly closed the door. Sinking against the hallway wall, she crossed her arms over her chest and drank in the peace in the silence and darkness.

She struggled with the weariness that tried to settle on her shoulders. "I can do this," she whispered. "I can be what those children need me to be." Although Amy had always considered herself a fighter, strong enough for herself and anyone weaker, she was surprised at how tiring being a mom was. She was even more surprised by the loneliness.

Pushing away from the wall, she resolved to keep her weariness to herself. In time, it would fade. She hoped it would fade. Rounding the corner to the kitchen ready to face the dinner dishes, she stopped short at the sight that greeted her. She'd been right about one thing, wrong about the other. Justin Langdon was long gone. But he'd done the dishes.

Her heart twisted. She skimmed her fingers over the clean counter. Justin was an enigma. She found him extremely compelling. Another time, she might try to solve some of the mysteries she saw in his eyes. Amy thought of the kids and shook her head. In another life.

Justin climbed the steps to the front door of his town home in his well-lit, well-patrolled, quietly affluent neighborhood. He strode through the door and listened to the silence. After the noise and chaos of Amy's home, his house felt a little too quiet.

Justin scowled. That was impossible. Her home

symbolized everything he'd always wanted to avoid in his life. Dependents. He'd filled out countless tax forms answering "None" to the question "How many dependents?" Justin had always been determined to keep his answer at the nice safe, round number of zero. As a kid, he'd been disappointed so much by those who'd claimed him as a dependent that he never wanted to be in the position to disappoint.

He felt an odd uneasiness when he thought about Amy and her situation. She was taking on a lot of responsibility without much visible means of support. The memory of his promise to the Almighty wafted through his mind like a feather. Justin still knew he needed to find the reason he'd been put on this earth. Could it be related to Amy and the kids? His stomach clenched and he shook his head. That would involve the *D* word—dependents. Walking down the hardwood floors of the hall to his den which housed state-of-the-art video and stereo systems, Justin reached for an old James Bond DVD. With its Italian leather furniture and soft light, the room oozed comfort. He could easily imagine the sight of Amy lounging in his den, her lips inviting, her curves seductive. When she'd kissed him, he'd felt a ripple shoot to his groin. Her combination of power and sensuality alternately aroused his admiration and his baser instincts. He remembered she'd smelled like apple juice and sex.

A fleeting image of Amy's rugrats, cute though they may be, running wild in his peaceful domain made him twitch.

Justin shook off the images and slid the DVD into the player. He'd done her dishes and he would donate a tidy sum to her after-school program, but he was certain there was nothing else in the cards for him and Amy.

Over the next week, Justin pushed Amy from his mind and returned to his daily routine of trading on the stock market. At odd times during the day, however, her smiling face would sneak into his mind, her laughter would ring in his ears, and the remembered sensation of her lips against his would make his mouth buzz. Knowing he was scheduled to meet with the other members of the Millionaires' Club soon to deliver an update, he left his home office as soon as the market closed and drove to meet her at her after-school program. He rounded the corner just as she was finishing her class.

"*P* words," she said, dressed in pink and purple for obvious reasons. She wore a giant pipe cleaner shaped into the letter *P* on her head. Something inside him lightened at the sight of her.

"Pretty!" yelled one little girl.

"Pirate," called a boy.

"Pancake," yelled another.

And so on until Amy held up her hands. "I think

you've got it," she said. "It's time for us to *part*,"
she said, grinning as she emphasized the last word.
"You've been practically perfect. Ask your parents
to talk to you about the letter *Q*. Bye for now."

She glanced around the room as the little ones left
and her gaze landed on Justin. She met his eyes for
a long moment that hit him like a gut punch. He
walked toward her.

"You've surprised me again," she said. "Just
please tell me you're not having a recurrence of your
ulcer."

He shook his head. "I'm still clear," he said, then
remembered the original purpose for his visit. "I
asked you about your program a few times and what
the financial needs were, but you never answered."

She nodded, the *P* pipe cleaner bobbing on her
head. "And you never told me why you were interested."

"I know someone who may be interested in helping."

She brightened. "Oh, that would be great. A
blank check would be great, too," she joked, then
her eyes clouded. "A new social worker would be
terrific."

"Ms. Hatcher still causing problems?" he asked.

Amy absently pulled the makeshift *P* hat from her
head and sighed. "Every time I think we're making
progress, she throws something else in front of me.

I'm starting to wonder if she really can prevent me from adopting the kids.''

Seeing her discouragement, Justin felt an odd need to fix her situation. He shouldn't care, he thought, but for some strange reason he did. "I have some connections. Would a different lawyer help?''

"I think I need to be about ten years older and married,'' she said wryly. "Got any miracles in your pocket?''

Miracle. The word jarred him. He swallowed over a knot of tension in his throat. Miracles were too closely associated with the man upstairs for Justin's comfort. "So you're saying that if you were either ten years older or married, you would have no problem with gaining custody of the children?''

"Both would be nice,'' she said. "But either would probably work at the moment.''

"You would give up ten years for those kids?'' he asked incredulously.

"Oh, yeah,'' she said without pause. "A stable loving parent during childhood can make all the difference in the world.''

She spoke as if she'd experienced a stable loving environment. Justin felt a sliver of envy. "Did yours make a big difference for you?''

She paused and met his gaze. "I didn't have the most stable upbringing. I always viewed my background as something I would overcome, and for the most part, I think I have. I want something different for my sister's children.''

In that moment Justin felt a bone-deep connection that reverberated throughout him like shifting plates of the earth's crust during an earthquake. Justin looked into the fire of Amy's brown eyes and had the sinking sense that he was staring into the face of his purpose.

Three

──────

"No, no and no," Justin muttered as he entered O'Malley's bar later that night. "This has got to be a joke," he said to himself. To God. "I thought we had this settled. You know more than anyone that I am not a choice candidate for marriage or anything involving kids." Continuing his conversation with the Almighty, Justin made his way to the opposite end of the bar where Michael and Dylan were seated. "I realize you're perfect and you don't make mistakes, but this looks like the makings of a whopper to me."

"Justin, who are you talking to?" Dylan asked.

Justin shrugged. "You wouldn't understand."

"Did you get the research taken care of?" Dylan grinned. "I realize how much you hate to part with your green, but we've been talking about the after-school reading program for months."

"I talked to the woman in charge of the program and she gave me a figure. I think it's low, though."

Dylan and Michael stared at him in surprise.

"Low?" Michael echoed. "Does that mean you think we should kick in more?"

Justin nodded. "Yeah, and maybe we can find a ladies' club or something to sponsor the program. It needs some visibility."

Dylan shook his head. "I never thought I'd see the day when you'd suggest we give *more.* I never thought I'd hear the word *more* come out of your mouth in association with giving away your money."

Justin shrugged. Giving away another thirty thousand bucks was the least of his worries at the moment. "Things change."

Dylan frowned. "What's happening with the market lately?"

"It's up and down like it always is. Why?"

"Are you still doing okay with it?"

Better than okay, actually, Justin thought. "Most days," he said. "Why? Do you need a tip?"

"No, you just seem different."

Justin accepted the beer Michael offered him. "I am different. It's not enough for me to make money and hoard it. It never felt right to spend it for the sake of spending."

"Like me," Dylan said, his eyes glinting with dark challenge. For all his fun and games, Justin knew Dylan had a deeper side.

"Let's just say you haven't had the same hang-ups about spending that I've had," Justin said wryly and took a long swallow of beer.

"I've had more time to spend my inheritance. Up to now, my position on the board of my dear departed father's company has been nonexistent. That's about to change, though," Dylan said, his voice holding a thread of steel.

"What brought this on? The trip to Belize?" Michael asked. "Without Alisa?"

"Belize was great," Dylan said. "No paved roads, not much to do except dive and pet nurse sharks. The breeze blows all the crap from your head. Alisa may be the one that got away, but the seat on the board is mine and it's time I took ownership."

"Watch out, Remington Pharmaceuticals," Michael said, lifting his bottle in salute. "If you guys would get married and have a kid, your lives would be a helluva lot better. Speaking of which, I've got new baby pictures of Michelle."

Justin and Dylan groaned. "Just because things worked out with you and Kate doesn't mean the rest of us should get married." Dylan elbowed Justin.

"Right? Justin my man is the poster boy for a forever bachelor. Right?"

Justin paused, hearing *M* words ring in his ears like a discordant bell. Miracle. Marriage. There was a reason both came to mind at the same time. As far as Justin could see, a successful marriage took a miracle.

Dylan elbowed him again. "Right?"

"Right," Justin muttered and took another long swallow of beer. He felt Michael's curious gaze on him and had no interest in answering any more questions. "The after-school research is done, so it's your turn with the medical research," he said to Dylan.

"No problem," Dylan said. "Any other business?"

"None from me except Kate wanted me to invite you two for a cookout this weekend."

"Will Alisa be there?" Dylan asked.

"I don't know," Michael said with a shrug. "I thought you said that was over."

"It is," Dylan said in a cold voice.

"Think you can make it?" Michael asked Justin.

"I'll let you know. You never know when a family emergency can crop up."

Michael screwed up his face in confusion. "But you don't have any family."

"Exactly," Justin said, thinking of Amy and her brood. If he ended up with a family, it would definitely be an emergency. "I've got some charts I need to check. Later," he said and left the bar knowing his two friends were shaking their heads over him.

James Bond didn't do the trick tonight. After Justin studied a few stock charts, he tried a DVD, but his mind kept wandering to Amy. He told himself he would write a check for the after-school program and get the best lawyer he could find, but his thoughts sat on his brain like an undigested meal. He finally went to bed and after an hour of tossing and turning, he fell asleep.

The Scrooge dreams returned with Amy's kids featured as poor and needy. Little Emily never smiled and the sparkle vanished from the twins' eyes. Ms. Hatcher played an evil housemother, but the star fool bore an uncanny resemblance to himself. He was the one who could have changed everything and made life better for Amy and her kids, but his reluctance kept him from it, and he died before he could change his mind. Desperate to gain custody of the children, Amy agreed to marry a man who would kill her spirit.

With sickening horror, Justin watched in Technicolor as Amy took her vows to such a man. Everything within him rebelled. *No. No.* "No!"

Justin sat straight up in bed, his body in a cold

sweat. The image disturbed him so much his heart pounded with his fury.

Taking several deep breaths, he cleared his head. He rose from the bed, naked, and walked to his window. He pushed aside the curtain and drank in the moonlight.

He wasn't dead. Amy and the kids were still safe. It had only been a dream. Only a dream.

"Yeah, right," Justin muttered and shook his head. This was no dream. This was a kick in the butt. No more running. Justin knew his purpose was clear. Heaven help him, he was supposed to marry Amy.

"You think we should what?" Amy said, unable to believe her ears as she stared at Justin. He'd called her and asked to come over to speak to her after she put the kids to bed. Although she'd been tired, she agreed.

"I think we should get married," Justin said. "You said you needed a husband to get custody of the children. I'm the one you need."

Her stomach took a dip at his words. "But we don't love each other."

"Exactly," he agreed.

"We don't really even like each other."

"I don't agree with that," he said. "I like you."

Amy dipped her head and covered her face with her hand. "I like you. Let's get married," she whispered to herself. She lifted her gaze to his again. "This just doesn't make sense to me. Why would you do this? I mean, you don't need a green card or anything, do you?"

He shook his head. "No. I'm a U.S. citizen," he said, then looked away. "This is hard to explain."

"Try me," she said.

"You know how you have this strong feeling that part of your purpose in life is to help those disadvantaged preschoolers?"

Amy nodded, but the connection eluded her. "Yes."

Justin stood and shoved his hands in his pockets. He walked restlessly to the other side of her den. "Well, when I had that medical emergency, I had a weird dream and I kinda got the message that there was a reason I'm on this earth and I needed to find out what it was."

"And?" she prompted, still not making any connection.

He turned to face her. "I had another weird dream last night. This one was about you and the kids, and I think—" His jaw hardened. "I *know* I'm supposed to marry you."

"Omigoodness," she said, realization sprinkling through her like a cold rain shower. "You think marrying me is your mission."

"I wouldn't say mission," he said, wincing.

"Then what would you call it?"

"The same reason you gave me when you took me to the hospital. You are one of my reasons for being on this planet."

He spoke with such rock-solid certainty that she blinked. She almost believed him. She would have believed him if the notion had not been so totally insane. "Please don't take this the wrong way, but does your family have a history of mental illness?"

His laugh was short and wry. "No. This is more sane than it appears. You need a husband, and I need to keep my deal with the Almighty."

"I didn't make your deal with the Almighty," she pointed out.

"But you made a deal with yourself to get custody of your sister's children and give them a loving home."

He was right, and Amy wasn't sure she liked him for it. "But I don't really need you to keep the deal I made with myself."

Justin just met her glare with an uplifted brow.

"I shouldn't need you," she said, standing and looking up at him. At the moment, she didn't like his height, and she didn't like the strength in his face. She especially didn't like the fact that he seemed far less rattled by this than she did. "I don't know anything about you. I don't know if you have a criminal record."

"I don't."

"I don't know what your education level is," she continued.

"I graduated from St. Albans with a B.S. in Finance."

"I don't know if you have a drinking problem."

"I don't."

His gaze was so open and level she couldn't not believe him. Desperation trickled through her. "Children are very expensive. You may not make good money. I can't afford to feed and house another person."

His eyes flickered with a touch of humor. "I make okay money."

"Children are expensive," she insisted.

"I make very good money," he said, his left eye twitching.

Amy felt a sinking sensation in her stomach. She would bite her tongue in two before she asked the obvious question.

"I'm a millionaire," he finally, reluctantly said.

Stunned, Amy blinked at him. "Pardon?"

"Million, six zeroes," he said.

She sucked in a quick breath. "But you don't look like a millionaire."

His lips twitched. "How does a millionaire look?"

"I don't know," she said, thinking Justin was entirely too attractive. "Bill Gates?"

"He's a billionaire," he said.

"Oh," she said. "Well, when you get up to six zeroes, who's counting?"

"A billion has nine zeroes."

"It doesn't matter," she said, waving her hand and looking at him sideways. "Are you sure you're not a kook?"

He met her with the most level, sane gaze she'd ever seen. "I'm not a kook. I'm proposing marriage because—"

"—it's your mission."

"Because I believe it's one of the reasons I'm here on earth," he said. "As crazy as it sounds, I bet you can respect that."

She could respect it. "Kinda," she agreed and rubbed her eyes. She felt as if she were in some other-worldly zone.

"Saturday okay?"

Amy sighed. "For what?"

"For getting married," he said in a calm voice.

Her eyes flew open. "That's four days away."

"Did you want to do it sooner?" he asked, again in a voice so calm she questioned his sanity.

Her heart shot into her throat. "No!" She shook her head. "I don't know if I can do this. I don't know if it's a good idea. I'm going to have to think about it."

"That's okay," he said. "I had a tough time with it at first, too."

She eyed him curiously. "What did you do?"

"Shook my head, said no a lot, broke out in a cold sweat."

"You don't look at all upset now," she said, and barely kept the accusation from her voice.

"It's right," he said. "I never thought I would say that, but it is." He leaned forward and squeezed her arm. "Sleep on it, but remember Ms. Hatcher."

"I'll never sleep if I think about Ms. Hatcher."

"I can make her go away," he said in a voice liquid with sensual promise.

Amy felt something inside her shift and quiver. That last statement was the most seductive offer she'd had in ages. Talk about a dream come true. Make Ms. Hatcher go away. "I'll think about it," she told him.

"Name the date," he said as if they could have been meeting for bagels and coffee. "And I'll get it done."

His casual tone belied the formidable look in his eyes, letting Amy know he would accomplish anything he set out to do.

"G'night," he said, and brushed his fingers over her cheek before he walked out the door.

Her cheek burning from his touch, she lifted her hand to cradle it as she watched him walk to his car. A swirl of emotions spun her head round and round. She had joked about needing a husband to pass muster with Ms. Hatcher, but it had been strictly a joke. Or so she'd thought.

All her experiences with Justin had been odd from the beginning. He'd proposed marriage when she had thought a date with him would be nice. Her head began to throb. How could he be so calm? Surely he must be insane.

Pushing away from the doorjamb, she pinched the bridge of her nose. She had never pictured herself married. Then again, she hadn't pictured herself mothering her sister's three children either. Locking the door, she walked down the hall and peeked in on the twins. Jeremy's covers were already kicked off and his thumb was tucked in his mouth. Nick slept on his tummy with his mouth open.

In sleep their rowdiness quieted and they looked so sweetly vulnerable. Amy's heart caught. They'd lost so much at such a young age, she thought, feeling the grief from her sister's death wash over her.

Amy tiptoed to Jeremy's bed and pulled up the covers. She leaned down and gave him the softest breath of a kiss. He sighed, and she smiled.

Leaving the room, she closed the door behind her to check on Emily. Everything inside her tightened at the sight of the little girl. Emily clutched an old stuffed teddy bear in her hands. She was old enough to have a better idea of what she'd lost. Amy could tell Emily wanted so badly to please. Emily tried very hard to act like an adult, as if she could handle anything. It was almost as if she was afraid to cry,

Amy thought, as if she didn't trust the security of her situation enough to relax.

Amy kneeled beside Emily's bed and gently stroked the little girl's forehead. Although the idea chafed at her feminist conscience, Amy suspected Emily would benefit from a man around the house. The solidity and security offered by the right man could work wonders. But was Justin the right man? Amy wondered.

An image of Ms. Hatcher flashed through her mind, sending a cold chill through her. Amy frowned. These children needed her. They needed her love and stability, and they needed to belong to her.

Amy thought again of Justin's proposal.

A long, long time ago, when she was much younger, she had dreamed of finding a man to love, a man who would provide a safe harbor from the bad stuff life threw at her or him. Then she grew up and realized she had to make her own safe harbor, her own security; and needing a man could actually make her more vulnerable instead of less.

Long before Amy became an adult, she'd preferred to pilot her own ship. The idea of sharing the helm unsettled her. It wouldn't be her top choice.

She glanced again at Emily as she lay sweetly sleeping. Emily hadn't gotten her top choice either, Amy thought, her sister's death weighing heavily on her shoulders. Justin's proposal dangled before her, alternately seducing and repelling her.

Justin's phone rang at 6:00 a.m. Amy wanted to meet him after the kids left. She had called the school and arranged to go in late. Justin pulled into her driveway behind her Volkswagen and threaded his way through the obstacle course of Big Wheel toys on the walkway to her porch. Glancing at his watch, he rang the doorbell. He hoped to make it back to his house in time for the opening of the market. If he was going to bear some responsibility for three children, he was going to need to continue to make money.

Three children. His stomach turned. Heaven help him. Heaven had better help him, he thought, because this sure as hell hadn't been his idea.

Amy greeted him at the door, her gaze wary, her smile absent. The thought struck him that he would have liked to see her smile. She led him into the den and waved her hand at the sofa.

Justin sat. She didn't. She paced, the hem of her flippy skirt emphasizing the length of her bare legs.

"There are too many unanswered questions about your pro—" She faltered. "—suggestion that we marry."

He noticed she couldn't cough up the word proposal. If he'd had any secret romantic fantasies about marriage, he supposed he would have had a tough time with it, too. The only fantasy Justin had ever had about marriage was avoiding it. But since this was the deal from the big guy upstairs, Justin had no choice.

"What questions?"

"Where we'll live, how long we'll remain married, if you like children," she said, looking at him sideways. "I have a feeling you don't."

Justin shifted in his seat. "I don't dislike children. I haven't spent much time around them. As to where we'll live—"

"We need to live here," she said. "The kids don't need any further disruption in their lives. They've been through enough."

He nodded slowly. "I'll need a room for an office."

"I have an extra bedroom," she said and took a deep breath. "If we decide to get mar—" She stumbled over the words and shook her head. "If we decide to do this, I think we should do it for two years, then decide if we want to go our separate ways."

Justin turned the terms over in his head. "That's fine. I can get a prenup worked up to provide for you and the kids."

Amy looked at him in horror. "Oh, no! I wouldn't expect alimony or child support once this was over."

He shrugged. "I think that would be best."

She stared at him a long moment and realization crossed her face. "Oh, because it's your mission?"

Her choice of words grated on him. Amy had the kind of voice that could bring men age three to ninety-three to their knees. And her body— Justin wasn't on his knees, but he damn well wouldn't deny she aroused a distinctly *un*mission-like response in him. "One of the reasons I was put on earth," he corrected.

She nodded. "Okay. I think we need to keep the surprises to a minimum, so you need to know that I'm very independent and I don't take orders or interference well at all."

"That doesn't surprise me," he said, thinking of Amy's interplay with Ms. Hatcher. "I'm not interested in interfering or giving orders. I'm here to provide you with a vehicle to get custody of your sister's children and financial assistance."

She gave a quick nod and looked at him uneasily.

"What else?" Justin asked, impatient.

She crossed her arms under her breasts. "We need to discuss sex."

Four

Justin went completely silent. In odd random moments when he hadn't been fighting the idea that this marriage would likely kill him financially, if not mentally, he'd thought about taking Amy to bed. It was no hardship to imagine her lithe legs wrapped around his hips and her full breasts massaging his chest while he thrust inside her. She lived her life so passionately he'd like to see how that passion translated in the bedroom.

Her brown eyes wide with a mixture of uncertainty and a sliver of forbidden curiosity, she twisted her fingers together. Despite her bravado, Justin saw the vulnerability underneath. ''You've thought about sex?'' he asked, rising to his feet. It occurred to him that his sanity could well be pushed to the brink living in such close proximity to Amy and not taking her for his own.

She bit her lip. ''Uh, kinda, well, not really,'' she quickly amended. ''You can sleep in the extra bedroom. It can double as your office.''

Justin studied her for a long moment. ''We can change that later.''

Relief washed over her face. ''Yes. Right, later. I mean, we haven't even gone out on a date. I don't know you. You don't know me. We may not want each other,'' she finished in an uncharacteristically breathless voice. She looked at him as if she'd just told the biggest whopper of a lie and prayed he wouldn't call her on it.

Amy looked as if she'd just offered the biggest dare in the world and wanted to call it back. Justin wondered if the seductive images of sharing a bed with him ever danced across her mind. He knew from her covert, fleeting glances at his body that she was aware of him as a man. If she hadn't felt she needed to save her sister's children and then save the rest of the world, he suspected she might just let herself go. Even Amy must struggle with her needs.

He walked toward her and touched her chin. ''You're a beautiful woman,'' he told her. ''I want you. You want me.''

Her eyes widened and she swallowed audibly. "That's a little arrogant, don't you think?"

He shook his head. "It's not arrogance when it's the truth. You have a body that could stop and rewind the clock of every man in St. Albans."

Amy felt the tiniest ripple of pleasure, but told herself not to be flattered. "There are lots of bodies."

"Yes, but not all move like yours," he said.

He'd noticed the way she walked. By the look in his green gaze, he'd noticed quite a bit more. Her heart skipped.

"You have a fire inside you. It shows in your eyes, in your voice, in lots of ways. Men have always liked to play with fire."

The visual of Justin, naked, touching her, made her feel suddenly hot. Before she knew it, he lowered his head and pressed his mouth over hers. He rubbed his lips from side to side, then slid his tongue inside. She was both shocked and mesmerized by his boldness. He kissed her as if he were opening the doors and windows to a house that had been shut for months. For years?

Amy felt a dangerous delicious temptation to lean closer, to feel the sensation of his hard chest against her breasts, to feel more of him. Her heart hammered. Her mind scrambled. This was crazy. Too crazy for today. She had more important things to do, she told herself. The motivation for his proposal to marry washed over her like a cool spray from Nick's water gun. She pushed away.

"*This* is not the reason you want to marry me," she said. "Technically, you don't even want to marry me," she reminded him and herself. "You want to marry me because you think it's your mission."

"One of the reasons I was put on the earth," he corrected in a curt voice, his eyes as turbulent as her emotions.

"Whatever," she said. "You didn't suggest we marry because of your overwhelming love and passion for me. I won't pretend that you did."

"Just as your agreement to marry me is not based on your feeling that you can't live without me," he said.

"I haven't agreed."

"You haven't? Who's pretending now?"

Amy scowled. At the moment, she didn't like him. She didn't like him at all for being right. "All right, dammit, I'll marry you. For the children. I may be a little attracted to you, but that doesn't mean I'm interested in going to bed with you," she said, and tamped down her loud protesting inner voice of truth. "I have my priorities straight here. I'd appreciate it if you'd do the same. I'm not marrying you to save me or take care of me. I learned a long time ago to do that for myself."

His eyes darkened. "Then we're well-matched. I learned the same lesson."

A dozen questions flitted through her mind. What had forced Justin to learn the same hard lesson she had? She burned to ask.

Justin glanced at his watch. "Speaking of priorities, I need to go. The market opens in fifteen minutes. When do you want to get married?"

Her head spun with his businesslike tone. "I'm not sure. Friday or Saturday," she said. "Or next week," she added at the same time she knew the sooner she did the deed, the sooner she would gain custody.

"I'd rather not do it during market hours," Justin said.

Amy nodded. She may never have envisioned herself as Cinderella, but this was a little chilly for even her. "Saturday, then," she said, grimly reminding herself this was for two years. She would do just about anything for two years to keep her sister's children safe.

"Saturday. I'll be in touch," he said and walked out the door.

Amy could have sworn she felt the weight of a noose settle around her neck.

Amy and Justin met downtown for blood tests and to make application for the marriage license. Before she knew it, Saturday arrived. Amy broke into a sweat. *What was she doing!*

Emily knocked on Amy's bedroom door and bounded into the room. She jumped onto Amy's bed, her eyes sparkling with excitement. "We're getting married today!"

Amy gulped and mustered a smile. "Yes, we are."

"Do you want me to make pancakes for breakfast?"

Amy's stomach shrank at the thought. "Oh, that's a lovely offer, but I'm so excited I don't think I could eat." Excited wasn't the most accurate word choice, but Amy refused to quibble with herself this morning. "Could you make pancakes another time?"

Emily dimpled. "Yeah, when Justin moves in."

Amy's stomach twisted. "Right. Great idea," she said and rose from the bed. "You chose your dress last night and the boys' clothes are laid out on their beds. How would you like your hair?"

"Ponytail," Emily said. "With a ribbon?"

"Can do," Amy said, grabbing a brush from the bureau.

Emily stood in front of her staring into the mirror as Amy brushed her hair. "Are you going to wear a long white dress like my Barbie doll has?"

What to wear had been the last thing on her mind. "Uh, no, sweetie. People who wear long dresses have usually planned their weddings a long time in advance.''

"Longer than a week?" Amy said.

Try four days, Amy thought. "Exactly."

"Then what are you going to wear?"

Amy still didn't know. Her brain felt as if it were playing hopscotch. Guessing at Justin's ring size, she'd bought his gold band yesterday. She'd ordered a few flowers from the florist which she planned to pick up on her way to the judge's chambers. She hoped ice cream and the sheet cake she'd bought from the bakery would distract the children from the lack of true emotion surrounding the occasion.

Emily tugged on her sleeve. "What are you going to wear?"

Still at a loss, Amy smiled. "A surprise," she said, and it would be a surprise to herself, too.

"This is what you call a family emergency?" Dylan asked as he entered the hall outside the judge's chambers.

"Any wedding would be to me," Justin said. He'd spent most of the night arguing with the Almighty, trying to convince Him that Justin was not a good choice for this job. It was the strangest coincidence. The thunderstorm had gotten louder and louder the more Justin had argued. When he finally shut up in defeat, so had the storm.

Coincidence, he told himself again, but he knew what he had to do. Marry Amy Monroe.

"I still don't understand this. You made a deal with God." Dylan shook his head. "Are you sure they didn't mess up your anesthesia during your emergency surgery? Maybe your brain was affected—"

"You're here to be a witness," Justin said. "If there's one thing I don't need right now, it's a psychoanalysis from St. Albans's *numero uno* babe magnet."

"Okay, but I have to ask, are you sure she isn't marrying you for your money?"

"I told you. This is not about money. It's about custody." He glanced up and felt a slight easing at the sight of Michael and his wife, Kate.

Michael wore an expression of subdued admiration. "You sure know how to take the fuss out of a wedding. No church, no reception."

"Cheap," Kate added with disapproval.

"Expedient," Justin said, grinding his teeth. "Thank you for coming."

"Oh, my goodness!" Kate said as Amy rounded the corner balancing a bouquet, and holding a hand of each twin. Dressed in a pink frilly dress with a slightly lopsided ponytail, Emily brought up the rear with a miniature bouquet.

Justin's heart stopped. Amy was dressed in a cream-colored lace dress that whispered and sighed over her curves with a hem that kissed her shapely calves. Her hair was pulled up in a topknot with a spray of baby's breath, but a few unruly curls escaped. Her cheeks flushed, she gnawed on her bottom lip in nervousness. She was his bride. The knowledge filled him with surprising warmth.

"The children are adorable," Kate whispered.

Dylan cleared his throat. "Why didn't you tell me she was—"

Justin blinked. "Was what?"

Dylan shrugged. "Well, hell, she's stacked better than the City Library. I gotta tell you," he said with a nudge. "This marriage may not be such a hardship after all."

He had no idea, Justin thought. Amy's gaze finally landed on him, skimming over him from head to toe, then returning to his eyes. If her eyes could talk, they would have said "Are we insane?"

He walked toward her. "You look beautiful," he said, instinctively taking her chilled hand in his.

"Thank you," she said, her gaze dropping to his shirt collar. "You look very nice, too."

He sensed she was trying to hide her apprehension.

"Emily helped," she said.

"You look pretty, too," he said to the little girl.

Emily grinned hugely. "Do you like our flowers?"

"They're almost as pretty as you."

"I gotta go to the bathroom," Nicholas said, shifting from one foot to the other.

Jeremy tugged at his collar. "Aunt Amy says we get cake and ice cream when we get home."

Amy gave a pained smile. "The reward system at work."

"Good idea for the kids."

"And me," she muttered. "I should take Nicholas before we have an accident."

"Let Justin take him," Kate interjected, stepping forward. "I'm Kate Hawkins. This is my husband, Michael, and friend, Dylan. Why don't you guys take the other two children for a drink of water at the fountain while I help the bride?"

Michael's face crinkled in confusion. "Help the bride do what?"

Kate rolled her eyes. "Get ready for the ceremony."

"The ceremony won't take five minutes, so—"

"Sweetheart, would you please take the children to get a drink at the water fountain?"

He blinked. "Sure. Come on," he said to the kids.

Nicholas shifted again. "I gotta go."

Amy didn't want an accident. "So should I."

Justin surprised her by stepping forward and taking Nick's hand. "I'll take him."

Amy paused in surprise. "Are you sure you know how—"

Justin lifted an eyebrow. "I think we can muddle through."

She watched them leave. "It may sound crazy, but I have a hard time believing Justin has ever helped a three-year-old visit the bathroom."

"Given his aversion to children, I'd be surprised, too," Kate said.

"Aversion?" Amy echoed, swerving to look at Kate. The slim brunette with curious warm eyes wore an easy air of sophistication.

Kate gave a wry grin. "That was pre-emergency surgery Justin. He seems to have changed. Some," she added grudgingly. "Would you like one last dash to the powder room?"

Amy nodded and walked toward the ladies' room. "So what was the pre-emergency surgery Justin like?"

"Ultracareful. I always got the impression he had no intention of ever getting married or having children."

Amy's stomach began to twist and turn. "He doesn't like children?"

"I can't say that," Kate said. "He's crazy about our baby, Michelle." She sighed. "These three guys have hidden depths. Maybe it has something to do with spending all that time at the Granger Home for Boys. Maybe—"

Amy's jaw dropped. "Justin lived at the Granger Home for Boys?"

Kate nodded, saving the bouquet from Amy's limp hand. "Oh, yes. All three of them lived there. You didn't know?"

Amy shook her head, trying to make sense of the new information. It reinforced her feeling that there was more to him than what he had revealed. If he'd lived at Granger then he had firsthand experience with the reason Amy wanted custody of the children and why she felt so strongly about making a safe place for them.

"But you know he trades stocks and is very successful at it?" Kate asked.

"Yes. When he suggested that we get married, I told him I couldn't afford another mouth to feed and he told me he was a millionaire."

"This has happened so fast I bet he didn't have time to get you to sign a prenup," Kate said, extremely amused by the idea.

"I signed it the same afternoon we got our blood taken. It was more than generous." She met Kate's gaze. "I'm not interested in his money." She hesitated revealing her feelings. "I'm marrying Justin to ease the process for gaining custody of the children. To be perfectly honest, I've never set my sights on marrying any man, let alone a rich man. It always appeared to me that a woman pays in self-esteem and autonomy for that decision."

Kate stared at her in surprise, then smiled. "I think you may be very good for Justin."

Looking in the mirror, Amy felt a swirl of contradicting emotions. In less than fifteen minutes, she would be a wife. "This marriage may not last long," she confessed in a whisper.

Kate gave her a considering glance. "Michael and I didn't marry under the best circumstances and I didn't think our marriage would last."

"You changed your mind?"

Kate smiled. "Michael changed my mind. For what it's worth, Michael says Justin is a stand-up guy. When the chips are down and everyone else has fallen, Justin is the one who'll still be standing by you."

That sounded so incredibly tempting to Amy. Sometimes she felt she'd spent her life being the stand-up woman. Her palms damp, she rubbed them on the sides of her dress. *For the children,* she repeated to herself like a mantra. She licked her lips. "I guess it's time."

Kate looked at her with sympathy in her eyes. "We'd already planned a cookout this afternoon. Why don't we let it double as a wedding party?"

"I already have cake and ice cream at home for the kids," Amy said.

"Bring it," Kate said. "Hey, it's one less meal you'll have to cook. And my little girl will worship your children because they can walk and run."

"Thanks for the offer. Let's get through the ceremony first,'' Amy said, feeling an overwhelming urge to hike up her dress and run.

"It'll be short,'' Kate told her in a reassuring tone as she returned the bouquet. "You look beautiful.''

Amy and Kate left the ladies' room and encountered the rest of the group in the hallway. Justin caught Amy's eye and strode to her side. "Ready?''

No. She nodded.

"I'm not an axe murderer,'' he assured her. "Just for my own peace of mind, you're not related to Lorena Bobbit, that woman who cut off her husband's…''

Amy almost laughed. "No. Did everything go okay with Nick?''

"No problem. Just unzipped and put him in front of the urinal and let it fly.''

Amy felt a tug on her dress and looked down to find Nick smiling broadly. "Justin showed me a new way to pee. It's a lot better than sitting. Jeremy wants to try it now.''

Amy looked up at Justin. "Thank you for your contribution. I think,'' she added.

"It was nothing,'' he said. "Guy-thing. You ready?''

No, but I'd really like to get it over with. "Let's do it,'' she said gamely and walked into the judge's chambers.

Judge Bishop, a friendly man in his fifties, had just arrived from a morning golf game, jubilant over his score. "This is a great day to get married," he said as he was introduced to Amy. "I shot a score of sixty-eight and left the rest of my foursome in the dust."

Amy pushed her lips into a smile, wondering if she would remember that little tidbit in years to come.

"I'll keep this short, so you can get to the good stuff," Judge Bishop said with a broad wink.

Amy felt her smile falter. Oxygen was suddenly in short supply. Justin continued to hold her hand.

"Do you take this man…" the judge began, and Amy feared she might hyperventilate. Out of desperation, she did something she rarely did except for children. She pretended. She pretended she was talking to an order taker at Burger Doodle.

"…to have and to hold from this day forward for richer and poorer…"

Amy translated, *Do you want mustard and pickles on your burger?*

"I do," she whispered.

"In sickness and in health…"

Do you want fries with that?

"I do," she whispered again.

"Till death do you part?"

And a hot apple pie?

"I do," she said, firmly aloud.

From the corner of her mind, she heard Justin answer the same way she had. The bubble surrounding her game of pretend began to deflate when the judge asked for the rings. Emily bounced to her side with Justin's ring attached to a ribbon on her little nosegay.

With trembling fingers, Amy pushed the band on Justin's finger and repeated the words, "With this ring, I thee wed."

She stared at the wide gold band with the diamond solitaire Justin placed on her third finger and heard his voice repeat the same words. The weight of it was unfamiliar. The metal felt cold against her skin. She was enormously glad she wouldn't have to say anything else because she was too stunned by the ring to make a sound. The ring was definitely not a cheeseburger with mustard and pickles, fries and an apple pie.

She glanced up to find him staring at his own gold band in shock.

"You may now kiss the bride," the judge said.

Justin met her gaze and she had the slipping, sliding feeling that she had just danced with fate, done the polka with eternity. Though she may have pretended it, those were not Burger Doodle vows she'd just made.

Justin lowered his mouth to hers, and all her pretending was over.

Five

Amy felt as if she'd spent the day at the circus, minus the fun. After the ceremony, everyone met at the Hawkins's for a barbecue. The children enjoyed themselves immensely and Amy relaxed a tad until Dylan gave a second toast. It was definitely time to leave. The children were on such a sugar high from the cake and ice cream that they skipped their afternoon naps and "helped" Justin move in.

She prepared a gourmet dinner of peanut butter and jelly sandwiches and chicken noodle-o's soup. God finally smiled on her when all the kids tuckered out early and she put them to bed. Leaning against the wall in the darkened hallway, she closed her eyes and let out a long sigh. The only sounds she heard were the faint ticking of the downstairs clock and the rustling of computer and modem cords as Justin continued to set up his office.

She rubbed her thumb over the still unfamiliar wide gold band on her finger. Needing solitude, but unwilling to go to her bedroom just yet, she walked downstairs and lay down on the sofa in the quiet den.

Moments later, Justin appeared in the doorway. A dark silhouette with broad shoulders, he emanated a quiet strength merely by his presence. Amy wondered if the strength was in her imagination. There was so much she didn't know about him.

"One question," he said, his voice low and intimate in the darkness. "With those kids helping, how do you get anything done?"

She smiled at the dismay in his voice. "The rule of thumb is if you're female, you add an hour to your estimated completion time for every child helping you."

He strolled toward her and looked down at her. "And if you're male?"

"Add eight," Amy said.

"Eight?"

Amy nodded, keeping her head on the pillow. "Eight for every child helping you. It's unfortunate, but men have difficulty focusing on more than one thing at a time. I'm not sure if it's due to hormones or the Y chromosome.''

''Where did you learn this fun fact?''

''Oh, it's well known. Ask any married mother.'' She took a breath and looked up at him, a male stranger in her house. Her husband. Her heart jumped. She closed her eyes, thinking he might not affect her so much if she didn't look at him. ''Is part of the reason you offered to marry me because you once lived at the Granger Home for Boys?''

''Kate's been talking.''

''A little,'' Amy said, wondering why his voice felt like it rubbed over her like a forbidden caress. ''It wasn't all bad. You didn't answer my question.''

''My experience at Granger may have influenced me, but it wasn't the deciding factor.''

''Your *mission* was the deciding factor,'' she said, reminding herself as much as him.

Feeling his hand close around her ankle, she opened her eyes in surprise.

''Do I have your attention?'' he asked.

''Yes, and my foot.''

''Good,'' he said, not releasing her ankle. ''If we're going to live together, we need to come to an understanding about a few things.''

The slow motion of his thumb on the inside of her ankle distracted her. ''What things?''

''Your annoying description of why I proposed to

you," he said, holding firm when she wiggled her foot.

"Mission," she said. "What's wrong with that?"

"I said it was part of my purpose," he corrected through gritted teeth.

"Semantics. Would you let go of my foot?"

"When we reach our understanding," he said. His thumb and middle finger formed a human ankle cuff. The sight of his hand on her bare skin disrupted her.

"You want me to call it your purpose," she said.

"That would be better."

"We understand each other," she said, noticing that his finger began its mesmerizing motion again. "You can let go of my foot."

"Not quite," he said. "We don't understand each other yet. We don't know each other."

Amy gave a little test jerk of her foot to no avail. "Your point?"

"We don't have to make this situation a living hell for each other."

She met his gaze, wondering how one of his fingers could make her insides turn to warm liquid. "And how do we accomplish that?"

"We get to know each other," he said in a voice that brought to mind hot nights and tangled sheets.

She wanted to say she didn't have time to get to know him, but he chose that moment to skim a fingertip up the sole of her foot. Her stomach dipped.

"For the sake of peace of mind," he said.

She searched her mind for a reason to disagree, but her brain had turned to sludge. "Okay."

"We start tonight. I ask you a question and then you ask me one."

"Truth or dare," Amy said, not at all sure this was a good idea.

"Just truth," Justin said.

"Okay, ladies first," she said, shifting into a more upright position, ready to ask the question that had been burning a hole in her mind all day. "How did you end up at Granger?"

His jaw tightened. "My mother was unable to care for me."

"Why?" she asked.

He shook his head. "That's two," he said. "My turn. The first time I met you I asked you to dinner. If you hadn't been caring for your sister's children, what would your answer have been?"

Amy squirmed slightly. It was much more fun asking questions than answering them. "Gosh, that was a long time ago, almost two months ago. And I got pretty distracted when you had the ulcer attack," she said, trying to lead him away from his original question.

"What would your answer have been?"

Amy made a face. "Maybe."

"Your answer would have been maybe," he said. Amy frowned at his disbelieving voice. How had

he known she'd been intrigued by him from the beginning? "Okay," she admitted. "Maybe yes."

"I'm not familiar with what 'maybe yes' means.
I'm sure it's my Y chromosome. Could you trans-
late?" he asked, massaging her ankle.

Amy glowered at him. "It means yes. You were
interested in my after-school program. How could I
resist?" she rhetorically asked. She told herself
she'd been completely unaffected by his watchful,
intelligent green eyes, chiseled facial features and
those broad shoulders that looked like they could
carry any problem a woman might face. Amy wondered why she felt as if she were back in pretending
land again.

He nodded and released her foot. Her ankle felt
surprisingly bereft. "Sleep tight, Amy," he said and
turned to leave.

Oddly miffed, she sprang up from the couch.
"Sleep tight? That's it?"

He glanced around at her with one lifted eyebrow.
"I stuck to my proposal. One question," he said.
"Did you want something else?"

His voice was like a velvet invitation over her
skin. The way he looked at her reminded her she
was a woman. She fought the urge to rub away the
effect of his touch on her ankle. She crossed her
arms over her chest and shook her head. "No.
G'night."

After watching him leave the room, she stood

there for several moments, trying to regain her calm, but it had vanished like Houdini. She climbed the stairs and entered her bedroom, stripped and pulled on a cotton nightshirt. As she climbed into bed, Amy tried not to think about the fact that a dark, masculine stranger lay just down the hall from her, and that the dark masculine stranger was her husband.

Justin lay in a lumpy bed in a room one half the size of his walk-in closet. His *bride,* who possessed a body designed to make him burn with lust every wretched night of his immediate future, lay approximately twenty-five feet away. He hoped God was very happy.

Justin was waiting for the peace he'd expected in exchange for fulfilling at least the initial phase of his purpose on earth. Instead, when he closed his eyes, he saw Amy sprawled out on the sofa downstairs, her hair a riot, her eyes filled with sensual curiosity. Even her ankles got to him, slim, creamy and delicate. He had wanted to trace his finger up her calf to the inside of her thigh and higher still.

Justin wondered if hell could possibly be worse than being married to a woman who resented you and needed you at the same time. He stifled a groan. Then he thought of the kids and the tight feeling in his chest eased slightly. Even though they were nosey, noisy and expensive, he wouldn't wish his upbringing on them. He admired Amy for her commitment and sacrifice. In a strange way, their shared goal bound them together.

All fine and good, he thought as he rolled over on the soft mattress, but he wondered if the next two years would drive him quietly insane and totally broke. That image kept him awake for hours.

Justin finally drifted into a dreamless sleep. A sound permeated his deep slumber. He buried his head further in the pillow, but the sound persisted. It wrenched at something deep inside him before he even identified it.

A child was crying. Justin sat upright and listened. "Nick."

Hustling out of bed, he ran into the hall and collided with Amy. He instinctively closed his arms around her when she began to fall. She gasped, and he dimly noted her breasts heaving pleasurably against his chest. Her fingers closed around his biceps.

"Omigod, are you naked?" she whispered.

"Boxers," he said, feeling the brush of her thighs against his. Nick let out another sob that would rip the heart from Atilla the Hun. "Nick's crying."

"I know," she whispered, disentangling herself. "He does this every few nights. It used to be every night. I think it's part of his way of working out his grief. I'll take care of it."

She carefully opened the door and moved quickly to his side. Quietly following, Justin watched her touch his arm and whisper to him. "It's okay, baby."

"Aunt Amy?" he asked in a husky voice, giving a hiccup.

"It's me," she said, stroking his face. "You're okay."

"I had a scary dream. I was at Chica's Pizza and everybody left me. I was all by myself and I couldn't find you."

"That's not gonna happen," she said. "You're stuck with me. Do you want to get a drink of water and use the bathroom?"

He nodded. "Can I pee the way Justin taught me?"

Justin smothered a chuckle and stepped forward. "Yep, and I'll help," he said, offering his hand to Nick.

Catching Amy's look of surprise, Justin guided the wobbly child to the bathroom and held him up so he could drink from the faucet, then helped him finish with the toilet. He returned the boy to Amy.

"He has never shown this much motivation to use the bathroom," Amy murmured.

"That Y chromosome comes in handy when you least expect it."

She shook her head, but smiled. "I'll tuck him in."

"What about me?" he asked, figuring he could blame his audacity on the late hour.

"What about you?" she asked.

"When are you going to tuck me in?" he asked. "It's my first night here. I might have a bad dream."

"Count sheep," she said.

Justin wondered how such a woman who was so warm and generous with the kids could be so heartless with him. He knew, however, that Amy resented needing him to accomplish her goal.

And so began the inauspicious, passionless marriage of Amy and Justin. The following day was a flurry of activity with Justin continuing to get *help* from the children setting up his computer. The boys fastened themselves to him like glue, and in the corner of her mind, Amy wondered about them growing attached to him.

That evening, he met her again in the den. This time she was ready for him. She crossed her legs Indian style so he wouldn't work his voodoo on her ankle again. "Why couldn't your mother take care of you? Was she sick?"

He walked behind the couch and touched her hair. She turned her head to look at him.

"She wasn't physically ill," he said. "Or mentally ill in the true sense. She just couldn't manage money. Every month she would receive a check for child support from my father and she would spend it all within three days. Bills piled up, the landlord threw us out, our electricity was cut off too many times to count. She would stay out all night some-

times. A neighbor found out and called social ser-
vices. Not long after that, I started living at Granger.''

Her heart twisted at the picture he'd drawn of his
childhood. Amy's upbringing may not have been a
fairy tale, but her mother was usually around even
if she'd passed out drunk more nights than not.

''Neglect,'' she murmured. ''How old were—''

He shook his head. ''—one question. My turn.
What made you decide you wanted to change the
world?''

Her lips twitched. More than one friend had
teased her for her crusader orientation. ''I don't have
to change the world, really,'' she said. ''Although
that would be nice. I can just be satisfied working
on my little corner of it.''

Justin shrugged. ''You didn't answer my question. What made you decide—''

Amy waved her hand. ''Okay. When I was about
thirteen or fourteen, I observed that there were two
kinds of people in the world. People who make a
difference and people who waste their lives. I saw
too many people waste their lives to know I didn't
want that for myself.''

She could see the follow-up questions on his face,
but he just nodded. ''Okay, good night.''

The same irritation spiced with indignation she'd
felt last night prickled through her. He clearly had
more control and less curiosity than she did, blast

him. "Good night," she said, trying to keep the edge from her voice.

Justin glanced over his shoulder. "It'll be a helluva lot better for both of us when you stop being angry that you accepted my help. Sleep tight," he said and climbed the stairs.

Amy gaped after him. *Angry! Me, angry?* She had half a mind to chase him up those stairs and show him what *angry* was. While it may be true that she was exasperated with the legal system, and she resented the fact that getting married would make it easier to gain custody of the children, she wasn't angry with Justin. She wasn't pleased she'd had to marry a stranger, and the marriage was turning her life upside down, but her anger was directed at lawyers and a certain social worker. Not Justin. Right.

Monday presented the usual problems associated with the first day of the week. Justin left early saying he would work at his home during market hours until he got the kinks out of his new computer system. Emily missed the school bus, Nick had an accident, and when Amy arrived at school, she faced a class with so many children sick from a virus her classroom should have been quarantined.

That evening Justin didn't arrive home by dinnertime, making Amy wonder if he was experiencing buyer's remorse. Probably sensing her edginess, the kids chose that night for a full-fledged arsenic hour.

Topping it off with a cherry, Ms. Hatcher arrived at the door. Amy just managed to beat Emily to the door. Moving her lips into what she hoped looked like a smile, Amy opened the door and greeted the woman.

"Good evening, Ms. Hatcher. Do come in. You've arrived just at dinner time again," Amy said, cheerfully trying to keep the edge from her voice.

"I nearly tripped over the tricycle on the side-walk," Ms. Hatcher grumbled as they headed away from the foyer.

"I'm so sorry," Amy said, thinking it was a shame the woman hadn't broken her neck. As soon as the thought whispered across her mind, she winced, hoping she wouldn't get struck by lightning. "I wish I could offer you dessert, but—"

Amy heard the front door open and close. She glanced past Ms. Hatcher to see Justin. Her stomach flipped. She and Justin hadn't prepared for this. She didn't know whether to kiss him or tell him to leave. A visit from Ms. Hatcher was too important to mud-dle, and she and Justin hadn't even made plans. "Justin," she said, biting her lip, "Ms. Hatcher is here."

"Hi, Justin!" the twins chorused.

Waving to the boys, he quickly surveyed the

scene and walked toward Amy. "Nice to see you, Ms. Hatcher. Has Amy had a chance to share our news with you?"

The woman frowned as Justin put his arm around Amy. "News? What news?"

"We were married over the weekend. You can be among the first to congratulate us."

Ms. Hatcher's eyes nearly popped out of her head. "You're married? So quickly?"

He nuzzled Amy's hair, surprising the dickens out of her. "When it's right, it's best not to wait. Amy and I have each other, and the children have two parents."

"B-b-but, what about your honeymoon?"

Amy stiffened.

Justin skimmed his fingers down the sensitive inside of her arm and laced his long fingers through hers. "I'd like nothing more than to have my bride all to myself, but we thought it would be much better for the children not to leave them for a while." He squeezed Amy's hand a little too tightly as if to wake her from a trance. "Right, sweetheart?"

Amy nodded. "Right. The children have really taken to Justin, and I think it will be wonderful for both the boys and Emily to have a successful male role model in the home." Amy resisted the urge to put her finger down her throat. Give her pearls, heels and a vacuum cleaner and she could have been a 1950s television wife.

"Well, we will need to interview Mr. Langdon and perform our routine check," Ms. Hatcher said, clearly still struggling with her surprise.

Amy battled another dart of anxiety. What if there was something detrimental in Justin's past?

"Feel free. It's important for you to do your job," Justin said and to Amy's ears he might as well have said "Have at it, you nosey hag. I have nothing to hide."

She needed to get Ms. Hatcher out the door. She wouldn't be able to sustain the 1950s television wife persona much longer. "Was there anything else you needed this evening?" she asked.

"Not that I can think—"

"Then let me escort you to the door," Justin said. Amy wondered if he'd noticed her squeaky tone of voice. She suspected he knew how tense she was.

He deliberately pried Amy's fingers from his and took Ms. Hatcher's arm.

"Thank you," she said under her breath and felt her shoulder twitch when the woman turned away. A moment later, it twitched again.

Emily looked at her curiously. "Aunt Amy, why are you moving your arm funny?"

"I don't know, sweetie," she said, rolling her shoulder. "I think I'm a little tense." *Or maybe I'm allergic to Ms. Hatcher.*

Justin returned and met Amy's gaze. "She's gone."

Amy heaved a sigh of relief and rushed toward him. She impulsively hugged him and pressed her mouth against his, then pulled backed. "I cannot tell you how much I appreciate you showing up at the exact moment you did. Thank you. Thank you. I owe you a big one."

Justin glanced down her body with a sensual once-over, then seared her from the inside out with a warm, yet challenging gaze. "How big a one do you owe me?"

Oops. Amy felt her heart skip. She wondered if she'd traded the Wicked Witch of the West, Ms. Hatcher, for the Big Bad Wolf, her husband.

Six

___

Amy felt a tugging sensation on her shorts. She glanced down at Jeremy.

"What's a honeymoon?" he asked.

Her shoulder twitched again. "It's when the bride and groom take a special trip."

His eyes lit up. "To Disney World?"

"Yes, or the beach. It could be anywhere."

"I think we should go on a honeymoon!" he said.

"Yeah!" Nicholas chorused. "Let's go on a honeymoon."

Emily rolled her eyes in sisterly superiority. "We can't go on a honeymoon, you guys. Kids don't get to go. Just grown-ups."

Jeremy frowned. "That stinks."

"Exactly," Amy said. "We would miss you too much, so we're not going on a honeymoon."

Jeremy's face cleared. "Okay. Do we have any cookies?"

"Did you eat your peas?" Amy asked, glancing at the table.

Jeremy squirmed. "Two of 'em." He slid a glance toward Justin. "Do you eat peas?"

"Yes, I do. Peas make you tall."

Jeremy's eyes widened and he took in Justin's height. "They do?"

Nick smiled. "I'm gonna be tall," he said. "I eat 'em with catsup."

Amy turned away from the kids and whispered to Justin, "Peas make you tall?"

"Can't hurt," he said with a shrug, and nodded toward the kitchen table. "It worked."

Amy turned around to see Jeremy eating his peas. "Amazing," she muttered. "Teaching the twins the boy-way to pee, scaring away Ms. Hatcher, and now getting Jeremy to eat his vegetables." She glanced at him. "I'd almost have to recommend you for sainthood."

"Oh, no," Justin said, raking her from head to toe with another glance that turned up her body temperature. "I guarantee I'm no saint. I look forward to collecting the big one."

Amy tried very hard to prevent her mind from

venturing into forbidden territory at his mention of the big one, but she would just bet Justin had…. Her face heated. She definitely needed to chill out. "Ice cream," she said brightly. "Who wants ice cream?"

Later that evening, Amy collapsed on the sofa in the den and closed her eyes. She heard Justin's footsteps and felt his presence in the room, but kept her eyes closed. There was an air of expectancy between them. She ran her thumb over her wedding band, then lifted her hand in the air. "Why did you get me such a nice ring? You could have gotten me cubic zirconia."

A brief silence followed. "How do you know it's not cubic zirconia?"

Amy popped her eyes open and stared at him. "Is it?"

His lips lifted in a wry half-smile. "No, it's not. I've been called a tightwad, but even I know it wouldn't be appropriate in this case."

She pulled herself up into a sitting position. "In a way, it would be very appropriate," she said. "Our marriage isn't normal."

He raised his eyebrows. "From what I hear, normal isn't always that great. The ring is more a reflection of you. I think you're genuine, so I think you deserve a genuine stone."

Touched, Amy looked down at her ring, and the meaning of the band grew on her. It was one of nicest, sincerest things a man had said to her and it made her feel vulnerable and a bit confused. She slowly lifted her gaze to him again, too aware of her confusing feelings, too aware of the way his jeans fit his body and long legs like a lover's hand. Her fingers itched to trace the slight wave of his hair and the hard line of his chin. Her mind longed to know the secrets behind his eyes. Dangerous, she thought, and searched her mind for a safe subject. "How was your day at the market?"

"Profitable," he said. "My turn. What is a big one?"

Her stomach did a little dip. Not that again, she thought. "It's a relative term. Your idea of big and my idea of big could be very far apart."

"What about duration?" he asked, sitting beside her.

Amy's heart picked up at his nearness. "Again, relative. I would guess no longer than, say, three minutes," she said, betting that three minutes of anything with Justin couldn't get her into too much trouble. Three minutes wasn't long enough to— Well, if three minutes was long enough, it wouldn't be very good. Her cheeks began to feel hot again.

"Three minutes," he said.

She nodded, mesmerized by the intent look in his eyes.

"Of anything?"

"Within reason," she said.

"Okay, I want the big one tonight," Justin said.

Her heart stuttered. "So soon?"

"I told you I wasn't a saint."

She swallowed. "But if you use up the big one, you won't have it for later."

"That's okay. Three minutes," he said.

She swallowed again. "Three minutes of what?"

"One thing," he said. "A three-minute kiss."

Amy's breath stopped in her throat. "That's a long kiss."

"Depends on who you're kissing," he said and leaned closer.

Her heart hammering, Amy inched backward.

"Scared?"

Pride roared through her. She lifted her chin. "Of course not, it's just a kiss. Should I get a timer from the kitchen?"

He chuckled. "I have a timer on my watch. I can set it," he said, and pushed a few buttons on his watch.

Then he looked at her, lifted his hands to slide his fingers through her hair and pulled her to him like a bunch of flowers. As if the clock weren't ticking, as if he were in no rush, he rubbed his lips back and forth against hers, savoring the sensation of her mouth.

She sighed at his relaxed approach. He suckled her bottom lip into his, rimming just the inside with the tip of his tongue. Secret longings twisted inside her. Gently tilting her head, he stroked her scalp with his fingertips while his tongue toyed with hers.

Her breasts glanced his chest and his groan vibrated sensually inside her. Deepening the kiss, he trailed one hand down to massage her jaw.

A burning sensation built inside her. Inhaling his musky, male scent, she struggled with a restless need to take his mouth the way he was taking hers, to touch him, to get closer. She balled her fists to keep from reaching for him at the same time she opened her mouth farther for his exploration.

In a second, the tone of the kiss changed from lazy to hot and compelling. He tasted like sex. Consuming her lips, he slid his hand down her throat to her arm, urging her to touch him.

Her breasts felt swollen and her nerve endings buzzed with forbidden excitement. Her mind clouded with arousal, she leaned into him and lifted her hand to his shoulder. His strength lured her. Amy had told herself she always had to be the strong one, but his power surrounded him like a cloak, and the temptation to lean into him and absorb his power was overwhelming. Justin meshed his chest against hers, and the heat of him aroused her further. His fingertips grazed the side of her breasts, and Amy suckled his tongue deep into her mouth.

She burned. She wanted. He rubbed his thumb in a teasing movement on the outer edge of her breast. She wanted more. She wanted him to slide his hand under her shirt and cup her fully. She wanted him to rub her aching nipple, to take it into his mouth.

His finger edged closer and a moan vibrated in her throat. As if he could read her need, he moved slowly, ever closer to the stiff peak of her breast. So close.

Beyond the rush of arousal crashing in her bloodstream, she heard a tiny pinging sound. Justin paused and swore under his breath. The pinging grew louder. He pulled back, and she fought the instinct to follow his mouth with hers.

The alarm, Amy realized. The alarm had gone off. Three minutes had passed. Her body screaming for more, she disentangled herself and inhaled sharp breaths. The sound of her breaths mingled with his in the darkness like a hot sultry night, emphasizing the thick atmosphere of impending intimacy.

Rattled by the way he'd affected her in just *three minutes,* she stood and wrapped her arms around her waist. She knew without a doubt that the way he tempted her was more than sexual; it was also emotional. The knowledge frightened her so much her hands shook. She clasped either arm to halt the trembling.

Her mind whirled. She had always suspected Justin could be dangerous to her. His combination of strength, intelligence, and the underlying thread of his sexuality was entirely too compelling. She closed her eyes to calm down.

He touched her shoulder and she nearly jumped out of her skin. "Don't!" she whispered and held her breath. She was more sensitive than if she'd been sunburned. "Please don't touch me."

He didn't touch her, but his low murmur was almost worse. "Okay," he said, so close to her ear, she could almost feel his lips again. A shiver ran through her. "I want to do much more than touch you. I want to listen to your body instead of that damn alarm. I want to kiss you all over, but three minutes wouldn't be enough time. Three hours wouldn't be either," he said and the sensual promise of his words might as well have been an intimate caress in all her secret places.

"Sleep tight," he said, but it sounded more like a sexy taunt or challenge. Amy suspected she wouldn't be sleeping well tonight. She had grossly underestimated the effect he had on her.

An hour later, Justin rolled over for the twentieth time. He was still aroused. Although he'd sensed Amy was a passionate woman, he'd had no idea her response would burn his control to cinders so quickly.

Every time he closed his eyes, he tasted her lips and remembered the sensation of her tongue. He felt her breasts begging for his touch. He recalled the way her restlessness signaled her arousal. Every little move she'd made had wound his spring tighter and tighter. It would have taken so little to go further, to push up her shirt and stare at her full breasts before he tasted her nipples with his tongue. It would have taken so little for him to push aside her shorts and feel the inviting moistness between her thighs.

She was his wife.

But she might as well not be.

Giving in to insomnia, Justin pushed back the covers, rose from his bed and flipped on his desk lamp. Turning on his computer, he scrubbed his face with his hand. If he couldn't sleep, he may as well study stock charts.

The following morning, Amy felt vulnerable and she was angry with herself for the vulnerability. She shouldn't have gotten so worked up over a kiss. *But what a kiss,* her honest, feminine and currently unhelpful mind said. She banged her glass of orange juice down, and it sloshed all over the counter.

''Oops,'' Nicholas said.

Jeremy giggled. ''Oops.''

Together, they chorused, ''Oops.''

Her frayed nerves stretched tighter when the twins joyfully chorused, ''Justin!''

They were always so happy to see him, she thought, and made a face in the direction of the sink. The problem was she often felt just as childishly happy to see him as the children did.

"Good morning," Amy said in a muted voice, noticing that his eyes were a little more narrowed than usual, and his hair was slightly mussed. Maybe he hadn't slept any better than she had, she thought hopefully at the same time she was ashamed for having such dark thoughts. He looked pretty darn good for having had a rough night.

"Morning, boys," he said cheerily, then offered the same muted tone back at Amy with a nod, "Good morning."

"G'mornin', Justin," Emily said in her sweet, sleepy tone as she spooned cereal into her mouth.

Justin returned the greeting. Amy's heart softened and she stroked her niece's hair. "I'll ask the Colemans if you can borrow their piano again today. Okay, sweetie?"

Her mouth full, Emily smiled and nodded.

"Who are the Colemans?" Justin asked.

"A family down the street. They've been kind enough to let Emily use their piano. I think she's interested in taking lessons." Amy hadn't figured out how she would afford a piano or the lessons, but she supposed that was a challenge for another day.

Justin nodded thoughtfully. "I'm heading over to my other home office, and I'm meeting some friends tonight, so I won't be home until late. You guys, give it your best shot to have a good day." He paused and met her gaze. "You too, Amy," he said in a deeper, almost intimate tone that tugged at something deep inside her.

That night, for the sake of sanity, Justin revisited his bachelor roots. He met Dylan at O'Malley's for beer and a burger.

"Michael will be late," Dylan said as he joined Justin at a table perfectly positioned for watching the wide-screen television playing the Baltimore Orioles game.

"Problem?" Justin said.

Dylan made a face. "Yeah, he's getting a home-cooked meal instead of a burger. I wouldn't be surprised if Kate has another baby soon."

"So soon?"

"I think they want a big family," Dylan said, and the look on his face reminded Justin of time spent at the Granger Home for Boys.

"Remember when everybody wanted a big family?" Justin said, taking a drink of beer.

"A big nuclear family," Dylan said. "We wanted Dad and Mom and a bunch of brothers and a sister or two to attract the girls when we were teenagers."

"It may not be nuclear, but you technically have a big family," Justin pointed out. "You're part Remington, so you've got two half-brothers and a half-sister."

Dylan laughed shortly. "Half is the operative word. Nothing would make them happier than if I disappeared. Especially Grant. He's the oldest and I know he thinks I'm trying to take over the entire company.''

Justin quirked his mouth in a partial grin. For the most part, Dylan concealed his competitive nature with a well-honed, cool untroubled air. ''And you're not?''

Dylan gave him a sideways glance. ''Careful, someone might find out I give a damn after all. I don't want control of the entire company, just part of it,'' he said in a voice that reminded Justin of a shark.

''No wonder Grant doesn't sleep well at night.''

''Enough about me. How's married life? How are the perks?'' he asked with a sly grin.

''Amy and I haven't known each other very long, so we're not to the perks stage yet.'' He gave a sigh of frustration. ''Besides I'm married to a descendent of Joan of Arc, so she doesn't believe she has any human needs.''

Dylan winced. ''Sorry, bud. But you know even Joan of Arc burned in the end. How's the rest of it? Are you spending money like water?''

''Not yet,'' Justin said, the prospect of uncontrolled spending threatening a bout of indigestion. ''I bought something today for one of the kids and I'm setting up accounts for their college education.''

Dylan raised his eyebrows. ''This sounds like the real thing to me.''

"The kids are very real," Justin said with a shrug that belied his true feelings. "Kids take a lot of planning. I always knew that. I didn't know they could be fun, too."

"And Amy?"

Justin thought about how responsive she'd felt last night and wanted to growl. "Amy could be a lot of fun if she'd quit trying to save the world for fifteen minutes."

"Maybe you can get her to save you," Dylan said with a wicked grin.

Amy sat alone in the darkness of her den. The children were blessedly asleep and she was blessedly alone. Justin still hadn't arrived home. She should be welcoming these precious moments of solitude with open arms.

Instead her gaze wandered to the clock. She wondered where he was and with whom. It was none of her business, she told herself and rose to pace the area carpet. After all, it wasn't as if they were married in the truest sense of the word. If his idea of going out with friends included seeing a woman who would meet his needs, then that should be fine with her. In sexual terms, she had no claim on him.

So why did the very thought of Justin with another woman make her heart pound with fury? If Amy looked in a mirror right now, she feared a green monster would be staring back at her.

The force of her emotion for him made it even worse. She should not care, she fumed. "This is why I didn't want to get married," she muttered. "Caring for a man too much just gets in the way," she muttered to herself. "Feeling too much for a man muddles the mind and saps the energy."

She glanced at the clock again. Eleven-thirty. She missed their questions. Her day felt incomplete without them. She missed those few moments when she allowed herself to give in to her curiosity about him. And she was frustrated with herself for caring so much.

Taking a deep breath to calm herself, she left the den and climbed the stairs. This was why she needed to rein in her feelings at all times. Tonight was a perfect reminder. Amy must depend on herself and no one else. Always.

Seven

The following afternoon, Amy found herself in a bind. The preschool children for the after-school program would be arriving any moment and her sitter had called with an emergency. She needed Amy to pick up Emily, Nicholas and Jeremy. Amy's back-up sitter was out of town on vacation.

Although she would almost rather chew nails, she tried to get in touch with Justin, first at his house. To her surprise, she found him at her home instead.

"What's up?" he asked.

Just hearing the strength in his voice calmed her. "I have a problem. My sitter's had an emergency, and I'm here doing the after-school program, so I need someone to pick up the kids from the sitter."

A long pause followed, and she held her breath. Regret seeped in. "Forget it," she said. "You don't—"

"For Pete's sake, give me a minute," he said. "The market's still open and I've got two possible trades left. I'll place limit orders. Where does the sitter live?"

Amy quickly gave him the address and directions all the while thinking how much she hated asking for his help at the same time she was heaving a sigh of relief. "I really appreciate this," she said. "I owe you a—" She broke off before she said "a big one." The big one had gotten her in big trouble last time.

"We'll see," he said. "See ya."

No sexy tease on the *big one* from him either, she noticed with an odd sense of loss as she slowly hung up the phone. Perhaps he wasn't so interested in the big one with her now. That was good, she insisted to herself over a huge sinking feeling in her stomach. That was wonderful.

She kept telling herself the same thing during the after-school program and while she ordered burgers at the drive-thru. Ordering burgers, however, reminded her of her wedding ceremony. Brushing aside her sadness, she lugged the paper sacks of fast food to the front door and prayed her day wouldn't be topped off by the arrival of Ms. Hatcher. Opening the door, she reminded herself to limit her gratitude to Justin. She didn't need any more of that kind of trouble.

It only took a second for Amy to hear the tinkling of piano keys. For a half-moment, she wondered if it was a recording, but the sound wasn't at all professional sounding. She quickly marched through the foyer to the formal living room to find Emily, and her brothers standing on either side like bookends, playing a spinet piano.

Amy nearly dropped the burgers.

"Emily?" she asked. "Where did the piano come from?"

The boys looked up. "Justin!" they chorused.

Emily whipped around on the small bench with a huge smile on her face. "Justin got it for us!"

Justin poked his head around the corner with the phone attached to his ear. He looked at Amy and didn't speak or wave. He just looked at her from head to toe and back again, making her nerve endings dance on end.

Amy took a deep breath and looked at the piano. Beautifully polished and golden brown with white ivory keys, the instrument fit perfectly in the room without taking up too much space. She couldn't have made a better selection. How exactly was she supposed to limit her gratitude on this?

Nicholas sniffed loudly and rubbed his belly. "I smell burgers."

"You can't have any cuz you puked in Justin's car," Jeremy said.

Amy winced. Oops. Men could be particular about their cars. She was surprised Justin was still in the house. She searched Nicholas for outward signs of illness. "Are you sick, sweetie?"

He shook his head.

"He got into the sitter's cookie jar and ate too many cookies," Emily said.

Nick stuck out his bottom lip. "Justin won't let me have anything to eat cuz he said he doesn't want me to get sick again."

Surprised at Justin's wisdom, Amy felt the force of all three gazes on her as if they were waiting for her verdict. "Justin is right. We need to let your tummy settle down before anything else goes in it."

Nick eyed the sack of fast food. "But what about my burger?"

"We'll see. I'll call the three of you in a few minutes," she said and headed for the kitchen. She rounded the corner and plowed into Justin. Still talking on the phone, he wrapped his arm around her to stabilize her.

Amy caught a mouthwatering whiff of his aftershave, and remnants of the emotions she'd felt when he'd kissed her rushed through her. Tough to hold a grudge after the way he'd come through for her today.

"Okay. I'll check my system tomorrow morning

for the correction,'' he said, then turned off the phone. ''My online trading system listed a wrong trade on my account and I just caught it.''

His green gaze searched hers, and Amy struggled with a deep vulnerability that swept through places she kept hidden inside her. ''What made you get the piano?''

His lips twitched ever so slightly. ''Who said I got it?''

She smiled and shook her head. ''Well, it's not Christmas, so I know Santa didn't bring it down the chimney. I thought you told me you were a tight-wad.''

''I am,'' he said. ''This is different.''

''How is it different?''

He shrugged with discomfort and took the food sacks from her arms to the kitchen counter. ''Emily wanted to take piano lessons, so she needed a piano.''

''Needed?''

''In the scheme of things, this wasn't a big deal, so don't make it one,'' he said, narrowing his eyes restlessly.

''It was a big deal for her and for me,'' she added, taking a breath and lowering her guard a millimeter. ''Thank you.''

Nicholas and Jeremy burst into the room, popping the bubble of intimacy forming between her and Justin. ''We want burgers! We want burgers!'' they chanted.

"The natives are restless," he said. "Better feed 'em."

Throughout the evening, Amy would almost swear there was an air of anticipation between her and Justin. It grew thicker with each passing minute. At unexpected moments, his gaze would catch and hold hers. Her heart was also doing unexpected things like softening toward him. Amy's emotions swung from attraction and fascination to fear. By the time she put the children to bed, she felt like she was stuck on a carnival ride.

She went downstairs to the den, waiting and wondering which question he would ask her tonight. Which of her many questions about him would she get answered tonight? After waiting several moments, she leaned back on the sofa. Forty-five minutes later she awakened, but Justin was nowhere in sight.

Both disappointed and peeved, she returned upstairs and saw the light under his door. Burning with questions and curiosity, she lifted her hand to knock. She stopped just before her hand connected with the wood. It was better to keep a little distance, she told herself. She needed to rein in her fascination. He might be her husband, but it was in name only.

Justin avoided Amy the following morning. Her eyes might be saying *yes*, but he knew what her mouth would say. *No*. And if he weren't careful, the idea of changing her no to a yes could become an obsession. Could? he thought with a mocking chuckle. Who did he think he was fooling?

Hearing the blessed sound of footsteps departing the house and the door closing, he headed to the kitchen for a cup of coffee. Spying a bag lunch on the counter, he wrestled with his conscience, then grabbed it and darted out the front door.

Amy was buckling Jeremy into his car seat.

"You forgot something," he said, running to her side.

She glanced at him and the bag, then shook her head. "No, I didn't."

Confused, he looked at the bag. "Isn't this a lunch?"

"Yes," she said, sliding into the driver's seat of her Volkswagen.

"Who's it for?"

She met his gaze and her lips tilted in a smile so sexy it affected him the same way it would if she were dragging her mouth across his bare abdomen. "It's for you," she said and pulled her door closed. "Gotta go. Have a nice day."

Justin managed, barely, not to gape as she pulled out of the driveway and the kids waved at him. He glanced down at the bag lunch in amazement. Amy couldn't know that no one had ever prepared a bag lunch for him before.

He opened it and looked inside to examine the contents. Turkey and cheese sandwich on wheat, granola bar and banana. And a note. *No cookies until I know your favorite. Peanut butter or chocolate chip?*

That red-haired witch, Justin thought and felt an itchy, impatient sensation crawl over his nerve endings. He'd gone to bed hard and wanting every night since he'd said his marriage vows to Amy. Ever since "I do" had meant "I don't," he'd been burning in his bed. He hadn't known Joan of Arc could be such a tease.

Both. Thanks, J.

For the third time, Amy looked at Justin's bold scrawl answering her cookie question and couldn't help smiling. So, she had more than one cookie monster living in her house. She slid the note back into her pocket and stored the information in her brain.

The kitchen timer dinged and she pulled the second batch of cookies from the oven. The aroma of fresh-baked sweets filled the air.

"Is it your mission in life to torture me to death?" Justin asked from the doorway.

Amy turned around to look at him and stopped short. His hair attractively damp and mussed from his recent shower, he wore no shirt and a pair of cotton lounging trousers that tied at the top and rode low on his hips. The sight of his bare torso and abdomen short-circuited her breathing.

"Well, is it?" he asked, moving toward her.

Amy swallowed and shook her head. "No. How am I torturing you?"

"Too many ways to count," he muttered under his breath and nodded toward the cookies. "The smell is distracting."

"They're a thank-you gift."

"For who?"

"For you."

He blinked, then shrugged his impressive shoulders and reached for one of the cookies. "I'm not going to argue, but why?"

"Because you picked up the kids for me and I heard your car sustained damage."

"You're welcome," he said and took a bite of the still-hot cookie.

His chest was extremely distracting.

"What are you staring at?"

Embarrassment rushed through Amy, and she swung around to avoid him. "Nothing," she said in a high-pitched voice while she quickly removed the cookies with a spatula.

"I don't think so," he said, his hand squeezing her shoulder. Urging her back around to face him, he studied her face. "What's going on?"

"Nothing," she insisted in the same damn unconvincing high-pitched voice.

"I don't believe you," he said bluntly. "Answer my question."

Darn. "If this is truth or dare, I think I'll take the dare this time."

"It's not truth or dare," he said, moving closer. "It's just plain old truth."

Amy sighed and looked past his right shoulder. "It's your chest."

He glanced down. "What's wrong with it?"

"Nothing," she muttered, unhappy with him for forcing her to answer. "That's the problem."

He wrinkled his face in confusion. "I don't get it."

"You don't have to," she said, knowing her cheeks were as red as tomatoes.

He lifted a hand to her face. "You're blushing."

She rolled her eyes. "You're so observant."

Holding her jaw, he studied her for a long moment. She saw the moment the light dawned. "There's nothing wrong with my chest and that's the problem," he echoed in surprise. "You like my chest."

She bit her lip. "I didn't really say—"

She broke off when he lifted her palm to his chest. His warm skin and the thud of his heart against her palm wholly distracted her.

"I can't believe Amy of Arc likes my chest."

"I'm not Amy of Arc," she protested, but there was no oomph in her words. He moved her hand in a sensual circle over his skin, over the pectoral muscles, then down the center to his belly.

Amy's mouth went dry. "You work out."

"A few times a week." He released her hand, but she couldn't quite find the will to remove it. Meeting her gaze, he lifted his hand to her hair, then circled the back of her nape and slowly drew her to him. He dipped his head and his mouth hovered a tantalizing breath from hers. "What do you want?"

She whispered the only word her lips would form. "More."

Justin's tongue drew a circle around her inner lips. Amy's temperature immediately rose ten degrees. He slid his fingers through her hair and drew her against him trapping her hand against his chest so that she felt his rapid heartbeat.

The sensual pleasure of touching his bare skin made her wish she could feel him against her naked breasts. He slid his thigh between hers and the thin cotton of his trousers both tantalized and frustrated her. There was no mistaking the hard bulge of his crotch rocking against her. Amy slipped her fingers to the back of his neck, urging him on. He drew out every carnal urge she'd never thought she possessed. In the eyes of the law, he was her husband. For Amy he was still forbidden territory, but she was finding him too tempting to resist.

She was consumed with his touch, his mouth, his attention. She wanted him to consume her. He guided her in a sweeping, sliding motion over his thigh that teased her, and turned her damp and swollen. She stroked his tongue with hers, unable to swallow a moan.

He slid his hand down over the outside of her breast to her waist, then lower to her bottom. He shifted slightly so his masculinity rubbed against her intimately as he guided her in an undulating provocative rhythm. Amy's mind grew hazy with desire.

"What do you want?" he asked against her lips, his breath coming as quickly as hers.

"More," she whispered again.

He dragged his other hand to the hem of her tank top and slowly slipped his fingers up her waist and each rib until he slid one finger just underneath her bra. "Do you want me to stop?"

"No," she said, and he unfastened the front clasp.

"You feel so good," he muttered "I want to taste you."

Amy shuddered at the dark desire in his voice.

He toyed with her nipples, drawing tiny moans from her throat. Suddenly, he lifted her onto the countertop and raised her shirt to reveal her swollen breasts. For a moment, he stared at them, then met her gaze with an expression of barely restrained passion. He lowered his mouth to her nipple and made love to it with his tongue. At the same time he slid his fingers inside her shorts, past her panties to where she ached for him.

"Oh, Amy," he said when he found her swollen. "So wet."

She couldn't recall ever wanting to be the sole source of a man's desire and satisfaction this much before. She couldn't recall feeling so utterly female, so powerful, yet vulnerable within the same moment.

This wasn't just her gratitude over Justin coming through for her. It wasn't her appreciation for the piano. This man called to her in a way no other ever had. She didn't completely understand it, and wrapped in the cloud of arousal, she couldn't begin to explain it even to herself, but she wanted him to know her. As a woman.

She arched her breast farther into his mouth, and Justin slipped his finger inside her. He gently nibbled on the hard tip of her breast, sending a shower of sensations through her.

Swearing, he drew back and scored her with his gaze. "I want to be in you. I want to feel you wet and tight all around me."

She shuddered at the provocative bluntness of his words.

"It's either the kitchen counter, your bed, or my bed," he told her. "You choose."

Her heart fluttered wildly. "Your—" She swallowed over her suddenly dry mouth.

"Good enough," he said and lifting her in his arms, he carried her into his bedroom. With excruciating slowness, he eased her down the front of his body. "Last chance. Are you sure about this?"

Absolutely not, she thought, but more than her body was urging her onward. Doubts, however, slithered and crawled through her mind like serpents. Teetering on the edge of the unknown, she took a deep breath. "What am I to you?"

He stared at her without answering for a long moment. "You're a witch," he said.

Amy's mouth fell open. "A wi—"

"You're the witch who makes me hard and keeps me from falling asleep every night," he said, and the insult felt more like praise.

"You're Amy of Arc determined to save the world."

Irritation trickled through her. "I'm not Amy of—"

"I'm a pretty selfish sonovabitch, so I admire you for it."

Surprised again, Amy swallowed the rest of her protest.

He lifted his hand to her jaw and shook his head. "You are, by some stroke of fate or insanity, my wife. I need to know you. In every way."

His words clicked deep inside her. She couldn't

imagine refusing him. Anticipation tinged with the metallic taste of fear filled her mouth. Theirs would be no easy coupling. He would touch her in ways she hadn't been touched, make her feel things she hadn't felt before. There were doors inside her she'd kept locked shut from everyone, and she wondered how she would keep those same doors locked from Justin.

She couldn't begin to answer all her unanswered questions. Except one. "If I'm a witch and I've been keeping you awake," she said, twining her arms around the back of his neck to bring his mouth closer to hers. "Then show me how to put you to sleep."

His eyes lit like twin flames. "This is gonna take a while."

Eight

He led her to the bed and pulled her down on his lap. Lifting her tank top over her head, he pushed her bra from her shoulders so her top was completely bare to him.

"Your breasts have driven me insane," he told her.

Amy glanced down at her chest, expecting to feel her usual detachment about her body. Instead she watched his hand cup her, making her nipple pout. He made her feel so sexy. "I don't usually think about them," she confessed.

"I have," he muttered and pulled her closer to worry her nipples with his tongue.

In the mirrored closet door, she caught sight of the provocative image of his dark head buried in her breast. The sight and sensation provided a double sensual whammy, surprising her with immediate force. That was the tip of *her breast* his mouth caressed.

She had never thought she was a particularly sexual woman. Was that woman in the mirror really her?

He lifted his head and looked at her. Suddenly self-conscious, she ducked her head. She felt caught.

"What is it?" he asked in a low, intimate voice.

"I've never watched—"

Realization crossed his face. He stood and stripped off his lounge pants in one smooth motion. Amy stared at him. His body was unrelentingly male. Tugging her to her feet, he took her mouth at the same time he unzipped her shorts and pushed them down over her hips along with her panties.

He brought her lower body against his, then tilted her head toward the mirror. "Now look."

Her mouth went dry at the soft, sensual image of her body entwined with his.

"Nothing to say?" he taunted, stroking her breast with his hand.

She closed her eyes, but the strong, knee-weakening visual burned in her brain. "You are such a show-off," she said, biting her lip.

"What do you mean?" he asked, his sexy chuckle vibrating against her.

"I mean," she said, "your body is—" She stifled a groan of embarrassment. "Your body is impressive," she hissed through her lips.

"You're impressed with my body? I hadn't thought you'd noticed."

Hearing the smile in his voice, she shot him a dark look. "Liar."

His gaze grew serious. "Don't you know what a turn-on it is knowing such a sexy woman is impressed with me?"

"I'm not a sex—" she automatically started to say before he covered her mouth with his hand.

He shook his head in disbelief. "Teacher, somewhere along the way, your education has been sadly neglected." He rubbed his mouth over hers. "And I'm gonna show you how much."

He took her mouth and the room began to spin. Stroking her tongue with his, he tempted and teased her to respond. She'd thought it would be heat and fury, and maybe it still would be. She hadn't thought he would make her laugh and ache for him at the same time. How did he do that? she wondered.

"Look," he said. "Look at you." He shifted her in front of him. Burying his face in her shoulder, he skimmed his hand over her breast, down over her abdomen, then lower still between her legs.

Through half-closed eyes, she peeked at the erotic

sight of his large hands arousing her. But his touch was too distracting, her feelings too overwhelming, and her hunger for him too strong. She turned into him.

"Why won't you watch?"

"I'd rather watch you," she said, and he groaned.

Nudging her onto the bed, he followed her down, kissing her breasts, dragging his tongue over her skin. The tension inside her tightened with breathtaking speed. He dropped open-mouth kisses over her abdomen, whispering words of praise.

When he kissed her intimately, she stiffened.

"I want to taste you," he said, and his words melted her resistance.

His tongue sought her tender recesses while his hands stroked her inner thighs. He found her swollen bead of femininity and caressed her until she began to squirm. She felt hot and needy, full to the point of spilling over.

"Justin," she said, her voice husky to her own ears. She wove her fingers through his hair.

"So close," he said, flicking his tongue over her again and again.

Helpless against his sensual onslaught, she twisted beneath him. He devoured her and the coil of tension tightened excruciatingly. She arched, and a power surge ricocheted through her. She gasped in shocked pleasure.

Justin kissed his way up her body to take her

mouth again. The taste of her pleasure on his lips spun her around again. Before she could catch her breath, he pushed her thighs apart and holding her gaze, he thrust inside her.

Amy gasped. Despite her arousal, she felt over-stretched. He was large and hard.

He made a sound that mixed pleasure with exquisite frustration. "Tight," he muttered and swore.

"It's been a while," she confessed.

"How long?"

She breathed and wiggled beneath him, feeling herself slowly begin to accommodate him. "A while."

He swore again at her movements. "How long?" he repeated.

"Do we have to discuss this now?" she asked, distracted by his sensual invasion. "Can't you think of something better to do?"

He looked at her as if she'd just completely shredded his patience. His gaze dark and primitive, he flexed his powerful thighs and pushed deeper inside her, stealing her breath again. He lifted her hands to the wooden posts on the headboard. "Hold on," he told her and began a mind-bending rhythm.

His chest brushed her breasts and he stole kisses with each thrust. She felt the friction of his legs against her thighs. With a long motion, he pulled his hardness nearly all the way out of her. Craving more of him, she arched and flexed around him in silent invitation.

He licked her lips. "You like the way I feel inside you, don't you?"

She felt him, tantalizingly out of reach, at her entrance. She wiggled.

He licked her lips again. "Answer me," he demanded.

Surrounded by him and her need for him, she felt as if she were at his mercy. It was humbling, liberating, and scary. Though she feared what she might be giving up, she closed her eyes and just for the moment surrendered to her humanness, to her need as a woman. "Yes," she whispered.

Covering her hands on the headboard with his, he took her with all the heat and fury his gaze had earlier promised. He stretched inside her, filling her so completely she felt as if every stroke of his masculinity provided the most exquisite, intimate massage.

She felt his tension rise with the force of a crashing earthquake. His body quaked and rippled as he took her to the top again. Amy fought her release, fought the dizzying oxygen-deprived moment of ecstasy. In a primitive feminine way, she wanted to experience every moment of his pleasure.

She felt it before she saw it. His body stiffened, then he closed his eyes. "Amy," he muttered in a sex-rough voice that called her to come with him.

His climax took her over the edge again, and her body joined his in a rocket to the sky, shooting like a star.

Moments passed before Amy could breathe normally. Her head was spinning, her ears ringing as if cannons had gone off. Distantly she felt Justin roll beside her, his chest pressed against her side.

Her heart pounded so hard she was sure he could hear it. She knew she had never given herself so thoroughly, and she couldn't remember feeling this vulnerable in her adult life. Ever. She wanted to be held. Badly.

"Are you okay?" he asked, and she closed her eyes to his inquiring gaze. If he couldn't see her eyes, then he couldn't read her turmoil.

She cleared her throat. "Yes."

"Sure?"

"Yes," she said too quickly. Why did she feel as if she'd splintered into a thousand pieces and all those pieces of Amy would never be arranged in quite the same way again? She suddenly felt the horrifying urge to weep. Gritting her teeth against the feeling, she stiffened her love-worn body.

Justin slid his arm around her waist and shifted her on her side so she was cocooned against him. He surrounded her and even though her mind was racing, some primitive part of her must have trusted him because her body relaxed.

"You blew me away," he murmured next to her ear, a secret that gave her a sliver of ease.

Although she suspected their "blowing away" scales were vastly different, the notion that she'd had a fraction of the impact on him that he'd made on her allowed her to breathe normally.

Several hours later, she awakened, disoriented. What was she doing here? This wasn't her bed. Justin's arm was still wrapped around her, serving as a reminder of their intimacy. Amy shifted slightly and her body reminded her more thoroughly with twinges from their lovemaking.

A silken thread of uneasiness twisted inside her. Something about this was too comfortable, she thought. It would be too easy to slide into a habit of counting on Justin. Even though they had connected in the most powerful, physical way last night, he hadn't spoken any words of love and neither had she. Her heart tightened.

She couldn't love Justin, she told herself. She didn't know him well enough to love him. Besides, if she gave her heart to him, then what would she have left after he left her?

Too disturbed to remain, she held her breath and slowly slid from his bed. Gathering her clothes, she bundled them against her and tiptoed to her room. She tugged on a nightshirt and panties and crawled into bed. She'd thought she would feel safer in her own bed, more like herself. But she still felt shaken up and bothered. Knowing tomorrow would require all the energy and clear-thinking she could muster, she told herself not to think about Justin. She mentally closed every door in her mind to him, and when he still crept in like a warm breeze, she pulled the sheet over her head.

Justin watched Amy from the kitchen doorway as she poured juice and cereal. He wondered why she had left. He remembered the intensity of their lovemaking, however, and combined with her inexperience, he'd guess she was knocked off-kilter.

She must have felt his gaze. She looked up from taking a sip of orange juice and choked. She rose quickly from the table and rushed to his side.

"I— You—" She cleared her throat. "Do you want some orange juice?"

"I can get it myself," he said, catching all the little signs of nervousness, stuttering, high-pitched voice, and fluttery eyelids. Deciding he might as well get it over with, he pulled her into the hallway for a moment of privacy. "You left," he said. "Why?"

She bit her lip. "I, uh…" Her eyes widened helplessly. "Too much," she said haltingly adding, "you."

"At first," he agreed, remembering how tight she'd felt. "But you got used to me."

Color bloomed in her cheeks. "I didn't mean that

way.'' She closed her eyes and shook her head as if this conversation was almost more than she could bear. ''I mean the whole thing was too much. I'm not used to making love like that.''

''I sure as hell hope not,'' Justin said.

Her eyes popped open. ''And I didn't think it all the way through, the ramifications to the children.''

Confused as the dickens, Justin put his hand on her shoulder. ''Amy, what are you talking about? Last night had nothing to do with the kids.''

Her gaze of distress slid away from his. ''Well, I didn't think about sleeping arrangements and how the children would feel about finding us in the same bed.''

''Wouldn't that be normal for a married couple?''

''If we were a normal married couple,'' she said. ''But we're not. And I started thinking about what we'll do when the two-year trial period is over and if you leave how much it will hurt the kids.''

But not her. Justin fought the stinging sensation he felt in his chest. He swallowed the bitter taste of regret. ''Sounds like morning-after remorse.''

''Some,'' she admitted.

''I can move out if that will make it easier,'' he said, thinking it would make life a damn sight easier for him.

Her eyes widened in fear. ''The children.''

He remembered and nodded at the bottom line. ''It's okay. I won't leave before the custody issues are resolved,'' he said, wondering if it would kill him. ''We'll just stay out of each other's way.''

She moved her head in an uncertain, helpless circle, but said nothing.

Justin wondered where he could find a pair of blinders so he wouldn't see her twenty times a day. And earplugs so he wouldn't hear her voice. And a clothespin for his nose so he wouldn't catch her scent at odd moments. He wondered how to wipe out the memory of how she'd felt in his arms and tasted in his mouth. He wondered how to erase the visual of burying himself inside her, feeling her let go and let him in.

He didn't know how he'd do it. He just knew he had to.

Amy left a bag lunch on the counter for Justin. When she returned that evening, she found it in the exact same spot she'd left it, uneaten. The cookies she'd made for him were also uneaten. When she caught a quick glance inside his room that evening, she spied a dozen stock charts posted on the wall. Remaining in his room, he didn't show up for dinner or afterward when she could have awkwardly attempted to explain her inexplicable behavior. Perhaps it was best that she hadn't had an opportunity to explain anything since she wasn't so sure she understood too much herself right now.

She only knew there wasn't much she wouldn't

do to give her sister's children a secure home and it felt as if Justin could threaten that goal at the same time he was helping to make it happen. He reminded her she was human, that she was a woman. With no effort at all, he made her aware of how much she could want. He added a dimension to her life that was thrilling and distracting.

The distracting part bothered her most. What she needed to accomplish was too important to get waylaid by a passion for a man with compelling green eyes and an inner core of power that drew her like a magnet.

So why was she thinking about him now? she asked herself as she prepared another bag lunch for him. She scowled, then wrapped two cookies in a plastic wrapper and put them in his bag. A vivid memory of Justin, his eyes lit with desire, his body naked as he thrust inside her, flashed across her mind. A rush of heat suffused Amy. Splashing her face with cool water from the water faucet, she decided she might have more in common with Joan of Arc than she'd thought. When it came to Justin, she felt like she was burning at the stake.

Finding the lunch untouched on the kitchen counter again the following afternoon, Amy reached the conclusion that Justin had put her on *ignore*. She couldn't, however, fault him for his treatment of the children. Emily drew some watercolor pictures for the walls of his bedroom as a thank-you for the piano. Amy noticed he praised the little girl for her effort. The boys swarmed around him for attention, and he took them outside to play a quick round of dodge ball.

She glanced at the lunch she'd left him and made a face. No surprise, but so far she was flunking Wife 101.

Justin acknowledged Amy with a quick nod as he headed for his room to bury himself in stock charts. Even in a wacky market, the stock charts made a helluva lot more sense than his witchy wife.

"Kate Hawkins called," Amy said.

Justin stopped. "What did she want?"

"To invite us to a barbecue. I accepted."

He nodded slowly.

"And the local stockbroker's association called asking whether you preferred beef tenderloin or seafood spinach crepes for the dinner where you'll be speaking. I told them beef. When the woman learned I was your wife, she invited me to come."

"You'd be bored," he told her.

She lifted her chin and met his gaze. "I told her to count me in."

Irritated and confused, he didn't bother hiding it. "Why?" he demanded.

"Careful," she said with a smile so sweet it made his teeth ache. "I might get the impression you don't want me to come with you."

"Like I got the impression you don't want to make love with me."

Her eyes widened in surprise and color rose in her face. She walked closer to him. "This is obviously difficult for you to understand, but nobody gave me an instruction manual for how to handle this situation. We don't have a normal relationship, whatever normal is. Believe me, I don't have one tenth your sexual experience, so if making love with you left me feeling totally unwrapped, it shouldn't come as a big surprise to anyone. Excuse me if I needed to catch my breath, catch my *mind!*" she nearly yelled.

Taken aback, he looked into her brown eyes flashing with misplaced indignation. He felt the slow drag of his gut, tugging him toward her again. It would be the death of him, he thought. "You never answered my question about your sexual experience."

"You're right. Unlike you, I could barely breathe let alone think," she fumed and turned on her heel.

He could just let her have her temper tantrum while he returned to his stock charts. In another life, he thought wryly and followed her into the den where she watched the children from the picture window. "How long had it been?"

She slid a sideways glance at him. "Three and a half years," she said in a low voice.

He blinked. "Why so long?"

She crossed her arms over her chest. "I was too busy. I worked while I was in college to help pay for my tuition. Relationships looked messy and I knew I didn't have the time or energy for them."

"Who was it?"

"A guy who was very persistent. He pursued me long enough to catch me at a moment when I was—" She shrugged.

"Weak," he supplied.

"Curious," she immediately corrected as if weak wasn't in her vocabulary.

"Did he satisfy your curiosity?"

She paused a moment. "Yes, but not much else."

Ouch. "Lousy lover?"

"I really didn't have any basis for comparison."

She surprised him again. "Your only lover?"

She nodded. "And last until you."

"You're telling me you've only had two sexual experiences in your life?" he asked, unable to believe it.

"No," she said. "After the first time with him, I gave it two more tries, then called it quits. Being with you was—" she said, taking a breath. "Very different. But you have such a huge—" she glanced at him "—ego, that I'm sure you've heard this kind of thing before."

Bowled over by her disclosure, he struggled with a weird assortment of emotions. He had an odd urge to punch the guy who'd taken her without taking care of her. On the other hand, Justin was fiercely glad he had been the man to show her the pleasure of lovemaking. He walked to her side and despite the fact that her back looked as stiff as a board, he curled his hand around the nape of her neck beneath her hair. Despite her *cajone*-breaking image, he suspected the woman needed gentleness, something he hadn't offered her so far. "I wouldn't have thought you were so inexperienced," he said.

She glanced up at him. "Why?"

"Well, hell, Amy, you're built like a woman who could pose for a man's fantasy magazine. You laugh and every male within earshot age four to ninety-four is vying for your attention."

"You really think I'm built like a woman who could pose for a men's magazine?"

Justin twitched at the thought. He rubbed his face. "Don't get any ideas. The local school board wouldn't approve and neither would I. I wish I'd known all this."

She took a deep breath. "That's what I've been saying. You don't know me. I don't know you. You don't love me," she said, searching his face. "But we're going to do this for at least two years, right?"

He nodded, wondering if two years would be long enough for him to learn everything about Amy he wanted to learn.

"If we had been dating for less than a month and

we made love, would you have necessarily expected me to stay the whole night?''

''After a night like that?'' he asked, and he watched her nod. ''I would have kept you in bed for three days straight.''

Her eyes widened. ''Oh.'' She gulped. ''I'm not familiar with the etiquette, so—''

He gently squeezed the back of her neck. ''Screw etiquette, Amy,'' he said as kindly as he could manage. ''This was about getting enough of you.''

Nine

Amy's stomach dipped and swirled at the expression on Justin's face. She was beginning to feel that every time she was around Justin, she was in over her head. She prayed that wasn't true.

How had they gotten into this discussion? she wondered desperately. How had they gone from a barbecue and stockbroker's dinner to the complete unabridged history of her dismal sex life? Eating glass would have been preferable to telling him about her lack of romance, but Amy had made a deal with herself. If she wanted Justin to answer her questions, and she grudgingly admitted she did, then she would have to attempt to answer his questions.

She cleared her throat. "Can we get back to the broker's dinner?"

"You'll be bored," he told her.

"No, I won't. It will give me a chance to understand more about what you do."

"I can show you charts anytime."

"It will be the first thing resembling a date that you and I have attempted," she said bluntly.

That stopped him. He looked at her curiously. "You want a date?" he asked, sounding surprised.

She stifled a sigh. "Yes."

He shook his head. "I wouldn't take anyone I liked to this meeting. Besides—" he said, breaking off as his gaze skimmed over her breasts and lower.

"Besides what?"

Clearly reluctant, he rubbed his mouth. "Besides, if I were taking you on a date, my mission would be to get you into bed."

His *mission*. At the thought of being Justin's singular sexual mission, Amy felt a shudder ripple through her.

"But not at a stockbrokers' meeting. In the past, I could have picked up a woman there, but—"

Anger shot through her. "Picked up a woman? Is that why you don't want me to go? I might be interrupting your happy hunting grounds."

"I said in the past," Justin told her.

All her doubts clamored to the surface. "Yes, and our marriage is a figure of speech for both of us, so what's to keep you from 'hunting'? For all I know you could be picking up women when you go out with your so-called friends.''

He looked at her with an incredulous expression. ''Are you jealous?''

Amy's fury increased tenfold. She sucked in a quick breath. ''I am not jealous,'' she insisted. ''But if you're going to seduce me, I might need to be concerned about safe sex.''

His eyes darkened and Amy quickly gleaned that she'd insulted him. ''I'm not the one sneaking away from your bed in the middle of the night,'' he told her. ''And if you were so concerned about safe sex, then why didn't you mention contraception the other night?''

Amy swallowed. ''I'm on the Pill.''

''Why?''

It was none of his business. ''Because my periods are irregular!'' she said through clenched teeth.

He paused a long moment. ''Okay,'' he said. ''You can come to the stockbrokers' dinner and meeting if you want.''

Too peeved to be reasonable, she barely resisted the urge to kick him. ''Never mind,'' she said with a sniff and went outside to play with the kids.

Justin felt the breeze from the door swinging in his face and thought about ripping it off its hinges. She was going to drive him insane, he thought. If his friends had been true friends, they would have locked him up and thrown away the key when he'd said he was getting married.

First she tortured him by not making love with him, then she blew him away by making love with him. Then she'd insulted the daylights out of him by sneaking away like a thief. When he tried to keep a sane distance, she insisted on attending a boring stockbrokers' meeting with him. She'd flattered him beyond measure when she'd told him she could neither breathe nor think after he'd made love to her, then she might as well have kneed him in the groin when she'd suggested he was *hunting*.

He swore under his breath. The only thing he'd been hunting for was his sanity. He glanced out the window watching her twirl Nick around in her arms. She was an angel and she was a mistress. She was exquisitely soft and unrelentingly tough. She was impossible to manage, and if he did what was best for him, he would get the hell out of her looney bin.

But heaven help him, now that he'd had her, he wanted her again.

Over the next few days, Amy was snooty to Justin in a friendly way if that were possible. She turned her nose up at him at night, but she always left a bag lunch for him. When he didn't eat it, the next day she left a Post-it Note on his monitor reminding him to eat lunch. That little Post-it Note gave him an odd, warm sensation. He tried to recall the last

time anyone had given a damn whether he ate or
not and he couldn't. That night they planned to join
the Hawkins's for a barbecue, and Justin found himself looking forward to the casual gathering. He
wryly wondered if his bride might unbend enough
to talk with him in the presence of other people.

"It's not nice to hold a grudge," Amy could hear
her mother say in her mind.

It may not be nice, but it's safe, she respectfully
replied. Much safer to hold a grudge and keep her
distance. It was difficult, however, to bear ill will
toward the man when he made Emily giggle with a
silly joke. He pulled into the long driveway of the
Hawkins's home and the children immediately
clamored to get out. Amy released Nick's car seat
belt while Justin took care of Jeremy's. Emily
climbed out with a large bag of chips in her hands.

"There you are," Kate Hawkins called, walking
toward them with her baby in her arms. "Michelle's
been waiting for you."

"May I push her in the swing?" Emily asked.

Kate smiled and smoothed Emily's bangs. "Of
course you can, angel."

The boys dashed forward. "Can we swing?"
Nick asked.

"It's all yours," Kate said, pointing to the swing
set. "Michael was determined to get the outdoor
gym up for the baby even though she's not ready

for it yet. I'm glad someone will enjoy it this summer.'' She glanced up at Amy and Justin and a wicked glint shimmered in her eyes. "Justin, you look remarkably at ease considering you're a family man, now. I expected twitches and shakes and ulcers.''

Amy was the one experiencing twitches. "He's actually very good with the children.''

"Wonders never cease,'' Kate said.

Justin gave a long-suffering sigh. "You're never going to forgive me for what I said at O'Malley's that night you overheard me, are you? Would it help any if I mentioned I've never seen Michael happier and you're the cause of it?''

Kate's face softened. She reached forward and gave him a hug. "Of course I forgive you. Something tells me you're facing your own challenges now.'' She glanced past them. "Oh, here comes Alisa. I'll be right back.''

"I bet Dylan will turn cartwheels when he finds out Alisa's here,'' he muttered.

Amy watched Kate greet a slim woman with long straight blond hair. She glanced at Justin. "Dylan doesn't like Alisa?''

"They go way back,'' he said, carrying the food from the car.

"How far back?''

"Back to the Granger Home for Boys. Her mother was the cafeteria manager and Alisa used to

steal cookies for some of us. She and Dylan developed a heavy-duty crush as teenagers. Dylan keeps
asking her out, but she won't have anything to do
with him." He cracked a half-grin. "As the stomach
turns. About the stockbrokers' dinner," he began.

Amy lifted her chin. "Never mind."

"You're not gonna get snooty again, are you?"

She stopped midstep. "I'm never snooty."

He stopped and looked at her. "Yes, you are.
You've been snooty since we talked about the dinner."

"I have not."

"Yes, you have," he said with maddening calm.

"I have not," she insisted.

He shrugged. "Then prove it."

She swallowed her trepidation. "How?"

"Kiss me," he dared her.

Her heart flipped over. She swallowed again.
"Your hands are full," she said in a weak protest.

"My mouth is free."

She stifled a sound of *help*. She wasn't prepared
to turn to brainless mush tonight, and she knew kissing Justin would affect her that way.

"Amy," Kate said, providing a ready distraction,
"I'd like you to meet Alisa Jennings."

"Saved by the bell," Justin murmured.

Amy felt a rush of relief and turned toward Kate
and the blond woman. "Gotta go," she said to Justin, quickly leaving his side.

"Amy, this is Alisa Jennings, and she met Justin when he was—" Kate broke off, waiting for Alisa to fill in the blank.

"Probably around ten," Alisa said, extending her hand to Amy. "I must congratulate you on getting a ring on Justin's finger. He's been antimarriage as long as I can remember, so you must be very special to make him change his ways."

Amy's stomach turned. Alisa obviously didn't know the circumstances surrounding her marriage to Justin. "Uh, I'm not sure I—"

"—well, you know what a good woman can do," Kate interrupted tongue-in-cheek and put a comforting hand on Amy's arm.

Alisa smiled. "Yes, I've watched what you've done with Michael."

Kate glanced at Amy. "See how smart she is? That's why I wanted you to meet her."

Amy couldn't help smiling at their female camaraderie.

"Plus she has all these stories about Michael and Justin when they were kids."

Her curiosity piqued, she met Alisa's friendly gaze. "Really? What do you remember about Justin?"

"He always worked, sometimes more than one job. He worked with the cleaning crew at Granger until he was old enough to get a better paying part-time job," Alisa said. "And he was the best money manager of any kid at the home. All the other boys would buy candy or sports equipment with their extra money." Alisa shook her head. "Not Justin. He saved it. Everybody was always trying to hit him up for a loan," she said with a grin. "But Justin set a limit of two bucks and he wouldn't lend any more until the previous loan was paid."

"Let's move toward the picnic tables," Kate said. "Did they call Justin a tightwad back then, too?"

Alisa's face softened. "No. One year, there was this kid who wanted to visit his family for Christmas, but they didn't have enough money for him to come home because his father was very sick. Justin paid for his bus ticket."

Kate stopped with a surprised look on her face. "Really? I would never have thought—"

Amy's chest grew tight at the image of Justin, as a child, sharing his very hard-earned money that way. Overwhelmed by a need to defend Justin, Amy had to interrupt. "I haven't seen this tightwad side of Justin," she blurted out, and bit her lip. "He describes himself that way, but I don't believe it. He bought a piano for Emily two days after I made an idle comment about her wanting to take lessons. And the after-school program I run has just received an anonymous donation."

Kate nodded in the direction of her husband. "Same thing happened with the home for unwed pregnant teenagers where I volunteer. When I asked

Michael about it, he was evasive. Sometimes I wonder if the three of them have been doing something together, but whenever I start to ask, he—'' She paused and smiled. ''He distracts me.''

Alisa cracked a grin. ''Isn't that one of the qualities of a good husband? The ability to distract?''

''Perhaps,'' Kate said. ''Have you found anyone distracting lately?''

Alisa's grin fell. ''Not really.''

''Kate,'' Michael called. ''Your mom's on the phone.''

''Oh, and there's Dylan. Excuse me,'' Kate said.

''I thought he wasn't coming,'' Alisa said under her breath after Kate left.

''Pardon?''

Alisa waved her hand in a dismissing gesture. ''Nothing. Dylan and I were close as kids, but we're not at all now.''

''Justin told me the two of you had a crush as teenagers,'' Amy said. ''He also said Dylan keeps trying to get your attention now, but you won't have anything to do with him.''

Alisa's mouth tilted in a sad, wry smile. ''Justin always had a knack for pinning the tail on the donkey. The way I look at it is history has already repeated itself where Dylan and I are concerned, and it doesn't need to repeat itself again. We met again in college and he—''

Amy could see Alisa's eyes deepen with pain and

even though she didn't know the woman, she felt the hurt echo inside her. "It didn't go well," she finished for her.

Alisa met her gaze and Amy had the sense that she'd just made a new friend. "Right," Alisa said and gave Amy a kind, but assessing glance. "I have a feeling Justin may have found exactly what he needs in you."

Amy looked across the yard at Justin, her *husband.* Her stomach dipped at all he was and wasn't to her. What if fate was involved between them in some strange, crazy way? What if this was about more than custody and the kids and Justin's deal with God? What if somebody somewhere had put them together because they were meant to be married?

The wayward thought danced lightly through her mind like a butterfly, but the implication hit her like a two-by-four. Fate? Meant to be? Those terms sounded awfully close to fairy tales, she thought, and she had given up on Cinderella before she hit twelve years old. Plus there was her history of non-romance.

But what if there really was a man in this world for her, and what if it was Justin?

Amy closed her eyes. Then heaven had better help them both.

The evening was a companionable time filled with children's chatter, lots of food, and threatening storm clouds. The sky finally burst open, and the group went scurrying toward the house.

Nicholas glanced back, pointing at the table in horror. "The cupcakes! I didn't get one!"

"I'll get them." Amy darted back to rescue the cupcakes, but Justin beat her and snatched the plastic container. Grabbing her hand, he tugged her out of the downpour to the closest dry spot next to the house.

Justin's hair was plastered to his head, raindrops dripped off his chin.

Amy shook her head and laughed. "You're so wet."

"And you think you're not?" He shook his head and sprayed her.

Amy lifted her hands to shield her face and laughed again. "Stop!"

She pushed her drenched hair away from her face and looked up to find his gaze lingering on her breasts. Glancing down, she saw that she was just as wet as he was. The rain had turned her T-shirt nearly transparent as it molded faithfully to her breasts. Embarrassed, she crossed her arms over her chest. "Oops."

His gaze met hers with a trace of something that looked very close to possessiveness. "Yeah. If there was a wet T-shirt contest, you would definitely win, but I don't want anyone else seeing you like that." He pulled his shirt over his head and transferred it to her.

It was such a chivalrous, protective gesture that she didn't know what to say. With the rain pouring down just two feet away, she stood there staring into Justin's eyes and a dozen feelings rose within her. Bare-chested because he'd just given her his own shirt, this was the same man who had survived the Granger Home for Boys and had given his money to a kid so he could visit his parents. This was the same man who always knew the bottom line, and this was the same man who had made love to her with a force stronger than the rain. Her husband.

Unable to stop herself, she stretched up on tiptoe and kissed him. She slid her arms around his neck and with her kiss, she tried to tell him things she wasn't able to articulate to herself let alone to him. She tasted his surprise and desire, and she felt the familiar insistent urge inside her for more.

He pulled back and studied her with hooded eyes. "What was that for?"

Speechless while her body hummed, and her mind and heart raced, she tried to make her brain work. "A thank-you," she improvised. "For giving me the shirt off your back."

He paused again, pushing her hair behind her ear. "Maybe you can return the favor sometime."

Later that night after the kids were tucked in, Justin found Amy downstairs looking out the window at the full moon. "I wondered if you'd come tonight. You've been pretty busy with your stock charts."

"It's getting near the end of the trading season," he told her, but he knew he'd been avoiding her. As he looked at the way the moonlight glimmered on her hair and he remembered the provocative image of her nearly naked breasts, he wondered if he should be avoiding her again tonight.

She looked at him curiously. "Trading season? I thought the stock market was open year-round."

"It is, but there's a theory that the best time for trading is between October and May. Since it's almost May, I keep a close watch on my short-term positions."

"What do you like most about trading?" she asked.

He enjoyed being the object of her feminine curiosity. "I like the illusion of control. I have no control over the market, but if I study stocks and apply different theories to the charts, then I find my percentage of wins goes up."

"Do you celebrate when you win?"

He shook his head. "Not usually."

She studied him for a moment. "You don't usually celebrate when you win because you win all the time."

"More often than not," he said.

She pushed away from the wall and pointed her finger at his chest. "If you're so good the stockbrokers want you to come talk to them, then 'more often than not' must be an understatement."

Capturing her hand in his, he lifted her impertinent finger to his mouth and gently nipped it, watching her eyes widen. "There's a fine line between confidence and overconfidence in trading. The difference can cost you a fortune. The reasons I've been successful are that I know the difference and I focus on the discipline and process of trading."

He darted his tongue out to taste and soothe her forefinger. As her gaze locked with his in sensual expectation, Justin wondered what it would take for a woman like Amy to fall for him. He wondered what life would be like to have a woman like Amy loving him. Dangerous thoughts. It was the kind of thing he'd never allowed himself to wish. He was pretty damn sure it wouldn't be wise to start wishing now.

She stepped closer so that her body barely brushed his every time she breathed. "You're like a book I never thought I wanted to read, but once I opened, it was hard to stop. Every time I learn something about you," she said in a low, husky voice tinged with frustration, "I want to know more."

She was so inviting she reminded him of a flower waiting to be plucked. In the corner of his mind, he remembered how she'd reacted the time they'd made love, but he allowed himself a kiss. Gently pushing her back against the wall, he lowered his mouth to hers, and she immediately responded by opening her lips and twining her tongue with his.

Her instantaneous, sensual response affected him like an intimate stroke. Aroused, he played with her mouth, tasting her and allowing her to taste him. With each stroke of her tongue over his, a visual formed in his mind of her kissing her way down his body. Her hair skimming over his bare skin, her hardened nipples taunting him with random touches in her movement down to his thighs. Even now, he could feel the tips of her on his chest.

His hands itching to touch her, he slid his hand under her T-shirt and cupped her breast. Her sexy sigh in his mouth was too irresistible an invitation and he slipped his other hand underneath her shirt so that he touched both breasts.

Amy moaned and undulated against him. Instinctively he pressed his arousal between her thighs and when she opened her legs, Justin began to sweat. He knew how she felt, how she tasted.

He felt one of her hands circle the back of his neck, urging his mouth against hers, as if she were hungry for him, as if she couldn't get enough.

The notion sent a firestorm throbbing through his blood. He rhythmically slid his tongue into her mouth and she suckled him in the same way her body would squeeze his hardness if he were taking her.

She moved restlessly against him and he felt her hand slide down to touch him intimately through the fabric of his shorts. He couldn't withhold a groan. He wanted her naked. He wanted her mouth on him. He wanted her.

"Touch me," he urged in a low voice against her sexy open mouth.

With unsteady hands, she unfastened his shorts and cupped his aching masculinity in her hand. The touch of her caresses made him feel as if he would burst. Looking into his gaze with eyes dark with desire, she rubbed the honey of his arousal with her thumb and lifted it to her tongue.

The sight was so erotic it nearly made him crazy. "I want to take you," he told her. "I don't care much where or how. I just want to take you now."

Everything about her was one big delicious, inviting *yes*. Justin slid his hands down to her hips. It would be so easy to push down her shorts and find her wetness. It would be easy to lift her and wrap her thighs around his hips. It would be so decadently easy to thrust inside her tight wet femininity.

His mind and body throbbing in anticipation, he took her mouth as he began to unfasten her shorts.

Distantly he heard a high-pitched sound outside the room. He was so intent on Amy that he let it slide. However, he heard it again. A child's broken sob.

Despite his raging arousal, the sound tugged at him. It cost him, but Justin pulled back to listen.

"Aunt Amy," Nicholas cried from the top of the stairs. "I had a bad dream."

Justin ducked his head and inhaled deeply. He could feel her body humming with the same need he had. He took another deep breath. "You need to go," he murmured.

Ten

An hour and half later after a chilly shower, Justin still burned for her. But he wouldn't go to her. Prowling his small room, he felt caged. As much as he wanted her, his *wife* was an incredibly complex creature. Bold and shy, she somehow also managed to be both fearless and vulnerable. Justin didn't want her running out on him again. When he made love to her again, he wanted her waking up beside him.

He wondered how their relationship might have progressed if they hadn't married for the reasons they did. He tried to picture dating Amy, but it was damn difficult with three kids, as good as they might be. He wondered again what it would be like for her to give her heart to him.

His chest grew tight at the thought. He'd never wanted a woman's heart before. Her body, her attention, maybe, but not her heart. That got messy. But hell, marriage was about as messy as a man could get. The problem with wanting Amy's heart was that he suspected if she gave her heart, she would want him to give his in return. Justin would almost rather give his wallet.

"Have fun," Amy called after Justin as he left for the stockbrokers' dinner. He looked almost as good in a tux as he did naked.

He made a face. "I'm speaking."

She shrugged. "Well, then break a leg."

"I'll try not to. Later," he said and the door closed behind him.

Amy immediately turned to the kids. "I'm going out tonight, so a sitter will give you pizza."

"Woo-hoo pizza!" Nicholas yelled.

Emily was more reserved. "Who's the sitter?"

"Jennifer Stallings. I think you've met her. She lives down the street and she's very nice and experienced."

Emily nodded hesitantly.

Concerned, Amy bent down and gazed at her niece. "What is it, sweetie? Do you feel sick?"

Emily shook her head. She hesitated again. "You won't get in an accident, will you?" she asked in a low voice.

Amy's heart twisted and she pulled Emily into her

arms. "I have every intention of not getting in an accident. I know it's hard not to feel scared, but we can't lock ourselves at home. Not you or me." She pulled back and gazed into her niece's pensive face. "I tell you what. I plan to be home by around midnight at the very latest, and when I get home, I'll pop in and give you a kiss. Okay?"

Emily relaxed slightly. "Okay. Where are you going?"

"To surprise Justin," Amy whispered.

Emily's eyes widened. "Is it his birthday?"

Amy chuckled. "No, but he's giving a speech, so I'm going to surprise him by showing up to listen to him. Could you keep an eye on your brothers while I get ready?"

Emily nodded, and Amy raced to her room and jerked open her closet door. Her clothing selection for a dinner party was dismally limited since during most of her life she dressed like an elementary school teacher. Fanning through her hangers, she finally chose a black sleeveless sweater-and-skirt combination. With heels and her trendy new faux pearl necklace, she should pass muster.

She didn't want to embarrass herself or Justin. Doubts niggled inside her. What if he wasn't pleased to see her in the audience? What if the reason he had discouraged her attendance was something other than boredom? Like a more experienced woman. Her stomach knotted at the thought.

Nerves rising to the surface, Amy dressed and applied make-up, smearing her eye shadow and reapplying. Horrified when a blob of mascara fell beneath her eye, she quickly blotted it, then approached her hair which balked at every effort she made to tame it.

"Why don't you put it up on top of your head like you did for the wedding?" Emily asked from the doorway.

Amy shook her head at herself and smiled at Emily. "Out of the mouth of my favorite girl. Perfect solution. What would I do without you?"

Emily beamed beneath her praise. "Do you want me to pick some flowers in the backyard?"

"Dandelions," Amy murmured picturing the backyard. Not weeds. She spritzed her hair with water, then scooped it up off her neck and began to pin it in place. "Thanks Em, but I have a few sparkly bobby pins I might use instead this time. Maybe you can help put them in?"

Emily did indeed help with the pins and Amy would have to say the five-year-old had far steadier hands than she did tonight. After giving the sitter instructions and kissing each child twice, Amy left.

The meeting was held at an exclusive club in downtown St. Albans. Amidst the luxury automobiles, she handed her car keys to the valet driver who looked at her car askance. Nerves and irritation bubbled inside her. "It's a classic," she said with a smile. "Make sure you take care of it."

She walked into the opulent lobby decorated with chandeliers, statues, and fountains and she located Justin's dinner party. Almost all the round tables of eight, including Justin's table, were filled. After a thorough search, she found one spot at a table near the center of the room and sat down.

Although she felt terribly out of place, she picked at her food and tried to remain invisible as the dinner conversation swirled around her. Stealing glances at the head table, she saw that Justin was seated between two beautiful, perfectly polished women who probably had not needed the assistance of a five-year-old to fix their hair. They were everything she wasn't, she thought and fought not to feel diminished. The brunette, Amy noticed, kept touching him. She fought a terrible tug of envy.

"It's packed tonight," the middle-aged man with the hideous tie beside her said. "Everyone wants to hear what St. Albans's premier stock stud, self-made millionaire has to say. I say he's been damn lucky and has just missed the speed bumps most of us hit."

Indignant on Justin's behalf even though the brunette was sitting entirely too close and he was smiling too frequently, Amy clamped back a hasty retort.

The young man on her other side shook his head. "I have to disagree. Haven't you heard? He's been

trading for years. He didn't make his fortune over-
night or with one big trade.''

"You sound like a Langdon groupie,'' Mr. Bad
Tie said.

The young man shrugged. "I'm intrigued, like
about three hundred other people who are here tonight. If he can share his secret, I'll be more than
happy to cash in on it.''

Mr. Bad Tie grunted. "If it were that easy, everyone would be doing it,'' he said then turned to her.
"Allan Walters. I haven't seen you before. Which
firm are you with?''

Taken off guard, Amy blinked before she shook
the man's hand. "I'm not with a brokerage. I
teach—''

"—business or marketing,'' he finished incor-
rectly for her with a nod of approval. "It's good for
anyone teaching business to be exposed to this kind
of thing, but I hope you tell your students this is rare
and people can lose the money as fast as they make
it.''

"Needs to retire,'' the young man beside her murmured for her ears only.

"I hear Langdon goes through women like penny
stocks,'' Allan said with a sigh as he eyed Amy's
cleavage. "One of the luxuries of being young and
wealthy.''

Insulted, Amy bit her tongue, then counted to ten.

"You seem to know a lot about Mr. Langdon. Have you met him?"

"No, but word gets around if you know what I mean."

"So, most of the basis for your opinion is rumor," Amy clarified.

Allan with the bad tie adjusted his tie. "Well, it's clear he plays the field. Look. He's got a woman on either side of him tonight."

"The only thing that's clear is that the seating for his table is arranged male, female, male, female," she said and tried to tell herself she was totally correct even though a part of her worried.

"Well, I know the guy isn't married because it would have been in the newspaper."

"I can't tell you much about Mr. Langdon's past romantic life, but I'm pretty sure he doesn't get his stock tips from the newspaper or rumor mill. Perhaps that's part of the reason he's so successful."

"Well said," the young man on her other side murmured to her. He extended his hand. "Ben Haynes," he said. "And you are?"

"Amy Monroe," she said, wondering if she would ever consider taking Justin's last name.

"You're not the usual type of woman who shows up for these things," Ben said as if it were a compliment.

"And the usual type is?"

He grinned. "Think barracuda."

Amy's stomach twisted. So her competition, if she were interested in competing for Justin's attention, which she wasn't, she assured herself, was a cunning sea animal that gnashed its prey to bits with sharp teeth. Her head started to throb. Maybe this hadn't been such a great idea after all.

At the head dinner table, Justin stifled a sigh. Despite the fact that he'd flashed his wedding ring and mentioned his *wife* several times throughout the meal, the brunette woman beside him, Gabi, whose name fit her perfectly, had hit on him so much he would need to check for bruises.

Justin wasn't chomping at the bit to step in front of this crowd. Although he knew many admired and respected him, just as many resented his success. They were professionals. He wasn't, therefore he wasn't supposed to be successful.

"Oh, Justin," Gabi continued, but he turned off his listening ear as he took a drink of water and the association's president climbed the small stairway to the platform.

"Ladies and gentlemen," the man began. "It is my privilege to introduce our guest speaker for the Spring meeting of the Virginia Stockbrokers' Association. This man started out on a shoestring budget trading low-dollar stocks, eventually building to high-dollar profits. His net worth is now well into the multiple six figures…."

Justin stifled a yawn and surreptitiously glanced at his watch. Another moment passed and the president finally said, "Ladies and gentlemen, I now present Justin Langdon." The applause seemed to fill every corner of the huge room, surprising the dickens out of Justin. He stood and climbed the stairs to the stage to stand behind the podium. The room was packed and the lighting so dark he couldn't make out many faces.

As if he were attending a twelve-step recovery meeting, he said, "Hello, my name is Justin Langdon, and I'm a—" he paused for effect "—tightwad."

In the audience, Amy's heart swelled with pride and something that felt very close to love. Justin was such an incredible man.

The crowd laughed, and Justin continued with his speech. "I know it must irritate the dickens out of most of you to know that I built my fortune off the stock market without the assistance of a stockbroker. More importantly, no stockbroker benefited with commission. But all I've done is become my own expert. My system of trading is designed specifically with me in mind—my goals, my never-ending study of the market, knowing how much I can risk and still sleep at night, and my commitment to trade with a minimum of emotion. You have to figure this out for each of your clients, and unfortunately, your clients aren't clones."

With the exception of the tightwad remark, everything he said resonated with his actions. From the beginning, Amy had sensed he was a man who knew himself well. He had been tested and tried and had grown stronger because of it. Amy sensed many people admired him for the money he'd made. She admired him for the man he'd become.

"Most of your clients aren't like me at all," Justin said, "so parts of my plan won't work for them. But I'm going to help you with a response for the next time one of your clients says something annoying like, 'I've read about how Justin Langdon turned his portfolio from three digits to seven digits all by himself. Maybe I should try that.'

"Here is the step-by-step process for how to do what Justin has done. Number one, cheap housing. Live in a one-room efficiency in an area of town where your lullabye each and every night will be the sound of fights in the streets followed by police sirens.

"Two, eat cheap. Your regular menu should consist of cans of beans and packaged macaroni. You're allowed to splurge and go out to eat once a year. To McDonald's." The sound of the crowd's chuckles rose to the podium. They thought he was joking, Justin thought, but he knew better. He had lived it.

"Three, no car for three years. Walk or take the bus. Every penny you would have spent on payments, maintenance, gas and parking goes into your trading account.

"Four, say goodbye to your sleep. After you start making significant money on the market, get a job working the midnight shift so you can stare at your monitor all day, then work all night.

"Five, no social life for three years straight. Beer is a luxury, decent wine is a dream." Justin smiled to himself figuring he'd eliminated ninety percent of the people who wanted to "do what Justin Langdon had done."

"Six, no dating for three years straight. Dating costs money and if you want to do what Justin did, you have to put every penny into the market."

He took a drink of water and surveyed the crowd again. Light glimmered on red hair about halfway back. He paused, narrowing his eyes. *Amy?*

His heart hammered with an odd kick of joy and confusion. When had she arrived? Why hadn't she let him know she was here? She glanced from side to side, then met his gaze and smiled as if she knew he was looking at her.

He took another drink of water and noted she was dressed in a man-killer black number that faithfully followed every curve. It looked like the men on either side of her were noticing her curves, too.

He continued with his speech a bit more quickly than he'd intended. Justin wanted his questions answered. When the older guy beside Amy locked his gaze on her cleavage, Justin had to resist the urge to jump down from the stage and punch him. Justin took a slightly more civilized course, deviating from his prepared remarks.

"I'd like to take this opportunity to introduce you to my wife. She came in a little late." Justin watched her face turn the color of her hair and her eyes shoot daggers. "Amy, don't be shy. Wave to everyone."

She did reluctantly, but her expression told him there would be hell to pay. Wrapping up his talk, he nodded to acknowledge applause, shook hands with the president, then strode directly to Amy's table.

A young man beside her stood and offered his hand. "Mr. Langdon, I'm a longtime fan."

Justin shook his hand and nodded, then reached for Amy.

"I was trying to be invisible," she whispered through gritted teeth.

"Not dressed like that," he retorted in a low voice against her ear.

"Amy," the older man said with sickening familiarity that matched his lecherous smile, "now I know why you were defending him."

Justin did a double take. "You defended me?" he asked quietly.

Although it seemed impossible, Amy felt her face grow hotter. "He was—" Flustered, she broke off and shook her head. "Later."

"She's a sweet little thing," the man said with a wink. "Nice work."

Amy felt so patronized by the man's attitude she wanted to throw water in his face. She glanced at Justin and saw his jaw tighten.

Justin smiled like a shark. "If you know what's good for you," he said in a voice frighteningly gentle, "you'll pick your eyeballs up out of my wife's sweater, you old goat. Let's go," he said to Amy and tugged her toward the exit.

"Why didn't you tell me you were coming?"

Amy scrambled to keep up with his long stride. "I wanted to surprise you."

"You succeeded," he said, leading her across the marble floor. "Why didn't you come to my table?"

"It was full," she said, and couldn't resist adding, "You were already surrounded by women. Attentive women. Where are we going?" she asked when he punched the button for the elevator.

He tugged his tux tie loose. "Just as you were surrounded by attentive men," he said with an edge to his voice that surprised her. "The association gave me a parlor room for my use this evening."

"Parlor room?"

The brass elevator doors whooshed open and he pulled her inside. "This may come as a surprise to you, but some people are actually impressed by me, Amy. Some people think I'm hot stuff."

"I do, too," Amy said, feeling defensive. "I just

probably think so for different reasons than many of the people in that ballroom.''

''And what would your reasons be?'' he asked, his green gaze glinting with challenge.

The elevator doors opened, giving Amy a moment to gather her wits. A moment didn't feel nearly adequate, she thought as he guided her around a corner and whisked her into a room.

''You were saying?'' Justin prompted.

Wondering at his mood, Amy laced her fingers together and wished she hadn't felt so off balance this evening. ''I admire you for giving a boy at Granger money so he could travel home to see his family.'' She saw a flicker of surprise cross his face and continued, ''I admire you for not wigging when Nicholas got sick in your car. I admire you for being able to deal with me.''

He cocked his head to one side. ''What do you mean about my being able to deal with you?''

Uneasy, Amy turned away and tried to focus on the beautifully furnished parlor. ''Well, you married me and I'm not really wife material,'' she said. ''In fact, you would be safe in calling me the nonwife.''

He walked up behind her. ''You're going to have to explain this. I've never heard of a nonwife.''

''In my case, it's a woman who didn't want to get married and has never believed she possessed an aptitude for wifely things. Add in the fact that I'm uncomfortable that I'm very attracted to you and have feelings for you, and dealing with me should be the most crazy-making thing you've ever attempted.''

The silence that followed was so swollen with secret hopes and fears that Amy prayed the floor would swallow her to put her out of her misery.

''Why did you come tonight?''

''I told you,'' she said. ''Because I wanted to surprise you and—'' She broke off. Too much soul-baring.

She felt him toy with a strand of her hair that had fallen from her upsweep. ''And I wanted us to have a few minutes without the kids. A few minutes of just you and me.''

''Just you and me would have been okay, but you shouldn't have worn this,'' he said and lightly circled the back of her neck with his hand.

She stiffened. She'd felt out of place and he was confirming that fact. ''Why? It's not nice enough?'' she asked, turning around. ''What's wrong with it? I thought I did pretty good considering I'm usually dressed like an elementary school teacher.''

''Your outfit's nice. It fits you fine. Too damn fine. The problem is every man in the whole blazing room wanted to see you *without* your clothes,'' he said, hands on his narrow hips.

Amy blinked. ''Oh.'' She felt her defiance seep out of her like air out of a popped balloon. She noticed again how attractive he looked in a tux. Curious, she met his gaze. "Well, I have a question. If every man in the room wanted to see me without my clothes, does every man include you?"

Eleven

He slowly walked toward her until he stood just a smidgeon away as he looked down at her. So much closer, but still too far away, Amy thought. Her heart beat faster at the expression on his face.

"I didn't mention any exceptions, did I, Amy of Arc?" he asked in a voice that had the potential to undo her.

"Don't call me that," she said.

"I just want my turn." He lifted his hand to her face.

She took a tiny breath. Her tight chest would allow no more. "Your turn?"

"You've been so busy saving the world. My

turn," he said, lifting her hand to his shoulder. "Save me."

Her breath completely evaporated. *Save me.* It was such a ridiculous statement coming from him. He was so strong, so centered. If ever a man didn't need saving, it was Justin. "The closest I came to that was when I drove you to the hospital," she said in a voice husky to her own ears.

He shook his head. "Come closer," he said, and lowered his mouth to hers.

He took his time as if he knew she needed time and attention. She needed these moments to give without the rest of the world pressing in on them. She didn't worry that the children would burst in on them or the phone would ring or Ms. Hatcher would pay a surprise visit. It was simply Justin and her. Mouth to mouth, heart to heart.

Although she knew there was a part of her still unwilling to surrender to this marriage because self-reliance had been her salvation for too long, she also knew there was a power to her growing feelings for Justin, a power she'd never experienced before.

She couldn't find the words, or maybe she feared saying them. She had to show him. The searching, sensual open-mouth kiss went on and on, warming her, building the coil of anticipation inside her.

"Too fast," he muttered. "I always want you too fast." He rolled his tongue around the inner lips of her mouth in an erotic motion that made her weak.

"I want to go slow," he said. "I want to kiss all of you."

He pulled her sweater over her head and disposed of her bra. He lowered his mouth to her swollen, aroused breasts and took first one nipple, then the other into his mouth. She went liquid and restless beneath his mouth. He moved his hands up her skirt and beneath her panties to touch her secret moistness. He slid his finger inside her and she gasped.

Unable to remain passive any longer, Amy unfastened his tux shirt and tugged it loose. Eager to feel his skin, she shoved both the shirt and jacket from him. She slowly rubbed her cheeks and mouth over his hard, warm chest, savoring the touch and taste of him, the clean masculine scent of him. The strength she felt here, she knew, permeated the entire man. The knowledge of that strength turned her on even more.

Strength deserved boldness. Her heart pounding, she lowered her hands to his waist, undid his pants, and eased the zipper down over his bulging masculinity. His quick intake of breath was a provocative invitation to go further, to give more, to take more.

Her inhibitions lowering with each beat of her heart, Amy felt the rise of feminine sensual power. It was a new heady and addictive sensation. She skimmed her mouth down the front of his chest and felt one of his hands in her hair.

"What are you doing?" he asked in a voice roughened by need.

"Getting closer," she told him and slid down his body to her knees, pulling his pants and briefs down as she went. She rubbed her cheek against his full masculinity, then kissed him. Taking him into her mouth, she savored the taste of his arousal and the sound of his pleasure. He grew harder and fuller in her mouth.

He tangled his fingers in her hair and muttered an oath. She lifted her gaze to his green eyes full of black heat.

He shuddered. "You have no idea how erotic you look between my legs with your bare breasts, sweet face and mouth on me." He groaned and tugged her to her feet. "I need to be in you."

In a blur of motion, he pushed away her skirt and panties. There was no bed in the room, only a love seat. Sitting down on it, he lifted her over him. "Hold on to my shoulders," he told her, and eased her down over him.

She sucked in a quick breath. He was so huge and so hard that for a moment Amy wasn't certain she could take him. She closed her eyes and felt herself accommodate him.

"You are almost too big," she whispered.

He gave a rough chuckle. "We just need to do this a lot so you'll get used to me."

"I'm not sure I'll ever—" She broke off when he guided her hips upward and down again. Pleasure rippled through her. He did it again, and Amy had never felt so voluptuous in her life. She began her own rhythm, riding him.

He took her breast into his mouth and the sensation zinged all the way to her core. She felt herself clench around him and he began a litany of oaths and prayers. Shuddering, she rode him until she went over the edge in a ripple of endless ecstatic spasms.

Justin thrust inside her, his face clenching from a scalding release. Aftershocks rocked through both of them.

Her knees weak, she gingerly slid to his side and wrapped her arms around him. She had never felt so powerful in a wholly feminine way, and at the same time so defenseless.

He drew her against him. "It's gonna take a long time for me to get enough of you, Amy."

Amy sighed and closed her eyes. For this moment, she would allow herself to lean on him and rely on his strength. Wouldn't it be wonderful if she could always count on him being there for her? The prospect filled her with a joy so intense it shook her. What if this truly didn't have to end?

Justin helped put her back together, making her laugh with how limp her limbs were as he dressed her. "What happened to your bones?" he asked.

"You melted them," she said, thinking he had also melted her heart.

He skimmed his hands up her bare legs to her

thigh. "I like you like this. I think I'd like to keep you this way. How long did you arrange for the sitter to stay? A week?" he asked with a ridiculous mock-serious tone.

She laughed. "You're so funny. Around midnight, I turn into a pumpkin."

Glancing at the clock, he noted the late hour and groaned. "Someday I will have you for a whole night."

She shuddered with pleasure at his wickedly intent expression. "If no one is sick and we find the right sitter," she said with a smile. "And the stars are in perfect alignment."

"It will happen soon," he assured her and walked her out of the hotel to her car. He helped her into her Volkswagen and kissed her before she left, making Amy feel savored and precious in a way she couldn't remember feeling before.

On the drive home, though, other, darker realities slid into her mind. Some very important things hadn't changed. They'd agreed to try this for two years. They'd signed a prenuptial agreement that defined the terms of the end of their marriage. They'd agreed they didn't love each other.

The final thought cut like a knife.

Justin paid the sitter before Amy could open her purse. "That wasn't necessary. I could've covered it," she told him.

He waved aside her protest and studied her carefully. She seemed uneasy with him again, and he wondered why. He wouldn't have thought it possible, but the sensual, giving woman who had taken him to the moon just hours before seemed to have erected a nearly invisible wall during the drive home.

"You're quiet," he said.

"I'm tired and I promised Emily I'd give her a kiss when I got home."

He nodded. "Okay."

She bit her lip and met his gaze. "You were wonderful during the speech and after," she said. "Wonderful. Good night."

Justin felt his mood sink. "Cold feet again?"

She paused, looking conflicted, and he had his answer. He bit back an oath of frustration.

"I think it's more because of a reality check than cold feet," she finally said in that too-quiet voice.

"Tonight wasn't real enough for you?"

She drew in a quick breath. "Our marriage doesn't feel real to me."

"Maybe if we slept together—"

"—I don't think that's the solution," she said. "It's more than that. When we made our vows, I pretended I was giving an order at Burger Doodle so I wouldn't hyperventilate. We promised to give this two years. If it were real, we would have given it forever." Her eyes filled with doubt he wanted to banish. She looked down. "We don't love each other," she said in a voice edged with pain. "And the cherry on top of the sundae is the prenup agreement.''

Justin tensed. His attorney had warned him that it wasn't unusual for wives to ask for changes after the marriage. It wasn't unusual for women to use emotional or sexual blackmail to get more money. Amy wasn't that way, he told himself. He hoped she wasn't that way. "What do you mean? Do you believe the agreement was unfair?''

She shook her head. "No, but think about it. A prenup is a plan to divorce. It's an instruction booklet for how to end our marriage.''

"Are you saying that if we throw out the agreement then you'll be willing to sleep with me through the night?''

Amy paled. She looked as if he'd slapped her. "No, I'm not saying that at all. You just don't get it. This is about much more than a stupid prenup agreement. Much more,'' she said and walked away from him.

After that, Justin felt a distance grow between them. Amy was polite and kind, but reserved. He felt he'd had something at his fingertips, something precious, and he'd lost it. They had been so close. He'd treasured her trust and generosity.

Now it was gone. Living in the same house with her was painful, much more painful than Justin had ever believed possible. He couldn't recall a time when he had felt this much pain. Not even when his mother had left him at Granger.

His frustration and dark desperation seemed to grow with each passing hour. One day he ran out to pick up some computer equipment. It took longer than he planned. When he returned, he saw a different, late-model car and pick-up truck in the driveway. Two men were unloading swings. Curious, Justin followed the path to the backyard.

Amy stood talking to the men while they put the finishing touches on a wooden swing set. Emily stood by Amy's side and the twins ran in circles. Nicholas looked up. "Justin, Justin! We're getting a swing set!" he hollered. "Right now! And I'm gonna be the first to swing on it."

"Nuh-uh," Jeremy said. "I am."

"Nuh-uh," Nicholas said. "I am."

"Nuh-uh," Jeremy said.

"Nuh-uh," Emily said. "Aunt Amy and I are gonna ride it first because we're being nice, and you're not."

Nicholas and Jeremy abruptly shut their mouths.

Amy glanced up and smiled at Justin. His heart stuttered. She looked at him with a light in her eyes as if their argument from last week was forgotten. He saw the moment she remembered. Her smile faded. "I bought a swing set."

"So I see," Justin said.

"These guys say they can have it up by the time we finish dinner."

"Woo-hoo!" Nicholas and Jeremy yelled.

"What's with the different car in the driveway?"

Amy smiled sheepishly. "Part impulse, part practicality. It's tough buckling those car seats in the Volkswageon. I stopped by an auto sales lot on the way home and voila, I have a new vehicle."

Justin felt a trickle of unease. "Why didn't you ask me? I could've helped you out with the swing set and car."

"No, the swing set's my treat. I've been planning this for weeks. And it was time to trade the Beetle." She laughed, mostly it seemed, at herself. "That's what payday is for, right?"

His gut tightened. "I guess."

"Besides, it'll all balance out with dinner tonight."

"What do you mean?"

"Cheap meal," she said. "Okay, you guys, let's go inside and eat and give these men a chance to get their work done. It might be dark, but we might all get a chance to swing a little tonight."

She led the kids inside and they rushed to wash up for dinner. A vague darkness hovered over him even during the kids' exuberance. He was concerned about Amy's purchases. He hadn't thought she was an impulsive buyer.

He watched her from the kitchen doorway as she chatted with Emily. "Time to eat," she said and laughed at the boys. "Are you going to be able to sit still enough to eat dinner?"

"How still do we have to sit?" Jeremy asked.

"Just a little bit still," Nicholas said.

"Good, cuz I feel like jumpin'."

"I feel like swingin'," Nicholas said.

"Me, too."

"Sit down," Amy said in a sing-song voice, and the boys scurried to their seats. "Sorry for the gourmet fare," she said to Justin, "but there are times when the only appropriate choice is beanee weenees."

Justin's stomach immediately rebelled. His brain screamed in protest. A flurry of images raced through his mind. His mother once bought him a shiny fire truck and herself a new dress and shoes. For dinner, they'd eaten beanee weenees. Another time at Christmas, his mother had bought herself a new refrigerator and television and for Justin she had bought video games. The electricity had been cut off due to lack of payment, and he remembered eating beanee weenees cooked in the fireplace. He had eaten beanee weenees himself when he'd been putting every penny into his trading account in an attempt to form the security he'd never experienced as a child.

It was just too much.

He went to Amy and spoke in a low voice for her ears only, "I'm going to my house. I'll let you know when I'll be back." He didn't wait for her response. He just walked out the door.

Hours later, Justin sat on the leather sofa in the

darkness of his home pre-Amy. The silence was initially soothing, but now it felt too quiet. He'd grown accustomed to the creaks and groans of Amy's older home and the sound of children's chatter and Amy's musical voice. He'd grown accustomed to limited solitude.

Glancing at the clock, he thought he might be helping to tuck in one of the twins or reading a book with Emily. And after the kids were put to bed, Justin never stopped feeling Amy's presence. She could be at the other end of the house or asleep when he was not, but he always felt her presence.

He wondered if she ever longed for him during the long hours between darkness and morning. He wondered if he would ever stop longing for her. He felt as if he could see the missing piece to the puzzle of his life, but he couldn't hold it, and it frustrated the hell out of him.

He'd returned to his house for solitude and peace, but the solitude was suffocating and there was no peace in sight.

Later that night, the phone woke him out of a restless sleep. Justin automatically answered it.

"Hi, this is Michael. I just heard from Dylan and I thought you might want to go see him. He's at the hospital."

Alarmed, Justin sat straight up in bed. "He's hurt?"

"No. Alisa Jennings was in some kind of accident. It's serious. She's unconscious in ICU and Dylan's determined to camp at the hospital until she wakes up.''

"How did Dylan know she was hurt?"

"Apparently her mother's out of the country on an extended trip, so they couldn't reach her. They found Dylan's business card in her purse, so they gave him a call. He doesn't sound good. I'll get over there soon, but you're closer to the West County Medical Center. I tried calling you at your bride's house first," Michael said and let the question hang between them.

"I needed some time to think," Justin said.

"Hmm. Okay. Don't take too much time," Michael advised as if he'd learned something along the way about waiting too long. "I'll see you at the hospital."

Pulling on his clothes, he grabbed his car keys and left for the hospital. After getting two cups of coffee from a machine, he found Dylan in the ICU waiting room, staring unseeing through the glass door at the nurse's station. Dylan, the most outwardly carefree guy Justin had ever met, looked as if he were facing death itself.

"Hey," Justin said, offering him a cup of coffee. "What happened?"

Dylan accepted the coffee, but didn't drink it. "She was running after a neighbor's dog that got loose and a car hit her."

"Oh, God," Justin said. A picture of Alisa as a child slid through his mind. "She was such a sweet kid, and she grew up to be a beautiful lady. This is a damn shame. What's the prognosis?''

"They won't tell me much," Dylan said. "Serious head injury, internal injuries. They don't know if she's gonna wake up at all," he said, his voice desolate.

"Did they let you see her?"

Dylan hesitated. "Yeah. I told them I was her fiancé.''

Justin did a double take. He'd known Dylan had carried a torch for Alisa, but he hadn't known the man was this determined.

"It was the only way I could make them talk to me. Besides, her mother is on one of those trips to Europe and Russia where they move around every two or three days. Alisa may not want me right now," he said grimly, "but she damn well needs me.''

"How long have you been in love with her?"

Dylan gave a wry humorless laugh. "Forever. She's what I wished for before I knew how to wish, but I screwed up big time when we got together in college. I was so full of myself. I didn't treat her well. I'm paying now. God, if she dies, I don't know what I'll do.''

"But you haven't been together," Justin said.

"You don't understand," he said looking at Justin with stark eyes. "Just knowing she exists and is alive makes the world right for me.''

Justin felt an echo of recognition inside him at Dylan's words. Knowing Amy existed made the world a better place for him. He wondered what he would do if something like this happened to Amy. Just the thought scared the living daylights out of him.

What if Amy died? What if she wasn't even on the earth? What if he lost even the possibility of being with her?

Justin's stomach churned with nausea.

"When you're in love," Dylan said, raking a hand through his sun-streaked hair, "there's only two places in the world—where she is and where she's not."

Justin sat with Dylan through the long night, but in his mind, he was going home to Amy. That was exactly what he did the following morning. On the way to her house, he called his attorney and instructed him to dissolve the prenup agreement. When his attorney argued against it, Justin would have none of it. "Either you cancel it, or I'll pay somebody else to cancel it."

Pulling into the driveway at dawn, he felt a sense of resolve that went deeper than his bones. He strode into the house and headed upstairs.

Amy's voice stopped him. "How is Alisa?" she asked quietly from behind him.

He slowly turned to face her and drank in the sight of her in a nightshirt. He shook his head. "She's still unconscious, still in ICU."

She crossed her arms as if to hug herself. "It's terrible. I couldn't sleep. I tried to call you after

Michael called me, but you must've already left for the hospital."

"Yeah, Michael's with him now. I needed to see you."

Amy nodded. Her nerves were shot. "You're right. I need to talk to you."

Justin held up a hand. "I have something to tell you."

Terrified he was totally giving up on their marriage, she shook her head and spoke in a rush. "No. I need to say I'm sorry. I know this has been impossible. I'm sorry I haven't been anything resembling a wife. I've just been so determined and so scared," she said, that admission costing her, "that I shouldn't rely on you. Justin, you're so strong. You're the strongest man I know, and I want to rely on you, but at the same time I'm afraid to do that. There has never been anyone I could rely on. Both my parents were alcoholics and I learned at a very early age to be self-reliant. I don't know how to be more balanced," she confessed, feeling her throat tighten with emotion. "But I'd like to learn with you."

Justin walked closer and stared at her. "I called my attorney on the way from the hospital."

Amy's stomach sank. He was already initiating a separation. She was too late.

"I told him to cancel the prenup. I want you to marry me, Amy," he said.

Her head reeled. Unable to assimilate his words,

she shook her head in confusion. "I don't understand. I thought you'd had enough of our marriage and wanted out."

"I've had enough of pretending this is temporary, because it's not temporary for me," he said, slamming her heart into overdrive with his revelation. "I can't explain it, and I know it sounds weird as hell, but I think you and I were meant for each other. You are the woman I would have wished for if I'd known you existed. You make the world make sense to me. I don't—" He broke off. "Why are you crying?" he asked in horror.

Overwhelmed, Amy felt tears slide down her cheeks. "I thought you were leaving for good."

He pulled her into his arms and held tight. "No, the beanee weenees pushed a button, but—"

"Excuse me?" she said. "Beanee weenees?"

"Long story," he said. "It's one of those bad memory foods."

She winced. "They're Jeremy's favorite."

"He can have my share."

Being in his arms filled Amy with such warmth and hope. "I don't understand what you were saying about the prenup."

"Cancelled," he said. "We don't need a prenup."

"You didn't have to do that," she said, knowing it had been important to his sense of security. More than anything Amy wanted Justin to feel all the security and love he'd missed as a child. She wanted to be the woman to give it.

"Yeah, I did," he said. "I want a lifetime with you. I want a commitment with you with every possible string attached. I don't want you to get away."

Her eyes filled with tears again. "I have been so afraid of loving you, but I do. I love the child you were, the man you are and I want the chance to love the man you'll become."

He lowered his mouth to hers and kissed her with such tenderness and love that she was humbled. How, she wondered, had she gotten so lucky?

"I used to think my mission was marrying you for the sake of the kids. Now, I know my mission is loving you for the sake of me."

One week later, Amy surprised Justin when she arrived home with Chinese food and champagne, but no children in tow.

"Where are the munchkins?" he asked, giving her a welcome kiss.

"They're at a sleepover at Kate and Michael's house," she said, unable to keep a smile from her face. "We passed inspection. The kids are really ours now."

"Hallelujah," he said. "We should celebrate."

"That's my plan."

"Oh, really," he said, his voice deepening in approval. "What kind of plan?"

"I think you should take off all your clothes and go to bed immediately."

He scooped her up into his arms and strode to-

ward the room they'd shared as husband and wife
for the last six nights. "I'm not arguing," he said.
"What about the food?"

"Later," she said, and they made very good use
of their time making love to each other. Justin never
ceased to amaze her with how easily he read her
body. With each passing day, he seemed to read her
mind and heart.

Afterward, Amy slipped on a chemise and brought
the boxes of Chinese food and champagne to the bedroom on a tray. They took turns feeding each other.
"Did you hear about Alisa? Kate told me she woke
up, but she can't remember anything."

Justin nodded. "Dylan called today. I think he's
just relieved she's going to live. He said he's stick-
ing to her like glue even though she'll probably spit
in his eye when she gets her memory back."

"I feel lucky," she said.

He nodded. "I don't even want to remember what
it was like before you were in my life."

Her heart filled to overflowing. "There's something I need to say to you," she told him and took
his strong, gentle hands in hers. No Burger Doodle
vows for her. Looking directly into the eyes of the
man she adored more than anything, Amy made
promises she knew she would keep. "I take you,
Justin Langdon, to be my lawfully wedded husband,
for richer, for poorer, in sickness and in health."

She leaned forward and kissed him with all the
love in her heart. "Forever and ever and ever."

''I take you, Amy Monroe, to be my lawfully wedded wife. I will love and stand by you forever and ever,'' he said solemnly, then lowered his head to whisper in her ear. ''Even if you serve beanee weenees.''

Amy laughed at the same time a tear fell down her cheek. He had told her many secrets during the last week including the beanee weenee story. ''Now that is love.''

* * * * *

Watch for Dylan Barrows to be the next Millionaire to find true love in

The Millionaire's Secret Wish

The latest book in Leanne Banks's exciting mini-series.

On sale next month in a volume called **MILLIONAIRE MARRIAGES**.

* * *

You can also read more from Leanne Banks in Labour of Love—*an exciting new three-in-one anthology that's on the shelves now.*

0302/51a

SILHOUETTE®
DESIRE™

AVAILABLE FROM 15TH MARCH 2002

FORBIDDEN ATTRACTION

GABRIEL'S GIFT Cait London

Part of Gabriel died when he sent Miranda away all those years ago. Now she was back, and pregnant! With a single touch Gabriel broke all his rules and re-ignited their passion…

VICTORIA'S CONQUEST Laurie Paige

Business tycoon Jason Broadrick had wanted Victoria from the instant he'd seen her—the day she'd married his cousin! Now, although free, Victoria was still off limits. And Jason knew better than to risk his most valuable asset—his heart.

MILLIONAIRE MARRIAGES

MILLIONAIRE BOSS Peggy Moreland

Penny Rawley hadn't travelled across the country to have sexy boss Erik Thompson order her around! She'd come to his firm with one thing in mind: marrying the man she'd always loved. Now, he had the nerve to ignore her… Well, *that* was going to change…

THE MILLIONAIRE'S SECRET WISH Leanne Banks

Millionaire Dylan Barrows made Alisa's amnesia much easier to handle. The sexy executive made her feel whole again. Dylan told her they were just friends so why did her instincts tell her that wasn't the whole truth?

HEIRESS IN HIS ARMS

IN BED WITH THE BOSS'S DAUGHTER
Bronwyn Jameson

Corporate tough-guy Jack Manning hadn't laid eyes on Paris Grantham since the night he'd rebuffed her teenage advances. But he'd been more than a little tempted by the boss's daughter—and was relieved when the sweet seductress had retreated to London. Until now…

THE HEIRESS & THE BODYGUARD Ryanne Corey

Undercover private investigator Billy Lucas never expected to fall for his beautiful target, society princess Julie Roper. All Billy wanted was to have Julie in his arms… But could he convince Julie that he wanted her and not her riches?

Fortune's Children
THE GROOMS

Welcome back to the Fortune dynasty

The drama and mystery of Fortune's Children continues with a new 12-part book continuity series.

**Fortune's Children: THE GROOMS
and
Fortune's Children: THE LOST HEIRS**

The drama, glamour and mystery begins with Fortune's Grooms, five strong, sexy men surrounded by intrigue, but destined for love and marriage!

SILHOUETTE®

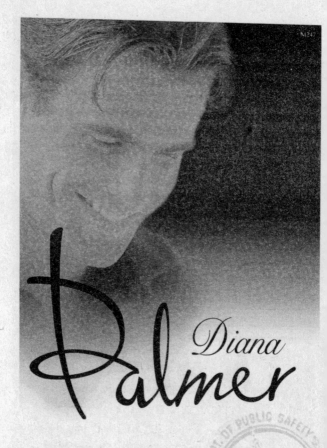

THE TEXAS RANGER
He has a passion for justice

Published 15th March 2002

▼ SILHOUETTE
SENSATION®

presents a new heart-pounding
twelve-book series:

A Year of Loving Dangerously

**When a top secret agency is threatened, twelve of the best
agents in the world put their lives—and their hearts—on
the line. But will justice...and true love...prevail?**

**SILHOUETTE®
SPECIAL EDITION™**

is proud to present

The Stockwells

Where family secrets, scandalous pasts and unexpected love wreak havoc on the lives of the rich and infamous Stockwells!

THE TYCOON'S INSTANT DAUGHTER
Christine Rimmer
January

SEVEN MONTHS AND COUNTING...
Myrna Temte
February

HER UNFORGETTABLE FIANCÉ
Allison Leigh
March

THE MILLIONAIRE AND THE MUM
Patricia Kay
April

THE CATTLEMAN AND THE VIRGIN HEIRESS
Jackie Merritt
May

1201/SH/LC24

FREE
1 BOOK
AND A SURPRISE GIFT!

We would like to take this opportunity to thank you for reading this Silhouette® book by offering you the chance to take another specially selected title from the Desire™ series absolutely FREE! We're also making this offer to introduce you to the benefits of the Reader Service™—

★ FREE home delivery
★ FREE monthly Newsletter
★ FREE gifts and competitions
★ Exclusive Reader Service discount
★ Books available before they're in the shops

Accepting this FREE book and gift places you under no obligation to buy; you may cancel at any time, even after receiving your free shipment. Simply complete your details below and return the entire page to the address below. **You don't even need a stamp!**

YES! Please send me 1 free Desire book and a surprise gift. I understand that unless you hear from me, I will receive 3 superb new titles every month for just £4.99 each, postage and packing free. I am under no obligation to purchase any books and may cancel my subscription at any time. The free book and gift will be mine to keep in any case.

D2ZEC

Ms/Mrs/Miss/Mr ....Initials.....................................
BLOCK CAPITALS PLEASE

Surname...

Address...

....

....Postcode ....

Send this whole page to:
UK: FREEPOST CN81, Croydon, CR9 3WZ
EIRE: PO Box 4546, Kilcock, County Kildare (stamp required)